UNDER THE WIDE
AND SCARY SKY

Lije Baley was going into space. That wasn't
so bad. The walls of the ship were around him,
protecting him, holding him within their limits,
like the familiar, comfortable walls of Earth's
totally enclosed environment. But after space
would come the planet!

It was a planet of wide-open spaces, where
the sky stretched on and on and on forever, space
without end, drawing a man's mind further and
further into nothingness. And there would be a
sun—a horrible, distant light in emptiness,
burning out a man's eyes when he looked at it.
Emptiness—emptiness right, left, and to all sides,
off into the distant, vanishing horizons!

It was unthinkable, not to be endured. Yet
Lije had to face it, to dare it. Otherwise, his
partner, R. Daneel Olivaw, would be amused,
however politely he might not show it.

A man couldn't let a robot laugh at him!

ISAAC ASIMOV

THE NAKED SUN

A Del Rey Book

BALLANTINE BOOKS • NEW YORK

To Noreen and Nick Falasca, for inviting me,
To Tony Boucher, for introducing me, and
To One Hundred Unusual Hours.

A Del Rey Book
Published by Ballantine Books

ISBN 0-345-33031-5

Selection of the Science Fiction Book Club, May 1971

This edition published by arrangement with Doubleday & Co., Inc.

Manufactured in the United States of America

First Ballantine Books Edition: December 1983
Fourth Printing: June 1985

Cover art by Michael Herring

CONTENTS

Introduction

THE STORY BEHIND THE ROBOT NOVELS

The writing side of my love affair with robots began on May 10, 1939, but as a science-fiction *reader* it began earlier still.

Robots were, after all, nothing new in science fiction, not even in 1939. Mechanical human beings are to be found in ancient and medieval myths and legends, and the word "robot" originally appeared in Karl Capek's play *R.U.R.*, which was first staged in 1921 in Czechoslovakia, but was soon translated into many languages.

R.U.R. stands for "Rossum's Universal Robots." Rossum, an English industrialist, produced artificial human beings designed to do the labor of the world and to free humanity for a life of creative leisure. (The word "robot" is from a Czech word meaning "compulsory labor.") Though Rossum meant well, it didn't work out as he planned: the robots rebelled, and the human species was destroyed.

It is perhaps not surprising that a technological advance, imagined in 1921, was seen as resulting in universal disaster. Remember that World War I, with its tanks, airplanes, and poison gas, had just ended and had showed people "the dark side of the force," to use *Star Wars* terminology.

R.U.R. added its somber view to that of the even more famous *Frankenstein*, in which the creation of another kind of artificial human being also ended in disaster, though on a more limited scale. Following these examples, it became very common, in the 1920s and 1930s, to picture robots as dangerous devices that invariably destroyed their creators. The moral was pointed out over and over again that "there are some things Man was not meant to know."

Even as a youngster, though, I could not bring myself to

believe that if knowledge presented danger, the solution was ignorance. To me, it always seemed that the solution had to be wisdom. You did not refuse to look at danger, rather you learned how to handle it safely.

After all, this has been the human challenge since a certain group of primates became human in the first place. *Any* technological advance can be dangerous. Fire was dangerous from the start, and so (even more so) was speech—and both are still dangerous to this day—but human beings would not be human without them.

At any rate, without quite knowing what dissatisfied me about the robot stories I read, I waited for something better, and I found it in the December 1938 issue of *Astounding Science Fiction*. That issue contained "Helen O'Loy" by Lester del Rey, a story in which a robot was portrayed sympathetically. It was, I believe, only his second story, but I was a del Rey fan forever after. (Please don't anybody tell him this. He must never know.)

At almost the same time, in the January 1939 issue of *Amazing Stories*, Eando Binder portrayed a sympathetic robot in *I, Robot*. This was much the poorer story of the two, but again I vibrated. Dimly, I began to feel that I wanted to write a story in which a robot would be portrayed lovingly. And on May 10, 1939, I began such a story. The job took me two weeks, for in those days it took me quite a while to write a story.

I called it "Robbie," and it was about a robot nursemaid, who was loved by the child it cared for and feared by the child's mother. Fred Pohl (who was also nineteen at the time, and who has matched me year for year ever since) was wiser than I, however. When he read it, he said that John Campbell, the all-powerful editor of *Astounding*, would not take it because it was too much like "Helen O'Loy." He was right. Campbell rejected it for that very reason.

However, Fred became editor of a pair of new magazines soon after, and *he* took "Robbie" on March 25, 1940. It appeared in the September 1940 issue of *Super-Science Stories*, though its name was changed to "Strange Playfellow." (Fred had an awful habit of changing titles, almost always for the worse. The story has appeared many times since, but always under my own original title.)

I was, in those days, dissatisfied with any sale not made to Campbell, however, and so I tried another robot story after a while. I discussed the idea with Campbell first, though, to make sure he wouldn't reject it for anything other than inadequate writing, and then I wrote "Reason," in which a robot got religion, so to speak.

Campbell bought it on November 22, 1940, and it appeared in the April 1941 issue of his magazine. It was my third sale to him and the first one he had taken as it stood, without requesting revision. I was so elated by this that I quickly wrote a third robot story, about a mind-reading robot, which I called "Liar!", and this one Campbell *also* took, and it appeared in the May 1941 issue. I had two robot stories in two successive issues.

After that, I did not intend to stop. I had a series going.

I had more than that. On December 23, 1940, when I was discussing my idea for a mind-reading robot with Campbell, we found ourselves discussing the rules that governed the way in which a robot behaved. It seemed to me that robots were engineering devices with built-in safeguards, and so the two of us began giving verbal form to those safeguards— these became the "Three Laws of Robotics."

I first worked out the final form of the Three Laws, and used them explicitly, in my fourth robot story, "Runaround," which appeared in the March 1942 issue of *Astounding*. The Three Laws first appear on page 100 of that issue. I looked that up, because where they appear there is the very first use of the word "robotics" in the history of the world, as far as I know.

I went on to write four more robot stories for *Astounding* in the 1940s. They were "Catch That Rabbit," "Escape" (which Campbell called "Paradoxical Escape" because two years before he had published a story with "Escape" as the title), "Evidence," and "The Evitable Conflict." These appeared in the February 1944, August 1945, September 1946, and June 1950 issues of *Astounding*.

By 1950, important publishing houses, notably Doubleday and Company, were beginning to publish hardcover science fiction. In January 1950, Doubleday published my first book, the science-fiction novel *Pebble in the Sky*, and I was hard at work on a second novel.

It occurred to Fred Pohl, who was my agent for a brief period at that time, that perhaps a book could be made out of my robot stories. Doubleday was not interested in short-story collections at the time, but a very small publishing house, Gnome Press, was.

On June 8, 1950, the collection was handed to Gnome Press, and the title I gave it was *Mind and Iron*. The publisher shook his head.

"Let's call it *I, Robot*," he said.

"We can't," I said. "Eando Binder wrote a short story with that title ten years ago."

"Who cares?" said the publisher (though that is a bowdlerized version of what he really said), and I allowed myself, rather uneasily, to be persuaded. *I, Robot* was my second book, and it came out just before the end of 1950.

The book contained my eight robot stories from *Astounding*, with their order rearranged to make a more logical progression. In addition, I included "Robbie," my first story, because I liked it despite Campbell's rejection.

I had written three other robot stories in the 1940s that Campbell had either rejected or never seen, but these were not in the direct path of progression of the stories, so I left them out. These, however, and other robot stories written in the decades since *I, Robot*, were included in later collections—all of them, without exception, appeared in *The Complete Robot*, published by Doubleday in 1982.

I, Robot did not make a big splash on publication, but it sold steadily, if slowly, year after year. Within five years, it had come out in an Armed Forces edition, in a cheaper hardcover edition, in a British edition, and in a German edition (my first foreign-language appearance). In 1956, it was even published in a paperback edition by New American Library.

The only trouble was that Gnome Press was just barely surviving, and it never did get around to giving me clear semiannual statements, or much in the way of payments. (That went for my three *Foundation* books, which Gnome Press also published.)

In 1961, Doubleday became aware of the fact that Gnome Press was having trouble, and they arranged to take over *I, Robot* (and the *Foundation* books, too). From then on, all the books did much better. In fact, *I, Robot* has remained in print ever since it was first published. That's thirty-three years now. In 1981, it was even sold to the movies, although no motion picture has yet been made. It has also appeared in eighteen different foreign languages that I know of, including Russian and Hebrew.

But I'm getting way ahead of the story.

Let's go back to 1952, at which time *I, Robot* was just plodding along as a Gnome Press book, and I had no hint of any real success.

By that time, new top-notch science-fiction magazines had come out and the field was in one of its periodic "booms." *The Magazine of Fantasy and Science Fiction* appeared in 1949, and *Galaxy Science Fiction* in 1950. With that John Campbell lost his monopoly of the field, and the "Golden Age" of the 1940s was over.

I began to write for Horace Gold, the editor of *Galaxy*, and with some relief, too. For a period of eight years, I had written for Campbell exclusively and I had come to feel that I was a one-editor writer and that if anything happened to Campbell, I would be through. My success in selling to Gold relieved my anxieties in this respect. Gold even serialized my second novel, *The Stars, Like Dust . . .* , although he changed its title to *Tyrann*, which I considered awful.

Nor was Gold my only new editor. I sold a robot story to Howard Browne, who edited *Amazing* during a brief period when it tried to be a quality magazine. The story, entitled "Satisfaction Guaranteed," appeared in the April 1951 issue of that magazine.

That was an exception, though. On the whole, I had no intention of writing further robot stories at that time. The appearance of *I, Robot* seemed to have brought that portion of my literary career to its natural close, and I was moving on to other things.

Gold, however, having published one serial by me, was perfectly willing to try another, especially since a new novel I had written, *The Currents of Space*, had been taken by Campbell for serialization.

On April 19, 1952, Gold and I were talking over the matter of a new novel that was to appear in *Galaxy*. He suggested a robot novel. I shook my head firmly. My robots had appeared only in short stories, and I was not at all sure I could write a whole novel based on robots.

"Sure you can," said Gold. "How about an overpopulated world in which robots are taking over human jobs?"

"Too depressing," I said. "I'm not sure I want to handle a heavy sociological story."

"Do it your way. You like mysteries. Put a murder in such a world and have a detective solve it with a robot partner. If the detective doesn't solve it, the robot will replace him."

That struck fire. Campbell had often said that a science-fiction mystery story was a contradiction in terms; that advances in technology could be used to get detectives out of their difficulties unfairly, and that the readers would therefore be cheated.

I sat down to write a story that would be a classic mystery and that would not cheat the reader—and yet would be a true science-fiction story. The result was *The Caves of Steel*. It appeared in *Galaxy* as a three-part serial in the October, November, and December 1953 issues, and in 1954, it was published by Doubleday as my eleventh book.

There was no question but that *The Caves of Steel* was my most successful book to date. It sold better than any of my earlier books; it elicited nicer letters from readers; and (best proof of all) Doubleday smiled at me with greater warmth than ever before. Until that point, they wanted outlines and chapters from me before handing me contracts, but after that I got my contracts on my mere statement that I was going to write another book.

The Caves of Steel was so successful, in fact, that it was inevitable that I write a sequel. I would have started it at once, I think, if I had not just begun to write science popularizations and found I enjoyed doing that tremendously. It was not till October 1955 that I actually began *The Naked Sun*.

Once begun, however, it went smoothly. In many ways, it balanced the earlier book. *The Caves of Steel* took place on Earth, a world of many human beings and few robots, while *The Naked Sun* took place on Solaria, a world of few human beings and many robots. What's more, although my books are generally devoid of romance, I actually introduced an understated love story into *The Naked Sun*.

I was entirely satisfied with the sequel, and in my heart,

thought it was even better than *The Caves of Steel*, but what was I to do with it? I had grown somewhat estranged from Campbell, who had taken up an odd bit of pseudoscience called dianetics and had managed to become interested in flying saucers, in psionics, and in various other questionable matters. On the other hand, I owed him a great deal and I felt rather guilty over having largely shifted to Gold, who had had two of my serials in a row. But as he had nothing to do with the planning of *The Naked Sun*, I could dispose of it as I wished.

I offered the novel to Campbell, therefore, and he took it at once. It appeared as a three-part serial in the October, November, and December 1956 issues of *Astounding*, and Campbell didn't change my title, either. In 1957, it was published by Doubleday as my twentieth book.

It did just as well as *The Caves of Steel*, if not better, and Doubleday at once pointed out I couldn't leave it there. I would have to write a third book and make it a trilogy, just as my three *Foundation* books made up a trilogy.

I fully agreed. I had a rough idea of the plot of the third book, and I had a title—*The Bounds of Infinity*.

In July 1958, the family was taking a three-week vacation in a house at the shore in Marshfield, Massachusetts, and it was my plan to get to work and do a sizable chunk of the new novel there. It was going to be set on Aurora, where the human/robot balance was to be neither overweighted in the direction of the human as in *The Caves of Steel* nor in the direction of the robot as in *The Naked Sun*. What's more, the element of romance was to be much strengthened.

I was all set—and yet, something was wrong. I had grown steadily more interested in non-fiction in the 1950s, and for the first time, I started a novel which wouldn't catch fire. After four chapters, I faded out and gave up. I decided that in my heart I felt I couldn't handle the romance, couldn't balance the human/robot mixture in properly equal fashion.

For twenty-five years, that was the way it remained. Neither *The Caves of Steel* nor *The Naked Sun* died or went out of print. They appeared together in *The Robot Novels*; they appeared with a group of short stories in *The Rest of the Robots*. And they appeared in various softcover editions.

For twenty-five years, therefore, readers had them available to read and, I presume, enjoy. As a result, many wrote me to ask for a third novel. At conventions they asked me directly. It became the most sure-fire request I was to receive (except the request for a fourth *Foundation* novel).

And whenever I was asked if I intended to write a third robot novel, I always answered, "Yes—someday—so pray for a long life for me."

Somehow, I felt I ought to, but as the years passed I grew more and more certain that I couldn't handle it, and more and more sadly convinced that the third novel was never going to be written.

And yet, in March of 1983, I presented Doubleday with the "long-awaited" third robot novel. It has no connection whatever with the ill-fated attempt of 1958, and its name is *The Robots of Dawn*. Doubleday will publish it in October of 1983.

But here I stop. This introduction is to appear in the new paperback editions of *The Caves of Steel* and *The Naked Sun* that Del Rey Books is republishing. The story of how the third novel came to be written is still to come.

—Isaac Asimov
New York City

1. A QUESTION IS ASKED

Stubbornly Elijah Baley fought panic.

For two weeks it had been building up. Longer than that, even. It had been building up ever since they had called him to Washington and there calmly told him he was being reassigned.

The call to Washington had been disturbing enough in itself. It came without details, a mere summons; and that made it worse. It included travel slips directing round trip by plane and that made it still worse.

Partly it was the sense of urgency introduced by any order for plane travel. Partly it was the thought of the plane; simply that. Still, that was just the beginning of uneasiness and, as yet, easy to suppress.

After all, Lije Baley had been in a plane four times before. Once he had even crossed the continent. So, while plane travel is never pleasant, it would, at least, not be a complete step into the unknown.

And then, the trip from New York to Washington would take only an hour. The take-off would be from New York Runway Number 2, which, like all official Runways, was decently enclosed, with a lock opening to the unprotected atmosphere only after air speed had been achieved. The arrival would be at Washington Runway Number 5, which was similarly protected.

Furthermore, as Baley well knew, there would be no windows on the plane. There would be good lighting, decent food, all necessary conveniences. The radio-controlled flight would be smooth; there would scarcely be any sensation of motion once the plane was air-borne.

He explained all this to himself, and to Jessie, his wife,

who had never been air-borne and who approached such matters with terror.

She said, "But I don't *like* you to take a plane, Lije. It isn't natural. Why can't you take the Expressways?"

"Because that would take ten hours"—Baley's long face was set in dour lines—"and because I'm a member of the City Police Force and have to follow the orders of my superiors. At least, I do if I want to keep my C-6 rating."

There was no arguing with that.

Baley took the plane and kept his eyes firmly on the news-strip that unreeled smoothly and continuously from the eye-level dispenser. The City was proud of that service: news, features, humorous articles, educational bits, occasional fiction. Someday the strips would be converted to film, it was said, since enclosing the eyes with a viewer would be an even more efficient way of distracting the passenger from his surroundings.

Baley kept his eyes on the unreeling strip, not only for the sake of distraction, but also because etiquette required it. There were five other passengers on the plane (he could not help noticing that much) and each one of them had his private right to whatever degree of fear and anxiety his nature and upbringing made him feel.

Baley would certainly resent the intrusion of anyone else on his own uneasiness. He wanted no strange eyes on the whiteness of his knuckles where his hands gripped the arm-rest, or the dampish stain they would leave when he took them away.

He told himself: I'm enclosed. This plane is just a little City.

But he didn't fool himself. There was an inch of steel at his left; he could feel it with his elbow. Past that, nothing——

Well, air! But that was nothing, really.

A thousand miles of it in one direction. A thousand in another. One mile of it, maybe two, straight down.

He almost wished he could see straight down, glimpse the top of the buried Cities he was passing over; New York, Philadelphia, Baltimore, Washington. He imagined the rolling, low-slung cluster-complexes of domes he had never seen but knew to be there. And under them, for a mile underground and dozens of miles in every direction, would be the Cities.

The endless, hiving corridors of the Cities, he thought, alive with people; apartments, community kitchens, factories, Expressways; all comfortable and warm with the evidence of man.

And he himself was isolated in the cold and featureless air in a small bullet of metal, moving through emptiness.

His hands trembled, and he forced his eyes to focus on the strip of paper and read a bit.

It was a short story dealing with Galactic exploration and it was quite obvious that the hero was an Earthman.

Baley muttered in exasperation, then held his breath momentarily in dismay at his boorishness in making a sound.

It was completely ridiculous, though. It was pandering to childishness, this pretense that Earthmen could invade space. Galactic exploration! The Galaxy was closed to Earthmen. It was pre-empted by the Spacers, whose ancestors had been Earthmen centuries before. Those ancestors had reached the Outer Worlds first, found themselves comfortable, and their descendants had lowered the bars to immigration. They had penned in Earth and their Earthman cousins. And Earth's City civilization completed the task, imprisoning Earthmen within the Cities by a wall of fear of open spaces that barred them from the robot-run farming and mining areas of their own planet; from even that.

Baley thought bitterly: Jehoshaphat! If we don't like it, let's do something about it. Let's not just waste time with fairy tales.

But there was nothing to do about it, and he knew it.

Then the plane landed. He and his fellow-passengers emerged and scattered away from one another, never looking.

Baley glanced at his watch and decided there was time for freshening before taking the Expressway to the Justice Department. He was glad there was. The sound and clamor of life, the huge vaulted chamber of the airport with City corridors leading off on numerous levels, everything else he saw and heard, gave him the feeling of being safely and warmly enclosed in the bowels and womb of the City. It washed away anxiety and only a shower was necessary to complete the job.

He needed a transient's permit to make use of one of the community bathrooms, but presentation of his travel orders eliminated any difficulties. There was only the routine stamping, with private-stall privileges (the date carefully marked to prevent abuse) and a slim strip of directions for getting to the assigned spot.

Baley was thankful for the feel of the strips beneath his feet. It was with something amounting to luxury that he felt himself accelerate as he moved from strip to moving strip inward toward the speeding Expressway. He swung himself aboard lightly, taking the seat to which his rating entitled him.

It wasn't a rush hour; seats were available. The bathroom, when he reached it, was not unduly crowded either. The stall assigned to him was in decent order with a launderette that worked well.

With his water ration consumed to good purpose and his clothing freshened he felt ready to tackle the Justice Department. Ironically enough, he even felt cheerful.

Undersecretary Albert Minnim was a small, compact man, ruddy of skin, and graying, with the angles of his body smoothed down and softened. He exuded an air of cleanliness and smelled faintly of tonic. It all spoke of the good things of life that came with the liberal rations obtained by those high in Administration.

Baley felt sallow and rawboned in comparison. He was conscious of his own large hands, deep-set eyes, a general sense of cragginess.

Minnim said cordially, "Sit down, Baley. Do you smoke?"

"Only a pipe, sir," said Baley.

He drew it out as he spoke, and Minnim thrust back a cigar he had half drawn.

Baley was instantly regretful. A cigar was better than nothing and he would have appreciated the gift. Even with the increased tobacco ration that went along with his recent promotion from C-5 to C-6 he wasn't exactly swimming in pipe fixings.

"Please light up, if you care to," said Minnim, and waited with a kind of paternal patience while Baley measured out a careful quantity of tobacco and affixed the pipe baffle.

Baley said, his eyes on his pipe, "I have not been told the reason for my being called to Washington, sir."

"I know that," said Minnim. He smiled. "I can fix that right now. You are being reassigned temporarily."

"Outside New York City?"

"Quite a distance."

Baley raised his eyebrows and looked thoughtful. "How temporarily, sir?"

"I'm not sure."

Baley was aware of the advantages and disadvantages of reassignment. As a transient in a City of which he was not a resident, he would probably live on a scale better than his official rating entitled him to. On the other hand, it would be very unlikely that Jessie and their son, Bentley, would be allowed to travel with him. They would be taken care of, to be sure, there in New York, but Baley was a domesticated creature and he did not enjoy the thought of separation.

Then, too, a reassignment meant a specific job of work, which was good, and a responsibility greater than that ordinarily expected of the individual detective, which could be uncomfortable. Baley had, not too many months earlier, survived the responsibility of the investigation of the murder of a Spacer just outside New York. He was not overjoyed at the prospect of another such detail, or anything approaching it.

He said, "Would you tell me where I'm going? The nature of the reassignment? What it's all about?"

He was trying to weigh the Undersecretary's "Quite a distance" and make little bets with himself as to his new base of operations. The "Quite a distance" had sounded emphatic and Baley thought: Calcutta? Sydney?

Then he noticed that Minnim was taking out a cigar after all and was lighting it carefully.

Baley thought: Jehoshaphat! He's having trouble telling me. He doesn't want to say.

Minnim withdrew his cigar from between his lips. He watched the smoke and said, "The Department of Justice is assigning you to temporary duty on Solaria."

For a moment Baley's mind groped for an illusive identification: Solaria, Asia; Solaria, Australia . . . ?

Then he rose from his seat and said tightly, "You mean, one of the Outer Worlds?"

Minnim didn't meet Baley's eyes. "That is right."

Baley said, "But that's impossible. They wouldn't allow an Earthman on an Outer World."

"Circumstances do alter cases, Plainclothesman Baley. There has been a murder on Solaria."

Baley's lips quirked into a sort of reflex smile. "That's a little out of our jurisdiction, isn't it?"

"They've requested help."

"From us? Earth?" Baley was torn between confusion and disbelief. For an Outer World to take any attitude other than contempt toward the despised mother planet or, at best, a patronizing social benevolence was unthinkable. To come for help?

"From Earth?" he repeated.

"Unusual," admitted Minnim, "but there it is. They want a Terrestrial detective assigned to the case. It's been handled through diplomatic channels on the highest levels."

Baley sat down again. "Why me? I'm not a young man. I'm forty-three. I've got a wife and child. I couldn't leave Earth."

"That's not our choice, Plainclothesman. You were specifically asked for."

"*I?*"

"Plainclothesman Elijah Baley, C-6, of the New York City Police Force. They knew what they wanted. Surely you see why."

Baley said stubbornly, "I'm not qualified."

"They think you are. The way you handled the Spacer murder has apparently reached them."

"They must have got it all mixed up. It must have seemed better than it was."

Minnim shrugged. "In any case, they've asked for you and we have agreed to send you. You are reassigned. The papers have all been taken care of and you must go. During your absence, your wife and child will be taken care of at a C-7 level since that will be your temporary rating during your discharge of this assignment." He paused significantly.

"Satisfactory completion of the assignment may make the rating permanent."

It was happening too quickly for Baley. None of this could be so. He *couldn't* leave Earth. Didn't they see that?

He heard himself ask in a level voice that sounded unnatural in his own ears, "What kind of a murder? What are the circumstances? Why can't they handle it themselves?"

Minnim rearranged small objects on his desk with carefully kept fingers. He shook his head. "I don't know anything about the murder. I don't know the circumstances."

"Then who does, sir? You don't expect me to go there cold, do you?" And again a despairing inner voice: But I *can't* leave Earth.

"Nobody knows anything about it. Nobody on Earth. The Solarians didn't tell us. That will be your job; to find out what is so important about the murder that they must have an Earthman to solve it. Or, rather, that will be *part* of your job."

Baley was desperate enough to say, "What if I refuse?" He knew the answer, of course. He knew exactly what declassification would mean to himself and, more than that, to his family.

Minnim said nothing about declassification. He said softly, "You can't refuse, Plainclothesman. You have a job to do."

"For Solaria? The hell with them."

"For *us*, Baley. For us." Minnim paused. Then he went on, "You know the position of Earth with respect to the Spacers. I don't have to go into that."

Baley knew the situation and so did every man on Earth. The fifty Outer Worlds, with a far smaller population, in combination, than that of Earth alone, nevertheless maintained a military potential perhaps a hundred times greater. With their underpopulated worlds resting on a positronic robot economy, their energy production per human was thousands of times that of Earth. And it was the amount of energy a single human could produce that dictated military potential, standard of living, happiness, and all besides.

Minnim said, "One of the factors that conspires to keep us in that position is ignorance. Just that. Ignorance. The Spacers know all about us. They send missions enough to

Earth, heaven knows. We know nothing about them except what they tell us. No man on Earth has ever as much as set foot on an Outer World. *You* will, though."

Baley began, "I can't..."

But Minnim repeated, "You *will*. Your position will be unique. You will be on Solaria on their invitation, doing a job to which they will assign you. When you return, you will have information useful to Earth."

Baley watched the Undersecretary through somber eyes. "You mean I'm to spy for Earth."

"No question of spying. You need do nothing they don't ask you to do. Just keep your eyes and mind open. Observe! There will be specialists on Earth when you return to analyze and interpret your observations."

Baley said, "I take it there's a crisis, sir."

"Why do you say that?"

"Sending an Earthman to an Outer World is risky. The Spacers hate us. With the best will in the world and even though I'm there on invitation, I could cause an interstellar incident. The Terrestrial Government could easily avoid sending me if they chose. They could say I was ill. The Spacers are pathologically afraid of disease. They wouldn't want me for any reason if they thought I were ill."

"Do you suggest," said Minnim, "we try that trick?"

"No. If the government had no other motive for sending me, they would think of that or something better without my help. So it follows that it is the question of spying that is the real essential. And if that is so, there must be more to it than just a see-what-you-can-see to justify the risk."

Baley half expected an explosion and would have half welcomed one as a relief of pressure, but Minnim only smiled frostily and said, "You can see past the nonessentials, it seems. But then, I expected no less."

The Undersecretary leaned across his desk toward Baley. "Here is certain information which you will discuss with no one, not even with other government officials. Our sociologists have been coming to certain conclusions concerning the present Galactic situation. Fifty Outer Worlds, underpopulated, roboticized, powerful, with people that are healthy and long-lived. We ourselves, crowded, technologically underdeveloped, short-lived, under their domination. It is unstable."

"Everything is in the long run."

"This is unstable in the short run. A hundred years is the most we're allowed. The situation will last our time, to be sure, but we have children. Eventually we will become too great a danger to the Outer Worlds to be allowed to survive. There are eight billions on Earth who hate the Spacers."

Baley said, "The Spacers exclude us from the Galaxy, handle our trade to their own profit, dictate to our government, and treat us with contempt. What do they expect? Gratitude?"

"True, and yet the pattern is fixed. Revolt, suppression, revolt, suppression—and within a century Earth will be virtually wiped out as a populated world. So the sociologists say."

Baley stirred uneasily. One didn't question sociologists and their computers. "But what do you expect me to accomplish if all this is so?"

"Bring us information. The big flaw in sociological forecast is our lack of data concerning the Spacers. We've had to make assumptions on the basis of the few Spacers they sent out here. We've had to rely on what they choose to tell us of themselves, so it follows we know their strengths and only their strengths. Damn it, they have their robots and their low numbers and their long lives. But do they have weaknesses? Is there some factor or factors which, if we but knew, would alter the sociologic inevitability of destruction; something that could guide our actions and better the chance of Earth's survival."

"Hadn't you better send a sociologist, sir?"

Minnim shook his head. "If we could send whom we pleased, we would have sent someone out ten years ago, when these conclusions were first being arrived at. This is our first excuse to send someone and they ask for a detective and that suits us. A detective is a sociologist, too; a rule-of-thumb, practicing sociologist, or he wouldn't be a good detective. Your record proves you a good one."

"Thank you, sir," said Baley mechanically. "And if I get into trouble?"

Minnim shrugged. "That's the risk of a policeman's job." He dismissed the point with a wave of his hand and added, "In any case, you must go. Your time of departure is set. The ship that will take you is waiting."

Baley stiffened. "Waiting? When do I leave?"

"In two days."

"I've got to get back to New York then. My wife——"

"*We* will see your wife. She can't know the nature of your job, you know. She will be told not to expect to hear from you."

"But this in inhuman. I must see her. I may never see her again."

Minnim said, "What I say now may sound even more inhuman, but isn't it true there is never a day you set about your duties on which you cannot tell yourself she may never see you again? Plainclothesman Baley, we must all do our duty."

Baley's pipe had been out for fifteen minutes. He had never noticed it.

No one had more to tell him. No one knew anything about the murder. Official after official simply hurried him on to the moment when he stood at the base of a spaceship, all unbelieving still.

It was like a gigantic cannon aimed at the heavens, and Baley shivered spasmodically in the raw, open air. The night closed in (for which Baley was thankful) like dark black walls melting into a black ceiling overhead. It was cloudy, and though he had been to Planetaria, a bright star, stabbing through a rift in the cloud, startled him when it caught his eyes.

A little spark, far, far away. He stared curiously, almost unafraid of it. It looked quite close, quite insignificant, and yet around things like that circled planets of which the inhabitants were lords of the Galaxy. The sun was a thing like that, he thought, except much closer, shining now on the other side of the Earth.

He thought of the Earth suddenly as a ball of stone with a film of moisture and gas, exposed to emptiness on every side, with its Cities barely dug into the outer rim, clinging precariously between rock and air. His skin crawled!

The ship was a Spacer vessel, of course. Interstellar trade was entirely in Spacer hands. He was alone now, just outside the rim of the City. He had been bathed and scraped and sterilized until he was considered safe, by Spacer standards, to board the ship. Even so, they sent only a robot out to meet him, bearing as he did a hundred varieties of disease germs from the sweltering City to which he himself was resistant but to which the eugenically hothoused Spacers were not.

The robot bulked dimly in the night, its eyes a dull red glow.

"Plainsclothesman Elijah Baley?"

"That's right," said Baley crisply, the hair on the nape of his neck stirring a bit. He was enough of an Earthman to get angry goose flesh at the sight of a robot doing a man's job. There had been R. Daneel Olivaw, who had partnered with him in the Spacer murder affair, but that had been different. Daneel had been——

"You will follow me, please," said the robot, and a white light flooded a path toward the ship.

Baley followed. Up the ladder and into the ship he went, along corridors, and into a room.

The robot said, "This will be your room, Plainclothesman Baley. It is requested that you remain in it for the duration of the trip."

Baley thought: Sure, seal me off. Keep me safe. Insulated.

The corridors along which he had traveled had been empty. Robots were probably disinfecting them now. The robot facing him would probably step through a germicidal bath when it left.

The robot said, "There is a water supply and plumbing. Food will be supplied. You will have viewing matter. The ports are controlled from this panel. They are closed now but if you wish to view space——"

Baley said with some agitation, "That's all right, boy. Leave the ports closed."

He used the "boy" address that Earthmen always used for robots, but the robot showed no adverse response. It couldn't, of course. Its responses were limited and controlled by the Laws of Robotics.

The robot bent its large metal body in the travesty of a respectful bow and left.

Baley was alone in his room and could take stock. It was better than the plane, at least. He could see the plane from end to end. He could see its limits. The spaceship was large. It had corridors, levels, rooms. It was a small City in itself. Baley could almost breathe freely.

Then lights flashed and a robot's metallic voice sounded over the communo and gave him specific instructions for guarding himself against take-off acceleration.

There was the push backward against webbing and a yielding hydraulic system, a distant rumble of force-jets heated to fury by the proton micro-pile. There was the hiss of tearing atmosphere, growing thinner and high-pitched and fading into nothingness after an hour.

They were in space.

It was as though all sensation had numbed, as though nothing were real. He told himself that each second found him thousands of miles farther from the Cities, from Jessie, but it didn't register.

On the second day (the third?—there was no way of telling time except by the intervals of eating and sleeping) there was a queer momentary sensation of being turned inside out. It lasted an instant and Baley knew it was a Jump, that oddly incomprehensible, almost mystical, momentary transition through hyperspace that transferred a ship and all it contained from one point in space to another, light-years away. Another lapse of time and another Jump, still another lapse, still another Jump.

Baley told himself now that he was light-years away, tens of light-years, hundreds, thousands.

He didn't know how many. No one on Earth as much as knew Solaria's location in space. He would bet on that. They were ignorant, every one of them.

He felt terribly alone.

There was the feel of deceleration and the robot entered. Its somber, ruddy eyes took in the details of Baley's harness. Efficiently it tightened a wing nut; quickly it surveyed the details of the hydraulic system.

It said, "We will be landing in three hours. You will remain, if you please, in this room. A man will come to escort you out and to take you to your place of residence."

"Wait," said Baley tensely. Strapped in as he was, he felt helpless. "When we land, what time of day will it be?"

The robot said at once, "By Galactic Standard Time, it will be——"

"Local time, boy. Local time! Jehoshaphat!"

The robot continued smoothly, "The day on Solaria is twenty-eight point thirty-five Standard hours in length. The Solarian hour is divided into ten decads, each of which is divided into a hundred centads. We are scheduled to arrive at an airport at which the day will be at the twentieth centad of the fifth decad."

Baley hated that robot. He hated it for its obtuseness in not understanding; for the way it was making him ask the question directly and exposing his own weakness.

He had to. He said flatly, "Will it be daytime?"

And after all that the robot answered, "Yes, sir," and left.

It would be day! He would have to step out onto the unprotected surface of a planet in daytime.

He was not quite sure how it would be. He had seen glimpses of planetary surfaces from certain points within the City; he had even been out upon it for moments. Always, though, he had been surrounded by walls or within reach of one. There was always safety at hand.

Where would there be safety now? Not even the false walls of darkness.

And because he would not display weakness before the Spacers—he'd be damned if he would—he stiffened his body against the webbing that held him safe against the forces of deceleration, closed his eyes, and stubbornly fought panic.

2. A FRIEND IS ENCOUNTERED

Baley was losing his fight. Reason alone was not enough.

Baley told himself over and over: Men live in the open all their lives. The Spacers do so now. Our ancestors on Earth did it in the past. There is no real harm in wall-lessness. It is only my mind that tells me differently, and it is wrong.

But all that did not help. Something above and beyond reason cried out for walls and would have none of space.

As time passed, he thought he would not succeed. He would be cowering at the end, trembling and pitiful. The Spacer they would send for him (with filters in his nose to keep out germs, and gloves on his hands to prevent contact) would not even honestly despise him. The Spacer would feel only disgust.

Baley held on grimly.

When the ship stopped and the deceleration harness automatically uncoupled, while the hydraulic system retracted into the wall, Baley remained in his seat. He was afraid, and determined not to show it.

He looked away at the first quiet sound of the door of his room opening. There was the eye-corner flash of a tall, bronze-haired figure entering; a Spacer, one of those proud descendants of Earth who had disowned their heritage.

The Spacer spoke. "Partner Elijah!"

Baley's head turned toward the speaker with a jerk. His eyes rounded and he rose almost without volition.

He stared at the face; at the broad, high cheekbones, the absolute calm of the facial lines, the symmetry of the body, most of all at that level look out of nerveless blue eyes.

"D-daneel."

The Spacer said, "It is pleasant that you remember me, Partner Elijah."

"Remember you!" Baley felt relief wash over him. This

being was a bit of Earth, a friend, a comfort, a savior. He had an almost unbearable desire to rush to the Spacer and embrace him, to hug him wildly, and laugh and pound his back and do all the foolish things old friends did when meeting once again after a separation.

But he didn't. He couldn't. He could only step forward, and hold out his hand and say, "I'm not likely to forget you, Daneel."

"That is pleasant," said Daneel, nodding gravely. "As you are well aware, it is quite impossible for me, while in working order, to forget you. It is well that I see you again."

Daneel took Baley's hand and pressed it with firm coolness, his fingers closing to a comfortable but not painful pressure and then releasing it.

Baley hoped earnestly that the creature's unreadable eyes could not penetrate Baley's mind and see that wild moment, just past and not yet entirely subsided, when all of Baley had concentrated into a feeling of an intense friendship that was almost love.

After all, one could not love as a friend this Daneel Olivaw, who was not a man at all, but only a robot.

The robot that looked so like a man said, "I have asked that a robot-driven ground-transport vessel be connected to this ship by air-tube——"

Baley frowned. "An air-tube?"

"Yes. It is a common technique, frequently used in space, in order that personnel and matériel be transferred from one vessel to another without the necessity of special equipment against vacuum. It would seem then that you are not acquainted with the technique."

"No," said Baley, "but I get the picture."

"It is, of course, rather complicated to arrange such a device between spaceship and ground vehicle, but I have requested that it be done. Fortunately, the mission on which you and I are engaged is one of high priority. Difficulties are smoothed out quickly."

"Are you assigned to the murder case too?"

"Have you not been informed of that? I regret not having told you at once." There was, of course, no sign of regret on the robot's perfect face. "It was Dr. Han Fastolfe, whom you met on Earth during our previous partnership and whom I hope you remember, who first suggested you as an appropriate investigator in this case. He made it a condition that I be assigned to work with you once more."

Baley managed a smile. Dr. Fastolfe was a native of Aurora and Aurora was the strongest of the Outer Worlds. Apparently the advice of an Auroran bore weight.

Baley said, "A team that works shouldn't be broken up, eh?" (The first exhilaration of Daneel's appearance was fading and the compression about Baley's chest was returning.)

"I do not know if that precise thought was in his mind, Partner Elijah. From the nature of his orders to me, I should think that he was interested in having assigned to work with you one who would have experience with your world and would know of your consequent peculiarities."

"Peculiarities!" Baley frowned and felt offended. It was not a term he liked in connection with himself.

"So that I could arrange the air-tube, for example. I am well aware of your aversion to open spaces as a result of your upbringing in the Cities of Earth."

Perhaps it was the effect of being called "peculiar," the feeling that he had to counterattack or lose caste to a machine, that drove Baley to change the subject sharply. Perhaps it was just that life-long training prevented him from leaving any logical contradiction undisturbed.

He said, "There was a robot in charge of my welfare on board this ship; a robot" (a touch of malice intruded itself here) "that looks like a robot. Do you know it?"

"I spoke to it before coming on board."

"What's its designation? How do I make contact with it?"

"It is RX-2475. It is customary on Solaria to use only serial numbers for robots." Daneel's calm eyes swept the control panel near the door. "This contact will signal it."

Baley looked at the control panel himself and, since the contact to which Daneel pointed was labeled RX, its identification seemed quite unmysterious.

Baley put his finger over it and in less than a minute, the robot, the one that looked like a robot, entered.

Baley said, "You are RX-2475."

"Yes, sir."

"You told me earlier that someone would arrive to escort me off the ship. Did you mean him?" Baley pointed at Daneel.

The eyes of the two robots met. RX-2475 said, "His papers identify him as the one who was to meet you."

"Were you told in advance anything about him other than his papers? Was he described to you?"

"No, sir. I was given his name, however."

"Who gave you the information?"

"The captain of the ship, sir."

"Who is a Solarian?"

"Yes, sir."

Baley licked his lips. The next question would be decisive.

He said, "What were you told would be the name of the one you were expecting?"

RX-2475 said, "Daneel Olivaw, sir."

"Good boy! You may leave now."

There was the robotic bow and then the sharp about-face. RX-2475 left.

Baley turned to his partner and said thoughtfully, "You are not telling me all the truth, Daneel."

"In what way, Partner Elijah?" asked Daneel.

"While I was talking to you earlier, I recalled an odd point. RX-2475, when it told me I would have an escort said a *man* would come for me. I remember that quite well."

Daneel listened quietly and said nothing.

Baley went on. "I thought the robot might have made a mistake. I thought also that perhaps a man had indeed been assigned to meet me and had later been replaced by you, RX-2475 not being informed of the change. But you heard me check that. Your papers were described to it and it was given your name. But it was not quite given your name at that, was it, Daneel?"

"Indeed, it was not given my entire name," agreed Daneel.

"Your name is not Daneel Olivaw, but R. Daneel Olivaw, isn't it? Or, in full, Robot Daneel Olivaw."

"You are quite correct, Partner Elijah."

"From which it all follows that RX-2475 was never informed that you are a robot. It was allowed to think of you as a man. With your manlike appearance, such a masquerade is possible."

"I have no quarrel with your reasoning."

"Then let's proceed." Baley was feeling the germs of a kind of savage delight. He was on the track of something. It couldn't be anything much, but this was the kind of tracking he could do well. It was something he could do well enough to be called half across space to do. He said, "Now why should anyone want to deceive a miserable robot? It doesn't matter to it whether you are man or robot. It follows orders in either case. A reasonable conclusion then is that the Solarian captain who informed the robot and the Solarian officials who informed the Captain did not themselves know you were a robot. As I say, that is one reasonable conclusion, but perhaps not the only one. Is this one true?"

"I believe it is."

"All right, then. Good guess. Now why? Dr. Han Fastolfe, in recommending you as my partner allows the Solarians to think you are a human. Isn't that a dangerous thing? The Solarians, if they find out, may be quite angry. Why was it done?"

The humanoid robot said, "It was explained to me thus, Partner Elijah. Your association with a human of the Outer Worlds would raise your status in the eyes of the Solarians. Your association with a robot would lower it. Since I was familiar with your ways and could work with you easily, it was thought reasonable to allow the Solarians to accept me as a man without actually deceiving them by a positive statement to that effect."

Baley did not believe it. It seemed like the kind of careful consideration for an Earthman's feelings that did not come naturally to a Spacer, not even to as enlightened a one as Fastolfe.

He considered an alternative and said, "Are the Solarians well known among the Outer Worlds for the production of robots?"

"I am glad," said Daneel, "that you have been briefed concerning the inner economy of Solaria."

"Not a word," said Baley. "I can guess the spelling of the word Solaria and there my knowledge stops."

"Then I do not see, Partner Elijah, what it was that impelled you to ask that question, but it is a most pertinent one. You have hit the mark. My mind-store of information includes the fact that, of the fifty Outer Worlds, Solaria is by far the best known for the variety and excellence of robot models it turns out. It exports specialized models to all the other Outer Worlds."

Baley nodded in grim satisfaction. Naturally Daneel did not follow an intuitive mental leap that used human weakness as a starting point. Nor did Baley feel impelled to explain the reasoning. *If* Solaria turned out to be a world expert in robotics, Dr. Han Fastolfe and his associates might have purely personal and very human motives for demonstrating their own prize robot. It would have nothing at all to do with an Earthman's safety or feelings.

They would be asserting their own superiority by allowing the expert Solarians to be fooled into accepting a robot of Auroran handiwork as a fellow-man.

Baley felt much better. Strange that all the thought, all the intellectual powers he could muster, could not succeed in lifting him out of panic; and yet a sop to his own vainglory succeeded at once.

The recognition of the vainglory of the Spacers helped too.

He thought: Jehoshaphat, we're all human; even the Spacers.

Aloud he said, almost flippantly, "How long do we have to wait for the ground-car? I'm ready."

The air-tube gave signs of not being well adapted to its present use. Man and humanoid stepped out of the spaceship erect, moving along flexible mesh that bent and swayed under their weight. (In space, Baley imagined hazily, men transferring weightlessly from ship to ship might easily skim along the length of the tube, impelled by an initial Jump.)

Toward the other end the tube narrowed clumsily, its meshing bunching as though some giant hand had constricted it. Daneel, carrying the flashlight, got down on all fours and so did Baley. They traveled the last twenty feet in that fashion, moving at last into what was obviously a ground-car.

Daneel closed the door through which they had entered, sliding it shut carefully. There was a heavy, clicking noise that might have been the detachment of the air-tube.

Baley looked about curiously. There was nothing too exotic about the ground-car. There were two seats in tandem, each of which could hold three. There were doors at each end of each seat. The glossy sections that might ordinarily have been windows were black and opaque, as a result, undoubtedly, of appropriate polarization. Baley was acquainted with that.

The interior of the car was lit by two round spots of yellow illumination in the ceiling and, in short, the only thing Baley felt to be strange was the transmitter set into the partition immediately before the front seat and, of course, the added fact that there were no visible controls.

Baley said, "I suppose the driver is on the other side of this partition."

Daneel said, "Exactly so, Partner Elijah. And we can give our orders in this fashion." He leaned forward slightly and flicked a toggle switch that set a spot of red light to flickering. He said quietly, "You may start now. We are ready."

There was a muted whir that faded almost at once, a very slight, very transitory pressing against the back of the seat, and then nothing.

Baley said in surprise, "Are we moving?"

Daneel said, "We are. The car does not move on wheels but glides along a diamagnetic force-field. Except for acceleration and deceleration, you will feel nothing."

"What about curves?"

"The car will bank automatically to compensate. Its level is maintained when traveling up- or downhill."

"The controls must be complicated," said Baley dryly.

"Quite automatic. The driver of the vehicle is a robot."

"Umm." Baley had about all he wanted on the ground-car. He said, "How long will this take?"

"About an hour. Air travel would have been speedier, but I was concerned to keep you enclosed and the aircraft models available on Solaria do not lend themselves to complete enclosure as does a ground-car such as that in which we are now riding."

Baley felt annoyed at the other's "concern." He felt like a baby in the charge of its nurse. He felt almost as annoyed, oddly enough, at Daneel's sentences. It seemed to him that such needlessly formal sentence structure might easily betray the robotic nature of the creature.

For a moment Baley stared curiously at R. Daneel Olivaw. The robot, looking straight ahead, was motionless and unself-conscious under the other's gaze.

Daneel's skin texture was perfect, the individual hair on head and body had been lovingly and intricately manufactured and placed. The muscle movement under the skin was most realistic. No pains, however extravagant, had been spared. Yet Baley knew, from personal knowledge, that limbs and chest could be split open along invisible seams so that repairs might be made. He knew there was metal and silicone under that realistic skin. He knew a positronic brain, most advanced but only positronic, nestled in the hollow of the skull. He knew that Daneel's "thoughts" were only short-lived positronic currents flowing along paths rigidly designed and foreordained by the manufacturer.

But what were the signs that would give that away to the expert eye that had no foreknowledge? The trifling unnaturalness of Daneel's manner of speech? The unemotional gravity that rested so steadily upon him? The very perfection of his humanity?

But he was wasting time. Baley said, "Let's get on with it, Daneel. I suppose that before arriving here, you were briefed on matters Solarian?"

"I was, Partner Elijah."

"Good. That's more than they did for me. How large is the world?"

"Its diameter is 9500 miles. It is the outermost of three planets and the only inhabited one. In climate and atmosphere it resembles Earth; its percentage of fertile land is higher; its useful mineral content lower, but of course less exploited. The world is self-supporting and can, with the aid of its robot exports, maintain a high standard of living."

Baley said, "What's the population?"

"Twenty thousand people, Partner Elijah."

Baley accepted that for a moment, then he said mildly, "You mean twenty million, don't you?" His scant knowledge of the Outer Worlds was enough to tell him that, although the worlds were underpopulated by Earthly standards, the individual populations *were* in the millions.

"Twenty thousand people, Partner Elijah," said the robot again.

"You mean the planet has just been settled?"

"Not at all. It has been independent for nearly two centuries, and it was settled for a century or more before that. The population is deliberately maintained at twenty thousand, that being considered optimum by the Solarians themselves."

"How much of the planet do they occupy?"

"All the fertile portions."

"Which is, in square miles?"

"Thirty million square miles, including marginal areas."

"For twenty thousand people?"

"There are also some two hundred million working positronic robots, Partner Elijah."

"Jehoshaphat! That's—that's ten thousand robots per human."

"It is by far the highest such ratio among the Outer Worlds, Partner Elijah. The next highest, on Aurora, is only fifty to one."

"What can they use so many robots for? What do they want with all that food?"

"Food is a relatively minor item. The mines are more important, and power production more important still."

Baley thought of all those robots and felt a trifle dizzy. Two hundred million robots! So many among so few humans. The robots must litter the landscape. An observer from without might think Solaria a world of robots altogether and fail to notice the thin human leaven.

He felt a sudden need to see. He remembered the conversation with Minnim and the sociologic prediction of Earth's danger. It seemed far off, a bit unreal, but he remembered. His personal dangers and difficulties since leaving Earth dimmed the memory of Minnim's voice stating enormities with cool and precise enunciation, but never blotted it out altogether.

Baley had lived too long with duty to allow even the overwhelming fact of open space to stop him in its performance. Data collected from a Spacer's words, or from those of a Spacer robot for that matter, was the sort of thing that was already available to Earth's sociologists. What was needed was direct observation and it was his job, however unpleasant, to collect it.

He inspected the upper portion of the ground-car. "Is this thing a convertible, Daneel?"

"I beg your pardon, Partner Elijah, but I do not follow your meaning."

"Can the car's top be pushed back? Can it be made open to the—the sky?" (He had almost said "dome" out of habit.)

"Yes, it can."

"Then have that done, Daneel. I would like to take a look."

The robot responded gravely, "I am sorry, but I cannot allow that."

Baley felt astonished. He said, "Look, R. Daneel" (he stressed the R.). "Let's rephrase that. I order you to lower the top."

The creature was a robot, manlike or not. It *had* to follow orders.

But Daneel did not move. He said, "I must explain that it is my first concern to spare you harm. It has been clear to me on the basis both of my instructions and of my own personal experience that you would suffer harm at finding yourself in large, empty spaces. I cannot, therefore, allow you to expose yourself to that."

Baley could feel his face darkening with an influx of blood and at the same time could feel the complete uselessness of anger. The creature *was* a robot, and Baley knew the First Law of Robotics well.

It went: *A robot may not injure a human being, or, through inaction, allow a human being to come to harm.*

Everything else in a robot's positronic brain—that of any robot on any world in the Galaxy—had to bow to that prime consideration. Of course a robot had to follow orders, but with one major, all-important qualification. Following orders was only the Second Law of Robotics.

It went: *A robot must obey the orders given it by human beings except where such orders would conflict with the First Law.*

Baley forced himself to speak quietly and reasonably. "I think I can endure it for a short time, Daneel."

"That is not my feeling, Partner Elijah."

"Let me be the judge, Daneel."

"If that is an order, Partner Elijah, I cannot follow it."

Baley let himself lounge back against the softly upholstered seat. The robot would, of course, be quite beyond the reach of force. Daneel's strength, if exerted fully, would be a hundred times that of flesh and blood. He would be perfectly capable of restraining Baley without ever hurting him.

Baley was armed. He could point a blaster at Daneel, but, except for perhaps a momentary sensation of mastery, that action would only succeed in greater frustration. A threat of destruction was useless against a robot. Self-preservation was only the Third Law.

It went: *A robot must protect its own existence, as long as such protection does not conflict with the First or Second Laws.*

It would not trouble Daneel to be destroyed if the alternative were breaking the First Law. And Baley did not wish to destroy Daneel. Definitely not.

Yet he did want to see out the car. It was becoming an obsession with him. He couldn't allow this nurse-infant relationship to build up.

For a moment he thought of pointing the blaster at his own temple. Open the car top or I'll kill myself. Oppose one application of the First Law by a greater and more immediate one.

Baley knew he couldn't do it. Too undignified. He disliked the picture conjured up by the thought.

He said wearily, "Would you ask the driver how close in miles we are to destination?"

"Certainly, Partner Elijah."

Daneel bent forward and pushed the toggle switch. But as he did so, Baley leaned forward too, crying out, "Driver! Lower the top of the car!"

And it was the human hand that moved quickly to the toggle switch and closed it again. The human hand held its place firmly thereafter.

Panting a bit, Baley stared at Daneel.

For a second Daneel was motionless, as though his positronic paths were momentarily out of stability in their effort to adjust to the new situation. But that passed quickly and then the robot's hand was moving.

Baley had anticipated that. Daneel would remove the human hand from the switch (gently, not hurting it), reactivate the transmitter, and countermand the order.

Baley said, "You won't get my hand away without hurting me. I warn you. You will probably have to break my fingers."

That was not so. Baley knew that. But Daneel's movements stopped. Harm against harm. The positronic brain had to weigh probabilities and translate them into opposing potentials. It meant just a bit more hesitation.

Baley said, "It's too late."

His race was won. The top was sliding back and pouring into the car, now open, was the harsh white light of Solaria's sun.

Baley wanted to shut his eyes in initial terror, but fought the sensation. He faced the enormous wash of blue and green, incredible quantities of it. He could feel the undisciplined rush of air against his face, but could make out no details of anything. A moving something flashed past. It might have been a robot or an animal or an unliving something caught in a puff of air. He couldn't tell. The car went past it too quickly.

Blue, green, air, noise, motion—and over it all, beating down, furiously, relentlessly, frighteningly, was the white light that came from a ball in the sky.

For one fleeting split moment he bent his head back and stared directly at Solaria's sun. He stared at it, unprotected by the diffusing glass of the Cities' uppermost-Level sunporches. He stared at the naked sun.

And at the very moment he felt Daneel's hands clamping down upon his shoulders. His mind crowded with thought during that unreal, whirling moment. He had to see! He had to see all he could. And Daneel must be there with him to keep him from seeing.

But surely a robot would not dare use violence on a man. That thought was dominant. Daneel could not prevent him forcibly, and yet Baley felt the robot's hands forcing him down.

Baley lifted his arms to force those fleshless hands away and lost all sensation.

3. A VICTIM IS NAMED

Baley was back in the safety of enclosure. Daneel's face wavered before his eyes, and it was splotched with dark spots that turned to red when he blinked.

Baley said, "What happened?"

"I regret," said Daneel, "that you have suffered harm despite my presence. The direct rays of the sun are damaging to the human eye, but I believe that the damage from the short exposure you suffered will not be permanent. When you looked up, I was forced to pull you down and you lost consciousness."

Baley grimaced. That left the question open as to whether he had fainted out of overexcitement (or fright?) or had been knocked unconscious. He felt his jaw and head and found no pain. He forbore asking the question direct. In a way he didn't want to know.

He said, "It wasn't so bad."

"From your reactions, Partner Elijah, I should judge you had found it unpleasant."

"Not at all," said Baley stubbornly. The splotches before his eyes were fading and they weren't tearing so. "I'm only sorry I saw so little. We were moving too fast. Did we pass a robot?"

"We passed a number of them. We are traveling across the Kinbald estate, which is given over to fruit orchards."

"I'll have to try again," said Baley.

"You must not, in my presence," said Daneel. "Meanwhile, I have done as you requested."

"As I requested?"

"You will remember, Partner Elijah, that before you ordered the driver to lower the top of the car, you had ordered me to ask the driver how close in miles we were to desti-

nation. We are ten miles away now and shall be there in
some six minutes."

Baley felt the impulse to ask Daneel if he were angry at
having been outwitted if only to see that perfect face become
imperfect, but he repressed it. Of course Daneel would
simply answer no, without rancor or annoyance. He would
sit there as calm and as grave as ever, unperturbed and
imperturbable.

Baley said quietly, "Just the same, Daneel, I'll have to
get used to it, you know."

The robot regarded his human partner. "To what is it
that you refer?"

"Jehoshaphat! To the—the outdoors. It's all this planet
is made of."

"There will be no necessity for facing the outdoors," said
Daneel. Then, as though that disposed of the subject, he
said, "We are slowing down, Partner Elijah. I believe we
have arrived. It will be necessary to wait now for the connection of another air-tube leading to the dwelling that will
serve as our base of operations."

"An air-tube is unnecessary, Daneel. If I am to be working outdoors, there is no point in delaying the indoctrina-
tion."

"There will be no reason for you to work outdoors, Partner Elijah."

The robot started to say more, but Baley waved him quiet
with a peremptory motion of the hand.

At the moment he was not in the mood for Daneel's
careful consolations, for soothings, for assurances that all
would be well and that he would be taken care of.

What he really wanted was an inner knowledge that he
could take care of himself and fulfill his assignment. The
sight and feel of the open had been hard to take. It might
be that when the time came he would lack the hardihood
to dare face it again, at the cost of his self-respect and,
conceivably, of Earth's safety. All over a small matter of
emptiness.

His face grew grim even at the glancing touch of that
thought. He would face air, sun, and empty space yet!

*   *   *

Elijah Baley felt like an inhabitant of one of the smaller Cities, say Helsinki, visiting New York and counting the Levels in awe. He had thought of a "dwelling" as something like an apartment unit, but this was nothing like it at all. He passed from room to room endlessly. Panoramic windows were shrouded closely, allowing no hint of disturbing day to enter. Lights came to life noiselessly from hidden sources as they stepped into a room and died again as quietly when they left.

"So many rooms," said Baley with wonder. "So many. It's like a very tiny City, Daneel."

"It would seem so, Partner Elijah," said Daneel with equanimity.

It seemed strange to the Earthman. Why was it necessary to crowd so many Spacers together with him in close quarters? He said, "How many will be living here with me?"

Daneel said, "There will be myself, of course, and a number of robots."

Baley thought: He ought to have said, a number of *other* robots.

Again he found it obvious that Daneel had the intention of playing the man thoroughly even for no other audience than Baley, who knew the truth so well.

And then that thought popped into nothing under the force of a second, more urgent one. He cried, "*Robots*? How many *humans*?"

"None, Partner Elijah."

They had just stepped into a room, crowded from floor to ceiling with book films. Three fixed viewers with large twenty-four-inch viewing panels set vertically were in three corners of the room. The fourth contained an animation screen.

Baley looked about in annoyance. He said, "Did they kick everyone out just to leave me rattling around alone in this mausoleum?"

"It is meant only for you. A dwelling such as this for one person is customary on Solaria."

"Everyone lives like this?"

"Everyone."

"What do they need all the rooms for?"

"It is customary to devote a single room to a single

purpose. This is the library. There is also a music room, a gymnasium, a kitchen, a bakery, a dining room, a machine shop, various robot-repair and testing rooms, two bedrooms——"

"Stop! How do you know all this?"

"It is part of the information pattern," said Daneel smoothly, "made available to me before I left Aurora."

"Jehoshaphat! Who takes care of all of this?" He swung his arm in a wide arc.

"There are a number of household robots. They have been assigned to you and will see to it that you are comfortable."

"But I don't need all this," said Baley. He had the urge to sit down and refuse to budge. He wanted to see no more rooms.

"We can remain in one room if you so desire, Partner Elijah. That was visualized as a possibility from the start. Nevertheless, Solarian customs being what they are, it was considered wiser to allow this house to be built——"

"*Built!*" Baley stared. "You mean this was built for me? All this? Specially?"

"A thoroughly roboticized economy——"

"Yes, I see what you're going to say. What will they do with the house when all this is over?"

"I believe they will tear it down."

Baley's lips clamped together. Of course! Tear it down! Build a tremendous structure for the special use of one Earthman and then tear down everything he touched. Sterilize the soil the house stood on! Fumigate the air he breathed! The Spacers might seem strong, but they, too, had their foolish fears.

Daneel seemed to read his thoughts, or to interpret his expression at any rate. He said, "It may appear to you, Partner Elijah, that it is to escape contagion that they will destroy the house. If such are your thoughts, I suggest that you refrain from making yourself uncomfortable over the matter. The fear of disease on the part of Spacers is by no means so extreme. It is just that the effort involved in building the house is, to them, very little. Nor does the waste involved in tearing it down once more seem great to them.

"And by law, Partner Elijah, this place cannot be allowed

to remain standing. It is on the estate of Hannis Gruer and there can only be one legal dwelling place on any estate, that of the owner. This house was built by special dispensation, for a specific purpose. It is meant to house us for a specific length of time, till our mission is completed."

"And who is Hannis Gruer?" asked Baley.

"The head of Solarian security. We are to see him on arrival."

"Are we? Jehoshaphat, Daneel, when do I begin to learn anything at all about anything? I'm working in a vacuum and I don't like it. I might as well go back to Earth. I might as well——"

He felt himself working up into resentment and cut himself short. Daneel never wavered. He merely waited his chance to speak. He said, "I regret the fact that you are annoyed. My general knowledge of Solaria does seem to be greater than yours. My knowledge of the murder case itself is as limited as is your own. It is Agent Gruer who will tell us what we must know. The Solarian Government has arranged this."

"Well, then, let's get to this Gruer. How long a trip will it be?" Baley winced at the thought of more travel and the familiar constriction in his chest was making itself felt again.

Daneel said, "No travel is necessary, Partner Elijah. Agent Gruer will be waiting for us in the conversation room."

"A room for conversation, too?" Baley murmured wryly. Then, in a louder voice, "Waiting for us now?"

"I believe so."

"Then let's get to him, Daneel!"

Hannis Gruer was bald, and that without qualification. There was not even a fringe of hair at the sides of his skull. It was completely naked.

Baley swallowed and tried, out of politeness, to keep his eyes off that skull, but couldn't. On Earth there was the continuous acceptance of Spacers at the Spacers' own evaluation. The Spacers were the unquestioned lords of the Galaxy; they were tall, bronze of skin and hair, handsome, large, cool, aristocratic.

In short, they were all R. Daneel Olivaw was, but with the fact of humanity in addition.

And the Spacers who were sent to Earth often did look

like that; perhaps were deliberately chosen for that reason.

But here was a Spacer who might have been an Earthman for all his appearance. He was bald. And his nose was misshapen, too. Not much, to be sure, but on a Spacer even a slight asymmetry was noteworthy.

Baley said, "Good afternoon, sir. I am sorry if we kept you waiting."

No harm in politeness. He would have to work with these people.

He had the momentary urge to step across the expanse of room (how ridiculously large) and offer his hand in greeting. It was an urge easy to fight off. A Spacer certainly would not welcome such a greeting: a hand covered with Earthly germs?

Gruer sat gravely, as far away from Baley as he could get, his hands resting within long sleeves, and probably there were filters in his nostrils, although Baley couldn't see them.

It even seemed to him that Gruer cast a disapproving look at Daneel as though to say: You're a queer Spacer, standing that close to an Earthman.

That would mean Gruer simply did not know the truth. Then Baley noticed suddenly that Daneel was standing at some distance, at that; farther than he usually did.

Of course! Too close, and Gruer might find the proximity unbelievable. Daneel was intent on being accepted as human.

Gruer spoke in a pleasant, friendly voice, but his eyes tended to remain furtively on Daneel; looking away, then drifting back. He said, "I haven't been waiting long. Welcome to Solaria, gentlemen. Are you comfortable?"

"Yes, sir. Quite," said Baley. He wondered if etiquette would require that Daneel as the "Spacer" should speak for the two, but rejected that possibility resentfully. Jehoshaphat! It was he, himself, who had been requested for the investigation and Daneel had been added afterward. Under the circumstances Baley felt he would not play the secondary to a genuine Spacer; it was out of the question when a robot was involved, even such a robot as Daneel.

But Daneel made no attempt to take precedence over Baley, nor did Gruer seem surprised or displeased at that.

Instead, he turned his attention at once to Baley to the exclusion of Daneel.

Gruer said, "You have been told nothing. Plainclothesman Baley, about the crime for which your services have been solicited. I imagine you are quite curious about that." He shook his arms so that the sleeves fell backward and clasped his hands loosely in his lap. "Won't you gentlemen sit down?"

They did so and Baley said, "We *are* curious." He noted that Gruer's hands were not protected by gloves.

Gruer went on. "That was on purpose, Plainclothesman. We wanted you to arrive here prepared to tackle the notions. You will have available to you shortly a full report of the details of the crime and of the investigations we have been able to conduct. I am afraid, Plainclothesman, that you will find our investigations ridiculously incomplete from the standpoint of your own experience. We have no police force on Solaria."

"None at all?" asked Baley.

Gruer smiled and shrugged. "No crime, you see. Our population is tiny and widely scattered. There is no occasion for crime; therefore no occasion for police."

"I see. But for all that, you *do* have crime now."

"True, but the first crime of violence in two centuries of history."

"Unfortunate, then, that you must begin with murder."

"Unfortunate, yes. More unfortunately still, the victim was a man we could scarcely afford to lose. A most inappropriate victim. And the circumstances of the murder were particularly brutal."

Baley said, "I suppose the murderer is completely unknown." (Why else would the crime be worth the importation of an Earthly detective?)

Gruer looked particularly uneasy. He glanced sideways at Daneel, who sat motionless, an absorptive, quiet mechanism. Baley knew than Daneel would, at any time in the future, be able to reproduce any conversation he heard, of whatever length. He was a recording machine that walked and talked like a man.

Did Gruer know that? His look at Daneel had certainly something of the furtive about it.

Gruer said, "No, I cannot say the murderer is completely unknown. In fact, there is only one person that can possibly have done the deed."

"Are you sure you don't mean only one person who is *likely* to have done the deed?" Baley distrusted overstatement and had no liking for the armchair deducer who discovered certainty rather than probability in the workings of logic.

But Gruer shook his bald head. "No. Only one possible person. Anyone else is impossible. Completely impossible."

"Completely?"

"I assure you."

"Then you have no problem."

"On the contrary. We do have a problem. That one person couldn't have done it either."

Baley said calmly, "Then no one did it."

"Yet the deed was done. Rikaine Delmarre is dead."

That's something, thought Baley. Jehoshaphat, I've got *something*. I've got the victim's name.

He brought out his notebook and solemnly made note of it, partly out of a wry desire to indicate that he had scraped up, at last, a nubbin of fact, and partly to avoid making it too obvious that he sat by the side of a recording machine who needed no notes.

He said, "How is the victim's name spelled?"

Gruer spelled it.

"His profession, sir?"

"Fetologist."

Baley spelled that as it sounded and let it go. He said, "Now who would be able to give me a personal account of the circumstances surrounding the murder? As firsthand as possible.

Gruer's smile was grim and his eyes shifted to Daneel again, and then away. "His wife, Plainclothesman."

"His wife . . . ?"

"Yes. Her name is Gladia." Gruer pronounced it in three syllables, accenting the second.

"Any children?" Baley's eyes were fixed on his notebook. When no answer came, he looked up. "Any children?"

But Gruer's mouth had pursed up as though he had tasted

something sour. He looked sick. Finally he said, "I would scarcely know."

Baley said, "What?"

Gruer added hastily, "In any case, I think you had better postpone actual operations till tomorrow. I know you've had a hard trip, Mr. Baley, and that you are tired and probably hungry."

Baley, about to deny it, realized suddenly that the thought of food had an uncommon attraction for him at the moment. He said, "Will you join us at our meal?" He didn't think Gruer would, being a Spacer. (Yet he had been brought to the point of saying "Mr. Baley" rather than "Plainclothesman Baley," which was something.)

As expected, Gruer said, "A business engagement makes that impossible. I will have to leave. I am sorry."

Baley rose. The polite thing would be to accompany Gruer to the door. In the first place, however, he wasn't at all anxious to approach the door and the unprotected open. And in the second he wasn't sure where the door was.

He remained standing in uncertainty.

Gruer smiled and nodded. He said, "I will see you again. Your robots will know the combination if you wish to talk to me."

And he was gone.

Baley exclaimed sharply.

Gruer and the chair he was sitting on were simply not there. The wall behind Gruer, the floor under his feet changed with explosive suddenness.

Daneel said calmly, "He was not there in the flesh at any time. It was a trimensional image. It seemed to me you would know. You have such things on Earth."

"Not like this," muttered Baley.

A trimensional image on Earth was encased in a cubic force-field that glittered against the background. The image itself had a tiny flicker. On Earth there was no mistaking image for reality. Here . . .

No wonder Gruer had worn no gloves. He needed no nose filters, for that matter.

Daneel said, "Would you care to eat now, Partner Elijah?"

Dinner was an unexpected ordeal. Robots appeared. One set the table, One brought in the food.

"How many are there in the house, Daneel?" Baley asked.

"About fifty, Partner Elijah."

"Will they stay here while we eat?" (One had backed into a corner, his glossy, glowing-eyed face turned toward Baley.)

"It is the usual practice," said Daneel, "for one to do so in case its service is called upon. If you do not wish that, you have only to order it to leave."

Baley shrugged. "Let it stay!"

Under normal conditions Baley might have found the food delicious. Now he ate mechanically. He noted abstractedly that Daneel ate also, with a kind of unimpassioned efficiency. Later on, of course, he would empty the fluorocarbon sac within him into which the "eaten" food was now being stored. Meanwhile Daneel maintained his masquerade.

"Is it night outside?" asked Baley.

"It is," replied Daneel.

Baley stared somberly at the bed. It was too large. The whole bedroom was too large. There were no blankets to burrow under, only sheets. They would make a poor enclosure.

Everything was difficult! He had already gone through the unnerving experience of showering in a stall that actually adjoined the bedroom. It was the height of luxury in a way, yet, on the other hand, it seemed an unsanitary arrangement.

He said abruptly, "How is the light put out?" The headboard of the bed gleamed with a soft light. Perhaps that was to facilate book viewing before sleeping, but Baley was in no mood for that.

"It will be taken care of once you're in bed, if you compose yourself for sleep."

"The robots watch, do they?"

"It is their job."

"Jehoshaphat! What do these Solarians do for *themselves*?" Baley muttered. "I wonder now why a robot didn't scrub my back in the shower."

With no trace of humor Daneel said, "One would have,

had you required it. As for the Solarians, they do what they choose. No robot performs his duty if ordered not to, except, of course, where the performance is necessary to the well-being of the human."

"Well, good night, Daneel."

"I will be in another bedroom, Partner Elijah. If, at any time during the night, you need anything——"

"I know. The robots will come."

"There is a contact patch on the side table. You have only to touch it. I will come too."

Sleep eluded Baley. He kept picturing the house he was in, balanced precariously at the outer skin of the world, with emptiness waiting just outside like a monster.

On Earth his apartment—his snug, comfortable, crowded apartment—sat nestled beneath many others. There were dozens of Levels and thousands of people between himself and the rim of Earth.

Even on Earth, he tried to tell himself, there were people on the topmost Level. They would be immediately adjacent to the outside. Sure! But that's what made those apartments low-rent.

Then he thought of Jessie, a thousand light-years away.

He wanted terribly to get out of bed right now, dress, and walk to her. His thoughts grew mistier. If there were only a tunnel, a nice, safe tunnel burrowing its way through safe, solid rock and metal from Solaria to Earth, he would walk and walk and walk. . . .

He would walk back to Earth, back to Jessie, back to comfort and security. . . .

Security.

Baley's eyes opened. His arms grew rigid and he rose up on his elbow, scarcely aware that he was doing so.

Security! This man, Hannis Gruer, was head of Solarian security. So Daneel had said. What did "security" mean? If it meant the same as it meant on Earth, and surely it must, this man Gruer was responsible for the protection of Solaria against invasion from without and subversion from within.

Why was he interested in a murder case? Was it because there were no police on Solaria and the Department of Security would come the closest to knowing what to do about a murder?

Gruer had seemed at ease with Baley, yet there had been those furtive glances, again and again, in the direction of Daneel.

Did Gruer suspect the motives of Daneel? Baley, himself, had been ordered to keep his eyes open and Daneel might very likely have received similar instructions.

It would be natural for Gruer to suspect that espionage was possible. His job made it necessary for him to suspect that in any case where it was conceivable. And he would not fear Baley overmuch, an Earthman, representative of the least formidable world in the Galaxy.

But Daneel was a native of Aurora, the oldest and largest and strongest of the Outer Worlds. That would be different.

Gruer, as Baley now remembered, had not addressed one word to Daneel.

For that matter, why should Daneel pretend so thoroughly to be a man? The earlier explanation that Baley had posed for himself, that it was a vainglorious game on the part of Daneel's Auroran designers, seemed trivial. It seemed obvious now that the masquerade was something more serious.

A man could be expected to receive diplomatic immunity; a certain courtesy and gentleness of treatment. A robot could not. But then why did not Aurora send a real man in the first place. Why gamble so desperately on a fake? The answer suggested itself instantly to Baley. A real man of Aurora, a real Spacer, would not care to associate too closely or for too long a time with an Earthman.

But if all this were true, why should Solaria find a single murder so important that it must allow an Earthman and an Auroran to come to their planet?

Baley felt trapped.

He was trapped on Solaria by the necessities of his assignment. He was trapped by Earth's danger, trapped in an environment he could scarcely endure, trapped by a responsibility he could not shirk. And, to add to all this, he was trapped somehow in the midst of a Spacer conflict the nature of which he did not understand.

4. A WOMAN IS VIEWED

He slept at last. He did not remember when he actually made the transition to sleep. There was just a period when his thoughts grew more erratic and then the headboard of his bed was shining and the ceiling was alight with a cool, daytime glow. He looked at his watch.

Hours had passed. The robots who ran the house had decided it was time for him to wake up and had acted accordingly.

He wondered if Daneel were awake and at once realized the illogic of the thought. Daneel could not sleep. Baley wondered if he had counterfeited sleep as part of the role he was playing. Had he undressed and put on nightclothes?

As though on cue Daneel entered. "Good morning, Partner Elijah."

The robot was completely dressed and his face was in perfect repose. He said, "Did you sleep well?"

"Yes," said Baley dryly, "did you?"

He got out of bed and tramped into the bathroom for a shave and for the remainder of the morning ritual. He shouted, "If a robot comes in to shave me, send him out again. They get on my nerves. Even if I don't see them, they get on my nerves."

He stared at his own face as he shaved, marveling a bit that it looked so like the mirrored face he saw on Earth. If only the image were another Earthman with whom he could consult instead of only the light-mimicry of himself. If he could go over what he had already learned, small as it was...

"Too small! Get more," he muttered to the mirror.

He came out, mopping his face, and pulled trousers over fresh shorts. (Robots supplied everything, damn them.)

He said, "Would you answer a few questions, Daneel?"

"As you know, Partner Elijah, I answer all questions to the best of my knowledge."

Or to the letter of your instructions, thought Baley. He said, "Why are there only twenty thousand people on Solaria?"

"That is a mere fact," said Daneel. "A datum. A figure that is the result of a counting process."

"Yes, but you're evading the matter. The planet can support millions; why, then, only twenty thousand? You said the Solarians consider twenty thousand optimum. Why?"

"It is their way of life."

"You mean they practice birth control?"

"Yes."

"And leave the planet empty?" Baley wasn't sure why he was pounding away at this one point, but the planet's population was one of the few hard facts he had learned about it and there was little else he could ask about.

Daneel said, "The planet is not empty. It is parceled out into estates, each of which is supervised by a Solarian."

"You mean each lives on his estate. Twenty thousand estates, each with a Solarian."

"Fewer estates than those, Partner Elijah. Wives share the estate."

"No Cities?" Baley felt cold.

"None at all, Partner Elijah. They live completely apart and never see one another except under the most extraordinary circumstances."

"Hermits?"

"In a way, yes. In a way, no."

"What does that mean?"

"Agent Gruer visited you yesterday by trimensional image. Solarians visit one another freely that way and in no other way."

Baley stared at Daneel. He said, "Does that include us? Are we expected to live that way?"

"It is the custom of the world."

"Then how do I investigate this case? If I want to see someone——"

"From this house, Partner Elijah, you can obtain a trimensional view of anyone on the planet. There will be no problem. In fact, it will save you the annoyance of leaving this house. It was why I said when we arrived that there would be no occasion for you to feel it necessary to grow accustomed to facing the outdoors. And that is well. Any other arrangement would be most distasteful to you."

"I'll judge what's distasteful to me," said Baley. "First thing today, Daneel, I get in touch with the Gladia woman, the wife of the murdered man. If the trimensional business is unsatisfactory, I will go out to her place, personally. It's a matter for my decision."

"We shall see what is best and most feasible, Partner Elijah," said Daneel noncommittally. "I shall arrange for breakfast." He turned to leave.

Baley stared at the broad robotic back and was almost amused. Daneel Olivaw acted the master. If his instructions had been to keep Baley from learning any more than was absolutely necessary, a trump card had been left in Baley's hand.

The other was only *R*. Daneel Olivaw, after all. All that was necessary was to tell Gruer, or any Solarian, that Daneel was a robot and not a man.

And yet, on the other hand, Daneel's pseudo humanity could be of great use, too. A trump card need not be played at once. Sometimes it was more useful in the hand.

Wait and see, he thought, and followed Daneel out to breakfast.

Baley said, "Now how does one go about establishing trimensional contact?"

"It is done for us, Partner Elijah," said Daneel, and his finger sought out one of the contact patches that summoned robots.

A robot entered at once.

Where do they come from, Baley wondered. As one wandered aimlessly about the uninhabited maze that constituted the mansion, not one robot was ever visible. Did they scramble out of the way as humans approached? Did they send messages to one another and clear the path?

Yet whenever a call went out, one appeared without delay.

Baley stared at the robotic newcomer. It was sleek, but

not glossy. Its surface had a muted, grayish finish, with a checkerboard pattern on the right shoulder as the only bit of color. Squares in white and yellow (silver and gold, really, from the metallic luster) were placed in what seemed an aimless pattern.

Daneel said, "Take us to the conversation room."

The robot bowed and turned, but said nothing.

Baley said, "Wait, boy. What's your name?"

The robot faced Baley. It spoke in clear tones and without hesitation. "I have no name, master. My serial number"— and a metal finger lifted and rested on the shoulder patch— "is ACX-2745."

Daneel and Baley followed into a large room, which Baley recognized as having held Gruer and his chair the day before.

Another robot was waiting for them with the eternal, patient nonboredom of the machine. The first bowed and left.

Baley compared shoulder patches of the two as the first bowed and started out. The pattern of silver and gold was different. The checkerboard was made up of a six-by-six square. The number of possible arrangements would be 2^{36} then, or seventy billion. More than enough.

Baley said, "Apparently, there is one robot for everything. One to show us here. One to run the viewer."

Daneel said, "There is much robotic specialization in Solaria, Partner Elijah."

"With so many of them, I can understand why." Baley looked at the second robot. Except for the shoulder patch, and, presumably, for the invisible positronic patterns within it spongy platinum-iridium brain it was the duplicate of the first. He said, "And your serial number?"

"ACC-1129, master."

"I'll just call you boy. Now I want to speak to a Mrs. Gladia Delmarre, wife of the late Rikaine Delmarre—— Daneel, is there an address, some way of pin-pointing her location?"

Daneel said gently, "I do not believe any further information is necessary. If I may question the robot——"

"Let me do that," Baley said. "All right, boy, do you know how the lady is to be reached?"

"Yes, master. I have knowledge of the connection pattern of all masters." This was said without pride. It was a mere fact, as though it were saying: I am made of metal, master.

Daneel interposed, "That is not surprising, Partner Elijah. There are less than ten thousand connections that need be fed into the memory circuits and that is a small number."

Baley nodded. "Is there more than one Gladia Delmarre, by any chance? There might be that chance of confusion."

"Master?" After the question the robot remained blankly silent.

"I believe," said Daneel, "that this robot does not understand your question. It is my belief that duplicate names do not occur on Solaria. Names are registered at birth and no name may be adopted unless it is unoccupied at the time."

"All right," said Baley, "we learn something every minute. Now see here, boy, you tell me how to work whatever it is I am supposed to work; give me the connection pattern, or whatever you call it, and then step out."

There was a perceptible pause before the robot answered. It said, "Do you wish to make contact yourself, sir?"

"That's right."

Daneel touched Baley's sleeve gently. "One moment, Partner Elijah."

"Now what is it?"

"It is my belief that the robot could make the necessary contact with greater ease. It is his specialization."

Baley said grimly, "I'm sure he can do it better than I can. Doing it myself, I may make a mess of it." He stared levelly at the impassive Daneel. "Just the same, I prefer to make contact myself. Do I give the orders or don't I?"

Daneel said, "You give the orders, Partner Elijah, and your orders, where First Law permits, will be obeyed. However, with your permission, I would like to give you what pertinent information I have concerning the Solarian robots. Far more than on any other world, the robots on Solaria are specialized. Although Solarian robots are physically capable of many things, they are heavily equipped mentally for one particular type of job. To perform functions outside their specialty requires the high potentials produced by direct application of one of the Three Laws. Again, for them *not* to perform the duty for which they *are* equipped also requires the direct application of the Three Laws."

"Well, then, a direct order from me brings the Second Law into play, doesn't it?"

"True. Yet the potential set up by it is 'unpleasant' to the robot. Ordinarily, the matter would not come up, since almost never does a Solarian interfere with the day-to-day workings of a robot. For one thing, he would not care to do a robot's work; for another, he would feel no need to."

"Are you trying to tell me, Daneel, that it hurts the robot to have me do its work?"

"As you know, Partner Elijah, pain in the human sense is not applicable to robotic reactions."

Baley shrugged. "Then?"

"Nevertheless," went on Daneel, "the experience which the robot undergoes is as upsetting to it as pain is to a human, as nearly as I can judge."

"And yet," said Baley, "I'm not a Solarian. I'm an Earthman. I don't like robots doing what I want to do."

"Consider, too," said Daneel, "that to cause distress to a robot might be considered on the part of our hosts to be an act of impoliteness since in a society such as this there must be a number of more or less rigid beliefs concerning how it is proper to treat a robot and how it is not. To offend our hosts would scarcely make our task easier."

"All right," said Baley. "Let the robot do its job."

He settled back. The incident had not been without its uses. It was an educational example of how remorseless a robotic society could be. Once brought into existence, robots were not so easily removed, and a human who wished to dispense with them even temporarily found he could not.

His eyes half closed, he watched the robot approach the wall. Let the sociologists on Earth consider what had just occurred and draw their conclusions. He was beginning to have certain notions of his own.

Half a wall slid aside and the control panel that was revealed would have done justice to a City Section power station.

Baley longed for his pipe. He had been briefed that smoking on non-smoking Solaria would be a terrible breach of decorum, so he had not even been allowed to take his fix-

ings. He sighed. There were moments when the feel of
pipestem between teeth and a warm bowl in his hand would
have been infinitely comforting.

The robot was working quickly, adjusting variable re-
sistances a trifle here and there and intensifying field-forces
in proper pattern by quick finger pressures.

Daneel said, "It is necessary first to signal the individual
one desires to view. A robot will, of course, receive the
message. If the individual being signaled is available and
wishes to receive the view, full contact is established."

"Are all those controls necessary?" asked Baley. "The
robot's hardly touching most of the panel."

"My information on the matter is not complete, Partner
Elijah. There is, however, the necessity of arranging, upon
occasion, for multiple viewings and for mobile viewings.
The latter, particularly, call for complicated and continuing
adjustments."

The robot said, "Masters, contact is made and approved.
When you are ready, it will be completed."

"Ready," growled Baley, and as though the word were
a signal, the far half of the room was alive with light.

Daneel said at once, "I neglected to have the robot specify
that all visible openings to the outside be draped. I regret
that and we must arrange——"

"Never mind," said Baley, wincing. "I'll manage. Don't
interfere."

It was a bathroom he was staring at, or he judged it to
be so from its fixtures. One end of it was, he guessed, a
kind of beautician's establishment and his imagination pictured a robot (or robots?) working with unerring swiftness
on the details of a woman's coiffure and on the externals
that made up the picture she presented to the world.

Some gadgets and fittings he simply gave up on. There
was no way of judging their purpose in the absence of
experience. The walls were inlaid with an intricate pattern
that all but fooled the eye into believing some natural object
was being represented before fading away into an abstraction. The result was soothing and almost hypnotic in the
way it monopolized attention.

What might have been the shower stall, a large one, was

shielded off by nothing that seemed material, but rather by
a trick of lighting that set up a wall of flickering opacity.
No human was in sight.

Baley's glance fell to the floor. Where did his room end
and the other begin? It was easy to tell. There was a line
where the quality of the light changed and that must be it.

He stepped toward the line and after a moment's hesitation pushed his hand beyond it.

He felt nothing, any more than he would have had he
shoved the hand into one of Earth's crude trimensionals.
There, at least, he would have seen his own hand still;
faintly, perhaps, and overlaid by the image, but he would
have seen it. Here it was lost completely. To his vision, his
arm ended sharply at the wrist.

What if he stepped across the line altogether? Probably
his own vision would become inoperative. He would be in
a world of complete blackness. The thought of such efficient
enclosure was almost pleasant.

A voice interrupted him. He looked up and stepped backward with an almost clumsy haste.

Gladia Delmarre was speaking. At least Baley assumed
it was she. The upper portion of the flickering light across
the shower stall had faded and a head was clearly visible.

It smiled at Baley. "I said hello, and I'm sorry to keep
you waiting. I'll be dry soon."

Hers was a triangular face, rather broad at the cheekbones
(which grew prominent when she smiled) and narrowing
with a gentle curve past full lips to a small chin. Her head
was not high above the ground. Baley judged her to be
about five feet two in height. (This was not typical. At least
not to Baley's way of thinking. Spacer women were supposed to lean toward the tall and stately.) Nor was her hair
the Spacer bronze. It was light brown, tinging toward yellow, and worn moderately long. At the moment it was
fluffed out in what Baley imagined must be a stream of
warm air. The whole picture was quite pleasing.

Baley said in confusion, "If you want us to break contact
and wait till you're through——"

"Oh no. I'm almost done, and we can talk meanwhile.
Hannis Gruer told me you would be viewing. You're from

Earth, I understand." Her eyes rested full on him, seemed to drink him in.

Baley nodded and sat down. "My companion is from Aurora."

She smiled and kept her glance fixed on Baley as though *he* remained the curiosity nevertheless, and of course, Baley thought, so he was.

She lifted her arms above her head, running her fingers through the hair and spreading it out as though to hasten drying. Her arms were slim and graceful. Very attractive, Baley thought.

Then he thought uneasily: Jessie wouldn't like this.

Daneel's voice broke in. "Would it be possible, Mrs. Delmarre, to have the window we see polarized or draped. My partner is disturbed by the sight of daylight. On Earth, as you may have heard——"

The young woman (Baley judged her to be twenty-five but had the doleful thought that the apparent ages of Spacers could be most deceptive) put her hands to her cheeks and said, "Oh my, yes. I know all about that. How ridiculously silly of me. Forgive me, please, but it won't take a moment. I'll have a robot in here——"

She stepped out of the drying cabinet, her hand extended toward the contact-patch, still talking. "I'm always thinking I ought to have more than one contact-patch in this room. A house is just no good if it doesn't have a patch within reach no matter where you stand—say not more than five feet away. It just——Why, what's the matter?"

She stared in shock at Baley, who, having jumped out of his chair and upset it behind him, had reddened to his hairline and hastily turned away.

Daneel said calmly, "It would be better, Mrs. Delmarre, if, after you have made contact with the robot, you would return to the stall or, failing that, proceed to put on some articles of clothing."

Gladia looked down at her nudity in surprise and said, "Well, of course."

5. A CRIME IS DISCUSSED

"It was only viewing, you see," said Gladia contritely. She was wrapped in something that left her arms and shoulders free. One leg showed to mid-thigh, but Baley, entirely recovered and feeling an utter fool, ignored it stoically.

He said, "It was the surprise, Mrs. Delmarre——"

"Oh, please. You can call me Gladia, unless—unless that's against your customs."

"Gladia, then. It's all right. I just want to assure you there was nothing repulsive about it, you understand. Just the surprise." Bad enough for him to have acted the fool, he thought, without having the poor girl think he found her unpleasant. As a matter of fact, it had been rather—rather...

Well, he didn't have the phrase, but he knew quite certainly that there was no way he would ever be able to talk of this to Jessie.

"I know I offended you," Gladia said, "but I didn't mean to. I just wasn't thinking. Of course I realize one must be careful about the customs of other planets, but the customs are so queer sometimes; at least, not queer," she hastened to add, "I don't mean queer. I mean strange, you know, and it's so easy to forget. As I forgot about keeping the windows darkened."

"Quite all right," muttered Baley. She was in another room now with all the windows draped and the light had the subtly different and more comfortable texture of artificiality.

"But about the other thing," she went on earnestly, "it's just *viewing*, you see. After all, you didn't mind talking to me when I was in the drier and I wasn't wearing anything then, either."

"Well," said Baley, wishing she would run down as far

48

as that subject was concerned, "hearing you is one thing, and seeing you is another."

"But that's exactly it. Seeing isn't involved." She reddened a trifle and looked down. "I hope you don't think I'd ever do anything like that, I mean, just step out of the drier, if anyone were *seeing* me. It was just *viewing*."

"Same thing, isn't it?" said Baley.

"Not at all the same thing. You're viewing me right now. You can't touch me, can you, or smell me, or anything like that. You could if you were seeing me. Right now, I'm two hundred miles away from you at *least*. So how can it be the same thing?"

Baley grew interested. "But I see you with my eyes."

"No, you don't see me. You see my image. You're viewing me."

"And that makes a difference?"

"All the difference there is."

"I see." In a way he did. The distinction was not one he could make easily, but it had a kind of logic to it.

She said, bending her head a little to one side, "Do you *really* see?"

"Yes."

"Does that mean you wouldn't mind if I took off my wrapper?" She was smiling.

He thought: She's teasing and I ought to take her up on it.

But aloud he said, "No, it would take my mind off my job. We'll discuss it another time."

"Do you mind my being in the wrapper, rather than something more formal? Seriously."

"I don't mind."

"May I call you by your first name?"

"If you have the occasion."

"What is your first name?"

"Elijah."

"All right." She snuggled into a chair that looked hard and almost ceramic in texture, but it slowly gave as she sat until it embraced her gently.

Baley said, "To business, now."

She said, "To business."

Baley found it all extraordinarily difficult. There was no

way even to make a beginning. On Earth he would ask name, rating, City and Sector of dwelling, a million different routine questions. He might even know the answers to begin with, yet it would be a device to ease into the serious phase. It would serve to introduce him to the person, make his judgment of the tactics to pursue something other than a mere guess.

But here? How could he be certain of anything? The very verb "to see" meant different things to himself and to the woman. How many other words would be different? How often would they be at cross-purposes without his being aware of it?

He said, "How long were you married, Gladia?"

"Ten years, Elijah."

"How old are you?"

"Thirty-three."

Baley felt obscurely pleased. She might easily have been a hundred thirty-three.

He said. "Were you happily married?"

Gladia looked uneasy. "How do you mean that?"

"Well——" For a moment Baley was at a loss. How do you define a happy marriage. For that matter, what would a Solarian consider a happy marriage? He said, "Well, you saw one another often?"

"What? I should hope not. We're not animals, you know."

Baley winced. "You did live in the same mansion? I thought——"

"Of course, we did. We were married. But I had my quarters and he had his. He had a very important career which took much of his time and I have my own work. We viewed each other whenever necessary."

"He *saw* you, didn't he?"

"It's not a thing one talks about but he *did* see me."

"Do you have any children?"

Gladia jumped to her feet in obvious agitation. "That's too much. Of all the indecent——"

"Now wait. *Wait!*" Baley brought his fist down on the arm of his chair. "Don't be difficult. This is a murder investigation. Do you understand? Murder. And it was your husband who was murdered. Do you want to see the murderer found and punished or don't you?"

"Then *ask* about the murder, not about—about——"

"I have to ask all sorts of things. For one thing I want to know whether you're sorry your husband is dead." He added with calculated brutality. "You don't seem to be."

She stared at him haughtily. "I'm sorry when anyone dies, especially when he's young and useful."

"Doesn't the fact that he was your husband make it just a little more than that?"

"He was assigned to me and, well, we *did* see each other when scheduled and—and"—she hurried the next words— "and, if you must know, we don't have children because none have been assigned us yet. I don't see what all that has to do with being sorry over someone being dead."

Maybe it had nothing to do with it, Baley thought. It depended on the social facts of life and with those he was not acquainted.

He changed the subject. "I'm told you have personal knowledge of the circumstances of the murder."

For a moment she seemed to grow taut. "I—discovered the body. Is that the way I should say it?"

"Then you didn't witness the actual murder?"

"Oh no," she said faintly.

"Well, suppose you tell me what happened. Take your time and use your own words." He sat back and composed himself to listen.

She began, "It was on three-two of the fifth——"

"When was that in Standard Time?" asked Baley quickly.

"I'm not sure. I really don't know. You can check, I suppose."

Her voice seemed shaky and her eyes had grown large. They were a little too gray to be called blue, he noted.

She said, "He came to my quarters. It was our assigned day for seeing and I knew he'd come."

"He always came on the assigned day?"

"Oh yes. He was a very conscientious man, a good Solarian. He never skipped an assigned day and always came at the same time. Of course, he didn't stay long. We have not been assigned ch——"

She couldn't finish the word, but Baley nodded.

"Anyway," she said, "he always came at the same time, you know, so that everything would be comfortable. We

spoke a few minutes; seeing *is* an ordeal, but he spoke quite
normally to me. It was his way. Then he left to attend to
some project he was involved with; I'm not sure what. He
had a special laboratory in my quarters to which he could
retire on seeing days. He had a much bigger one in his
quarters, of course."

Baley wondered what he did in those laboratories. Fe-
tology, perhaps, whatever that was.

He said, "Did he seem unnatural in any way? Worried?"

"No. No. He was never worried." She came to the edge
of a small laugh and buried it at the last moment. "He always
had perfect control, like your friend there." For a brief
moment her small hand reached out and indicated Daneel,
who did not stir.

"I see. Well, go on."

Gladia didn't. Instead she whispered, "Do you mind if
I have myself a drink?"

"Please do."

Gladia's hand slipped along the arm of her chair momentarily. In less than a minute, a robot moved in silently
and a warm drink (Baley could see the steam) was in her
hand. She sipped slowly, then set the drink down.

She said, "That's better. May I ask a personal question?"

Baley said, "You may always ask."

"Well, I've read a lot about Earth. I've always been
interested, you know. It's such a *queer* world." She gasped
and added immediately, "I didn't mean that."

Baley frowned a little. "Any world is queer to people
who don't live on it."

"I mean it's different. You know. Anyway, I want to
ask a rude question. At least, I hope it doesn't seem rude
to an Earthman. I wouldn't ask it of a Solarian, of course.
Not for anything."

"Ask what, Gladia?"

"About you and your friend—Mr. Olivaw, is it?"

"Yes."

"You two aren't viewing, are you?"

"How do you mean?"

"I mean each other. You're seeing. You're there, both
of you."

Baley said, "We're physically together. Yes."

"You could touch him, if you wanted to."

"That's right."

She looked from one to the other and said, "Oh."

It might have meant anything. Disgust? Revulsion?

Baley toyed with the idea of standing up, walking to Daneel and placing his hand flat on Daneel's face. It might be interesting to watch her reaction.

He said, "You were about to go on with the events of that day when your husband came to see you." He was morally certain that her digression, however interesting it might have been intrinsically to her, was primarily motivated by a desire to avoid just that.

She returned to her drink for a moment. Then: "There isn't much to tell. I saw he would be engaged, and I knew he would be, anyway, because he was always at some sort of constructive work, so I went back to my own work. Then, perhaps fifteen minutes later, I heard a shout."

There was a pause and Baley prodded her. "What kind of a shout?"

She said, "Rikaine's. My husband's. Just a shout. No words. A kind of fright. No! Surprise, shock. Something like that. I'd never heard him shout before."

She lifted her hands to her ears as though to shut out even the memory of the sound and her wrapper slipped slowly down to her waist. She took no notice and Baley stared firmly at his notebook.

He said, "What did you do?"

"I ran. I ran. I didn't know where he was——"

"I thought you said he had gone to the laboratory he maintained in your quarters."

"He did, E-Elijah, but *I* didn't know where that was. Not for sure, anyway. I never went there. It was his. I had a general idea of its direction. I knew it was somewhere in the west, but I was so upset, I didn't even think to summon any robot. One of them would have guided me easily, but of course none came without being summoned. When I did get there—I found it somehow—he was dead."

She stopped suddenly and, to Baley's acute discomfort, she bent her head and wept. She made no attempt to obscure her face. Her eyes simply closed and tears slowly trickled down her cheeks. It was quite soundless. Her shoulders barely trembled.

Then her eyes opened and looked at him through swimming tears. "I never saw a dead man before. He was all bloody and his head was—just—all——I managed to get a robot and he called others and I suppose they took care of me and of Rikaine. I don't remember. I don't——"

Baley said, "What do you mean, they took care of Rikaine?"

"They took him away and cleaned up." There was a small wedge of indignation in her voice, the lady of the house careful of its condition. "Things were a mess."

"And what happened to the body?"

She shook her head. "I don't know. Burned, I suppose. Like any dead body."

"You didn't call the police?"

She looked at him blankly and Baley thought: No police!

He said, "You told somebody, I suppose. People found out about the matter."

She said, "The robots called a doctor. And I had to call Rikaine's place of work. The robots there had to know he wouldn't be back."

"The doctor was for you, I suppose."

She nodded. For the first time, she seemed to notice her wrapper draped about her hips. She pulled it up into position, murmuring forlornly, "I'm sorry, I'm sorry."

Baley felt uncomfortable, watching her as she sat there helpless, shivering, her face contorted with the absolute terror that had come over her with the memory.

She had never seen a dead body before. She had never seen blood and a crushed skull. And if the husband-wife relationship on Solaria was something thin and shallow, it was still a dead human being with whom she had been confronted.

Baley scarcely knew what to say or do next. He had the impulse to apologize, and yet, as a policeman, he was doing only his duty.

But there were no police on this world. Would she understand that this was his duty?

Slowly, and as gently as he could, he said, "Gladia, did

you hear anything at all? Anything besides your husband's shout."

She looked up, her face as pretty as ever, despite its obvious distress—perhaps because of it. She said, "Nothing."

"No running footsteps? No other voice?"

She shook her head. "I didn't hear anything."

"When you found your husband, he was completely alone? You two were the only ones present?"

"Yes."

"No signs of anyone else having been there?"

"None that I could see. I don't see how anyone could have been there, anyway."

"Why do you say that?"

For a moment she looked shocked. Then she said dispiritedly, "You're from Earth. I keep forgetting. Well, it's just that nobody could have been there. My husband never saw anybody except me; not since he was a boy. He certainly wasn't the sort to see anybody. Not Rikaine. He was very strict; very custom-abiding."

"It might not have been his choice. What if someone had just come to see him without an invitation, without your husband knowing anything about it? He couldn't have helped seeing the intruder regardless of how custom-abiding he was."

She said, "Maybe, but he would have called robots at once and had the man taken away. He would have! Besides, no one would try to see my husband without being invited to. I couldn't conceive of such a thing. And Rikaine certainly would never invite anyone to see him. It's ridiculous to think so."

Baley said softly, "Your husband was killed by being struck on the head, wasn't he? You'll admit that."

"I suppose so. He was—all——"

"I'm not asking for the details at the moment. Was there any sign of some mechanical contrivance in the room that would have enabled someone to crush his skull by remote control."

"Of course not. At least, I didn't see any."

"If anything like that had been there, I imagine you would have seen it. It follows then that a hand held something capable of crushing a man's skull and that hand swung it. Some person had to be within four feet of your husband to do that. So someone did see him."

"No one would," she said earnestly. "A Solarian just wouldn't see anyone."

"A Solarian who would commit murder wouldn't stick at a bit of seeing, would he?"

(To himself that statement sounded dubious. On Earth he had known the case of a perfectly conscienceless murderer who had been caught only because he could not bring himself to violate the custom of absolute silence in the community bathroom.)

Gladia shook her head. "You don't understand about seeing. Earthmen just see anybody they want to all the time, so you don't understand it. . . ."

Curiosity seemed to be struggling within her. Her eyes lightened a bit. "Seeing does seem perfectly normal to you, doesn't it?"

"I've always taken it for granted," said Baley.

"It doesn't trouble you?"

"Why should it?"

"Well, the films don't say, and I've always wanted to know——Is it all right if I ask a question?"

"Go ahead," said Baley stolidly.

"Do you have a wife assigned to you?"

"I'm married. I don't know about the assignment part."

"And I know you see your wife any time you want to and she sees you and neither of you thinks anything of it."

Baley nodded.

"Well, when you see her, suppose you just want to——" She lifted her hands elbow-high, pausing as though searching for the proper phrase. She tried again, "Can you just—any time . . ." She let it dangle.

Baley didn't try to help.

She said, "Well, never mind. I don't know why I should bother you with that sort of thing now anyway. Are you through with me?" She looked as though she might cry again.

Baley said, "One more try, Gladia. Forget that no one would see your husband. Suppose someone *did*. Who might it have been?"

"It's just useless to guess. It couldn't be anyone."

"It has to be someone. Agent Gruer says there is reason to suspect some one person. So you see there must be someone."

A small, joyless smile flickered over the girl's face. "I know who he thinks did it."

"All right. Who?"

She put a small hand on her breast. "I."

6. A THEORY IS REFUTED

"I should have said, Partner Elijah," said Daneel, speaking suddenly, "that that is an obvious conclusion."

Baley cast a surprised look at his robot partner. "Why obvious?" he asked.

"The lady herself," said Daneel, "states that she was the only person who did or who would see her husband. The social situation on Solaria is such that even she cannot plausibly present anything else as the truth. Certainly Agent Gruer would find it reasonable, even obligatory, to believe that a Solarian husband would be seen only by his wife. Since only one person could be in seeing range, only one person could be the murderer. Or murderess, rather. Agent Gruer, you will remember, said that only one person could have done it. Anyone else he considered impossible. Well?"

"He also said," said Baley, "that that one person couldn't have done it, either."

"By which he probably meant that there was no weapon found at the scene of the crime. Presumably Mrs. Delmarre could explain that anomaly."

He gestured with cool robotic politeness toward where Gladia sat, still in viewing focus, her eyes cast down, her small mouth compressed.

Jehoshaphat, thought Baley, we're forgetting the lady.

Perhaps it was annoyance that had caused him to forget. It was Daneel who annoyed him, he thought, with his unemotional approach to problems. Or perhaps it was himself, with his emotional approach. He did not stop to analyze the matter.

He said, "That will be all for now, Gladia. However one goes about it, break contact. Good-by."

She said softly, "Sometimes one says, 'Done viewing,'"

but I like 'Good-by' better. You seem disturbed, Elijah. I'm sorry, because I'm used to having people think I did it, so you don't need to feel disturbed."

Daneel said, "*Did* you do it, Gladia?"

"No," she said angrily.

"Good-by, then."

With the anger not yet washed out of her face she was gone. For a moment, though, Baley could still feel the impact of those quite extraordinary gray eyes.

She might say she was used to having people think her a murderess, but that was very obviously a lie. Her anger spoke more truly than her words. Baley wondered of how many other lies she was capable.

And now Baley found himself alone with Daneel. He said, "All right, Daneel, I'm not altogether a fool."

"I have never thought you were, Partner Elijah."

"Then tell me what made you say there was no murder weapon found at the site of the crime? There was nothing in the evidence so far, nothing in anything I've heard that would lead us to that conclusion."

"You are correct. I have additional information not yet available to you."

"I was sure of that. What kind?"

"Agent Gruer said he would send a copy of the report of their own investigation. I have that copy. It arrived this morning."

"Why haven't you shown it to me?"

"I felt that it would perhaps be more fruitful for you to conduct your investigation, at least in the initial stages, according to your own ideas, without being prejudiced by the conclusions of other people who, self-admittedly, have reached no satisfactory conclusions. It was because I, myself, felt my logical processes might be influenced by those conclusions that I contributed nothing to the discussion."

Logical processes! Unbidden, there leaped into Baley's mind the fragment of a conversation he had once had with a roboticist. A robot, the man had said, is logical but not reasonable.

He said, "You entered the discussion at the end."

"So I did, Partner Elijah, but only because by that time

I had independent evidence bearing out Agent Gruer's suspicions."

"What kind of independent evidence?"

"That which could be deduced from Mrs. Delmarre's own behavior."

"Let's be specific, Daneel."

"Consider that if the lady were guilty and were attempting to prove herself innocent, it would be useful to her to have the detective in the case believe her innocent."

"Well?"

"If she could warp his judgment by playing upon a weakness of his, she might do so, might she not?"

"Strictly hypothetical."

"Not at all," was the calm reply. "You will have noticed, I think, that she concentrated her attention entirely on you."

"I was doing the talking," said Baley.

"Her attention was on you from the start; even before she could guess that you would be doing the talking. In fact, one might have thought she would, logically, have expected that I, as an Auroran, would take the lead in the investigation. Yet she concentrated on you."

"And what do you deduce from this?"

"That it was upon you, Partner Elijah, that she pinned her hopes. You were the Earthman."

"What of that?"

"She had studied Earth. She implied that more than once. She knew what I was talking about when I asked her to blank out the outer daylight at the very start of the interview. She did not act surprised or uncomprehending, as she would most certainly have done had she not had actual knowledge of conditions on Earth."

"Well?"

"Since she has studied Earth, it is quite reasonable to suppose that she discovered one weakness Earthmen possess. She must know of the nudity tabu, and of how such a display must impress an Earthman."

"She—she explained about viewing——"

"So she did. Yet did it seem entirely convincing to you? Twice she allowed herself to be seen in what you would consider a state of improper clothing——"

"Your conclusion," said Baley, "is that she was trying to seduce me. Is that it?"

"Seduce you away from your professional impersonality. So it would seem to me. And though I cannot share human reactions to stimuli, I would judge, from what has been imprinted on my instruction circuits, that the lady meets any reasonable standard of physical attractiveness. From your behavior, moreover, it seems to me that you were aware of that and that you approved her appearance. I would even judge that Mrs. Delmarre acted rightly in thinking her mode of behavior would predispose you in her favor."

"Look," said Baley uncomfortably, "regardless of what effect she might have had on me, I am still an officer of the law in full possession of my sense of professional ethics. Get that straight. Now let's see the report."

Baley read through the report in silence. He finished, turned back, and read it through a second time.

"That brings in a new item," he said. "The robot."

Daneel Olivaw nodded.

Baley said thoughtfully, "She didn't mention it."

Daneel said, "You asked the wrong question. You asked if he was alone when she found the body. You asked if anyone else had been present at the death scene. A robot isn't 'anybody else.'"

Baley nodded. If he himself were a suspect and were asked who else had been at the scene of a crime, he would scarcely have replied: "No one but this table."

He said, "I suppose I should have asked if any robots were present?" (Damn it, what questions does one ask anyway on a strange world?) He said, "How legal is robotic evidence, Daneel?"

"What do you mean?"

"Can a robot bear witness on Solaria? Can it give evidence?"

"Why should you doubt it?"

"A robot isn't human, Daneel. On Earth, it cannot be a legal witness."

"And yet a footprint can, Partner Elijah, although that is much less a human than a robot is. The position of your planet in this respect is illogical. On Solaria, robotic evidence, when competent, is admissible."

Baley did not argue the point. He rested his chin on the knuckles of one hand and went over this matter of the robot in his mind.

In the extremity of terror Gladia Delmarre, standing over her husband's body, had summoned robots. By the time they came she was unconscious.

The robots reported having found her there together with the dead body. And something else was present as well; a robot. That robot had not been summoned; it was already there. It was not one of the regular staff. No other robot had seen it before or knew its function or assignment.

Nor could anything be discovered from the robot in question. It was not in working order. When found, its motions were disorganized and so, apparently, was the functioning of its positronic brain. It could give none of the proper responses, either verbal or mechanical, and after exhaustive investigation by a robotics expert it was declared a total loss.

Its only activity that had any trace of organization was its constant repetition of "You're going to kill me—you're going to kill me—you're going to kill me . . ."

No weapon that could possibly have been used to crush the dead man's skull was located.

Baley said suddenly, "I'm going to eat, Daneel, and then we see Agent Gruer again—or view him, anyway."

Hannis Gruer was still eating when contact was established. He ate slowly, choosing each mouthful carefully from a variety of dishes, peering at each anxiously as though searching for some hidden combination he would find most satisfactory.

Baley thought: He may be a couple of centuries old. Eating may be getting dull for him.

Gruer said, "I greet you, gentlemen. You received our report, I believe." His bald head glistened, as he leaned across the table to reach a titbit.

"Yes. We have spent an interesting session with Mrs. Delmarre also," said Baley.

"Good, good," said Gruer. "And to what conclusion, if any, did you come?"

Baley said, "That she is innocent, sir."

Gruer looked up sharply. "Really?"

Baley nodded.

Gruer said, "And yet she was the only one who could see him, the only one who could possibly be within reach. . . ."

Baley said, "That's been made clear to me, and no matter how firm social customs are on Solaria, the point is not conclusive. May I explain?"

Gruer had returned to his dinner. "Of course."

"Murder rests on three legs," said Baley, "each equally important. They are motive, means, and opportunity. For a good case against any suspect, each of the three must be satisfied. Now I grant you that Mrs. Delmarre had the opportunity. As for the motive, I've heard of none."

Gruer shrugged. "We know of none." For a moment his eyes drifted to the silent Daneel.

"All right. The suspect has no known motive, but perhaps she's a pathological killer. We can let the matter ride for a while, and continue. She is in his laboratory with him and there's some reason why she wants to kill him. She waves some club or other heavy object threateningly. It takes him a while to realize that his wife really intends to hurt him. He shouts in dismay, 'You're going to kill me,' and so she does. He turns to run as the blow descends and it crushes the back of his head. Did a doctor examine the body, by the way?"

"Yes and no. The robots called a doctor to attend Mrs. Delmarre and, as a matter of course, he looked at the dead body, too."

"That wasn't mentioned in the report."

"It was scarcely pertinent. The man was dead. In fact, by the time the doctor could view the body, it had been stripped, washed, and prepared for cremation in the usual manner."

"In other words, the robots had destroyed evidence," said Baley, annoyed. Then: "Did you say he *viewed* the body? He didn't *see* it?"

"Great Space," said Gruer, "what a morbid notion. He

viewed it, of course, from all necessary angles and at close focus, I'm sure. Doctors can't avoid seeing patients under some conditions, but I can't conceive of any reason why they should have to see corpses. Medicine is a dirty job, but even doctors draw the line somewhere."

"Well, the point is this. Did the doctor report anything about the nature of the wound that killed Dr. Delmarre?"

"I see what you've driving at. You think that perhaps the wound was too severe to have been caused by a woman."

"A woman is weaker than a man, sir. And Mrs. Delmarre is a small woman."

"But quite athletic, Plainclothesman. Given a weapon of the proper type, gravity and leverage would do most of the work. Even not allowing for that, a woman in frenzy can do surprising things."

Baley shrugged. "You speak of a weapon. Where is it?"

Gruer shifted position. He held out his hand toward an empty glass and a robot entered the viewing field and filled it with a colorless fluid that might have been water.

Gruer held the filled glass momentarily, then put it down as though he had changed his mind about drinking. He said, "As is stated in the report, we have not been able to locate it."

"I know the report says that. I want to make absolutely certain of a few things. The weapon was searched for?"

"Thoroughly."

"By yourself?"

"By robots, but under my own viewing supervision at all times. We could locate nothing that might have been the weapon."

"That weakens the case against Mrs. Delmarre, doesn't it?"

"It does," said Gruer calmly. "It is one of several things about the case we don't understand. It is one reason why we have not acted against Mrs. Delmarre. It is one reason why I told you that the guilty party could not have committed the crime, either. Perhaps I should say that she apparently could not have committed the crime."

"Apparently?"

"She must have disposed of the weapon someway. So far, we have lacked the ingenuity to find it."

Baley said dourly, "Have you considered all possibilities?"

"I think so."

"I wonder. Let's see. A weapon has been used to crush a man's skull and it is not found at the scene of the crime. The only alternative is that it has been carried away. It could not have been carried away by Rikaine Delmarre. He was dead. Could it have been carried away by Gladia Delmarre?"

"It must have been," said Gruer.

"How? When the robots arrived, she was on the floor unconscious. Or she may have been feigning unconsciousness, but anyway she was there. How long a time between the murder and the arrival of the first robot?"

"That depends upon the exact time of the murder, which we don't know," said Gruer uneasily.

"I read the report, sir. One robot reported hearing a disturbance and a cry it identified as Dr. Delmarre's. It was apparently the closest to the scene. The summoning signal flashed five minutes afterward. It would take the robot less than a minute to appear on the scene." (Baley remembered his own experiences with the rapid-fire appearance of robots when summoned.) "In five minutes, even ten, how far could Mrs. Delmarre have carried a weapon and returned in time to assume unconsciousness?"

"She might have destroyed it in a disposer unit."

"The disposer unit was investigated, according to the report, and the residual gamma-ray activity was quite low. Nothing sizable had been destroyed in it for twenty-four hours."

"I know that," said Gruer. "I simply present it as an example of what might have been done."

"True," said Baley, "but there may be a very simple explanation. I suppose the robots belonging to the Delmarre household have been checked and all were accounted for."

"Oh yes."

"And all in reasonable working order?"

"Yes."

"Could any of those have carried away the weapon, perhaps without being aware of what it was?"

"Not one of them had removed anything from the scene of the crime. Or touched anything, for that matter."

"That's not so. They certainly removed the body and prepared it for cremation."

"Well, yes, of course, but that scarcely counts. You would expect them to do that."

"Jehoshaphat!" muttered Baley. He had to struggle to keep calm.

He said, "Now suppose someone else had been on the scene."

"Impossible," said Gruer. "How could someone invade Dr. Delmarre's personal presence?"

"Suppose!" cried Baley. "Now there was never any thought in the robots' minds that an intruder might have been present. I don't suppose any of them made an immediate search of the grounds about the house. It wasn't mentioned in the report."

"There was no search till we looked for the weapon, but that was a considerable time afterward."

"Nor any search for signs of a ground-car or an air vehicle on the grounds?"

"No."

"Then if someone had nerved himself to invade Dr. Delmarre's personal presence, as you put it, he could have killed him and then walked away leisurely. No one would have stopped him or even seen him. Afterward, he could rely on everyone being sure no one could have been there."

"And no one could," said Gruer positively.

Baley said, "One more thing. Just one more. There was a robot involved. A robot was at the scene."

Daneel interposed for the first time. "The robot was not at the scene. Had it been there, the crime would not have been committed."

Baley turned his head sharply. And Gruer, who had lifted his glass a second time as though about to drink, put it down again to stare at Daneel.

"Is that not so?" asked Daneel.

"Quite so," said Gruer. "A robot would have stopped one person from harming another. First Law."

"All right," said Baley. "Granted. But it must have been close. It was on the scene when the other robots arrived. Say it was in the next room. The murderer is advancing on Delmarre and Delmarre cries out, 'You're going to kill me.'

The robots of the household did not hear those words; at most they heard a cry, so, unsummoned, they did not come. But this particular robot heard the words and First Law made it come unsummoned. It was too late. Probably, it actually saw the murder committed."

"It must have seen the last stages of the murder," agreed Gruer. "That is what disordered it. Witnessing harm to a human without having prevented it is a violation of the First Law and, depending upon circumstances, more or less damage to the positronic brain is induced. In this case, it was a great deal of damage."

Gruer stared at his fingertips as he turned the glass of liquid to and fro, to and fro.

Baley said, "Then the robot was a witness. Was it questioned?"

"What use? He was disordered. It could only say 'You're going to kill me.' I agree with your reconstruction that far. They were probably Delmarre's last words burned into the robot's consciousness when everything else was destroyed."

"But I'm told Solaria specializes in robots. Was there no way in which the robot could be repaired? No way in which its circuits could be patched?"

"None," said Gruer sharply.

"And where is the robot, now?"

"Scrapped," said Gruer.

Baley raised his eyebrows. "This is a rather peculiar case. No motive, no means, no witnesses, no evidence. Where there was some evidence to begin with, it was destroyed. You have only one suspect and everyone seems convinced of her guilt; at least, everyone is certain no one else can be guilty. That's your opinion, too, obviously. The question then is: Why was I sent for?"

Gruer frowned. "You seem upset, Mr. Baley." He turned abruptly to Daneel. "Mr. Olivaw."

"Yes, Agent Gruer."

"Won't you please go through the dwelling and make sure all windows are closed and blanked out? Plainclothesman Baley may be feeling the effects of open space."

The statement astonished Baley. It was his impulse to deny Gruer's assumption and order Daneel to keep his place when, on the brink, he caught something of panic in Gruer's voice, something of glittering appeal in his eyes.

He sat back and let Daneel leave the room.

It was as though a mask had dropped from Gruer's face, leaving it naked and afraid. Gruer said, "That was easier than I had thought. I'd planned so many ways of getting you alone. I never thought the Auroran would leave at a simple request, and yet I could think of nothing else to do."

Baley said, "Well, I'm alone now."

Gruer said, "I couldn't speak freely in his presence. He's an Auroran and he is here because he was forced on us as the price of having you." The Solarian leaned forward. "There's something more to this than murder. I am not concerned only with the matter of who did it. There are parties on Solaria, secret organizations. . . ."

Baley stared. "Surely, I can't help you there."

"Of course you can. Now understand this: Dr. Delmarre was a Traditionalist. He believed in the old ways, the good ways. But there are new forces among us, forces for change, and Delmarre has been silenced."

"By Mrs. Delmarre?"

"Hers must have been the hand. That doesn't matter. There is an organization behind her and that is the important matter."

"Are you sure? Do you have evidence?"

"Vague evidence, only. I can't help that. Rikaine Delmarre was on the track of something. He assured me *his* evidence was good, and I believe him. I knew him well enough to know him as neither fool nor child. Unfortunately, he told me very little. Naturally, he wanted to complete his investigation before laying the matter completely open to the authorities. He must have gotten close to completion, too, or they wouldn't have dared the risk of having him openly slaughtered by violence. One thing Delmarre told me, though. The whole human race is in danger."

Baley felt himself shaken. For a moment it was as though he were listening to Minnim again, but on an even larger scale. Was *everyone* going to turn to him with cosmic dangers?

"Why do you think I can help?" he asked.

"Because you're an Earthman," said Gruer. "Do you understand? We on Solaria have no experience with these things. In a way, we don't understand people. There are too few of us here."

He looked uneasy. "I don't like to say this, Mr. Baley. My colleagues laugh at me and some grow angry, but it is a definite feeling I have. It seems to me that you Earthmen *must* understand people far better than we do, just by living among such crowds of them. And a detective more than anyone. Isn't that so?"

Baley half nodded and held his tongue.

Gruer said, "In a way, this murder was fortunate. I have not dared speak to the others about Delmarre's investigation, since I wasn't sure who might be involved in the conspiracy, and Delmarre himself was not ready to give any details till his investigation was complete. And even if Delmarre had completed his work, how would we deal with the matter afterward? How does one deal with hostile human beings? I don't know. From the beginning, I felt we needed an Earthman. When I heard of your work in connection with the murder in Spacetown on Earth, I knew we needed you. I got in touch with Aurora, with whose men you have worked most closely, and through them approached the Earth government. Yet my own colleagues could not be persuaded into agreeing to this. Then came the murder and that was enough of a shock to give me the agreement I needed. At the moment, they would have agreed to anything."

Gruer hesitated, then added, "It's not easy to ask an Earthman to help, but I must do so. Remember, whatever it is, the human race is in danger. Earth, too."

Earth was doubly in danger, then. There was no mistaking the desperate sincerity in Gruer's voice.

But then, if the murder were so fortunate a pretext for allowing Gruer to do what he so desperately wanted to do all the time, was it entirely fortune? It opened new avenues of thought that were not reflected in Baley's face, eyes, or voice.

Baley said, "I have been sent here, sir, to help. I will do so to the best of my ability."

Gruer finally lifted his long-delayed drink and looked over the rim of the glass at Baley. "Good," he said. "Not a word to the Auroran, please. Whatever this is about,

Aurora may be involved. Certainly they took an unusually intense interest in the case. For instance, they insisted on including Mr. Olivaw as your partner. Aurora is powerful; we had to agree. They say they include Mr. Olivaw only because he worked with you before, but it may well be that they wish a reliable man of their own on the scene, eh?"

He sipped slowly, his eyes on Baley.

Baley passed the knuckles of one hand against his long cheek, rubbing it thoughtfully. "Now if that——"

He didn't finish, but leaped from his chair and almost hurled himself toward the other, before remembering it was only an image he was facing.

For Gruer, staring wildly at his drink, clutched his throat, whispered hoarsely, "Burning . . . burning . . ."

The glass fell from his hand, its contents spilling. And Gruer dropped with it, his face distorted with pain.

7. A DOCTOR IS PRODDED

Daneel stood in the doorway. "What happened, Partner Eli——"

But no explanation was needed. Daneel's voice changed to a loud ringing shout. "Robots of Hannis Gruer! Your master is hurt! Robots!"

At once a metal figure strode into the dining room and after it, in a minute or two, a dozen more entered. Three carried Gruer gently away. The others busily engaged in straightening the disarray and picking up the tableware strewn on the floor.

Daneel called out suddenly, "You there, robots, never mind the crockery. Organize a search. Search the house for any human being. Alert any robots on the grounds outside. Have them go over every acre of the estate. If you find a master, hold him. Do not hurt him" (unnecessary advice) "but do not let him leave, either. If you find no master present, let me know. I will remain at this viewer combination."

Then, as robots scattered, Elijah muttered to Daneel, "That's a beginning. It was poison, of course."

"Yes. That much is obvious, Partner Elijah." Daneel sat down queerly, as though there were a weakness in his knees. Baley had never seen him give way so, not for an instant, to any action that resembled anything so human as a weakness in the knees.

Daneel said, "It is not well with my mechanism to see a human being come to harm."

"There was nothing you could do."

"That I understand and yet it is as though there were certain cloggings in my thought paths. In human terms what I feel might be the equivalent to shock."

"If that's so, get over it." Baley felt neither patience nor sympathy for a queasy robot. "We've got to consider the little matter of responsibility. There is no poison without a poisoner."

"It might have been food-poisoning."

"Accidental food-poisoning? On a world this neatly run? Never. Besides, the poison was in a liquid and the symptoms were sudden and complete. It was a poisoned dose and a large one. Look, Daneel, I'll go into the next room to think this out a bit. You get Mrs. Delmarre. Make sure she's at home and check the distance between her estate and Gruer's."

"Is it that you think she——"

Baley held up a hand. "Just find out, will you?"

He strode out of the room, seeking solitude. Surely there could not be two independent attempts at murder so close together in time on a world like Solaria. And if a connection existed, the easiest assumption to make was that Gruer's story of a conspiracy was true.

Baley felt a familiar excitement growing within him. He had come to this world with Earth's predicament in his mind, and his own. The murder itself had been a faraway thing, but now the chase was really on. The muscles in his jaw knotted.

After all, the murderer or murderers (or murderess) had struck in his presence and he was stung by that. Was he held in so little account? It was professional pride that was hurt and Baley knew it and welcomed the fact. At least it gave him a firm reason to see this thing through as a murder case, simply, even without reference to Earth's dangers.

Daneel had located him now and was striding toward him. "I have done as you asked me to, Partner Elijah. I have viewed Mrs. Delmarre. She is at home, which is somewhat over a thousand miles from the estate of Agent Gruer."

Baley said, "I'll see her myself later. View her, I mean." He stared thoughtfully at Daneel. "Do you think she has any connection with this crime?"

"Apparently not a direct connection, Partner Elijah."

"Does that imply there might be an indirect connection?"

"She might have persuaded someone else to do it."

"Someone else?" Baley asked quickly. "Who?"

"That, Partner Elijah, I cannot say."

"If someone were acting for her, that someone would have to be at the scene of the crime."

"Yes," said Daneel, "someone must have been there to place the poison in the liquid."

"Isn't it possible that the poisoned liquid might have been prepared earlier in the day? Perhaps much earlier?"

Daneel said quietly, "I had thought of that, Partner Elijah, which is why I used the word 'apparently' when I stated that Mrs. Delmarre had no direct connection with the crime. It is within the realm of possibility for her to have been on the scene earlier in the day. It would be well to check her movements."

"We will do that. We will check whether she was physically present at any time."

Baley's lips twitched. He had guessed that in some ways robotic logic must fall short and he was convinced of it now. As the roboticist had said: Logical but not reasonable.

He said, "Let's get back into the viewing room and get Gruer's estate back in view."

The room sparkled with freshness and order. There was no sign at all that less than an hour before a man had collapsed in agony.

Three robots stood, backs against the wall, in the usual robotic attitude of respectful submission.

Baley said, "What news concerning your master?"

The middle robot said, "The doctor is attending him, master."

"Viewing or seeing?"

"Viewing, master."

"What does the doctor say? Will your master live?"

"It is not yet certain, master."

Baley said, "Has the house been searched?"

"Thoroughly, master."

"Was there any sign of another master beside your own?"

"No, master."

"Were there any signs of such presence in the near past?"

"Not at all, master."

"Are the grounds being searched?"

"Yes, master."

"Any results so far?"

"No, master."

Baley nodded and said, "I wish to speak to the robot that served at the table this night."

"It is being held for inspection, master. Its reactions are erratic."

"Can it speak?"

"Yes, master."

"Then get it here without delay."

There *was* delay and Baley began again. "I said——"

Daneel interrupted smoothly. "There is interradio communication among these Solarian types. The robot you desire is being summoned. If it is slow in coming, it is part of the disturbance that has overtaken it as the result of what has occurred."

Baley nodded. He might have guessed at interradio. In a world so thoroughly given over to robots some sort of intimate communication among them would be necessary if the system were not to break down. It explained how a dozen robots could follow when one robot had been summoned, but only when needed and not otherwise.

A robot entered. It limped, one leg dragging. Baley wondered why and then shrugged. Even among the primitive robots on Earth reactions to injury of the positronic paths were never obvious to the layman. A disrupted circuit might strike a leg's functioning, as here, and the fact would be most significant to a roboticist and completely meaningless to anyone else.

Baley said cautiously, "Do you remember a colorless liquid on your master's table, some of which you poured into a goblet for him?"

The robot said, "Yeth, mathter."

A defect in oral articulation, too!

Baley said, "What was the nature of the liquid?"

"It wath water, mathter."

"Just water? Nothing else?"

"Jutht water, mathter."

"Where did you get it?"

"From the rethervoir tap, mathter."

"Had it been standing in the kitchen before you brought it in?"

"The mathter preferred it not too cold, mathter. It wath

a thtanding order that it be poured an hour before mealth."

How convenient, thought Baley, for anyone who knew that fact.

He said, "Have one of the robots connect me with the doctor viewing your master as soon as he is available. And while that is being done, I want another one to explain how the reservoir tap works. I want to know about the water supply here."

The doctor was available with little delay. He was the oldest Spacer Baley had ever seen, which meant, Baley thought, that he might be over three hundred years old. The veins stood out on his hands and his close-cropped hair was pure white. He had a habit of tapping his ridged front teeth with a fingernail, making a little clicking noise that Baley found annoying. His name was Altim Thool.

The doctor said, "Fortunately, he threw up a good deal of the dose. Still, he may not survive. It is a tragic event." He sighed heavily.

"What was the poison, Doctor?" asked Baley.

"I'm afraid I don't know." (Click-click-click.)

Baley said, "What? Then how are you treating him?"

"Direct stimulation of the neuromuscular system to prevent paralysis, but except for that I am letting nature take its course." His face, with its faintly yellow skin, like well-worn leather of superior quality, wore a pleading expression. "We have very little experience with this sort of thing. I don't recall another case in over two centuries of practice."

Baley stared at the other with contempt. "You know there are such things as poisons, don't you?"

"Oh, yes." (Click-click.) "Common knowledge."

"You have book-film references where you can gain some knowledge."

"It would take days. There are numerous mineral poisons. We make use of insecticides in our society, and it is not impossible to obtain bacterial toxins. Even with descriptions in the films it would take a long time to gather the equipment and develop the techniques to test for them."

"If no one on Solaria knows," said Baley grimly, "I'd suggest you get in touch with one of the other worlds and find out. Meanwhile, you had better test the reservoir tap in Gruer's mansion for poison. Get there in person, if you have to, and do it."

Baley was prodding a venerable Spacer roughly, ordering him about like a robot and was quite unconscious of the incongruity of it. Nor did the Spacer make any protest.

Dr. Thool said doubtfully, "How could the reservoir tap be poisoned? I'm sure it couldn't be."

"Probably not," agreed Baley, "but test it anyway to make sure."

The reservoir tap was a dim possibility indeed. The robot's explanation had shown it to be a typical piece of Solarian self-care. Water might enter it from whatever source and be tailored to suit. Microorganisms were removed and non-living organic matter eliminated. The proper amount of aeration was introduced, as were various ions in just those trace amounts best suited to the body's needs. It was very unlikely that any poison could survive one or another of the control devices.

Still, if the safety of the reservoir were directly established, then the time element would be clear. There would be the matter of the hour before the meal, when the pitcher of water (exposed to *air*, thought Baley sourly) was allowed to warm slowly, thanks to Gruer's idiosyncrasy.

But Dr. Thool, frowning, was saying. "But how would I test the reservoir tap?"

"Jehoshaphat! Take an animal with you. Inject some of the water you take out of the tap into its veins, or have it drink some. Use your head, man. And do the same for what's left in the pitcher, and if that's poisoned, as it must be, run some of the tests the reference films describe. Find some simple one. Do *some*thing."

"Wait, wait. What pitcher?"

"The pitcher in which the water was standing. The pitcher from which the robot poured the poisoned drink."

"Well, dear me—I presume it has been cleaned up. The household retinue would surely not leave it standing about."

Baley groaned. Of course not. It was *impossible* to retain evidence with eager robots forever destroying it in the name of household duty. He should have *ordered* it preserved, but of course, this society was not his own and he never reacted properly to it.

Jehoshaphat!

Word eventually came through that the Gruer estate was clear; no sign of any unauthorized human present anywhere.

Daneel said, "That rather intensifies the puzzle, Partner Elijah, since it seems to leave no one in the role of poisoner."

Baley, absorbed in thought, scarcely heard. He said, "What? . . . Not at all. Not at all. It clarifies the matter." He did not explain, knowing quite well that Daneel would be incapable of understanding or believing what Baley was certain was the truth.

Nor did Daneel ask for an explanation. Such an invasion of a human's thoughts would have been most unrobotic.

Baley prowled back and forth restlessly, dreading the approach of the sleep period, when his fears of the open would rise and his longing for Earth increase. He felt an almost feverish desire to keep things happening.

He said to Daneel, "I might as well see Mrs. Delmarre again. Have the robot make contact."

They walked to the viewing room and Baley watched a robot work with deft metal fingers. He watched through a haze of obscuring thought that vanished in startled astonishment when a table, elaborately spread for dinner, suddenly filled half the room.

Gladia's voice said, "Hello." A moment later she stepped into view and sat down. "Don't look surprised, Elijah. It's just dinnertime. And I'm very carefully dressed. See?"

She was. The dominant color of her dress was a light blue and it shimmered down the length of her limbs to wrists and ankles. A yellow ruff clung about her neck and shoulders, a little lighter than her hair, which was now held in disciplined waves.

Baley said, "I did not mean to interrupt your meal."

"I haven't begun yet. Why don't you join me?"

He eyed her suspiciously. "Join you?"

She laughed. "You Earthmen are so funny. I don't mean join me in personal presence. How could you do that? I mean, go to your own dining room and then you and the other one can dine with me."

"But if I leave——"

"Your viewing technician can maintain contact."

Daneel nodded gravely at that, and with some uncertainty Baley turned and walked toward the door. Gladia, together with her table, its setting, and its ornaments moved with him.

Gladia smiled encouragingly. "See? Your viewing technician is keeping us in contact."

Baley and Daneel traveled up a moving ramp that Baley did not recall having traversed before. Apparently there were numerous possible routes between any two rooms in this impossible mansion and he knew only few of them. Daneel, of course, knew them all.

And, moving through walls, sometimes a bit below floor level, sometimes a bit above, there was always Gladia and her dinner table.

Baley stopped and muttered, "This takes getting used to."

Gladia said at once, "Does it make you dizzy?"

"A little."

"Then I tell you what. Why don't you have your technicians freeze me right here. Then when you're in your dining room and all set, he can join us up."

Daneel said, "I will order that done, Partner Elijah."

Their own dinner table was set when they arrived, the plates steaming with a dark brown soup in which diced meat was bobbing, and in the center a large roast fowl was ready for the carving. Daneel spoke briefly to the serving robot and, with smooth efficiency, the two places that had been set were drawn to the same end of the table.

As though that were a signal, the opposite wall seemed to move outward, the table seemed to lengthen and Gladia was seated at the opposite end. Room joined to room and table to table so neatly that but for the varying pattern in wall and floor covering and the differing designs in tableware it would have been easy to believe they were all dining together in actual fact.

"There," said Gladia with satisfaction. "Isn't this comfortable?"

"Quite," said Baley. He tasted his soup gingerly, found it delicious, and helped himself more generously. "You know about Agent Gruer?"

Trouble shadowed her face at once and she put her spoon down. "Isn't it terrible? Poor Hannis."

"You use his first name. Do you know him?"

"I know almost all the important people on Solaria. Most Solarians do know one another. Naturally."

Naturally, indeed, thought Baley. How many of them were there, after all?

Baley said, "Then perhaps you know Dr. Altim Thool. He's taking care of Gruer."

Gladia laughed gently. Her serving robot sliced meat for her and added small, browned potatoes and slivers of carrots. "Of course I know him. He treated me."

"Treated you when?"

"Right after the—the trouble. About my husband, I mean."

Baley said in astonishment, "Is he the only doctor on the planet?"

"Oh no." For a moment her lips moved as though she were counting to herself. "There are at least ten. And there's one youngster I know of who's studying medicine. But Dr. Thool is one of the best. He has the most experience. Poor Dr. Thool."

"Why poor?"

"Well, you know what I mean. It's such a nasty job, being a doctor. Sometimes you just have to see people when you're a doctor and even touch them. But Dr. Thool seems so resigned to it and he'll always do some seeing when he feels he must. He's always treated me since I was a child and was always so friendly and kind and I honestly feel I almost wouldn't mind if he did have to see me. For instance, he saw me this last time."

"After your husband's death, you mean?"

"Yes. You can imagine how he felt when he saw my husband's dead body and me lying there."

"I was told he viewed the body," said Baley.

"The body, yes. But after he made sure I was alive and in no real danger, he ordered the robots to put a pillow under my head and give me an injection of something or other, and then get out. He came over by jet. Really! By jet. It took less than half an hour and he took care of me and made sure all was well. I was so woozy when I came to that I was sure I was only viewing him, you know, and it wasn't till he touched me that I knew we were seeing, and I screamed. Poor Dr. Thool. He was awfully embarrassed, but I knew he meant well."

Baley nodded. "I suppose there's not much use for doctors on Solaria?"

"I should hope *not*."

"I know there are no germ diseases to speak of. What about metabolic disorders? Atherosclerosis? Diabetes? Things like that?"

"It happens and it's pretty awful when it does. Doctors can make life more livable for such people in a physical way, but that's the least of it."

"Oh?"

"Of course. It means the gene analysis was imperfect. You don't suppose we allow defects like diabetes to develop on purpose. Anyone who develops such things has to undergo very detailed re-analysis. The mate assignment has to be retracted, which is terribly embarrassing for the mate. And it means no—no"—her voice sank to a whisper—"children."

Baley said in a normal voice, "No children?"

Gladia flushed. "It's a terrible thing to say. Such a word! Ch-children!"

"It comes easy after a while," said Baley dryly.

"Yes, but if I get into the habit, I'll say it in front of another Solarian someday and I'll just sink into the ground. . . . Anyway, if the two of them have had children (see, I've said it again) already, the children have to be found and examined—that was one of Rikaine's jobs, by the way—and well, it's just a mess."

So much for Thool, thought Baley. The doctor's incompetence was a natural consequence of the society, and held nothing sinister. Nothing *necessarily* sinister. Cross him off, he thought, but lightly.

He watched Gladia as she ate. She was neat and precisely delicate in her movements and her appetite seemed normal. (His own fowl was delightful. In one respect, anyway—food—he could easily be spoiled by these Outer Worlds.)

He said, "What is your opinion of the poisoning, Gladia?"

She looked up. "I'm trying not to think of it. There are

so many horrors lately. Maybe it wasn't poisoning."

"It was."

"But there wasn't anyone around?"

"How do you know?"

"There couldn't have been. He has no wife, these days, since he's all through with his quota of ch—you know what. So there was no one to put the poison in anything, so how could he be poisoned?"

"But he was poisoned. That's a fact and must be accepted."

Her eyes clouded over. "Do you suppose," she said, "he did it himself?"

"I doubt it. Why should he? And so publicly?"

"Then it couldn't be done, Elijah. It just couldn't."

Baley said, "On the contrary, Gladia. It could be done very easily. And I'm sure I know exactly how."

8. A SPACER IS DEFIED

Gladia seemed to be holding her breath for a moment. It came out through puckered lips in what was almost a whistle. She said, "I'm sure *I* don't see how. Do you know *who* did it?"

Baley nodded. "The same one who killed your husband."

"Are you sure?"

"Aren't you? Your husband's murder was the first in the history of Solaria. A month later there is another murder. Could that be a coincidence? Two separate murderers striking within a month of each other on a crime-free world? Consider, too, that the second victim was investigating the first crime and therefore represented a violent danger to the original murderer."

"Well!" Gladia applied herself to her dessert and said between mouthfuls, "If you put it that way, I'm innocent."

"How so, Gladia?"

"Why, Elijah. I've never been near the Gruer estate, never in my whole life. So I certainly couldn't have poisoned Agent Gruer. And if I haven't—why, neither did I kill my husband."

Then, as Baley maintained a stern silence, her spirit seemed to fade and the corners of her small mouth drooped. "Don't you think so, Elijah?"

"I can't be sure," said Baley. "I've told you I know the method used to poison Gruer. It's an ingenious one and anyone on Solaria could have used it, whether they were ever on the Gruer estate or not."

Gladia clenched her hands into fists. "Are you saying I did it?"

"I'm not saying that."

"You're implying it." Her lips were thin with fury and her high cheekbones were splotchy. "Is that all your interest in viewing me? To ask me sly questions? To trap me?"

"Now wait——"

"You seemed so sympathetic. So understanding. You—you Earthman!"

Her contralto had become a tortured rasp with the last word.

Daneel's perfect face leaned toward Gladia and he said, "If you will pardon me, Mrs. Delmarre, you are holding a knife rather tightly and may cut yourself. Please be careful."

Gladia stared wildly at the short, blunt, and undoubtedly quite harmless knife she held in her hand. With a spasmodic movement she raised it high.

Baley said, "You couldn't reach me, Gladia."

She gasped. "Who'd want to reach you? Ugh!" She shuddered in exaggerated disgust and called out, "Break contact at once!"

The last must have been to a robot out of the line of sight, and Gladia and her end of the room were gone and the original wall sprang back.

Daneel said, "Am I correct in believing you now consider this woman guilty?"

"No," said Baley flatly. "Whoever did this needed a great deal more of certain characteristics than this poor girl has."

"She has a temper."

"What of that? Most people do. Remember, too, that she has been under a considerable strain for a considerable time. If I had been under a similar strain and someone had turned on me as she imagined I had turned on her, I might have done a great deal more than wave a foolish little knife."

Daneel said, "I have not been able to deduce the technique of poisoning at a distance, as you say you have."

Baley found it pleasant to be able to say, "I know you haven't. You lack the capacity to decipher this particular puzzle."

He said it with finality and Daneel accepted the statement as calmly and as gravely as ever.

Baley said, "I have two jobs for you, Daneel."

"And what are they, Partner Elijah?"

"First, get in touch with this Dr. Thool and find out Mrs.

Delmarre's condition at the time of the murder of her husband. How long she required treatment and so on."

"Do you want to determine something in particular?"

"No. I'm just trying to accumulate data. It isn't easy on this world. Secondly, find out who will be taking Gruer's place as head of security and arrange a viewing session for me first thing in the morning. As for me," he said without pleasure in his mind, and with none in his voice, "I'm going to bed and eventually, I hope, I'll sleep." Then, almost petulantly, "Do you suppose I could get a decent book-film in this place?"

Daneel said, "I would suggest that you summon the robot in charge of the library."

Baley felt only irritation at having to deal with the robot. He would much rather have browsed at will.

"No," he said, "not a classic; just an ordinary piece of fiction dealing with everyday life on contemporary Solaria. About half a dozen of them."

The robot submitted (it would have to) but even as it manipulated the proper controls that plucked the requisite book-films out of their niches and transferred them first to an exit slot and then to Baley's hand, it rattled on in respectful tones about all the other categories in the library.

The master might like an adventure romance of the days of exploration, it suggested, or an excellent view of chemistry, perhaps, with animated atom models, or a fantasy, or a Galactography. The list was endless.

Baley waited grimly for his half dozen, said, "These will do," reached with his own hands (his *own* hands) for a scanner and walked away.

When the robot followed and said, "Will you require help with the adjustment, master?" Baley turned and snapped, "No. Stay where you are."

The robot bowed and stayed.

Lying in bed, with the headboard aglow, Baley almost regretted his decision. The scanner was like no model he had ever used and he began with no idea at all as to the method for threading the film. But he worked at it obstinately, and, eventually, by taking it apart and working it out bit by bit, he managed something.

At least he could view the film and, if the focus left a bit to be desired, it was small payment for a moment's independence from the robots.

In the next hour and a half he had skipped and switched through four of the six films and was disappointed.

He had had a theory. There was no better way, he had thought, to get an insight into Solarian ways of life and thought than to read their novels. He needed that insight if he were to conduct the investigation sensibly.

But now he had to abandon his theories. He had viewed novels and had succeeded only in learning of people with ridiculous problems who behaved foolishly and reacted mysteriously. Why should a woman abandon her job on discovering her child had entered the same profession and refuse to explain her reasons until unbearable and ridiculous complications had resulted? Why should a doctor and an artist be humiliated at being assigned to one another and what was so noble about the doctor's insistence on entering robotic research?

He threaded the fifth novel into the scanner and adjusted it to his eyes. He was bone-weary.

So weary, in fact, that he never afterward recalled anything of the fifth novel (which he believed to be a suspense story) except for the opening in which a new estate owner entered his mansion and looked through the past account films presented him by a respectful robot.

Presumably he fell asleep then with the scanner on his head and all lights blazing. Presumably a robot, entering respectfully, had gently removed the scanner and put out the lights.

In any case, he slept and dreamed of Jessie. All was as it had been. He had never left Earth. They were ready to travel to the community kitchen and then to see a subetheric show with friends. They would travel over the Expressways and see people and neither of them had a care in the world. He was happy.

And Jessie was beautiful. She had lost weight somehow. Why should she be so slim? And so beautiful?

And one other thing was wrong. Somehow the sun shone down on them. He looked up and there was only the vaulted base of the upper Levels visible, yet the sun shone down, blazing brightly on everything, and no one was afraid.

Baley woke up, disturbed. He let the robots serve breakfast and did not speak to Daneel. He said nothing, asked nothing, downed excellent coffee without tasting it.

Why had he dreamed of the visible-invisible sun? He could understand dreaming of Earth and of Jessie, but what had the sun to do with it? And why should the thought of it bother him, anyway?

"Partner Elijah," said Daneel gently.

"What?"

"Corwin Attlebish will be in viewing contact with you in half an hour. I have arranged that."

"Who the hell is Corwin Whatchamacullum?" asked Baley sharply, and refilled his coffee cup.

"He was Agent Gruer's chief aide, Partner Elijah, and is now Acting Head of Security."

"Then get him now."

"The appointment, as I explained, is for half an hour from now."

"I don't care when it's for. Get him now. That's an order."

"I will make the attempt, Partner Elijah. He may not, however, agree to receive the call."

"Let's take the chance, and get on with it, Daneel."

The Acting Head of Security accepted the call and, for the first time on Solaria, Baley saw a Spacer who looked the usual Earthly conception of one. Attlebish was tall, lean, and bronze. His eyes were a light brown, his chin large and hard.

He looked faintly like Daneel. But whereas Daneel was idealized, almost godlike, Corwin Attlebish had lines of humanity in his face.

Attlebish was shaving. The small abrasive pencil gave out its spray of fine particles that swept over cheek and chin, biting off the hair neatly and then disintegrating into impalpable dust.

Baley recognized the instrument through hearsay but had never seen one used before.

"You the Earthman?" asked Attlebish slurringly through

barely cracked lips, as the abrasive dust passed under his nose.

Baley said, "I'm Elijah Baley, Plainclothesman C-7. I'm from Earth."

"You're early." Attlebish snapped his shaver shut and tossed it somewhere outside Baley's range of vision. "What's on your mind, Earthman?"

Baley would not have enjoyed the other's tone of voice at the best of times. He burned now. He said, "How is Agent Gruer?"

Attlebish said, "He's still alive. He may stay alive."

Baley nodded. "Your poisoners here on Solaria don't know dosages. Lack of experience. They gave Gruer too much and he threw it up. Half the dose would have killed him."

"Poisoners? There is no evidence for poison."

Baley stared. "Jehoshaphat! What else do you think it is?"

"A number of things. Much can go wrong with a person." He rubbed his face, looking for roughness with his fingertips. "You would scarcely know the metabolic problems that arise past the age of two fifty."

"If that's the case, have you obtained competent medical advice?"

"Dr. Thool's report——"

That did it. The anger that had been boiling inside Baley since waking burst through. He cried at the top of his voice, "I don't care about Dr. Thool. I said competent medical advice. Your doctors don't know anything, any more than your detectives would, if you had any. You had to get a detective from Earth. Get a doctor as well."

The Solarian looked at him coolly. "Are you telling me what to do?"

"Yes, and without charge. Be my guest. Gruer *was* poisoned. I witnessed the process. He drank, retched, and yelled that his throat was burning. What do you call it when you consider that he was investigating——" Baley came to a sudden halt.

"Investigating what?" Attlebish was unmoved.

Baley was uncomfortably aware of Daneel at his usual

position some ten feet away. Gruer had not wanted Daneel, as an Auroran, to know of the investigation. He said lamely, "There were political implications."

Attlebish crossed his arms and looked distant, bored, and faintly hostile. "We have no politics on Solaria in the sense we hear of it on other worlds. Hannis Gruer has been a good citizen, but he is imaginative. It was he who, having heard some story about you, urged that we import you. He even agreed to accept an Auroran companion for you as a condition. I did not think it necessary. There is no mystery. Rikaine Delmarre was killed by his wife and we shall find out how and why. Even if we do not, she will be genetically analyzed and the proper measures taken. As for Gruer, your fantasy concerning poisoning is of no importance."

Baley said incredulously, "You seem to imply that I'm not needed here."

"I believe not. If you wish to return to Earth, you may do so. I may even say we urge you to."

Baley was amazed at his own reaction. He cried, "No, sir. I don't budge."

"We hired you, Plainclothesman. We can discharge you. You will return to your home planet."

"*No!* You listen to me. I'd advise you to. You're a big-time Spacer and I'm an Earthman, but with all respect, with deepest and most humble apologies, you're scared."

"Withdraw that statement!" Attlebish drew himself to his six-foot-plus, and stared down at the Earthman haughtily.

"You're scared as hell. You think you'll be next if you pursue this thing. You're giving in so they'll let you alone; so they'll leave you your miserable life." Baley had no notion who the "they" might be or if there were any "they" at all. He was striking out blindly at an arrogant Spacer and enjoying the thud his phrases made as they hit against the other's self-control.

"You will leave," said Attlebish, pointing his finger in cold anger, "within the hour. There'll be no diplomatic considerations about this, I assure you."

"Save your threats, Spacer. Earth is nothing to you, I admit, but I'm not the only one here. May I introduce my partner, Daneel Olivaw. He's from Aurora. He doesn't talk much. He's not here to talk. I handle that department. But he listens awfully well. He doesn't miss a word.

"Let me put it straight, Attlebish"—Baley used the un-adorned name with relish—"whatever monkeyshines are going on here on Solaria, Aurora and forty-odd other Outer Worlds are interested. If you kick us off, the next deputation to visit Solaria will consist of warships. I'm from Earth and I know how the system works. Hurt feelings mean warships by return trip."

Attlebish transferred his regard to Daneel and seemed to be considering. His voice was gentler. "There is nothing going on here that need concern anyone outside the planet."

"Gruer thought otherwise and my partner heard him." This was no time to cavil at a lie.

Daneel turned to look at Baley, at the Earthman's last statement, but Baley paid no attention. He drove on: "I intend to pursue this investigation. Ordinarily, there's nothing I wouldn't do to get back to Earth. Even just dreaming about it gets me so restless I can't sit. If I owned this robot-infested palace I'm living in now, I'd give it with the robots thrown in and you and all your lousy world to boot for a ticket home.

"But I won't be ordered off by you. Not while there's a case to which I've been assigned that's still open. Try getting rid of me against my will and you'll be looking down the throats of space-based artillery.

"What's more, from now on, this murder investigation is going to be run *my* way. I'm in charge. I see the people I want to see. I *see* them. I don't view them. I'm used to seeing and that's the way it's going to be. I'll want the official approval of your office for all of that."

"This is impossible, unbearable——"

"Daneel, you tell him."

The humanoid's voice said dispassionately, "As my part-ner has informed you, Agent Attlebish, we have been sent here to conduct a murder investigation. It is essential that we do so. We, of course, do not wish to disturb any of your customs and perhaps actual seeing will be unnecessary, although it would be helpful if you were to give approval for such seeing as becomes necessary as Plainclothesman Baley has requested. As to leaving the planet against our will, we feel that would be inadvisable, although we regret any feeling on your part or on the part of any Solarian that our remaining would be unpleasant."

Baley listened to the stilted sentence structure with a dour stretching of his lips that was not a smile. To one who knew Daneel as a robot, it was all an attempt to do a job without giving offense to any human, not to Baley and not to Attlebish. To one who thought Daneel was an Auroran, a native of the oldest and most powerful militarily of the Outer Worlds, it sounded like a series of subtly courteous threats.

Attlebish put the tips of his fingers to his forehead. "I'll think about it."

"Not too long," said Baley, "because I have some visiting to do within the hour, and not by viewer. Done viewing!"

He signaled the robot to break contact, then he stared with surprise and pleasure at the place where Attlebish had been. None of this had been planned. It had all been impulse born of his dream and of Attlebish's unnecessary arrogance. But now that it had happened, he was glad. It was what he had wanted, really—to take control.

He thought: Anyway, that was telling the dirty Spacer!

He wished the entire population of Earth could have been here to watch. The man *looked* such a Spacer, and that made it all the better, of course. All the better.

Only, why this feeling of vehemence in the matter of seeing? Baley scarcely understood that. He knew what he planned to do, and seeing (not viewing) was part of it. All right. Yet there had been the tight lift to his spirit when he spoke of seeing, as though he were ready to break down the walls of this mansion even though it served no purpose.

Why?

There was something impelling him besides the case, something that had nothing to do even with the question of Earth's safety. But what?

Oddly, he remembered his dream again; the sun shining down through all the opaque layers of the gigantic underground Cities of Earth.

Daneel said with thoughtfulness (as far as his voice could carry a recognizable emotion), "I wonder, Partner Elijah, if this is entirely safe."

"Bluffing this character? It worked. And it wasn't really

a bluff. I think it *is* important to Aurora to find out what's going on on Solaria, and that Aurora knows it. Thank you, by the way, for not catching me out in a misstatement."

"It was the natural decision. To have borne you out did Agent Attlebish a certain rather subtle harm. To have given you the lie would have done you a greater and more direct harm."

"Potentials countered and the higher one won out, eh, Daneel?"

"So it was, Partner Elijah. I understand that this process, in a less definable way, goes on within the human mind. I repeat, however, that this new proposal of yours is not safe."

"Which new proposal is this?"

"I do not approve your notion of seeing people. By that I mean seeing as opposed to viewing."

"I understand you. I'm not asking for your approval."

"I have my instructions, Partner Elijah. What it was that Agent Hannis Gruer told you during my absence last night I cannot know. That he did say something is obvious from the change in your attitude toward this problem. However, in the light of my instructions, I can guess. He must have warned you of the possibility of danger to other planets arising from the situation on Solaria."

Slowly Baley reached for his pipe. He did that occasionally and always there was the feeling of irritation when he found nothing and remembered he could not smoke. He said, "There are only twenty thousand Solarians. What danger can they represent?"

"My masters on Aurora have for some time been uneasy about Solaria. I have not been told all the information at their disposal——"

"And what little you have been told you have been told not to repeat to me. Is that it?" demanded Baley.

Daneel said, "There is a great deal to find out before this matter can be discussed freely."

"Well, what are the Solarians doing? New weapons? Paid subversion? A campaign of individual assassination? What can twenty thousand people do against hundreds of millions of Spacers?"

Daneel remained silent.

Baley said, "I intend to find out, you know."

"But not the way you have now proposed, Partner Elijah. I have been instructed most carefully to guard your safety."

"You would have to anyway. First Law!"

"Over and above that, as well. In conflict between your safety and that of another I must guard yours."

"Of course. I understand that. If anything happens to me, there is no further way in which you can remain on Solaria without complications that Aurora is not yet ready to face. As long as I'm alive, I'm here at Solaria's original request and so we can throw our weight around, if necessary, and make them keep us. If I'm dead, the whole situation is changed. Your orders are, then, to keep Baley alive. Am I right, Daneel?"

Daneel said, "I cannot presume to interpret the reasoning behind my orders."

Baley said, "All right, don't worry. The open space won't kill me, if I do find it necessary to see anyone. I'll survive. I may even get used to it."

"It is not the matter of open space alone, Partner Elijah," said Daneel. "It is this matter of seeing Solarians. I do not approve of it."

"You mean the Spacers won't like it. Too bad if they don't. Let them wear nose filters and gloves. Let them spray the air. And if it offends their nice morals to see me in the flesh, let them wince and blush. But I intend to see them. I consider it necessary to do so and I *will* do so."

"But I cannot allow you to."

"*You* can't allow *me*?"

"Surely you see why, Partner Elijah."

"I do not."

"Consider, then, that Agent Gruer, the key Solarian figure in the investigation of this murder, has been poisoned. Does it not follow that if I permit you to proceed in your plan for exposing yourself indiscriminately in actual person, the next victim will necessarily be you yourself. How then can I possibly permit you to leave the safety of this mansion?"

"How will you stop me, Daneel?"

"By force, if necessary, Partner Elijah," said Daneel calmly. "Even if I must hurt you. If I do not do so, you will surely die."

9. A ROBOT IS STYMIED

Baley said, "So the higher potential wins out again, Daneel. You will hurt me to keep me alive."

"I do not believe hurting you will be necessary, Partner Elijah. You know that I am superior to you in strength and you will not attempt a useless resistance. If it should become necessary, however, I will be compelled to hurt you."

"I could blast you down where you stand," said Baley. "Right now! There is nothing in *my* potentials to prevent me."

"I had thought you might take this attitude at some time in our present relationship, Partner Elijah. Most particularly, the thought occurred to me during our trip to this mansion, when you grew momentarily violent in the ground-car. The destruction of myself is unimportant in comparison with your safety, but such destruction would cause you distress eventually and disturb the plans of my masters. It was one of my first cares, therefore, during your first sleeping period, to deprive your blaster of its charge."

Baley's lips tightened. He was left without a charged blaster! His hand dropped instantly to his holster. He drew his weapon and stared at the charge reading. It hugged zero.

For a moment he balanced the lump of useless metal as though to hurl it directly into Daneel's face. What good? The robot would dodge efficiently.

Baley put the blaster back. It could be recharged in good time.

Slowly, thoughtfully, he said, "I'm not fooled by you, Daneel."

"In what way, Partner Elijah?"

"You are too much the master. I am too completely stopped by you. Are you a robot?"

"You have doubted me before," said Daneel.

"On Earth last year I doubted whether R. Daneel Olivaw was truly a robot. It turned out he was. I believe he still is. My question, however is this: Are you R. Daneel Olivaw?"

"I am."

"Yes? Daneel was designed to imitate a Spacer closely. Why could not a Spacer be made up to imitate Daneel closely?"

"For what reason?"

"To carry on an investigation here with greater initiative and capacity than ever a robot could. And yet by assuming Daneel's role, you could keep me safely under control by giving me a false consciousness of mastery. After all, you are working through me and I must be kept pliable."

"All this is not so, Partner Elijah."

"Then why do all the Solarians we meet assume you to be human? They are robotic experts. Are they so easily fooled? It occurs to me that I cannot be one right against many wrong. It is far more likely that I am one wrong against many right."

"Not at all, Partner Elijah."

"Prove it," said Baley, moving slowly toward an end table and lifting a scrap-disposal unit. "You can do that easily enough, if you *are* a robot. Show the metal beneath your skin."

Daneel said. "I assure you——"

"Show the metal," said Baley crisply. "That is an order! Or don't you feel compelled to obey orders?"

Daneel unbuttoned his shirt. The smooth, bronze skin of his chest was sparsely covered with light hair. Daneel's fingers exerted a firm pressure just under the right nipple, and flesh and skin split bloodlessly the length of the chest, with the gleam of metal showing beneath.

And as that happened, Baley's fingers, resting on the end table, moved half an inch to the right and stabbed at a contact patch. Almost at once a robot entered.

"Don't move, Daneel," cried Baley. "That's an order! Freeze!"

Daneel stood motionless, as though life, or the robotic imitation thereof, had departed from him.

Baley shouted to the robot, "Can you get two more of

the staff in here without yourself leaving? If so, do it."

The robot said, "Yes, master."

Two more robots entered, answering a radioed call. The three lined up abreast.

"Boys!" said Baley. "Do you see this creature whom you thought a master?"

Six ruddy eyes had turned solemnly on Daneel. They said in unison, "We see him, master."

Baley said, "Do you also see that this so-called master is actually a robot like yourself since it is metal within. It is only designed to look like a man."

"Yes, master."

"You are not required to obey any order it gives you. Do you understand that?"

"Yes, master."

"I, on the other hand," said Baley, "am a true man."

For a moment the robots hesitated. Baley wondered if, having had it shown to them that a thing might seem a man yet be a robot, they would accept *anything* in human appearance as a man, anything at all.

But then one robot said, "You are a man, master," and Baley drew breath again.

He said, "Very well, Daneel. You may relax."

Daneel moved into a more natural position and said calmly, "Your expressed doubt as to my identity, then, was merely a feint designed to exhibit my nature to these others, I take it."

"So it was," said Baley, and looked away. He thought: The thing is a machine, not a man. You can't doublecross a machine.

And yet he couldn't entirely repress a feeling of shame. Even as Daneel stood there, chest open, there seemed something so human about him, something capable of being betrayed.

Baley said, "Close your chest, Daneel, and listen to me. Physically, you are no match for three robots. You see that, don't you?"

"That is clear, Partner Elijah."

"Good! . . . Now you boys," and he turned to the other robots again. "You are to tell no one, human or master, that this creature is a robot. Never at any time, without further instructions from myself and myself alone."

"I thank you," interposed Daneel softly.

"However," Baley went on, "this manlike robot is not to be allowed to interfere with my actions in any way. If it attempts any such interference, you will restrain it by force, taking care not to damage it unless absolutely necessary. Do not allow it to establish contact with humans other than myself, or with robots other than yourselves, either by seeing or by viewing. And do not leave it at any time. Keep it in this room and remain here yourselves. Your other duties are suspended until further notice. Is all this clear?"

"Yes, master," they chorused.

Baley turned to Daneel again. "There is nothing you can do now, so don't try to stop me."

Daneel's arms hung loosely at his side. He said, "I may not, through inaction, allow you to come to harm, Partner Elijah. Yet under the circumstances, nothing but inaction is possible. The logic is unassailable. I shall do nothing. I trust you will remain safe and in good health."

There it was, thought Baley. Logic was logic and robots had nothing else. Logic told Daneel he was completely stymied. Reason might have told him that all factors are rarely predictable, that the opposition might make a mistake.

None of that. A robot is logical only, not reasonable.

Again Baley felt a twinge of shame and could not forbear an attempt at consolation. He said, "Look, Daneel, even if I were walking into danger, *which I'm not*" (he added that hurriedly, with a quick glance at the other robots) "it would only be my job. It is what I'm paid to do. It is as much my job to prevent harm to mankind as a whole as yours is to prevent harm to man as an individual. Do you see?"

"I do not, Partner Elijah."

"Then that is because you're not made to see. Take my word for it that if you were a man, you would see."

Daneel bowed his head in acquiescence and remained standing, motionless, while Baley walked slowly toward the door of the room. The three robots parted to make room for him and kept their photo-electric eyes fixed firmly on Daneel.

Baley was walking to a kind of freedom and his heart beat rapidly in anticipation of the fact, then skipped a beat.

Another robot was approaching the door from the other side.

Had something gone wrong?

"What is it, boy?" he snapped.

"A message has been forwarded to you, master, from the office of Acting Head of Security Attlebish."

Baley took the personal capsule handed to him and it opened at once. A finely inscribed strip of paper unrolled. (He wasn't startled. Solaria would have his fingerprints on file and the capsule would be adjusted to open at the touch of his particular convolutions.)

He read the message and his long face mirrored satisfaction. It was his official permission to arrange "seeing" interviews, subject to the wishes of the interviewees, who were nevertheless urged to give "Agents Baley and Olivaw" every possible co-operation.

Attlebish had capitulated, even to the extent of putting the Earthman's name first. It was an excellent omen with which to begin, finally, an investigation conducted as it should be conducted.

Baley was in an air-borne vessel again, as he had been on that trip from New York to Washington. This time, however, there was a difference. The vessel was not closed in. The windows were left transparent.

It was a clear bright day and from where Baley sat the windows were so many patches of blue. Unrelieved, featureless. He tried not to huddle. He buried his head in his knees only when he could absolutely no longer help it.

The ordeal was of his own choosing. His state of triumph, his unusual sense of freedom at having beaten down first Attlebish and then Daneel, his feeling of having asserted the dignity of Earth against the Spacers, almost demanded it.

He had begun by stepping across open ground to the waiting plane with a kind of lightheaded dizziness that was almost enjoyable, and he had ordered the windows left unblanked in a kind of manic self-confidence.

I have to get used to it, he thought, and stared at the blue until his heart beat rapidly and the lump in his throat swelled beyond endurance.

He had to close his eyes and bury his head under the

protective cover of his arms at shortening intervals. Slowly his confidence trickled away and even the touch of the holster of his freshly recharged blaster could not reverse the flow.

He tried to keep his mind on his plan of attack. First, learn the ways of the planet. Sketch in the background against which everything must be placed or fail to make sense.

See a sociologist!

He had asked a robot for the name of the Solarian most eminent as a sociologist. And there was that comfort about robots; they asked no questions.

The robot gave the name and vital statistics, and paused to remark that the sociologist would most probably be at lunch and would, therefore, possibly ask to delay contact.

"Lunch!" said Baley sharply. "Don't be ridiculous. It's not noon by two hours."

The robot said, "I am using local time, master."

Baley stared, then understood. On Earth, with its buried Cities, day and night, waking and sleeping, were man-made periods, adjusted to suit the needs of the community and the planet. On a planet such as this one, exposed nakedly to the sun, day and night were not a matter of choice at all, but were imposed on man willy-nilly.

Baley tried to picture a world as a sphere being lit and unlit as it turned. He found it hard to do and felt scornful of the so-superior Spacers who let such an essential thing as time be dictated to them by the vagaries of planetary movements.

He said, "Contact him anyway."

Robots were there to meet the plane when it landed and Baley, stepping out into the open again, found himself trembling badly.

He muttered to the nearest of the robots, "Let me hold your arm, boy."

The sociologist waited for him down the length of a hall, smiling tightly. "Good afternoon, Mr. Baley."

Baley nodded breathlessly. "Good evening, sir. Would you blank out the windows?"

The sociologist said, "They are blanked out already. I

know something of the ways of Earth. Will you follow me?"

Baley managed it without robotic help, following at a considerable distance, across and through a maze of hallways. When he finally sat down in a large and elaborate room, he was glad of the opportunity to rest.

The walls of the room were set with curved, shallow alcoves. Statuary in pink and gold occupied each niche; abstract figures that pleased the eye without yielding instant meaning. A large, boxlike affair with white and dangling cylindrical objects and numerous pedals suggested a musical instrument.

Baley looked at the sociologist standing before him. The Spacer looked precisely as he had when Baley had viewed him earlier that day. He was tall and thin and his hair was pure white. His face was strikingly wedge-shaped, his nose prominent, his eyes deep-set and alive.

His name was Anselmo Quemot.

They stared at one another until Baley felt he could trust his voice to be reasonably normal. And then his first remark had nothing to do with the investigation. In fact it was nothing he had planned.

He said, "May I have a drink?"

"A drink?" The sociologist's voice was a trifle too high-pitched to be entirely pleasant. He said, "You wish water?"

"I'd prefer something alcoholic."

The sociologist's look grew sharply uneasy, as though the obligations of hospitality were something with which he was unacquainted.

And that, thought Baley, was literally so. In a world where viewing was the thing, there would be no sharing of food and drink.

A robot brought him a small cup of smooth enamel. The drink was a light pink in color. Baley sniffed at it cautiously and tasted it even more cautiously. The small sip of liquid evaporated warmly in his mouth and sent a pleasant message along the length of his esophagus. His next sip was more substantial.

Quemot said, "If you wish more——"

"No, thank you, not now. It is good of you, sir, to agree to see me."

Quemot tried a smile and failed rather markedly, "It has

been a long time since I've done anything like this. Yes."

He almost squirmed as he spoke.

Baley said, "I imagine you find this rather hard."

"Quite." Quemot turned away sharply and retreated to a chair at the opposite end of the room. He angled the chair so that it faced more away from Baley than toward him and sat down. He clasped his gloved hands and his nostrils seemed to quiver.

Baley finished his drink and felt warmth in his limbs and even the return of something of his confidence.

He said, "Exactly how *does* it feel to have me here, Dr. Quemot?"

The sociologist muttered, "That is an uncommonly personal question."

"I know it is. But I think I explained when I viewed you earlier that I was engaged in a murder investigation and that I would have to ask a great many questions, some of which were bound to be personal."

"I'll help if I can," said Quemot. "I hope the questions will be decent ones." He kept looking away as he spoke. His eyes, when they struck Baley's face, did not linger, but slipped away.

Baley said, "I don't ask about your feelings out of curiosity only. This is essential to the investigation."

"I don't see how."

"I've got to know as much as I can about this world. I must understand how Solarians feel about ordinary matters. Do you see that?"

Quemot did not look at Baley at all now. He said slowly, "Ten years ago, my wife died. Seeing her was never very easy, but, of course, it is something one learns to bear in time and she was not the intrusive sort. I have been assigned no new wife since I am past the age of—of"—he looked at Baley as though requesting him to supply the phrase, and when Baley did not do so, he continued in a lower voice— "siring. Without even a wife, I have grown quite unused to this phenomenon of seeing."

"But how does it feel?" insisted Baley. "Are you in panic?" He thought of himself on the plane.

"No. Not in panic." Quemot angled his head to catch a glimpse of Baley and almost instantly withdrew. "But I will be frank, Mr. Baley. I imagine I can smell you."

Baley automatically leaned back in his chair, painfully self-conscious. "Smell me?"

"Quite imaginary, of course," said Quemot. "I cannot say whether you do have an odor or how strong it is, but even if you had a strong one, my nose filters would keep it from me. Yet, imagination . . ." He shrugged.

"I understand."

"It's worse. You'll forgive me, Mr. Baley, but in the actual presence of a human, I feel strongly as though something slimy were about to touch me. I keep shrinking away. It is most unpleasant."

Baley rubbed his ear thoughtfully and fought to keep down annoyance. After all, it was the other's neurotic reaction to a simple state of affairs.

He said. "If all this is so, I'm surprised you agreed to see me so readily. Surely you anticipated this unpleasantness."

"I did. But you know, I was curious. You're an Earthman."

Baley thought sardonically that that should have been another argument against seeing, but he said only, "What does that matter?"

A kind of jerky enthusiasm entered Quemot's voice. "It's not something I can explain easily. Not even to myself, really. But I've worked on sociology for ten years now. Really worked. I've developed propositions that are quite new and startling, and yet basically true. It is one of these propositions that makes me most extraordinarily interested in Earth and Earthmen. You see, if you were to consider Solaria's society and way of life carefully, it will become obvious to you that the said society and way of life is modeled directly and closely on that of Earth itself."

10. A CULTURE IS TRACED

Baley could not prevent himself from crying out, "What!"

Quemot looked over his shoulder as the moments of silence passed and said finally, "Not Earth's present culture. No."

Baley said, "Oh."

"But in the past, yes. Earth's ancient history. As an Earthman, you know it, of course."

"I've viewed books," said Baley cautiously.

"Ah. Then you understand."

Baley, who did not, said, "Let me explain exactly what I want, Dr. Quemot. I want you to tell me what you can about why Solaria is so different from the other Outer Worlds, why there are so many robots, why you behave as you do. I'm sorry if I seem to be changing the subject."

Baley most definitely wanted to change the subject. Any discussion of a likeness or unlikeness between Solaria's culture and Earth's would prove too absorbing by half. He might spend the day there and come away none the wiser as far as useful information was concerned.

Quemot smiled. "You want to compare Solaria and the other Outer Worlds and not Solaria and Earth."

"I know Earth, sir."

"As you wish." The Solarian coughed slightly. "Do you mind if I turn my chair completely away from you? It would be more—more comfortable."

"As you wish, Dr. Quemot," said Baley stiffly.

"Good." A robot turned the chair at Quemot's low-voiced order, and as the sociologist sat there, hidden from Baley's eyes by the substantial chair back, his voice took on added life and even deepened and strengthened in tone.

Quemot said, "Solaria was first settled about three hundred

years ago. The original settlers were Nexonians. Are you acquainted with Nexon?"

"I'm afraid not."

"It is close to Solaria, only about two parsecs away. In fact, Solaria and Nexon represented the closest pair of inhabited worlds in the Galaxy. Solaria, even when uninhabited by man, was life-bearing and eminently suited for human occupation. It represented an obvious attraction to the well-to-do of Nexon, who found it difficult to maintain a proper standard of living as their own planet filled up."

Baley interrupted. "Filled up? I thought Spacers practiced population control."

"Solaria does, but the Outer Worlds in general control it rather laxly. Nexon was completing its second million of population at the time I speak of. There was sufficient crowding to make it necessary to regulate the number of robots that might be owned by a particular family. So those Nexonians who could established summer homes on Solaria, which was fertile, temperate, and without dangerous fauna.

"The settlers on Solaria could still reach Nexon without too much trouble and while on Solaria they could live as they pleased. They could use as many robots as they could afford or felt a need for. Estates could be as large as desired since, with an empty planet, room was no problem, and with unlimited robots, exploitation was no problem.

"Robots grew to be so many that they were outfitted with radio contact and that was the beginning of our famous industries. We began to develop new varieties, new attachments, new capabilities. Culture dictates invention; a phrase I believe I have invented." Quemot chuckled.

A robot responding to some stimulus Baley could not see beyond the barrier of the chair, brought Quemot a drink similar to that Baley had had earlier. None was brought to Baley, and he decided not to ask for one.

Quemot went on, "The advantages of life on Solaria were obvious to all who watched. Solaria became fashionable. More Nexonians established homes, and Solaria became what I like to call a 'villa planet.' And of the settlers, more and more took to remaining on the planet all year round and carrying on their business on Nexon through proxies. Robot factories were established on Solaria. Farms and mines began to be exploited to the point where exports were possible.

"In short, Mr. Baley, it became obvious that Solaria, in the space of a century or less, would be as crowded as Nexon had been. It seemed ridiculous and wasteful to find such a new world and then lose it through lack of foresight.

"To spare you a great deal of complicated politics, I need say only that Solaria managed to establish its independence and make it stick without war. Our usefulness to other Outer Worlds as a source of specialty robots gained us friends and helped us, of course.

"Once independent, our first care was to make sure that population did not grow beyond reasonable limits. We regulate immigration and births and take care of all needs by increasing and diversifying the robots we use."

Baley said, "Why is it the Solarians object to seeing one another?" He felt annoyed at the manner in which Quemot chose to expound sociology.

Quemot peeped round the corner of his chair and retreated almost at once. "It follows inevitably. We have huge estates. An estate ten thousand square miles in area is not uncommon, although the largest ones contain considerable unproductive areas. My own estate is nine hundred fifty square miles in area but every bit of it is good land.

"In any case, it is the size of an estate, more than anything else, that determines a man's position in society. And one property of a large estate is this: You can wander about in it almost aimlessly with little or no danger of entering a neighbor's territory and thus encountering your neighbor. You see?"

Baley shrugged. "I suppose I do."

"In short, a Solarian takes pride in not meeting his neighbor. At the same time, his estate is so well run by robots and so self-sufficient that there is no reason for him to have to meet his neighbor. The desire not to do so led to the development of ever more perfect viewing equipment, and as the viewing equipment grew better there was less and less need ever to see one's neighbor. It was a reinforcing cycle, a kind of feed-back. Do you see?"

Baley said, "Look here, Dr. Quemot. You don't have to make all this so simple for me. I'm not a sociologist but

I've had the usual elementary courses in college. It's only an Earth college, of course," Baley added with a reluctant modesty designed to ward off the same comment, in more insulting terms, from the other, "but I can follow mathematics."

"Mathematics?" said Quemot, his voice squeaking the last syllable.

"Well, not the stuff they use in robotics, which I *wouldn't* follow, but sociological relationships I can handle. For instance, I'm familiar with the Teramin Relationship."

"The what, sir?"

"Maybe you have a different name for it. The differential of inconveniences suffered with privileges granted: dee eye sub jay taken to the nth——"

"What are you talking about?" It was the sharp and peremptory tone of a Spacer that Baley heard and he was silenced in bewilderment.

Surely the relationship between inconveniences suffered and privileges granted was part of the very essentials of learning how to handle people without an explosion. A private stall in the community bathroom for one person, given for cause, would keep x persons waiting patiently for the same lightning to strike them, the value of x varying in known ways with known variations in environment and human temperament, as quantitatively described in the Teramin Relationship.

But then again, in a world where all was privilege and nothing inconvenience, the Teramin Relationship might reduce to triviality. Perhaps he had chosen the wrong example.

He tried again. "Look, sir, it's one thing to get a qualitative fill-in on the growth of this prejudice against seeing, but it isn't helpful for my purposes. I want to know the exact analysis of the prejudice so I can counteract it effectively. I want to persuade people to see me, as you are doing now."

"Mr. Baley," said Quemot, "you can't treat human emotions as though they were built about a positronic brain."

"I'm not saying you can. Robotics is a deductive science and sociology an inductive one. But mathematics can be made to apply in either case."

There was silence for a moment. Then Quemot spoke in

a voice that trembled. "You have admitted you are not a sociologist."

"I know. But I was told you *were* one. The best on the planet."

"I am the only one. You might almost say I have invented the science."

"Oh?" Baley hesitated over the next question. It sounded impertinent even to himself. "Have you viewed books on the subject?"

"I've looked at some Auroran books."

"Have you looked at books from Earth?"

"Earth?" Quemot laughed uneasily. "It wouldn't have occurred to me to read any of Earth's scientific productions. No offense intended."

"Well, I'm sorry. I had thought I would be able to get specific data that would make it possible for me to interview others face to face without having to——"

Quemot made a queer, grating, inarticulate sound and the large chair in which he sat scraped backward, then went over with a crash.

A muffled "My apologies" was caught by Baley.

Baley had a momentary glimpse of Quemot running with an ungainly stride, then he was out the room and gone.

Baley's eyebrows lifted. What the devil had he said this time? Jehoshaphat! What wrong button had he pushed?

Tentatively he rose from his seat, and stopped halfway as a robot entered.

"Master," said the robot, "I have been directed to inform you that the master will view you in a few moments."

"*View* me, boy?"

"Yes, master. In the meanwhile, you may desire further refreshment."

Another beaker of the pink liquid was at Baley's elbow and this time a dish of some confectionary, warm and fragrant, was added.

Baley took his seat again, sampled the liquor cautiously and put it down. The confectionary was hard to the touch and warm, but the crust broke easily in the mouth and the inner portion was at once considerably warmer and softer. He could not identify the components of the taste and wondered if it might not be a product of the native spices or condiments of Solaria.

Then he thought of the restricted, yeast-derived dietary of Earth and wondered if there might be a market for yeast strains designed to imitate the tastes of Outer World products.

But his thoughts broke off sharply as sociologist Quemot appeared out of nowhere and faced him. *Faced* him this time! He sat in a smaller chair in a room in which the walls and floor clashed sharply with those surrounding Baley. And he was smiling now, so that fine wrinkles in his face deepened and, paradoxically, gave him a more youthful appearance by accentuating the life in his eyes.

He said, "A thousand pardons, Mr. Baley. I thought I was enduring personal presence so well, but that was a delusion. I was quite on edge and your phrase pushed me over it, in a manner of speaking."

"What phrase was that, sir?"

"You said something about interviewing people face to——" He shook his head, his tongue dabbing quickly at his lips. "I would rather not say it. I think you know what I mean. The phrase conjured up the most striking picture of the two of us breathing—breathing one another's breath." The Solarian shuddered. "Don't you find that repulsive?"

"I don't know that I've ever thought of it so."

"It seems so filthy a habit. And as you said it and the picture rose in my mind, I realized that after all we *were* in the same room and even though I was not facing you, puffs of air that had been in your lungs must be reaching me and entering mine. With my sensitive frame of mind——"

Baley said, "Molecules all over Solaria's atmosphere have been in thousands of lungs. Jehoshaphat! They've been in the lungs of animals and the gills of fish."

"That *is* true," said Quemot with a rueful rub of his cheek, "and I'd just as soon not think of that, either. However there was a sense of immediacy to the situation with yourself actually there and with both of us inhaling and exhaling. It's amazing the relief I feel in viewing."

"I'm still in the same house, Dr. Quemot."

"That's precisely what is so amazing about the relief.

You are in the same house and yet just the use of the trimensionals makes all the difference. At least I know what seeing a stranger feels like now. I won't try it again."

"That sounds as though you were experimenting with seeing."

"In a way," said the Spacer, "I suppose I was. It was a minor motivation. And the results were interesting, even if they were disturbing as well. It was a good test and I may record it."

"Record what?" asked Baley, puzzled.

"My feelings!" Quemot returned puzzled stare for puzzled stare.

Baley sighed. Cross-purposes. Always cross-purposes. "I only asked because somehow I assumed you would have instruments of some sort to measure emotional responses. An electroencephalograph, perhaps." He looked about fruitlessly, "Though I suppose you could have a pocket version of the same that works without direct electrical connection. We don't have anything like that on Earth."

"I trust," said the Solarian stiffly, "that I am able to estimate the nature of my own feelings without an instrument. They were pronounced enough."

"Yes, of course, but for quantitative analysis . . ." began Baley.

Quemot said querulously, "I don't know what you're driving at. Besides, I'm trying to tell you something else, my own theory, in fact, something I have viewed in no books, something I am quite proud of——"

Baley said, "Exactly what is that, sir?"

"Why, the manner in which Solaria's culture is based on one existing in Earth's past."

Baley sighed. If he didn't allow the other to get it off his chest, there might be very little co-operation thereafter. He said, "And that is?"

"Sparta!" said Quemot, lifting his head so that for a moment his white hair glistened in the light and seemed almost a halo. "I'm sure you've heard of Sparta!"

Baley felt relieved. He had been mightily interested in Earth's ancient past in his younger days (it was an attractive study to many Earthmen—an Earth supreme because it was an Earth alone; Earthmen the masters because there were no Spacers), but Earth's past was a large one. Quemot might well have referred to some phase with which Baley was unacquainted and that would have been embarrassing.

As it was, he could say cautiously, "Yes, I've viewed films on the subject."

"Good. Good. Now Sparta in its heyday consisted of a relatively small number of Spartiates, the only full citizens, plus a somewhat larger number of second-class individuals, the Perioeci, and a really large number of outright slaves, the Helots. The Helots outnumbered the Spartiates a matter of twenty to one, and the Helots were men with human feelings and human failings.

"In order to make certain that a Helot rebellion could never be successful despite their overwhelming numbers, the Spartans became military specialists. Each lived the life of a military machine, and the society achieved its purpose. There was never a successful Helot revolt.

"Now we human beings on Solaria are equivalent, in a way, to the Spartiates. We have our Helots, but our Helots aren't men but machines. They cannot revolt and need not be feared even though they outnumber us a thousand times as badly as the Spartans' human Helots outnumbered them. So we have the advantage of Spartiate exclusiveness without any need to sacrifice ourselves to rigid mastery. We can, instead, model ourselves on the artistic and cultural way of life of the Athenians, who were contemporaries of the Spartans and who——"

Baley said, "I viewed films on the Athenians, too."

Quemot grew warmer as he spoke. "Civilizations have always been pyramidal in structure. As one climbs toward the apex of the social edifice, there is increased leisure and increasing opportunity to pursue happiness. As one climbs, one finds also fewer and fewer people to enjoy this more and more. Invariably, there is a preponderance of the dispossessed. And remember this, no matter how well off the bottom layers of the pyramid might be on an absolute scale, they are always dispossessed in comparison with the apex. For instance, even the most poorly off humans on Aurora are better off than Earth's aristocrats, but they are dispossessed with respect to Aurora's aristocrats, and it is with the masters of their own world that they compare themselves.

"So there is always social friction in ordinary human societies. The action of social revolution and the reaction of guarding against such revolution or combating it once it has begun are the causes of a great deal of the human misery with which history is permeated.

"Now here on Solaria, for the first time, the apex of the pyramid stands alone. In the place of the dispossessed are the robots. We have the first new society, the first really new one, the first great social invention since the farmers of Sumeria and Egypt invented cities."

He sat back now, smiling.

Baley nodded. "Have you published this?"

"I may," said Quemot with an affectation of carelessness, "someday. I haven't yet. This is my third contribution."

"Were the other two as broad as this?"

"They weren't in sociology. I have been a sculptor in my time. The work you see about you"—he indicated the statuary—"is my own. And I have been a composer, too. But I am getting older and Rikaine Delmarre always argued strongly in favor of the applied arts rather than the fine arts and I decided to go into sociology."

Baley said, "That sounds as though Delmarre was a good friend of yours."

"We knew one another. At my time in life, one knows all adult Solarians. But there is no reason not to agree that Rikaine Delmarre and I were well acquainted."

"What sort of a man was Delmarre?" (Strangely enough, the name of the man brought up the picture of Gladia in Baley's mind and he was plagued with a sudden, sharp recall of her as he had last seen her, furious, her face distorted with anger at him.)

Quemot looked a bit thoughtful. "He was a worthy man; devoted to Solaria and to its way of life."

"An idealist, in other words."

"Yes. Definitely. You could see that in the fact that he volunteered for his job as—as fetal engineer. It was an applied art, you see, and I told you his feelings about that."

"Was volunteering unusual?"

"Wouldn't *you* say——But I forget you're an Earthman. Yes, it is unusual. It's one of those jobs that must be done, yet finds no voluntary takers. Ordinarily, someone must be assigned to it for a period of so many years and it isn't pleasant to be the one chosen. Delmarre volunteered, and for life. He felt the position was too important to be left to reluctant draftees, and he persuaded me into that opinion, too. Yet I certainly would never have volunteered. I couldn't possibly make the personal sacrifice. And it was more of a sacrifice for him, since he was almost a fanatic in personal hygiene."

"I'm still not certain I understand the nature of his job."

Quemot's old cheeks flushed gently. "Hadn't you better discuss that with his assistant?"

Baley said, "I would certainly have done so by now, sir, if anyone had seen fit to tell me before this moment that he had an assistant."

"I'm sorry about that," said Quemot, "but the existence of the assistant is another measure of his social responsibility. No previous occupant of the post provided for one. Delmarre, however, felt it necessary to find a suitable youngster and conduct the necessary training himself so as to leave a professional heir behind when the time came for him to retire or, well, to die." The old Solarian sighed heavily. "Yet I outlived him and he was so much younger. I used to play chess with him. Many times."

"How did you manage that?"

Quemot's eyebrows lifted. "The usual way."

"You saw one another?"

Quemot looked horrified. "What an idea! Even if I could stomach it, Delmarre would never allow it for an instant. Being fetal engineer didn't blunt his sensibilities. He was a finicky man."

"Then how——"

"With two boards as any two people would play chess." The Solarian shrugged in a sudden gesture of tolerance. "Well, you're an Earthman. My moves registered on his board, and his on mine. It's a simple matter."

Baley said, "Do you know Mrs. Delmarre?"

"We've viewed one another. She's a field colorist, you know, and I've viewed some of her showings. Fine work in a way but more interesting as curiosities than as creations. Still, they're amusing and show a perceptive mind."

"Is she capable of killing her husband, would you say?"

"I haven't given it thought. Women are surprising creatures. But then, there's scarcely room for argument, is there? Only Mrs. Delmarre could have been close enough to Rikaine to kill him. Rikaine would never, under any circumstances, have allowed anyone else seeing privileges for any reason. Extremely finicky. Perhaps finicky is the wrong word. It was just that he lacked any trace of abnormality; anything of the perverse. He was a good Solarian."

"Would you call your granting me seeing privileges perverse?" asked Baley.

Quemot said, "Yes, I think I would. I should say there was a bit of scatophilia involved."

"Could Delmarre have been killed for political reasons?"

"What?"

"I've heard him called a Traditionalist."

"Oh, we all are."

"You mean there is no group of Solarians who are *not* Traditionalists?"

"I dare say there are some," said Quemot slowly, "who think it is dangerous to be too Traditionalist. They are over-conscious of our small population, of the way the other worlds outnumber us. They think we are defenseless against possible aggression from the other Outer Worlds. They're quite foolish to think so and there aren't many of them. I don't think they're a force."

"Why do you say they are foolish? Is there anything about Solaria that would affect the balance of power in spite of the great disadvantage of numbers? Some new type of weapon?"

"A weapon, certainly. But not a new one. The people I speak of are more blind than foolish not to realize that such a weapon is in operation continuously and cannot be resisted."

Baley's eyes narrowed. "Are you serious?"

"Certainly."

"Do you know the nature of the weapon?"

"All of us must. *You* do, if you stop to think of it. I see it a trifle easier than most, perhaps, since I am a sociologist.

To be sure, it isn't used as a weapon ordinarily is used. It doesn't kill or hurt, but it is irresistible even so. All the more irresistible because no one notices it."

Baley said with annoyance, "And just what is this non-lethal weapon?"

Quemot said, "The positronic robot."

11. A FARM IS INSPECTED

For a moment Baley went cold. The positronic robot was the symbol of Spacer superiority over Earthmen. That was weapon enough.

He kept his voice steady. "It's an economic weapon. Solaria is important to the other Outer Worlds as a source of advanced models and so it will not be harmed by them."

"That's an obvious point," said Quemot indifferently. "That helped us establish our independence. What I have in mind is something else, something more subtle and more cosmic." Quemot's eyes were fixed on his fingers' ends and his mind was obviously fixed on abstractions.

Baley said, "Is this another of your sociological theories?"

Quemot's poorly suppressed look of pride all but forced a short smile out of the Earthman.

The sociologist said, "It is indeed mine. Original, as far as I know, and yet obvious if population data on the Outer Worlds is carefully studied. To begin with, ever since the positronic robot was invented, it has been used more and more intensively everywhere."

"Not on Earth," said Baley.

"Now, now, Plainclothesman. I don't know much of your Earth, but I know enough to know that robots are entering your economy. You people live in large Cities and leave most of your planetary surface unoccupied. Who runs your farms and mines, then?"

"Robots," admitted Baley. "But if it comes to that, Doctor, Earthmen invented the positronic robot in the first place."

"They did? Are you sure?"

"You can check. It's true."

"Interesting. Yet robots made the least headway there."

114

The sociologist said thoughtfully, "Perhaps that is because of Earth's large population. It would take that much longer. Yes . . . Still, you have robots even in your Cities."

"Yes," said Baley.

"More now than, say, fifty years ago."

Baley nodded impatiently. "Yes."

"Then it fits. The difference is only one of time. Robots tend to displace human labor. The robot economy moves in only one direction. More robots and fewer humans. I've studied population data *very* carefully and I've plotted it and made a few extrapolations." He paused in sudden surprise. "Why, that's rather an application of mathematics to sociology, isn't it?"

"It is," said Baley.

"There may be something to it, at that. I will have to give the matter thought. In any case, these are the conclusions I have come to, and I am convinced there is no doubt as to their correctness. The robot-human ratio in any economy that has accepted robot labor tends continuously to increase despite any laws that are passed to prevent it. The increase is slowed, but never stopped. At first the human population increases, but the robot population increases much more quickly. Then, after a certain critical point is reached . . ."

Quemot stopped again, then said, "Now let's see. I wonder if the critical point could be determined exactly; if you could really put a figure to it. There's your mathematics again."

Baley stirred restlessly. "What happens after the critical point is reached, Dr. Quemot?"

"Eh? Oh, the human population begins actually to decline. A planet approaches a true social stability. Aurora will have to. Even your Earth will have to. Earth may take a few more centuries, but it is inevitable."

"What do you mean by social stability?"

"The situation here. In Solaria. A world in which the humans are the leisure class only. So there is no reason to fear the other Outer Worlds. We need only wait a century perhaps and they shall all be Solarias. I suppose that will be the end of human history, in a way; at least, its fulfillment. Finally, finally, all men will have all they can need and want. You know, there is a phrase I once picked up; I don't know where it comes from; something about the pursuit of happiness."

Baley said thoughtfully, "All men are 'endowed by their Creator with certain unalienable rights . . . among these are life, liberty, and the pursuit of happiness.'"

"You've hit it. Where's that from?"

"Some old document," said Baley.

"Do you see how that is changed here on Solaria and eventually in all the Galaxy? The pursuit will be over. The rights mankind will be heir to will be life, liberty, and happiness. Just that. Happiness."

Baley said dryly. "Maybe so, but a man has been killed on your Solaria and another may yet die."

He felt regret almost the moment he spoke, for the expression on Quemot's face was as though he had been struck with an open palm. The old man's head bowed. He said without looking up, "I have answered your questions as well as I could. Is there anything else you wish?"

"I have enough. Thank you, sir. I am sorry to have intruded on your grief at your friend's death."

Quemot looked up slowly. "It will be hard to find another chess partner. He kept our appointments most punctually and he played an extraordinarily even game. He was a good Solarian."

"I understand," said Baley softly. "May I have your permission to use your viewer to make contact with the next person I must see?"

"Of course," said Quemot. "My robots are yours. And now I will leave you. Done viewing."

A robot was at Baley's side within thirty seconds of Quemot's disappearance and Baley wondered once again how these creatures were managed. He had seen Quemot's fingers move toward a contact as he had left and that was all.

Perhaps the signal was quite a generalized one, saying only, "Do your duty!" Perhaps robots listened to all that went on and were always aware of what a human might desire at any given moment, and if the particular robot was not designed for a particular job in either mind or body, the radio web that united all robots went into action and the correct robot was spurred into action.

For a moment Baley had the vision of Solaria as a robotic net with holes that were small and continually growing smaller, with every human being caught neatly in place. He thought of Quemot's picture of worlds turning into Solarias; of nets forming and tightening even on Earth, until——

His thoughts were disrupted as the robot who had entered spoke with the quiet and even respect of the machine.

"I am ready to help you, master."

Baley said, "Do you know how to reach the place where Rikaine Delmarre once worked?"

"Yes, master."

Baley shrugged. He would never teach himself to avoid asking useless questions. The robots knew. Period. It occurred to him that, to handle robots with true efficiency, one must needs be expert, a sort of roboticist. How well did the average Solarian do, he wondered? Probably only so-so.

He said, "Get Delmarre's place and contact his assistant. If the assistant is not there, locate him wherever he is."

"Yes, master."

As the robot turned to go, Baley called after it, "Wait! What time is it at the Delmarre workplace?"

"About 0630, master."

"In the morning?"

"Yes, master."

Again Baley felt annoyance at a world that made itself victim of the coming and going of a sun. It was what came of living on bare planetary surface.

He thought fugitively of Earth, then tore his mind away. While he kept firmly to the matter in hand, he managed well. Slipping into homesickness would ruin him.

He said, "Call the assistant, anyway, boy, and tell him it's government business—and have one of the other boys bring something to eat. A sandwich and a glass of milk will do."

* * *

He chewed thoughtfully at the sandwich, which contained a kind of smoked meat, and with half his mind thought that Daneel Olivaw would certainly consider every article of food suspect after what had happened to Gruer. And Daneel might be right, too.

He finished the sandwich without ill effects, however (immediate ill effects, at any rate), and sipped at the milk. He had not learned from Quemot what he had come to learn, but he had learned something. As he sorted it out in his mind, it seemed he had learned a good deal.

Little about the murder, to be sure, but more about the larger matter.

The robot returned. "The assistant will accept contact, master."

"Good. Was there any trouble with it?"

"The assistant was asleep, master."

"Awake now, though?"

"Yes, master."

The assistant was facing him suddenly, sitting up in bed and wearing an expression of sullen resentment.

Baley reared back as though a force-barrier had been raised before him without warning. Once again a piece of vital information had been withheld from him. Once again he had not asked the right questions.

No one had thought to tell him that Rikaine Delmarre's assistant was a woman.

Her hair was a trifle darker than ordinary Spacer bronze and there was a quantity of it, at the moment in disorder. Her face was oval, her nose a trifle bulbous, and her chin large. She scratched slowly at her side just above the waist and Baley hoped the sheet would remain in position. He remembered Gladia's free attitude toward what was permitted while viewing.

Baley felt a sardonic amusement at his own disillusion at that moment. Earthmen assumed, somehow, that all Spacer women were beautiful, and certainly Gladia had reinforced that assumption. This one, though, was plain even by Earthly standards.

It therefore surprised Baley that he found her contralto attractive when she said, "See here, do you know what time it is?"

"I do," said Baley, "but since I will be seeing you, I felt I should warn you."

"*Seeing* me? Skies above——" Her eyes grew wide and she put a hand to her chin. (She wore a ring on one finger, the first item of personal adornment Baley had yet seen on Solaria.) "Wait, you're not my new assistant, are you?"

"No. Nothing like that. I'm here to investigate the death of Rikaine Delmarre."

"Oh? Well, investigate, then."

"What is your name?"

"Klorissa Cantoro."

"And how long have you been working with Dr. Delmarre?"

"Three years."

"I assume you're now at the place of business." (Baley felt uncomfortable at that noncommittal phrase, but he did not know what to call a place where a fetal engineer worked.)

"If you mean, am I at the farm?" said Klorissa discontentedly, "I certainly am. I haven't left it since the old man was done in, and I won't leave it, looks like, till an assistant is assigned me. Can *you* arrange that, by the way?"

"I'm sorry, ma'am. I have no influence with anyone here."

"Thought I'd ask."

Klorissa pulled off the sheet and climbed out of bed without any self-consciousness. She was wearing a one-piece sleeping suit and her hand went to the notch of the seam, where it ended at the neck.

Baley said hurriedly, "Just one moment. If you'll agree to see me, that will end my business with you for now and you may dress in privacy."

"In privacy?" She put out her lower lip and stared at Baley curiously. "You're finicky, aren't you? Like the boss."

"Will you see me? I would like to look over the farm."

"I don't get this business about seeing, but if you want to view the farm I'll tour you. If you'll give me a chance to wash and take care of a few things and wake up a little, I'll enjoy the break in routine."

"I don't want to view anything. I want to *see*."

The woman cocked her head to one side and her keen look had something of professional interest in it. "Are you a pervert or something? When was the last time you underwent a gene analysis?"

"Jehoshaphat!" muttered Baley. "Look, I'm Elijah Baley. I'm from Earth."

"From Earth?" She cried vehemently. "Skies above! Whatever are you doing here? Or is this some kind of complicated joke?"

"I'm not joking. I was called in to investigate Delmarre's death. I'm a plainclothesman, a detective."

"You mean that kind of investigation. But I thought everyone knew his wife did it."

"No, ma'am, there's some question about it in my mind. May I have your permission to see the farm and you. As an Earthman, you understand, I'm not accustomed to viewing. It makes me uncomfortable. I have permission from the Head of Security to see people who might help me. I will show you the document, if you wish."

"Let's see it."

Baley held the official strip up before her imaged eyes.

She shook her head. "Seeing! It's filthy. Still, skies above, what's a little more filth in this filthy job? Look here, though, don't you come close to me. You stay a good distance away. We can shout or send messages by robot, if we have to. You understand?"

"I understand."

Her sleeping suit split open at the seam just as contact broke off and the last word he heard from her was a muttered: "Earthman!"

"That's close enough," said Klorissa.

Baley, who was some twenty-five feet from the woman, said, "It's all right this distance, but I'd like to get indoors quickly."

It had not been so bad this time, somehow. He had scarcely minded the plane trip, but there was no point in overdoing it. He kept himself from yanking at his collar to allow himself to breathe more freely.

Klorissa said sharply, "What's wrong with you? You look kind of beat."

Baley said, "I'm not used to the outdoors."

"That's right! Earthman! You've got to be cooped up or

something. Skies above!" Her tongue passed over her lips as though it tasted something unappetizing. "Well, come in, then, but let me move out of the way first. All right. Get in."

Her hair was in two thick braids that wound about her head in a complicated geometrical pattern. Baley wondered how long it took to arrange like that and then remembered that, in all probability, the unerring mechanical fingers of a robot did the job.

The hair set off her oval face and gave it a kind of symmetry that made it pleasant if not pretty. She did not wear any facial make-up, nor, for that matter, were her clothes meant to do more than cover her serviceably. For the most part they were a subdued dark blue except for her gloves, which covered her to mid-arm and were a badly clashing lilac in color. Apparently they were not part of her ordinary costume. Baley noted the thickening of one finger of the gloves owing to the presence of the ring underneath.

They remained at opposite ends of the room, facing one another.

Baley said, "You don't like this, do you, ma'am?"

Klorissa shrugged. "Why should I like it? I'm not an animal. But I can stand it. You get pretty hardened, when you deal with—with"—she paused, and then her chin went up as though she had made up her mind to say what she had to say without mincing—"with children." She pronounced the word with careful precision.

"You sound as though you don't like the job you have."

"It's an important job. It must be done. Still, I don't like it."

"Did Rikaine Delmarre like it?"

"I suppose he didn't, but he never showed it. He was a good Solarian."

"And he was finicky."

Klorissa looked surprised.

Baley said, "You yourself said so. When we were viewing and I said you might dress in private, you said I was finicky like the boss."

"Oh. Well, he *was* finicky. Even viewing he never took any liberties. Always proper."

"Was that unusual?"

"It shouldn't be. Ideally, you're supposed to be proper, but no one ever is. Not when viewing. There's no personal presence involved so why take any pains? You know? I don't take pains when viewing, except with the boss. You had to be formal with him."

"Did you admire Dr. Delmarre?"

"He was a good Solarian."

Baley said, "You've called this place a farm and you've mentioned children. Do you bring up children here?"

"From the age of a month. Every fetus on Solaria comes here."

"Fetus?"

"Yes." She frowned. "We get them a month after conception. Does this embarrass you?"

"No," Baley said shortly. "Can you show me around?"

"I can. But keep your distance."

Baley's long face took on a stony grimness as he looked down the length of the long room from above. There was glass between the room and themselves. On the other side, he was sure, was perfectly controlled heat, perfectly controlled humidity, perfectly controlled asepsis. Those tanks, row on row, each contained its little creature floating in a watery fluid of precise composition, infused with a nutrient mixture of ideal proportions. Life and growth went on.

Little things, some smaller than half his fist, curled on themselves, with bulging skulls and tiny budding limbs and vanishing tails.

Klorissa, from her position twenty feet away, said, "How do you like it, Plainclothesman?"

Baley said, "How many do you have?"

"As of this morning, one hundred and fifty-two. We receive fifteen to twenty each month and we graduate as many to independence."

"Is this the only such institution on the planet?"

"That's right. It's enough to keep the population steady, counting on a life expectancy of three hundred years and a population of twenty thousand. This building is quite new. Dr. Delmarre supervised its construction and made many changes in our procedures. Our fetal death rate now is virtually zero."

Robots threaded their way among the tanks. At each tank

they stopped and checked controls in a tireless, meticulous way, looking in at the tiny embryos within.

"Who operates on the mother?" asked Baley. "I mean, to get the little things."

"Doctors," answered Klorissa.

"Dr. Delmarre?"

"Of course not. *Medical* doctors. You don't think Dr. Delmarre would ever stoop to——Well, never mind."

"Why can't robots be used?"

"Robots in surgery? First Law makes that very difficult, Plainclothesman. A robot might perform an appendectomy to save a human life, if he knew how, but I doubt that he'd be usable after that without major repairs. Cutting human flesh would be quite a traumatic experience for a positronic brain. Human doctors can manage to get hardened to it. Even to the personal presence required."

Baley said, "I notice that robots tend the fetuses, though. Do you and Dr. Delmarre ever interfere?"

"We have to, sometimes, when things go wrong. If a fetus has developmental trouble, for instance. Robots can't be trusted to judge the situation accurately when human life is involved."

Baley nodded. "Too much risk of a misjudgment and a life lost, I suppose."

"Not at all. Too much risk of overvaluing a life and saving one improperly." The woman looked stern. "As fetal engineers, Baley, we see to it that healthy children are born; *healthy* ones. Even the best gene analysis of parents can't assure that all gene permutations and combinations will be favorable, to say nothing of the possibility of mutations. That's our big concern, the unexpected mutation. We've got the rate of those down to less than one in a thousand, but that means that, on the average, once a decade, we have trouble."

She motioned him along the balcony and he followed her.

She said, "I'll show you the infants' nurseries and the youngsters' dormitories. They're much more a problem than the fetuses are. With them, we can rely on robot labor only to a limited extent."

"Why is that?"

"You would know, Baley, if you ever tried to teach a robot the importance of discipline. First Law makes them almost impervious to that fact. And don't think youngsters don't learn that about as soon as they can talk. I've seen a three-year-old holding a dozen robots motionless by yelling, 'You'll hurt me. I'm hurt.' It takes an extremely advanced robot to understand that a child might be deliberately lying."

"Could Delmarre handle the children?"

"Usually."

"How did he do that? Did he get out among them and shake sense into them?"

"Dr. Delmarre? Touch them? Skies above! Of course not! But he could *talk* to them. And he could give a robot specific orders. I've seen him viewing a child for fifteen minutes, and keeping a robot in spanking position all that time, getting it to spank—spank—spank. A few like that and the child would risk fooling with the boss no more. And the boss was skillful enough about it so that usually the robot didn't need more than a routine readjustment afterward."

"How about you? Do you get out among the children?"

"I'm afraid I have to sometimes. I'm not like the boss. Maybe someday I'll be able to handle the long-distance stuff, but right now if I tried, I'd just ruin robots. There's an art to handling robots really well, you know. When I think of it, though. Getting out among the children. Little animals!"

She looked back at him suddenly. "I suppose you wouldn't mind seeing them."

"It wouldn't bother me."

She shrugged and stared at him with amusement. "Earthman!" She walked on again. "What's this all about, anyway? You'll have to end up with Gladia Delmarre as murderess. You'll *have* to."

"I'm not quite sure of that," said Baley.

"How could you be anything else but sure? Who else could it possibly be?"

"There are possibilities, ma'am."

"Who, for instance?"

"Well, you, for instance!"

And Klorissa's reaction to that quite surprised Baley.

12. A TARGET IS MISSED

She laughed.

The laughter grew and fed on itself till she was gasping for breath and her plump face had reddened almost to purple. She leaned against the wall and gasped for breath.

"No, don't come—closer," she begged. "I'm all right."

Baley said gravely, "Is the possibility that humorous?"

She tried to answer and laughed again. Then, in a whisper, she said, "Oh, you *are* an Earthman? How could it ever be me?"

"You knew him well," said Baley. "You knew his habits. You could have planned it."

"And you think I would *see* him? That I would get close enough to bash him over the head with something? You just don't know anything at all about it, Baley."

Baley felt himself redden. "Why couldn't you get close enough to him, ma'am. You've had practice—uh—mingling."

"With the *children*."

"One thing leads to another. You seem to be able to stand my presence."

"At twenty feet," she said contemptuously.

"I've just visited a man who nearly collapsed because he had to endure my presence for a while."

Klorissa sobered and said, "A difference in degree."

"I suggest that a difference in degree is all that is necessary. The habit of seeing children makes it possible to endure seeing Delmarre just long enough."

"I would like to point out, Mr. Baley," said Klorissa, no longer appearing the least amused, "that it doesn't matter a speck what I can endure. Dr. Delmarre was the finicky one. He was almost as bad as Leebig himself. Almost. Even

if I could endure seeing him, he would never endure seeing
me. Mrs. Delmarre is the only one he could possibly have
allowed within seeing distance."

Baley said, "Who's this Leebig you mentioned?"

Klorissa shrugged. "One of these odd-genius types, if
you know what I mean. He'd done work with the boss on
robots."

Baley checked that off mentally and returned to the matter
at hand. He said, "It could also be said you had a motive."

"What motive?"

"His death put you in charge of this establishment, gave
you position."

"You call that a motive? Skies above, who could *want*
this position? Who on Solaria? This is a motive for keeping
him alive. It's a motive for hovering over him and protecting
him. You'll have to do better than that, Earthman."

Baley scratched his neck uncertainly with one finger. He
saw the justice of that.

Klorissa said, "Did you notice my ring, Mr. Baley?"

For a moment it seemed she was about to strip the glove
from her right hand, but she refrained.

"I noticed it," said Baley.

"You don't know its significance, I suppose?"

"I don't." (He would never have done with ignorance,
he thought bitterly.)

"Do you mind a small lecture, then?"

"If it will help me make sense of this damned world,"
blurted out Baley, "by all means."

"Skies above!" Klorissa smiled. "I suppose we seem to
you as Earth would seem to us. Imagine. Say, here's an
empty chamber. Come in here and we'll sit down—no, the
room's not big enough. Tell you what, though. You take a
seat in there and I'll stand out here."

She stepped farther down the corridor, giving him space
to enter the room, then returned, taking up her stand against
the opposite wall at a point which she could see him.

Baley took his seat with only the slightest quiver of
chivalry countering it. He thought rebelliously: Why not?
Let the Spacer woman stand.

Klorissa folded her muscular arms across her chest and
said, "Gene analysis is the key to our society. We don't

analyze for genes directly, of course. Each gene, however, governs one enzyme, and we can analyze for enzymes. Know the enzymes, know the body chemistry. Know the body chemistry, know the human being. You see all that?"

"I understand the theory," said Baley. "I don't know how it's applied."

"That part's done here. Blood samples are taken while the infant is still in the late fetal stage. That gives us our rough first approximation. Ideally, we should catch all mutations at that point and judge whether birth can be risked. In actual fact, we still don't quite know enough to eliminate all possibility of mistake. Someday, maybe. Anyway, we continue testing after birth; biopsies as well as body fluids. In any case, long before adulthood, we know exactly what our little boys and girls are made of."

(Sugar and spice . . . A nonsense phrase went unbidden through Baley's mind.)

"We wear coded rings to indicate our gene constitution," said Klorissa. "It's an old custom, a bit of the primitive left behind from the days when Solarians had not yet been weeded eugenically. Nowadays, we're all healthy."

Baley said, "But you still wear yours. Why?"

"Because I'm exceptional," she said with an unembarrassed, unblunted pride. "Dr. Delmarre spent a long time searching for an assistant. He *needed* someone exceptional. Brains, ingenuity, industry, stability. Most of all, stability. Someone who could learn to mingle with children and not break down."

"He couldn't, could he? Was that a measure of his instability?"

Klorissa said, "In a way, it was, but at least it was a desirable type of instability under most circumstances. You wash your hands, don't you?"

Baley's eyes dropped to his hands. They were as clean as need be. "Yes," he said.

"All right. I suppose it's a measure of instability to feel such revulsion at dirty hands as to be unable to clean an oily mechanism by hand even in an emergency. Still, in the *ordinary* course of living, the revulsion keeps you clean, which is good."

"I see. Go ahead."

"There's nothing more. My genic health is the third-highest ever recorded on Solaria, so I wear my ring. It's a record I enjoy carrying with me."

"I congratulate you."

"You needn't sneer. It may not be my doing. It may be the blind permutation of parental genes, but it's a proud thing to own, anyway. And no one would believe me capable of so seriously psychotic an act as murder. Not with my gene make-up. So don't waste accusations on me."

Baley shrugged and said nothing. The woman seemed to confuse gene make-up and evidence and presumably the rest of Solaria would do the same.

Klorissa said, "Do you want to see the youngsters now?"

"Thank you. Yes."

The corridors seemed to go on forever. The building was obviously a tremendous one. Nothing like the huge banks of apartments in the Cities of Earth, of course, but for a single building clinging to the outside skin of a planet it must be a mountainous structure.

There were hundreds of cribs, with pink babies squalling, or sleeping, or feeding. Then there were playrooms for the crawlers.

"They're not too bad even at this age," said Klorissa grudgingly, "though they take up a tremendous sum of robots. It's practically a robot per baby till walking age."

"Why is that?"

"They sicken if they don't get individual attention."

Baley nodded. "Yes, I suppose the requirement for affection is something that can't be done away with."

Klorissa frowned and said brusquely, "Babies require attention."

Baley said, "I am a little surprised that robots can fulfill the need for affection."

She whirled toward him, the distance between them not sufficing to hide her displeasure. "See here, Baley, if you're trying to shock me by using unpleasant terms, you won't succeed. Skies above, don't be childish."

"Shock you?"

"I can use the word too. Affection! Do you want a short word, a good four-letter word. I can say that, too. Love!

Love! Now if it's out of your system, behave yourself."

Baley did not trouble to dispute the matter of obscenity. He said, "Can robots really give the necessary attention, then?"

"Obviously, or this farm would not be the success it is. They fool with the child. They nuzzle it and snuggle it. The child doesn't care that it's only a robot. But then, things grow more difficult between three and ten."

"Oh?"

"During that interval, the children insist on playing with one another. Quite indiscriminately."

"I take it you let them."

"We have to, but we never forget our obligation to teach them the requirements of adulthood. Each has a separate room that can be closed off. Even from the first, they must sleep alone. We insist on that. And then we have an isolation time every day and that increases with the years. By the time a child reaches ten, he is able to restrict himself to viewing for a week at a time. Of course, the viewing arrangements are elaborate. They can view outdoors, under mobile conditions, and can keep it up all day."

Baley said, "I'm surprised you can counter an instinct so thoroughly. You do counter it; I see that. Still, it surprises me."

"What instinct?" demanded Klorissa.

"The instinct of gregariousness. There is one. You say yourself that as children they insist on playing with each other."

Klorissa shrugged. "Do you call that instinct? But then, what if it is? Skies above, a child has an instinctive fear of falling, but adults can be trained to work in high places even where there is constant danger of falling. Haven't you ever seen gymnastic exhibitions on high wires? There are some worlds where people live in tall buildings. And children have instinctive fear of loud noises, too, but are you afraid of them?"

"Not within reason," said Baley.

"I'm willing to bet that Earth people couldn't sleep if things were really quiet. Skies above, there isn't an instinct around that can't give way to a good, persistent education. Not in human beings, where instincts are weak anyway. In fact, if you go about it right, education gets easier with each generation. It's a matter of evolution."

Baley said, "How is that?"

"Don't you see? Each individual repeats his own evolutionary history as he develops. Those fetuses back there have gills and a tail for a time. Can't skip those steps. The youngster has to go through the social-animal stage in the same way. But just as a fetus can get through in one month a stage that evolution took a hundred million years to get through, so our children can hurry through the social-animal stage. Dr. Delmarre was of the opinion that with the generations, we'd get through that stage faster and faster."

"Is that so?"

"In three thousand years, he estimated, at the present rate of progress, we'd have children who'd take to viewing at once. The boss had other notions, too. He was interested in improving robots to the point of making them capable of disciplining children without becoming mentally unstable. Why not? Discipline today for a better life tomorrow is a true expression of First Law if robots could only be made to see it."

"Have such robots been developed yet?"

Klorissa shook her head. "I'm afraid not. Dr. Delmarre and Leebig had been working hard on some experimental models."

"Did Dr. Delmarre have some of the models sent out to his estate? Was he a good enough roboticist to conduct tests himself?"

"Oh yes. He tested robots frequently."

"Do you know that he had a robot with him when he was murdered?"

"I've been told so."

"Do you know what kind of a model it was?"

"You'll have to ask Leebig. As I told you, he's the roboticist who worked with Dr. Delmarre."

"You know nothing about it?"

"Not a thing."

"If you think of anything, let me know."

"I will. And don't think new robot models are all that Dr. Delmarre was interested in. Dr. Delmarre used to say the time would come when unfertilized ova would be stored

in banks at liquid-air temperatures and utilized for artificial
insemination. In that way, eugenic principles could be truly
applied and we could get rid of the last vestige of any need
for seeing. I'm not sure that I quite go along with him so
far, but he was a man of advanced notions; a very good
Solarian."

She added quickly, "Do you want to go outside? The
five-through-eight group are encouraged to take part in outdoor play and you could see them in action."

Baley said cautiously, "I'll try that. I may have to come
back inside on rather short notice."

"Oh yes, I forgot. Maybe you'd rather not go out at all?"

"No." Baley forced a smile. "I'm trying to grow accustomed to the outdoors."

The wind was hard to bear. It made breathing difficult.
It wasn't cold, in a direct physical sense, but the feel of it,
the feel of his clothes moving against his body, gave Baley
a kind of chill.

His teeth chattered when he tried to talk and he had to
force his words out in little bits. It hurt his eyes to look so
far at a horizon so hazy green and blue and there was only
limited relief when he looked at the pathway immediately
before his toes. Above all, he avoided looking up at the
empty blue, empty, that is, but for the piled-up white of
occasional clouds and the glare of the naked sun.

And yet he could fight off the urge to run, to return to
enclosure.

He passed a tree, following Klorissa by some ten paces,
and he reached out a cautious hand to touch it. It was rough
and hard to the touch. Frondy leaves moved and rustled
overhead, but he did not raise his eyes to look at them. A
living tree!

Klorissa called out. "How do you feel?"

"All right."

"You can see a group of youngsters from here," she said.
"They're involved in some kind of game. The robots organize the games and see to it that the little animals don't
kick each other's eyes out. With personal presence you can
do just that, you know."

Baley raised his eyes slowly, running his glance along

the cement of the pathway out to the grass and down the slope, farther and farther out—very carefully—ready to snap back to his toes if he grew frightened—feeling with his eyes...

There were the small figures of boys and girls racing madly about, uncaring that they raced at the very outer rim of a world with nothing but air and space above them. The glitter of an occasional robot moved nimbly among them. The noise of the children was a far-off incoherent squeaking in the air.

"They love it," said Klorissa. "Pushing and pulling and squabbling and falling down and getting up and just generally contacting. Skies above! How do children ever manage to grow up?"

"What are those older children doing?" asked Baley. He pointed at a group of isolated youngsters standing to one side.

"They're viewing. They're not in a state of personal presence. By viewing, they can walk together, talk together, race together, play together. Anything except physical contact."

"Where do children go when they leave here?"

"To estates of their own. The number of deaths is, on the average, equal to the number of graduations."

"To their parents' estates?"

"Skies above, no! It would be an amazing coincidence, wouldn't it, to have a parent die just as a child is of age. No, the children take any one that falls vacant. I don't know that any of them would be particularly happy, anyway, living in a mansion that once belonged to their parents, supposing, of course, they knew who their parents were."

"Don't they?"

She raised her eyebrows. "Why should they?"

"Don't parents visit their children here?"

"What a mind you have. Why should they want to?"

Baley said, "Do you mind if I clear up a point for myself? Is it bad manners to ask a person if they have had children?"

"It's an intimate question, wouldn't you say?"

"In a way."

"I'm hardened. Children are my business. Other people aren't."

Baley said, "Have you any children?"

Klorissa's Adam's apple made a soft but clearly visible motion in her throat as she swallowed. "I deserve that, I suppose. And you deserve an answer. I haven't."

"Are you married?"

"Yes, and I have an estate of my own and I would be there but for the emergency here. I'm just not confident of being able to control all the robots if I'm not here in person."

She turned away unhappily, and then pointed. "Now there's one of them gone tumbling and of course he's crying."

A robot was running with great space-devouring strides.

Klorissa said, "He'll be picked up and cuddled and if there's any real damage, I'll be called in." She added nervously, "I hope I don't have to be."

Baley took a deep breath. He noted three trees forming a small triangle fifty feet to the left. He walked in that direction, the grass soft and loathsome under his shoes, disgusting in its softness (like walking through corrupting flesh, and he nearly retched at the thought).

He was among them, his back against one trunk. It was almost like being surrounded by imperfect walls. The sun was only a wavering series of flitters through the leaves, so disconnected as almost to be robbed of horror.

Klorissa faced him from the path, then slowly shortened the distance by half.

"Mind if I stay here awhile?" asked Baley.

"Go ahead," said Klorissa.

Baley said, "Once the youngsters graduate out of the farm, how do you get them to court one another?"

"Court?"

"Get to know one another," said Baley, vaguely wondering how the thought could be expressed safely, "so they can marry."

"That's not their problem," said Klorissa. "They're matched by gene analysis, usually when they are quite young. That's the sensible way, isn't it?"

"Are they always willing?"

"To be married? They never are! It's a very traumatic process. At first they have to grow accustomed to one another, and a little bit of seeing each day, once the initial queasiness is gone, can do wonders."

"What if they don't like their partner?"

"What? If the gene analysis indicates a partnership what difference does it——"

"I understand," said Baley hastily. He thought of Earth and sighed.

Klorissa said, "Is there anything else you would like to know?"

Baley wondered if there were anything to be gained from a longer stay. He would not be sorry to be done with Klorissa and fetal engineering so that he might pass on to the next stage.

He had opened his mouth to say as much, when Klorissa called out at some object far off, "You, child, you there! What are you doing?" Then, over her shoulder: "Earthman! Baley! Watch out! Watch *out!*"

Baley scarcely heard her. He responded to the note of urgency in her voice. The nervous effort that held his emotions taut snapped wide and he flamed into panic. All the terror of the open air and the endless vault of heaven broke in upon him.

Baley gibbered. He heard himself mouth meaningless sounds and felt himself fall to his knees and slowly roll over to his side as though he were watching the process from a distance.

Also from a distance he heard the sighing hum piercing the air above him and ending with a sharp thwack.

Baley closed his eyes and his fingers clutched a thin tree root that skimmed the surface of the ground and his nails burrowed into dirt.

He opened his eyes (it must only have been moments after). Klorissa was scolding sharply at a youngster who remained at a distance. A robot, silent, stood closer to Klorissa. Baley had only time to notice the youngster held a stringed object in his hand before his eyes sheered away.

Breathing heavily, Baley struggled to his feet. He stared at the shaft of glistening metal that remained in the trunk of the tree against which he had been standing. He pulled at it and it came out readily. It had not penetrated far. He looked at the point but did not touch it. It was blunted, but it would have sufficed to tear his skin had he not dropped when he did.

It took him two tries to get his legs moving. He took a step toward Klorissa and called. "You. Youngster."

Klorissa turned, her face flushed. She said, "It was an accident. Are you hurt?"

"No! What is this thing?"

"It's an arrow. It is fired by a bow, which makes a taut string do the work."

"Like this," called the youngster impudently, and he shot another arrow into the air, then burst out laughing. He had light hair and a lithe body.

Klorissa said, "You will be disciplined. Now leave!"

"Wait, wait," cried Baley. He rubbed his knee where a rock had caught and bruised him as he had fallen. "I have some questions. What is your name?"

"Bik," he said carelessly.

"Did you shoot that arrow at me, Bik?"

"That's right," said the boy.

"Do you realize you would have hit me if I hadn't been warned in time to duck?"

Bik shrugged. "I was aiming to hit."

Klorissa spoke hurriedly. "You must let me explain. Archery is an encouraged sport. It is competitive without requiring contact. We have contests among the boys using viewing only. Now I'm afraid some of the boys will aim at robots. It amuses them and it doesn't hurt the robots. I'm the only adult human on the estate and when the boy saw you, he must have assumed you were a robot."

Baley listened. His mind was clearing, and the natural dourness of his long face intensified. He said, "Bik, did you think I was a robot?"

"No," said the youngster. "You're an Earthman."

"All right. Go now."

Bik turned and raced off whistling. Baley turned to the robot. "You! How did the youngster know I was an Earthman, or weren't you with him when he shot?"

"I was with him, master. I told him you were an Earthman."

"Did you tell him what an Earthman was?"

"Yes, master."

"What is an Earthman?"

"An inferior sort of human that ought not to be allowed on Solaria because he breeds disease, master."

"And who told you that, boy?"

The robot maintained silence.

Baley said, "Do you know who told you?"

"I do not, master. It is in my memory store."

"So you told the boy I was a disease-breeding inferior and he immediately shot at me. Why didn't you stop him?"

"I would have, master. I would not have allowed harm to come to a human, even an Earthman. He moved too quickly and I was not fast enough."

"Perhaps you thought I was just an Earthman, not completely a human, and hesitated a bit."

"No, master."

It was said with quiet calm, but Baley's lips quirked grimly. The robot might deny it in all faith, but Baley felt that was exactly the factor involved.

Baley said, "What were you doing with the boy?"

"I was carrying his arrows, master."

"May I see them?"

He held out his hand. The robot approached and delivered a dozen of them. Baley put the original arrow, the one that had hit the tree, carefully at his feet, and looked the others over one by one. He handed them back and lifted the original arrow again.

He said, "Why did you give this particular arrow to the boy?"

"No reason, master. He had asked for an arrow some time earlier and this was the one my hand touched first. He looked about for a target, then noticed you and asked who the strange human was. I explained——"

"I know what you explained. This arrow you handed him is the only one with gray vanes at the rear. The others have black vanes."

The robot simply stared.

Baley said, "Did you guide the youngster here?"

"We walked randomly, master."

The Earthman looked through the gap between two trees through which the arrow had hurled itself toward its mark.

He said, "Would it happen, by any chance, that this youngster, Bik, was the best archer you have here?"

The robot bent his head. "He is the best, master."

Klorissa gaped. "How did you ever come to guess that?"

"It follows," said Baley dryly. "Now please observe this gray-vaned arrow and the others. The gray-vaned arrow is the only one that seems oily at the point. I'll risk melodrama, ma'am, by saying that your warning saved my life. This arrow that missed me is poisoned."

13. A ROBOTICIST IS CONFRONTED

Klorissa said, "Impossible! Skies above, absolutely impossible!"

"Above or below or any way you wish it. Is there an animal on the farm that's expendable? Get it and scratch it with the arrow and see what happens."

"But why should anyone want to——"

Baley said harshly, "I know why. The question is, who?"

"No one."

Baley felt the dizziness returning and he grew savage. He threw the arrow at her and she eyed the spot where it fell.

"Pick it up," Baley cried, "and if you don't want to test it, destroy it. Leave it there and you'll have an accident if the children get at it."

She picked it up hurriedly, holding it between forefinger and thumb.

Baley ran for the nearest entrance to the building and Klorissa was still holding the arrow, gingerly, when she followed him back indoors.

Baley felt a certain measure of equanimity return with the comfort of enclosure. He said, "Who poisoned the arrow?"

"I can't imagine."

"I suppose it isn't likely the boy did it himself. Would you have any way of telling who his parents were?"

"We could check the records," said Klorissa gloomily.

"Then you do keep records of relationships?"

"We have to for gene analysis."

"Would the youngster know who his parents were?"

"Never," said Klorissa energetically.

"Would he have any way of finding out?"

"He would have to break into the records room. Impossible."

"Suppose an adult visited the estate and wanted to know who his child was——"

Klorissa flushed. "Very unlikely."

"But suppose. Would he be told if he were to ask?"

"I don't know. It isn't exactly illegal for him to know. It certainly isn't customary."

"Would *you* tell him?"

"I'd try not to. I know Dr. Delmarre wouldn't have. He believed knowledge of relationship was for gene analysis only. Before him things may have been looser. . . . Why do you ask all this, anyway?"

"I don't see how the youngster could have a motive on his own account. I thought that through his parents he might have."

"This is all horrible." In her disturbed state of mind Klorissa approached more closely than at any previous time. She even stretched out an arm in his direction. "How can it all be happening? The boss killed; you nearly killed. We have no motives for violence on Solaria. We all have all we can want, so there is no personal ambition. We have no knowledge of relationship, so there is no family ambition. We are all in good genetic health."

Her face cleared all at once. "Wait. This arrow can't be poisoned. I shouldn't let you convince me it is."

"Why have you suddenly decided that?"

"The robot with Bik. He would never have allowed poison. It's inconceivable that he could have done anything that might bring harm to a human being. The First Law of Robotics makes sure of that."

Baley said, "Does it? What is the First Law, I wonder?"

Klorissa stared blankly. "What do you mean?"

"Nothing. You have the arrow tested and you will find it poisoned." Baley himself was scarcely interested in the matter. He knew it for poison beyond any internal questionings. He said, "Do you still believe Mrs. Delmarre to have been guilty of her husband's death?"

"She was the only one present."

"I see. And you are the only other human adult present on this estate at a time when I have just been shot at with a poisoned arrow."

She cried energetically, "I had nothing to do with it."

"Perhaps not. And perhaps Mrs. Delmarre is innocent as well. May I use your viewing apparatus?"

"Yes, of course."

Baley knew exactly whom he intended to view and it was *not* Gladia. It came as a surprise to himself then to hear his voice say, "Get Gladia Delmarre."

The robot obeyed without comment, and Baley watched the manipulations with astonishment, wondering why he had given the order.

Was it that the girl had just been the subject of discussion, or was it that he had been a little disturbed over the manner of the end of their last viewing, or was it simply the sight of the husky, almost overpoweringly practical figure of Klorissa that finally enforced the necessity of a glimpse of Gladia as a kind of counterirritant?

He thought defensively: Jehoshaphat! Sometimes a man has to play things by ear.

She was there before him all at once, sitting in a large, upright chair that made her appear smaller and more defenseless then ever. Her hair was drawn back and bound into a loose coil. She wore pendant earrings bearing gems that looked like diamonds. Her dress was a simple affair that clung tightly at the waist.

She said in a low voice, "I'm glad you viewed, Elijah. I've been trying to reach you."

"Good morning, Gladia." (Afternoon? Evening? He didn't know Gladia's time and he couldn't tell from the manner in which she was dressed what time it might be.) "Why have you been trying to reach me?"

"To tell you I was sorry I had lost my temper last time we viewed. Mr. Olivaw didn't know where you were to be reached."

Baley had a momentary vision of Daneel still bound fast by the overseeing robots and almost smiled. He said, "That's all right. In a few hours, I'll be seeing you."

"Of course, if——*Seeing* me?"

"Personal presence," said Baley gravely.

Her eyes grew wide and her fingers dug into the smooth plastic of the chair arms. "Is there any reason for that?"

"It is necessary."

"I don't think——"

"Would you allow it?"

She looked away. "Is it absolutely necessary?"

"It is. First, though, there is someone else I must see. Your husband was interested in robots. You told me that, and I have heard it from other sources, but he wasn't a roboticist, was he?"

"That wasn't his training, Elijah." She still avoided his eyes.

"But he worked with a roboticist, didn't he?"

"Jothan Leebig," she said at once. "He's a good friend of mine."

"He is?" said Baley energetically.

Gladia looked startled. "Shouldn't I have said that?"

"Why not, if it's the truth?"

"I'm always afraid that I'll say things that will make me seem as though——You don't know what it's like when everyone is sure you've done something."

"Take it easy. How is it that Leebig is a friend of yours?"

"Oh, I don't know. He's in the next estate, for one thing. Viewing energy is just about nil, so we can just view all the time in free motion with hardly any trouble. We go on walks together all the time; or we did, anyway."

"I didn't know you could go on walks together with anyone."

Gladia flushed. "I said *viewing*. Oh well, I keep forgetting you're an Earthman. Viewing in free motion means we focus on ourselves and we can go anywhere we want to without losing contact. I walk on my estate and he walks on his and we're together." She held her chin high. "It can be pleasant."

Then, suddenly, she giggled. "Poor Jothan."

"Why do you say that?"

"I was thinking of you thinking we walked together without viewing. He'd die if he thought anyone could think that."

"Why?"

"He's terrible that way. He told me that when he was five years old he stopped seeing people. Insisted on viewing only. Some children are like that. Rikaine"—she paused in confusion, then went on—"Rikaine, my husband, once told me, when I talked about Jothan, that more and more children would be like that too. He said it was a kind of social evolution that favored survival of pro-viewing. Do you think that's so?"

"I'm no authority," said Baley.

"Jothan won't even get married. Rikaine was angry with him, told him he was anti-social and that he had genes that were necessary in the common pool, but Jothan just refused to consider it."

"Has he a right to refuse?"

"No-o," said Gladia hesitantly, "but he's a very brilliant roboticist, you know, and roboticists are valuable on Solaria. I suppose they stretched a point. Except I think Rikaine was going to stop working with Jothan. He told me once Jothan was a bad Solarian."

"Did he tell Jothan that?"

"I don't know. He was working with Jothan to the end."

"But he thought Jothan was a bad Solarian for refusing to marry?"

"Rikaine once said that marriage was the hardest thing in life, but that it had to be endured."

"What did you think?"

"About what, Elijah?"

"About marriage. Did you think it was the hardest thing in life?"

Her expression grew slowly blank as though she were painstakingly washing emotion out of it. She said, "I never thought about it."

Baley said, "You said you go on walks with Jothan Leebig all the time, then corrected yourself and put that in the past. You don't go on walks with him any more, then?"

Gladia shook her head. Expression was back in her face. Sadness. "No. We don't seem to. I viewed him once or twice. He always seemed busy and I didn't like to——You know."

"Was this since the death of your husband?"

"No, even some time before. Several months before."

"Do you suppose Dr. Delmarre ordered him not to pay further attention to you?"

Gladia looked startled. "Why should he? Jothan isn't a robot and neither am I. How can we take orders and why should Rikaine give them?"

Baley did not bother to try to explain. He could have done so only in Earth terms and that would make things no clearer to her. And if it did manage to clarify, the result could only be disgusting to her.

Baley said, "Only a question. I'll view you again, Gladia, when I'm done with Leebig. What time do you have, by the way?" He was sorry at once for asking the question. Robots would answer in Terrestrial equivalents, but Gladia might answer in Solarian units and Baley was weary of displaying ignorance.

But Gladia answered in purely qualitative terms. "Mid-afternoon," she said.

"Then that's it for Leebig's estate also?"

"Oh yes."

"Good. I'll view you again as soon as I can and we'll make arrangements for seeing."

Again she grew hesitant. "Is it absolutely necessary?"

"It is."

She said in a low voice, "Very well."

There was some delay in contacting Leebig and Baley utilized it in consuming another sandwich, one that was brought to him in its original packaging. But he had grown more cautious. He inspected the seal carefully before breaking it, then looked over the contents painstakingly.

He accepted a plastic container of milk, not quite un-frozen, bit an opening with his own teeth, and drank from it directly. He thought gloomily that there were such things as odorless, tasteless, slow-acting poisons that could be introduced delicately by means of hypodermic needles or high-pressure needle jets, then put the thought aside as being childish.

So far murders and attempted murders had been com-mitted in the most direct possible fashion. There was nothing delicate or subtle about a blow on the head, enough poison in a glass to kill a dozen men, or a poisoned arrow shot openly at the victim.

And then he thought, scarcely less gloomily, that as long as he hopped between time zones in this fashion, he was scarcely likely to have regular meals. Or, if this continued, regular sleep.

The robot approached him. "Dr. Leebig directs you to call sometime tomorrow. He is engaged in important work."

Baley bounced to his feet and roared, "You tell that guy——"

He stopped. There was no use in yelling at a robot. That is, you could yell if you wished, but it would achieve results no sooner than a whisper.

He said in a conversational tone, "You tell Dr. Leebig, or his robot if that is as far as you've reached, that I am investigating the murder of a professional associate of his and a good Solarian. You tell him that I cannot wait on his work. You tell him that if I am not viewing him in five minutes, I will be in a plane and at his estate *seeing* him in less than an hour. You use that word, seeing, so there's no mistake."

He returned to his sandwich.

The five minutes were not quite gone, when Leebig, or at least a Solarian whom Baley presumed to be Leebig, was glaring at him.

Baley glared back. Leebig was a lean man, who held himself rigidly erect. His dark, prominent eyes had a look of intense abstraction about them, compounded now with anger. One of his eyelids dropped slightly.

He said, "Are you the Earthman?"

"Elijah Baley," said Baley, "Plainclothesman C-7, in charge of the investigation into the murder of Dr. Rikaine Delmarre. What is your name?"

"I'm Dr. Jothan Leebig. Why do you presume to annoy me at my work?"

"It's easy," said Baley quietly. "It's my business."

"Then take your business elsewhere."

"I have a few questions to ask first, Doctor. I believe you were a close associate of Dr. Delmarre. Right?"

One of Leebig's hands clenched suddenly into a fist and

he strode hastily toward a mantelpiece on which tiny clockwork contraptions went through complicated periodic motions that caught hypnotically at the eye.

The viewer kept focused on Leebig so that his figure did not depart from central projection as he walked. Rather the room behind him seemed to move backward in little rises and dips as he strode.

Leebig said, "If you are the foreigner whom Gruer threatened to bring in——"

"I am."

"Then you are here against my advice. Done viewing."

"Not yet. Don't break contact." Baley raised his voice sharply and a finger as well. He pointed it directly at the roboticist, who shrank visibly away from it, full lips spreading into an expression of disgust.

Baley said, "I wasn't bluffing about seeing you, you know."

"No Earthman vulgarity, please."

"A straightforward statement is what it is intended to be. I will see you, if I can't make you listen any other way. I will grab you by the collar and make you listen."

Leebig stared back. "You are a filthy animal."

"Have it your way, but I will do as I say."

"If you try to invade my estate, I will—I will——"

Baley lifted his eyebrows. "Kill me? Do you often make such threats?"

"I made no threat."

"Then talk now. In the time you have wasted, a good deal might have been accomplished. You were a close associate of Dr. Delmarre. Right?"

The roboticist's head lowered. His shoulders moved slightly to a slow, regular breathing. When he looked up, he was in command of himself. He even managed a brief, sapless smile.

"I was."

"Delmarre was interested in new types of robots, I understand."

"He was."

"What kind?"

"Are you a roboticist?"

"No. Explain it for the layman."

"I doubt that I can."

"Try! For instance, I think he wanted robots capable of disciplining children. What would that involve?"

Leebig raised his eyebrows briefly and said, "To put it very simply, skipping all the subtle details, it means a strengthening of the C-integral governing the Sikorovich tandem route response at the W-65 level."

"Double-talk," said Baley.

"The truth."

"It's double-talk to me. How else can you put it?"

"It means a certain weakening of the First Law."

"Why so? A child is disciplined for its own future good. Isn't that the theory?"

"Ah, the future good!" Leebig's eyes glowed with passion and he seemed to grow less conscious of his listener and correspondingly more talkative. "A simple concept, you think. How many human beings are willing to accept a trifling inconvenience for the sake of a large future good? How long does it take to train a child that what tastes good now means a stomach-ache later, and what tastes bad now will correct the stomach-ache later? Yet you want a robot to be able to understand?

"Pain inflicted by a robot on a child sets up a powerful disruptive potential in the positronic brain. To counteract that by an anti-potential triggered through a realization of future good requires enough paths and bypaths to increase the mass of the positronic brain by 50 per cent, unless other circuits are sacrificed."

Baley said, "Then you haven't succeeded in building such a robot."

"No, nor am I likely to succeed. Nor anyone."

"Was Dr. Delmarre testing an experimental model of such a robot at the time of his death?"

"Not of *such* a robot. We were interested in other more practical things also."

Baley said quietly, "Dr. Leebig, I am going to have to learn a bit more about robotics and I am going to ask you to teach me."

Leebig shook his head violently, and his drooping eyelid dipped further in a ghastly travesty of a wink. "It should be obvious that a course in robotics takes more than a moment. I lack the time."

"Nevertheless, you must teach me. The smell of robots is the one thing that pervades everything on Solaria. If it is time we require, then more than ever I must see you. I am an Earthman and I cannot work or think comfortably while viewing."

It would not have seemed possible to Baley for Leebig to stiffen his stiff carriage further, but he did. He said, "Your phobias as an Earthman don't concern me. Seeing is impossible."

"I think you will change your mind when I tell you what I chiefly want to consult you about."

"It will make no difference. Nothing can."

"No? Then listen to this. It is my belief that throughout the history of the positronic robot, the First Law of Robotics has been deliberately misquoted."

Leebig moved spasmodically. "Misquoted? Fool! Madman! Why?"

"To hide the fact," said Baley with complete composure, "that robots can commit murder."

14. A MOTIVE IS REVEALED

Leebig's mouth widened slowly. Baley took it for a snarl at first and then, with considerable surprise, decided that it was the most unsuccessful attempt at a smile that he had ever seen.

Leebig said, "Don't say that. Don't ever say that."

"Why not?"

"Because anything, however small, that encourages distrust of robots is harmful. Distrusting robots is a human *disease*!"

It was as though he were lecturing a small child. It was as though he were saying something gently that he wanted to yell. It was as though he were trying to persuade when what he really wanted was to enforce on penalty of death.

Leebig said, "Do you know the history of robotics?"

"A little."

"On Earth, you should. Yes. Do you know robots started with a Frankenstein complex against them? They were suspect. Men distrusted and feared robots. Robotics was almost an undercover science as a result. The Three Laws were first built into robots in an effort to overcome distrust and even so Earth would never allow a robotic society to develop. One of the reasons the first pioneers left Earth to colonize the rest of the Galaxy was so that they might establish societies in which robots would be allowed to free men of poverty and toil. Even *then*, there remained a latent suspicion not far below, ready to pop up at any excuse."

"Have you yourself had to counter distrust of robots?" asked Baley.

"Many times," said Leebig grimly.

"Is that why you and other roboticists are willing to distort the facts just a little in order to avoid suspicion as much as possible?"

"There is no distortion!"

"For instance, aren't the Three Laws misquoted?"

"No!"

"I can demonstrate that they are, and unless you convince me otherwise, I will demonstrate it to the whole Galaxy, if I can."

"You're mad. Whatever argument you may think you have is fallacious, I assure you."

"Shall we discuss it?"

"If it does not take too long."

"Face to face? Seeing?"

Leebig's thin face twisted. *"No!"*

"Good-by, Dr. Leebig. Others will listen to me."

"Wait. Great Galaxy, man, wait!"

"Seeing?"

The roboticist's hands wandered upward, hovered about his chin. Slowly a thumb crept into his mouth and remained there. He stared, blankly, at Baley.

Baley thought: Is he regressing to the pre-five-year-old stage so that it will be legitimate for him to see me?

"Seeing?" he said.

But Leebig shook his head slowly. "I can't. I can't," he moaned, the words all but stifled by the blocking thumb. "Do whatever you want."

Baley stared at the other and watched him turn away and face the wall. He watched the Solarian's straight back bend and the Solarian's face hide in shaking hands.

Baley said, "Very well, then, I'll agree to view."

Leebig said, back still turned, "Excuse me a moment. I'll be back."

Baley tended to his own needs during the interval and stared at his fresh-washed face in the bathroom mirror. Was he getting the feel of Solaria and Solarians? He wasn't sure.

He sighed and pushed a contact and a robot appeared. He didn't turn to look at it. He said, "Is there another viewer at the farm, besides the one I'm using?"

"There are three other outlets, master."

"Then tell Klorissa Cantoro—tell your mistress that I will be using this one till further notice and that I am not to be disturbed."

"Yes, master."

Baley returned to his position where the viewer remained focused on the empty patch of room in which Leebig had stood. It was still empty and he settled himself to wait.

It wasn't long. Leebig entered and the room once more jiggled as the man walked. Evidently focus shifted from room center to man center without delay. Baley remembered the complexity of viewing controls and began to feel a kind of appreciation of what was involved.

Leebig was quite master of himself now, apparently. His hair was slicked back and his costume had been changed. His clothes fitted loosely and were of a material that glistened and caught highlights. He sat down in a slim chair that folded out of the wall.

He said soberly, "Now what is this notion of yours concerning First Law?"

"Will we be overheard?"

"No. I've taken care."

Baley nodded. He said, "Let me quote the First Law."

"I scarcely need that."

"I know, but let me quote it, anyway: A robot may not harm a human being or, through inaction, allow a human being to come to harm."

"Well?"

"Now when I first landed on Solaria, I was driven to the estate assigned for my use in a ground-car. The ground-car was a specially enclosed job designed to protect me from exposure to open space. As an Earthman——"

"I know about that," said Leebig impatiently. "What has this to do with the matter?"

"The robots who drove the car did *not* know about it. I asked that the car be opened and was at once obeyed. Second Law. They had to follow orders. I was uncomfortable, of course, and nearly collapsed before the car was enclosed again. Didn't the robots harm me?"

"At your order," snapped Leebig.

"I'll quote the Second Law: A robot must obey the orders

given it by human beings except where such orders would conflict with the First Law. So you see, my order should have been ignored."

"This is nonsense. The robot lacked knowledge——"

Baley leaned forward in his chair. "Ah! We have it. Now let's recite the First Law as it should be stated: A robot may do nothing that, *to its knowledge*, will harm a human being; nor, through inaction, *knowingly* allow a human being to come to harm."

"This is all understood."

"I think not by ordinary men. Otherwise, ordinary men would realize robots could commit murder."

Leebig was white. "Mad! Lunacy!"

Baley stared at his finger ends. "A robot may perform an innocent task, I suppose; one that has no damaging effect on a human being?"

"If ordered to do so," said Leebig.

"Yes, of course. If ordered to do so. And a second robot may perform an innocent task, also, I suppose; one that also can have no damaging effect on a human being? If ordered to do so?"

"Yes."

"And what if the two innocent tasks, each completely innocent, completely, amount to murder when added together?"

"What?" Leebig's face puckered into a scowl.

"I want your expert opinion on the matter," said Baley. "I'll set you a hypothetical case. Suppose a man says to a robot, 'Place a small quantity of this liquid into a glass of milk that you will find in such and such a place. The liquid is harmless. I wish only to know its effect on milk. Once I know the effect, the mixture will be poured out. After you have performed this action, forget you have done so.'"

Leebig, still scowling, said nothing.

Baley said, "If I had told the robot to add a mysterious liquid to milk and then offer it to a man, First Law would force it to ask, 'What is the nature of the liquid? Will it harm a man?' And if it were assured the liquid was harmless, First Law might still make the robot hesitate and refuse to offer the milk. Instead, however, it is told the milk will be poured out. First Law is not involved. Won't the robot do as it is told?"

Leebig glared.

Baley said, "Now a second robot has poured out the milk in the first place and is unaware that the milk has been tampered with. In all innocence, it offers the milk to a man and the man dies."

Leebig cried out, *"No!"*

"Why not? Both actions are innocent in themselves. Only together are they murder. Do you deny that that sort of thing can happen?"

"The murderer would be the man who gave the order," cried Leebig.

"If you want to be philosophical, yes. The robots would have been the immediate murderers, though, the instruments of murder."

"No man would give such orders."

"A man would. A man has. It was exactly in this way that the murder attempt on Dr. Gruer must have been carried through. You've heard about that, I suppose."

"On Solaria," muttered Leebig, "one hears about everything."

"Then you know Gruer was poisoned at his dinner table before the eyes of myself and my partner, Mr. Olivaw of Aurora. Can you suggest any other way in which the poison might have reached him? There was no other human on the estate. As a Solarian, you must appreciate that point."

"I'm not a detective. I have no theories."

"I've presented you with one. I want to know if it is a possible one. I want to know if two robots might not perform two separate actions, each one innocent in itself, the two together resulting in murder. You're the expert, Dr. Leebig. *Is it possible?"*

And Leebig, haunted and harried, said, "Yes," in a voice so low that Baley scarcely heard him.

Baley said, "Very well, then. So much for the First Law."

Leebig stared at Baley and his drooping eyelid winked once or twice in a slow tic. His hands, which had been clasped, drew apart, though the fingers maintained their clawed shape as though each hand still entwined a phantom hand of air. Palms turned downward and rested on knees and only then did the fingers relax.

Baley watched it all in abstraction.

Leebig said, "Theoretically, yes. Theoretically! But don't dismiss the First Law that easily, Earthman. Robots would have to be ordered very cleverly in order to circumvent the First Law."

"Granted," said Baley. "I am only an Earthman. I know next to nothing about robots and my phrasing of the orders was only by way of example. A Solarian would be much more subtle and do much better. I'm sure of that."

Leebig might not have been listening. He said loudly, "If a robot can be manipulated into doing harm to a man, it means only that we must extend the powers of the positronic brain. One *might* say we ought to make the human better. That is impossible, so we will make the robot more foolproof.

"We advance continuously. Our robots are more varied, more specialized, more capable, and more unharming than those of a century ago. A century hence, we will have still greater advances. Why have a robot manipulate controls when a positronic brain can be built into the controls itself? That's specialization, but we can generalize, also. Why not a robot with replaceable and interchangeable limbs. Eh? Why not? If we——"

Baley interrupted. "Are you the only roboticist on Solaria?"

"Don't be a fool."

"I only wondered. Dr. Delmarre was the only—uh—fetal engineer, except for an assistant."

"Solaria has over twenty roboticists."

"Are you the best?"

"I am," Leebig said without self-consciousness.

"Delmarre worked with you."

"He did."

Baley said, "I understand that he was planning to break the partnership toward the end."

"No sign of it. What gave you the idea?"

"I understand he disapproved of your bachelorhood."

"He may have. He was a thorough Solarian. However,

it did not affect our business relationships."

"To change the subject. In addition to developing new model robots, do you also manufacture and repair existing types?"

Leebig said, "Manufacture and repair are largely robot-conducted. There is a large factory and maintenance shop on my estate."

"Do robots require much in the way of repair, by the way?"

"Very little."

"Does that mean that robot repair is an undeveloped science?"

"Not at all." Leebig said that stiffly.

"What about the robot that was at the scene of Dr. Delmarre's murder?"

Leebig looked away, and his eyebrows drew together as though a painful thought were being barred entrance to his mind. "It was a complete loss."

"Really complete? Could it answer any questions at all?"

"None at all. It was absolutely useless. Its positronic brain was completely short-circuited. Not one pathway was left intact. Consider! It had witnessed a murder it had been unable to halt——"

"Why was it unable to halt the murder, by the way?"

"Who can tell? Dr. Delmarre was experimenting with that robot. I do not know in what mental condition he had left it. He might have ordered it, for instance, to suspend all operations while he checked one particular circuit element. If someone whom neither Dr. Delmarre nor the robot suspected of harm were suddenly to launch a homicidal attack, there might be a perceptible interval before the robot could use First Law potential to overcome Dr. Delmarre's freezing order. The length of the interval would depend on the nature of the attack and the nature of Dr. Delmarre's freezing order. I could invent a dozen other ways of explaining why the robot was unable to prevent the murder. Being unable to do so was a First Law violation, however, and that was sufficient to blast every positronic pathway in the robot's mind."

"But if the robot was physically unable to prevent the

murder, was it responsible? Does the First Law ask impossibilities?"

Leebig shrugged. "The First Law, despite your attempts to make little of it, protects humanity with every atom of possible force. It allows no excuses. If the First Law is broken, the robot is ruined."

"That is a universal rule, sir?"

"As universal as robots."

Baley said, "Then I've learned something."

"Then learn something else. Your theory of murder by a series of robotic actions, each innocent in itself, will not help you in the case of Dr. Delmarre's death."

"Why not?"

"The death was not by poisoning, but by bludgeoning. Something had to hold the bludgeon, and that had to be a human arm. No robot could swing a club and smash a skull."

"Suppose," said Baley, "a robot were to push an innocent button which dropped a booby-trap weight on Delmarre's head."

Leebig smiled sourly. "Earthman, I've viewed the scene of the crime. I've heard all the news. The murder was a big thing here on Solaria, you know. So I know there was no sign of any machinery at the scene of the crime, or of any fallen weight."

Baley said, "Or of any blunt instrument, either."

Leebig said scornfully, "You're a detective. Find it."

"Granting that a robot was not responsible for Dr. Delmarre's death, who was, then?"

"Everyone knows who was," shouted Leebig. "His wife! Gladia!"

Baley thought: At least there's a unanimity of opinion.

Aloud he said, "And who was the mastermind behind the robots who poisoned Gruer?"

"I suppose..." Leebig trailed off.

"You don't think there are two murderers, do you? If Gladia was responsible for one crime, she must be responsible for the second attempt, also."

"Yes. You must be right." His voice gained assurance. "No doubt of it."

"No doubt?"

"Nobody else could get close enough to Dr. Delmarre to kill him. He allowed personal presence no more than I did, except that he made an exception in favor of his wife, and I make no exceptions. The wiser I." The roboticist laughed harshly.

"I believe you knew her," said Baley abruptly.

"Whom?"

"Her. We are discussing only one 'her.' Gladia!"

"Who told you I knew her any more than I know anyone else?" demanded Leebig. He put his hand to his throat. His fingers moved slightly and opened the neckseam of his garment for an inch downward, leaving more freedom to breathe.

"Gladia herself did. You two went for walks."

"So? We were neighbors. It is a common thing to do. She seemed a pleasant person."

"You approved of her, then?"

Leebig shrugged. "Talking to her was relaxing."

"What did you talk about?"

"Robotics." There was a flavor of surprise about the word as though there were wonder that the question could be asked.

"And she talked robotics too?"

"She knew nothing about robotics. Ignorant! But she listened. She has some sort of field-force rigmarole she plays with; field coloring, she calls it. I have no patience with that, but I listened."

"All this without personal presence?"

Leebig looked revolted and did not answer.

Baley tried again, "Were you attracted to her?"

"What?"

"Did you find her attractive? Physically?"

Even Leebig's bad eyelid lifted and his lips quivered. "Filthy animal," he muttered.

"Let me put it this way, then. When did you cease finding Gladia pleasant? You used that word yourself, if you remember."

"What do you mean?"

"You said you found her pleasant. Now you believe she murdered her husband. That isn't the mark of a pleasant person."

"I was mistaken about her."

"But you decided you were mistaken before she killed her husband, if she did so. You stopped walking with her some time before the murder. Why?"

Leebig said, "Is that important?"

"Everything is important till proven otherwise."

"Look, if you want information from me as a roboticist, ask it. I won't answer personal questions."

Baley said, "You were closely associated with both the murdered man and the chief suspect. Don't you see that personal questions are unavoidable? Why did you stop walking with Gladia?"

Leebig snapped, "There came a time when I ran out of things to say; when I was too busy; when I found no reason to continue the walks."

"When you no longer found her pleasant, in other words."

"All right. Put it so."

"Why was she no longer pleasant?"

Leebig shouted, "I have no reason."

Baley ignored the other's excitement. "You are still someone who has known Gladia well. What could her motive be?"

"Her motive?"

"No one has suggested any motive for the murder. Surely Gladia wouldn't commit murder without a motive."

"Great Galaxy!" Leebig leaned his head back as though to laugh, but didn't. "No one told you? Well, perhaps no one knew. I knew, though. She told me. She told me frequently."

"Told you what, Dr. Leebig?"

"Why, that she quarreled with her husband. Quarreled bitterly and frequently. She hated him, Earthman. Didn't anyone tell you that? Didn't *she* tell you?"

15. A PORTRAIT IS COLORED

Baley took it between the eyes and tried not to show it.

Presumably, living as they did, Solarians considered one another's private lives to be sacrosanct. Questions concerning marriage and children were in bad taste. He supposed then that chronic quarreling would exist between husband and wife and be a matter into which curiosity was equally forbidden.

But even when murder had been committed? Would no one commit the social crime of asking the suspect if she quarreled with her husband? Or of mentioning the matter if they happened to know of it?

Well, Leebig had.

Baley said, "What did the quarrel concern?"

"You had better ask her, I think."

He better had, thought Baley. He rose stiffly, "Thank you, Dr. Leebig, for your co-operation. I may need your help again later. I hope you will keep yourself available."

"Done viewing," said Leebig, and he and the segment of his room vanished abruptly.

For the first time Baley found himself not minding a plane flight through open space. Not minding it at all. It was almost as though he were in his own element.

He wasn't even thinking of Earth or of Jessie. He had been away from Earth only a matter of weeks, yet it might as well have been years. He had been on Solaria only the better part of three days and yet it seemed forever.

How fast could a man adapt to nightmare?

Or was it Gladia? He would be seeing her soon, not viewing her. Was that what gave him confidence and this odd feeling of mixed apprehension and anticipation?

Would she endure it? he wondered. Or would she slip away after a few moments of seeing, begging off as Quemot had done?

She stood at the other end of a long room when he entered. She might almost have been an impressionistic representation of herself, she was reduced so to essentials.

Her lips were faintly red, her eyebrows lightly penciled, her earlobes faintly blue, and, except for that, her face was untouched. She looked pale, a little frightened, and very young.

Her brown-blond hair was drawn back, and her gray-blue eyes were somehow shy. Her dress was a blue so dark as to be almost black, with a thin white edging curling down each side. She wore long sleeves, white gloves, and flat-heeled shoes. Not an inch of skin showed anywhere but in her face. Even her neck was covered by a kind of unobtrusive ruching.

Baley stopped where he was. "Is this close enough, Gladia?"

She was breathing with shallow quickness. She said, "I had forgotten what to expect really. It's just like viewing, isn't it? I mean, if you don't think of it as seeing."

Baley said, "It's all quite normal to me."

"Yes, on Earth." She closed her eyes. "Sometimes I try to imagine it. Just crowds of people everywhere. You walk down a road and there are others walking with you and still others walking in the other direction. Dozens——"

"Hundreds," said Baley. "Did you ever view scenes on Earth in a book-film? Or view a novel with an Earth setting?"

"We don't have many of those, but I've viewed novels set on the other Outer Worlds where seeing goes on all the time. It's different in a novel. It just seems like a multiview."

"Do people ever kiss in novels?"

She flushed painfully. "I don't read that kind."

"Never?"

"Well—there are always a few dirty films around, you know, and sometimes, just out of curiosity——It's sickening, really."

"Is it?"

She said with sudden animation, "But Earth is so different. So many people. When you walk, Elijah, I suppose you even t-touch people. I mean, by accident."

Baley half smiled. "You even knock them down by accident." He thought of the crowds on the Expressways, tugging and shoving, bounding up and down the strips, and for a moment, inevitably, he felt the pang of homesickness.

Gladia said, "You don't have to stay way out there."

"Would it be all right if I came closer?"

"I think so. I'll tell you when I'd rather you wouldn't any more."

Stepwise Baley drew closer, while Gladia watched him, wide-eyed.

She said suddenly, "Would you like to see some of my field colorings?"

Baley was six feet away. He stopped and looked at her. She seemed small and fragile. He tried to visualize her, something in her hand (what?), swinging furiously at the skull of her husband. He tried to picture her, mad with rage, homicidal with hate and anger.

He had to admit it could be done. Even a hundred and five pounds of woman could crush a skull if she had the proper weapon and were wild enough. And Baley had known murderesses (on Earth, of course) who, in repose, were bunny rabbits.

He said, "What are field colorings, Gladia?"

"An art form," she said.

Baley remembered Leebig's reference to Gladia's art. He nodded. "I'd like to see some."

"Follow me, then."

Baley maintained a careful six-foot distance between them. At that, it was less than a third the distance Klorissa had demanded.

They entered a room that burst with light. It glowed in every corner and every color.

Gladia looked pleased, proprietary. She looked up at Baley, eyes anticipating.

Baley's response must have been what she expected, though he said nothing. He turned slowly, trying to make out what he saw, for it was light only, no material object at all.

The gobbets of light sat on embracing pedestals. They

were living geometry, lines and curves of color, entwined into a coalescing whole yet maintaining distinct identities. No two specimens were even remotely alike.

Baley groped for appropriate words and said, "Is it supposed to mean anything?"

Gladia laughed in her pleasant contralto. "It means whatever you like it to mean. They're just light-forms that might make you feel angry or happy or curious or whatever *I* felt when I constructed one. I could make one for you, a kind of portrait. It might not be very good, though, because I would just be improvising quickly."

"Would you? I would be very interested."

"All right," she said, and half-ran to a light-figure in one corner, passing within inches of him as she did so. She did not seem to notice.

She touched something on the pedestal of the light-figure and the glory above died without a flicker.

Baley gasped and said, "Don't do that."

"It's all right. I was tired of it, anyway. I'll just fade the others temporarily so they don't distract me." She opened a panel along one featureless wall and moved a rheostat. The colors faded to something scarcely visible.

Baley said, "Don't you have a robot to do this? Closing contacts?"

"Shush, now," she said impatiently. "I don't keep robots in here. This is *me*." She looked at him, frowning. "I don't know you well enough. That's the trouble."

She wasn't looking at the pedestal, but her fingers rested lightly on its smooth upper surface. All ten fingers were curved, tense, waiting.

One finger moved, describing a half curve over smoothness. A bar of deep yellow light grew and slanted obliquely across the air above. The finger inched backward a fraction and the light grew slightly less deep in shade.

She looked at it momentarily. "I suppose that's it. A kind of strength without weight."

"Jehoshaphat," said Baley.

"Are you offended?" Her fingers lifted and the yellow slant of light remained solitary and stationary.

"No, not at all. But what is it? How do you do it?"

"That's hard to explain," said Gladia, looking at the

pedestal thoughtfully, "considering I don't really understand it myself. It's a kind of optical illusion, I've been told. We set up force-fields at different energy levels. They're extrusions of hyperspace, really, and don't have the properties of ordinary space at all. Depending on the energy level, the human eye sees light of different shades. The shapes and colors are controlled by the warmth of my fingers against appropriate spots on the pedestal. There are all sorts of controls inside each pedestal."

"You mean if I were to put my finger there——" Baley advanced and Gladia made way for him. He put a hesitant forefinger down upon the pedestal and felt a soft throbbing.

"Go ahead. Move your finger, Elijah," said Gladia.

Baley did so and a dirty-gray jag of light lifted upward, skewing the yellow light. Baley withdrew his finger sharply and Gladia laughed and then was instantly contrite.

"I shouldn't laugh," she said. "It's really very hard to do, even for people who've tried a long time." Her own hand moved lightly and too quickly for Baley to follow and the monstrosity he had set up disappeared, leaving the yellow light in isolation again.

"How did you learn to do this?" asked Baley.

"I just kept on trying. It's a new art form, you know, and only one or two really know how——"

"And you're the best," said Baley somberly. "On Solaria everyone is either the only or the best or both."

"You needn't laugh. I've had some of my pedestals on display. I've given shows." Her chin lifted. There was no mistaking her pride.

She continued, "Let me go on with your portrait." Her fingers moved again.

There were few curves in the light-form that grew under her ministrations. It was all sharp angles. And the dominant color was blue.

"That's Earth, somehow," said Gladia, biting her lower lip. "I always think of Earth as blue. All those people and seeing, seeing, seeing. Viewing is more rose. How does it seem to you?"

"Jehoshaphat, I can't picture things as colors."

"Can't you?" she asked abstractedly. "Now you say 'Jehoshaphat' sometimes and that's just a little blob of violet.

A little sharp blob because it usually comes out ping, like that." And the little blob was there, glowing just off-center.

"And then," she said, "I can finish it like this." And a flat, lusterless hollow cube of slate gray sprang up to enclose everything. The light within shone through it, but dimmer; imprisoned, somehow.

Baley felt a sadness at it, as though it were something enclosing him, keeping him from something he wanted. He said, "What's that last?"

Gladia said, "Why, the walls about you. That's what's most in you, the way you can't go outside, the way you have to be inside. You *are* inside there. Don't you see?"

Baley saw and somehow he disapproved. He said, "Those walls aren't permanent. I've been out today."

"You have? Did you mind?"

He could not resist a counterdig. "The way you mind seeing me. You don't like it but you can stand it."

She looked at him thoughtfully. "Do you want to come out now? With me? For a walk?"

It was Baley's impulse to say: Jehoshaphat, no.

She said, "I've never walked with anyone, seeing. It's still daytime, and it's pleasant weather."

Baley looked at his abstractionist portrait and said, "If I go, will you take away the gray?"

She smiled and said, "I'll see how you behave."

The structure of light remained as they left the room. It stayed behind, holding Baley's imprisoned soul fast in the gray of the Cities.

Baley shivered slightly. Air moved against him and there was a chill to it.

Gladia said, "Are you cold?"

"It wasn't like this before," muttered Baley.

"It's late in the day now, but it isn't really cold. Would you like a coat? One of the robots could bring one in a minute."

"No. It's all right." They stepped forward along a narrow paved path. He said, "Is this where you used to walk with Dr. Leebig?"

"Oh no. We walked way out among the fields, where you can only see an occasional robot working and you can hear the animal sounds. You and I will stay near the house though, just in case."

"In case what?"

"Well, in case you want to go in."

"Or in case you get weary of seeing?"

"It doesn't bother me," she said recklessly.

There was the vague rustle of leaves above and an all-pervading yellowness and greenness. There were sharp, thin cries in the air about, plus a strident humming, and shadows, too.

He was especially aware of the shadows. One of them stuck out before him, in shape like a man, that moved as he did in horrible mimicry. Baley had heard of shadows, of course, and he knew what they were, but in the pervasive indirect lighting of the Cities he had never been specifically aware of one.

Behind him, he knew, was the Solarian sun. He took care not to look at it, but he knew it was there.

Space was large, space was lonely, yet he found it drawing him. His mind pictured himself striding the surface of a world with thousands of miles and light-years of room all about him.

Why should he find attraction in this thought of loneliness? He didn't want loneliness. He wanted Earth and the warmth and companionship of the man-crammed Cities.

The picture failed him. He tried to conjure up New York in his mind, all the noise and fullness of it, and found he could remain conscious only of the quiet, air-moving chill of the surface of Solaria.

Without quite willing it Baley moved closer to Gladia until he was two feet away, then grew aware of her startled face.

"I beg your pardon," he said at once, and drew off.

She gasped, "It's all right. Won't you walk this way? We have some flower beds you might like."

The direction she indicated lay away from the sun. Baley followed silently.

Gladia said, "Later in the year, it will be wonderful. In the warm weather I can run down to the lake and swim, or just run across the fields, run as fast as I can until I'm just glad to fall down and lie still."

She looked down at herself. "But this is no costume for it. With all this on, I've *got* to walk. Sedately, you know."

"How would you prefer to dress?" asked Baley.

"Halter and shorts at the *most*," she cried, lifting her arms as though feeling the freedom of that in her imagination. "Sometimes less. Sometimes just sandals so you can feel the air with every inch——Oh, I'm sorry, I've offended you."

Baley said, "No. It's all right. Was that your costume when you went walking with Dr. Leebig?"

"It varied. It depended on the weather. Sometimes I wore very little, but it was viewing, you know. You *do* understand, I hope."

"I understand. What about Dr. Leebig, though? Did he dress lightly too?"

"Jothan dress lightly?" Gladia smiled flashingly. "Oh no. He's very solemn, always." She twisted her face into a thin look of gravity and half winked, catching the very essence of Leebig and forcing a short grunt of appreciation out of Baley.

"This is the way he talks," she said. "'My dear Gladia, in considering the effect of a first-order potential on positron flow——'"

"Is that what he talked to you about? Robotics?"

"Mostly. Oh, he takes it so seriously, you know. He was always trying to teach me about it. He never gave up."

"Did you learn anything?"

"Not one thing. Nothing. It's just all a complete mix-up to me. He'd get angry with me sometimes, but when he'd scold, I'd dive into the water, if we were anywhere near the lake, and splash him."

"*Splash* him? I thought you were viewing."

She laughed. "You're *such* an Earthman. I'd splash where he was standing in his own room or on his own estate. The water couldn't touch him, but he would duck just the same. Look at that."

Baley looked. They had circled a wooded patch and now came upon a clearing, centered about an ornamental pond. Small bricked walks penetrated the clearing and broke it up. Flowers grew in profusion and order. Baley knew them for flowers from book-films he had viewed.

In a way the flowers were like the light-patterns that Gladia constructed and Baley imagined that she constructed them in the spirit of flowers. He touched one cautiously, then looked about. Reds and yellows predominated.

In turning to look about Baley caught a glimpse of the sun.

He said uneasily, "The sun is low in the sky."

"It's late afternoon," called Gladia back to him. She had run toward the pond and was sitting on a stone bench at its edge. "Come here," she shouted, waving. "You can stand if you don't like to sit on stone."

Baley advanced slowly. "Does it get this low every day?" and at once he was sorry he asked. If the planet rotated, the sun must be low in the sky both mornings and afternoons. Only at midday could it be high.

Telling himself this couldn't change a lifetime of pictured thought. He knew there was such a thing as night and had even experienced it, with a planet's whole thickness interposing safely between a man and the sun. He knew there were clouds and a protective grayness hiding the worst of outdoors. And still, when he thought of planetary surfaces, it was always a picture of a blaze of light with a sun high in the sky.

He looked over his shoulder, just quickly enough to get a flash of sun, and wondered how far the house was if he should decide to return.

Gladia was pointing to the other end of the stone bench.

Baley said, "That's pretty close to you, isn't it?"

She spread out her little hands, palms up. "I'm getting used to it. Really."

He sat down, facing toward her to avoid the sun.

She leaned over backward toward the water and pulled a small cup-shaped flower, yellow without and white-streaked within, not at all flamboyant. She said, "This is a native plant. Most of the flowers here are from Earth originally."

Water dripped from its severed stem as she extended it gingerly toward Baley.

Baley reached for it as gingerly. "You killed it," he said.

"It's only a flower. There are thousands more." Suddenly, before his fingers more than touched the yellow cup, she snatched it away, her eyes kindling. "Or are you trying to imply I could kill a human being because I pulled a flower?"

Baley said in soft conciliation, "I wasn't implying anything. May I see it?"

Baley didn't really want to touch it. It had grown in wet soil and there was still the effluvium of mud about it. How could these people, who were so careful in contact with Earthmen and even with one another, be so careless in their contact with ordinary dirt?

But he held the stalk between thumb and forefinger and looked at it. The cup was formed of several thin pieces of papery tissue, curving up from a common center. Within it was a white convex swelling, damp with liquid and fringed with dark hairs that trembled lightly in the wind.

She said, "Can you smell it?"

At once Baley was aware of the odor that emanated from it. He leaned toward it and said, "It smells like a woman's perfume."

Gladia clapped her hands in delight. "How like an Earthman. What you really mean is that a woman's perfume smells like *that*."

Baley nodded ruefully. He was growing weary of the outdoors. The shadows were growing longer and the land was becoming somber. Yet he was determined not to give in. He wanted those gray walls of light that dimmed his portrait removed. It was quixotic, but there it was.

Gladia took the flower from Baley, who let it go without reluctance. Slowly she pulled its petals apart. She said, "I suppose every woman smells different."

"It depends on the perfume," said Baley indifferently.

"Imagine being close enough to tell. I don't wear perfume because no one is close enough. Except now. But I suppose you smell perfume often, all the time. On Earth, your wife is always with you, isn't she?" She was concentrating very hard on the flower, frowning as she plucked it carefully to pieces.

"She's not always with me," said Baley. "Not every minute."

"But most of the time. And whenever you want to——"

Baley said suddenly, "Why did Dr. Leebig try so hard

to teach you robotics, do you suppose?"

The dismembered flower consisted now of a stalk and the inner swelling. Gladia twirled it between her fingers, then tossed it away, so that it floated for a moment on the surface of the pond. "I think he wanted me to be his assistant," she said.

"Did he tell you so, Gladia?"

"Toward the end, Elijah. I think he grew impatient. Anyway, he asked me if I didn't think it would be exciting to work in robotics. Naturally, I told him I could think of nothing duller. He was quite angry."

"And he never walked with you again after that."

She said, "You know, I think that may have been it. I suppose his feelings were hurt. Really, though, what could I do?"

"It was before that, though, that you told him about your quarrels with Dr. Delmarre."

Her hands became fists and held so in a tight spasm. Her body held stiffly to its position, head bent and a little to one side. Her voice was unnaturally high. "What quarrels?"

"Your quarrels with your husband. I understand you hated him."

Her face was distorted and blotched as she glared at him. "Who told you that? Jothan?"

"Dr. Leebig mentioned it. I think it's true."

She was shaken. "You're still trying to prove I killed him. I keep thinking you're my friend and you're only—only a detective."

She raised her fists and Baley waited.

He said, "You know you can't touch me."

Her hands dropped and she began crying without a sound. She turned her head away.

Baley bent his own head and closed his eyes, shutting out the disturbing long shadows. He said, "Dr. Delmarre was not a very affectionate man, was he?"

She said in a strangled way, "He was a very busy man."

Baley said, "You *are* affectionate, on the other hand. You find a man interesting. Do you understand?"

"I c-can't help it. I know it's disgusting, but I can't help it. It's even disgusting t-to talk about it."

"You did talk about it to Dr. Leebig, though?"

"I *had* to do something and Jothan was handy and he didn't seem to mind and it made me feel better."

"Was this the reason you quarreled with your husband? Was it that he was cold and unaffectionate and you resented it?"

"Sometimes I hated him." She shrugged her shoulders helplessly. "He was just a good Solarian and we weren't scheduled for ch—for ch——" She broke down.

Baley waited. His own stomach was cold and open air pressed down heavily upon him. When Gladia's sobs grew quieter, he asked, as gently as he could, "Did you kill him, Gladia?"

"No-no." Then, suddenly, as though all resistance had corroded within her: "I haven't told you everything."

"Well, then, please do so now."

"We were quarreling that time, the time he died. The old quarrel. I screamed at him but he never shouted back. He hardly ever even said anything and that just made it worse. I was so angry, so angry. I don't remember after that."

"Jehoshaphat!" Baley swayed slightly and his eyes sought the neutral stone of the bench. "What do you mean you don't remember?"

"I mean he was dead and I was screaming and the robots came——"

"Did you kill him?"

"I don't remember it, Elijah, and I would remember it if I did, wouldn't I? Only I don't remember anything else, either, and I've been so frightened, so frightened. Help me, please, Elijah."

"Don't worry, Gladia. I'll help you." Baley's reeling mind fastened on the murder weapon. What happened to it? It must have been removed. If so, only the murderer could have done it. Since Gladia was found immediately after the murder on the scene, she could not have done it. The murderer would have to be someone else. No matter how it looked to everyone in Solaria, it had to be someone else.

Baley thought sickly: I've got to get back to the house. He said, "Gladia——"

Somehow he was staring at the sun. It was nearly at the

horizon. He had to turn his head to look at it and his eyes locked with a morbid fascination. He had never seen it so. Fat, red, and dim somehow, so that one could look at it without blinding, and see the bleeding clouds above it in thin lines, with one crossing it in a bar of black.

Baley mumbled, "The sun is so red."

He heard Gladia's choked voice say drearily, "It's always red at sunset, red and dying."

Baley had a vision. The sun was moving down to the horizon because the planet's surface was moving away from it, a thousand miles an hour, spinning under that naked sun, spinning with nothing to guard the microbes called men that scurried over its spinning surface, spinning madly forever, spinning—spinning . . .

It was his head that was spinning and the stone bench that was slanting beneath him and the sky heaving, blue, dark blue, and the sun was gone, and the tops of trees and the ground rushing up and Gladia screaming thinly and another sound . . .

16. A SOLUTION IS OFFERED

Baley was aware first of enclosure, the absence of the open, and then of a face bending over him.

He stared for a moment without recognition. Then: "*Daneel*!"

The robot's face showed no sign of relief or of any other recognizable emotion at being addressed. He said, "It is well that you have recovered consciousness, Partner Elijah. I do not believe you have suffered physical injury."

"I'm all right," said Baley testily, struggling to his elbows. "Jehoshaphat, am I in bed? What for?"

"You have been exposed to the open a number of times today. The effects upon you have been cumulative and you need rest."

"I need a few answers first." Baley looked about and tried to deny to himself that his head was spinning just a little. He did not recognize the room. The curtains were drawn. Lights were comfortably artificial. He was feeling much better. "For instance, where am I?"

"In a room of Mrs. Delmarre's mansion."

"Next, let's get something straight. What are *you* doing here?" How did you get away from the robots I set over you?"

Daneel said, "It had seemed to me that you would be displeased at this development and yet in the interests of your safety and of my orders, I felt that I had no choice but——"

"What did you *do*? Jehoshaphat!"

"It seems Mrs. Delmarre attempted to view you some hours ago."

"Yes." Baley remembered Gladia saying as much earlier in the day. "I know that."

"Your order to the robots that held me prisoner was, in your words: 'Do not allow him' (meaning myself) 'to establish contact with other humans or other robots, either by seeing or by viewing.' However, Partner Elijah, you said nothing about forbidding other humans or robots to contact me. You see the distinction?"

Baley groaned.

Daneel said, "No need for distress, Partner Elijah. The flaw in your orders was instrumental in saving your life, since it brought me to the scene. You see, when Mrs. Delmarre viewed me, being allowed to do so by my robot guardians, she asked after you and I answered, quite truthfully, that I did not know of your whereabouts, but that I could attempt to find out. She seemed anxious that I do so. I said I thought it possible you might have left the house temporarily and that I would check that matter and would she, in the meanwhile, order the robots in the room with me, to search the mansion for your presence."

"Wasn't she surprised that you didn't deliver the orders to the robots yourself?"

"I gave her the impression, I believe, that as an Auroran I was not as accustomed to robots as she was; that she might deliver the orders with greater authority and effect a more speedy consummation. Solarians, it is quite clear, are vain of their skill with robots and contemptuous of the ability of natives of other planets to handle them. Is that not your opinion as well, Partner Elijah?"

"And she ordered them away, then?"

"With difficulty. They protested previous orders but, of course, could not state the nature thereof since you had ordered them to tell no one of my own true identity. She overrode them, although the final orders had to be shrilled out in fury."

"And then you left."

"I did, Partner Elijah."

A pity, thought Baley, that Gladia did not consider that episode important enough to relay to him when he viewed her. He said, "It took you long enough to find me, Daneel."

"The robots on Solaria have a network of information through subetheric contact. A skilled Solarian could obtain information readily, but, mediated as it is through millions of individual machines, one such as myself, without experience in the matter, must take time to unearth a single datum. It was better than an hour before the information as to your whereabouts reached me. I lost further time by visiting Dr. Delmarre's place of business after you had departed."

"What were you doing there?"

"Pursuing researches of my own. I regret that this had to be done in your absence, but the exigencies of the investigation left me no choice."

Baley said, "Did you view Klorissa Cantoro, or see her?"

"I viewed her, but from another part of her building, not from our own estate. There were records at the farm I had to see. Ordinarily viewing would have been sufficient, but it might have been inconvenient to remain on our own estate since three robots knew my real nature and might easily have imprisoned me once more."

Baley felt almost well. He swung his legs out of bed and found himself in a kind of nightgown. He stared at it with distaste. "Get me my clothes."

Daneel did so.

As Baley dressed, he said, "Where's Mrs. Delmarre?"

"Under house arrest, Partner Elijah."

"What? By whose order?"

"By my order. She is confined to her bedroom under robotic guard and her right to give orders other than to meet personal needs has been neutralized."

"By yourself?"

"The robots on this estate are not aware of my identity."

Baley finished dressing. "I know the case against Gladia," he said. "She had the opportunity; more of it, in fact, than we thought at first. She did not rush to the scene at the sound of her husband's cry, as she first said. She was there all along."

"Does she claim to have witnessed the murder and seen the murderer?"

"No. She remembers nothing of the crucial moments. That happens sometimes. It turns out, also, that she has a motive."

"What was it, Partner Elijah?"

"One that I had suspected as a possibility from the first.

I said to myself, if this were Earth, and Dr. Delmarre were as he was described to be and Gladia Delmarre as she seemed to be, I would say that she was in love with him, or had been, and that he was in love only with himself. The difficulty was to tell whether Solarians felt love or reacted to love in any Earthly sense. My judgment as to their emotions and reactions wasn't to be trusted. It was why I had to see a few. *Not* view them, but see them."

"I do not follow you, Partner Elijah."

"I don't know if I can explain it to you. These people have their gene possibilities carefully plotted before birth and the actual gene distribution tested after birth."

"I know that."

"But genes aren't everything. Environment counts too, and environment can bend into actual psychosis where genes indicate only a potentiality for a particular psychosis. Did you notice Gladia's interest in Earth?"

"I remarked upon it, Partner Elijah, and considered it an assumed interest designed to influence your opinions."

"Suppose it were a real interest, even a fascination. Suppose there were something about Earth's crowds that excited her. Suppose she were attracted against her will by something she had been taught to consider filthy. There was possible abnormality. I had to test it by seeing Solarians and noticing how *she* reacted to it. It was why I had to get away from you, Daneel, at any cost. It was why I had to abandon viewing as a method for carrying on the investigation."

"You did not explain this, Partner Elijah."

"Would the explanation have helped against what you conceived your duty under First Law to be?"

Daneel was silent.

Baley said, "The experiment worked. I saw or tried to see several people. An old sociologist tried to see me and had to give up midway. A roboticist refused to see me at all even under terrific force. The bare possibility sent him into an almost infantile frenzy. He sucked his finger and wept. Dr. Delmarre's assistant was used to personal presence in the way of her profession and so she tolerated me, but at twenty feet only. Gladia, on the other hand——"

"Yes, Partner Elijah?"

"Gladia consented to see me without more than a slight hesitation. She tolerated my presence easily and actually showed signs of decreasing strain as time went on. It all fits into a pattern of psychosis. She didn't mind seeing me; she was interested in Earth; she might have felt an abnormal interest in her husband. All of it could be explained by a strong and, for this world, psychotic interest in the personal presence of members of the opposite sex. Dr. Delmarre, himself, was not the type to encourage such a feeling or co-operate with it. It must have been very frustrating for her."

Daneel nodded. "Frustrating enough for murder in a moment of passion."

"In spite of everything, I don't think so, Daneel."

"Are you perhaps being influenced by extraneous motives of your own, Partner Elijah? Mrs. Delmarre is an attractive woman and you are an Earthman in whom a preference for the personal presence of an attractive woman is not psychotic."

"I have better reasons," said Baley uneasily. (Daneel's cool glance was too penetrating and soul-dissecting by half. Jehoshaphat! The thing was only a machine.) He said, "If she were the murderess of her husband, she would also have to be the attempted murderess of Gruer." He had almost the impulse to explain the way murder could be manipulated through robots, but held back. He was not sure how Daneel would react to a theory that made unwitting murderers of robots.

Daneel said, "And the attempted murderess of yourself as well."

Baley frowned. He had had no intention of telling Daneel of the poisoned arrow that had missed; no intention of strengthening the other's already too strong protective complex vis-à-vis himself.

He said angrily, "What did Klorissa tell you?" He ought to have warned her to keep quiet, but then, how was he to know that Daneel would be about, asking questions?

Daneel said calmly, "Mrs. Cantoro had nothing to do with the matter. I witnessed the murder attempt myself."

Baley was thoroughly confused. "You were nowhere about."

Daneel said, "I caught you myself and brought you here an hour ago."

"What are you talking about?"

"Do you not remember, Partner Elijah? It was almost a perfect murder. Did not Mrs. Delmarre suggest that you go into the open? I was not a witness to that, but I feel certain she did."

"She did suggest it. Yes."

"She may even have enticed you to leave the house."

Baley thought of the "portrait" of himself, of the enclosing gray walls. Could it have been clever psychology? Could a Solarian have that much intuitive understanding of the psychology of an Earthman?

"No," he said.

Daneel said, "Was it she who suggested you go down to the ornamental pond and sit on the bench?"

"Well, yes."

"Does it occur to you that she might have been watching you, noticing your gathering dizziness?"

"She asked once or twice if I wanted to go back."

"She might not have meant it seriously. She might have been watching you turn sicker on that bench. She might even have pushed you, or perhaps a push wasn't necessary. At the moment I reached you and caught you in my arms, you were in the process of falling backward off the stone bench and into three feet of water, in which you would surely have drowned."

For the first time Baley recalled those last fugitive sensations. "Jehoshaphat!"

"Moreover," said Daneel with calm relentlessness, "Mrs. Delmarre sat beside you, watching you fall, without a move to stop you. Nor would she have attempted to pull you out of the water. She would have let you drown. She might have called a robot, but the robot would surely have arrived too late. And afterward, she would explain merely that, of course, it was impossible for her to touch you even to save your life."

True enough, thought Baley. No one would question her inability to touch a human being. The surprise, if any, would come at her ability to be as close to one as she was.

Daneel said, "You see, then, Partner Elijah, that her guilt

can scarcely be in question. You stated that she would have
to be the attempted murderess of Agent Gruer as though
this were an argument against her guilt. You see now that
she must have been. Her only motive to murder you was
the same as her motive for trying to murder Gruer; the
necessity of getting rid of an embarrassingly persistent investigator of the first murder."

Baley said, "The whole sequence might have been an
innocent one. She might never have realized how the outdoors would affect me."

"She studied Earth. She knew the peculiarities of Earthmen."

"I assured her I had been outdoors today and that I was
growing used to it."

"She may have known better."

Baley pounded fist against palm. "You're making her
too clever. It doesn't fit and I don't believe it. In any case,
no murder accusation can stick unless and until the absence
of the murder weapon can be accounted for."

Daneel looked steadily at the Earthman, "I can do that,
too, Partner Elijah."

Baley looked at his robot partner with a stunned expression. "How?"

"Your reasoning, you will remember, Partner Elijah, was
this. Were Mrs. Delmarre the murderess, then the weapon,
whatever it was, must have remained at the scene of the
murder. The robots, appearing almost at once, saw no sign
of such a weapon, hence it must have been removed from
the scene, hence the murderer must have removed it, hence
the murderer could not be Mrs. Delmarre. Is all that correct?"

"Correct."

"Yet," continued the robot, "there is one place where
the robots did not look for the weapon."

"Where?"

"Under Mrs. Delmarre. She was lying in a faint, brought
on by the excitement and passion of the moment, whether
murderess or not, and the weapon, whatever it was, lay
under her and out of sight."

Baley said, "Then the weapon would have been discovered as soon as she was moved."

"Exactly," said Daneel, "but she was not moved by the robots. She herself told us yesterday at dinner that Dr. Thool ordered the robots to put a pillow under her head and leave her. She was first moved by Dr. Altim Thool, himself, when he arrived to examine her."

"So?"

"It follows, therefore, Partner Elijah, that a new possibility arises. Mrs. Delmarre was the murderess, the weapon was at the scene of the crime, but Dr. Thool carried it off and disposed of it to protect Mrs. Delmarre."

Baley felt contemptuous. He had almost been seduced into expecting something reasonable. He said, "Completely motiveless. Why should Dr. Thool do such a thing?"

"For a very good reason. You remember Mrs. Delmarre's remarks concerning him: 'He always treated me since I was a child and was always so friendly and kind.' I wondered if he might have some motive for being particularly concerned about her. It was for that reason that I visited the baby farm and inspected the records. What I had merely guessed at as a possibility turned out to be the truth."

"What?"

"Dr. Altim Thool was the father of Gladia Delmarre, and what is more, he knew of the relationship."

Baley had no thought of disbelieving the robot. He felt only a deep chagrin that it had been Robot Daneel Olivaw and not himself that had carried through the necessary piece of logical analysis. Even so, it was not complete.

He said, "Have you spoken to Dr. Thool?"

"Yes. I have placed him under house arrest, also."

"What does he say?"

"He admits that he is the father of Mrs. Delmarre. I confronted him with the records of the fact and the records of his inquiries into her health when she was a youngster. As a doctor, he was allowed more leeway in this respect than another Solarian might have been allowed."

"Why should he have inquired into her health?"

"I have considered that, too, Partner Elijah. He was an old man when he was given special permission to have an

additional child and, what is more, he succeeded in pro-
ducing one. He considers this a tribute to his genes and to
his physical fitness. He is prouder of the result, perhaps,
than is quite customary on this world. Moreover, his position
as physician, a profession little regarded on Solaria because
it involves personal presences, made it the more important
to him to nurture this sense of pride. For that reason, he
maintained unobtrusive contact with his offspring."

"Does Gladia know anything of it?"

"As far as Dr. Thool is aware, Partner Elijah, she does
not."

Baley said, "Does Thool admit removing the weapon?"

"No. That he does not."

"Then you've got nothing, Daneel."

"Nothing?"

"Unless you can find the weapon and prove he took it,
or at the very least induce him to confess, you have no
evidence. A chain of deduction is pretty, but it isn't evidence."

"The man would scarcely confess without considerable
questioning of a type I myself could not carry through. His
daughter is dear to him."

"Not at all," said Baley. "His feeling for his daughter is
not at all what you and I are accustomed to. Solaria is
different!"

He strode the length of the room and back, letting himself
cool. He said, "Daneel, you have worked out a perfect
exercise in logic, but none of it is reasonable, just the same."
(Logical but not reasonable. Wasn't that the definition of a
robot?)

He went on, "Dr. Thool is an old man and past his best
years, regardless of whether he was capable of siring a
daughter thirty years or so ago. Even Spacers get senile.
Picture him then examining his daughter in a faint and his
son-in-law dead by violence. Can you imagine the unusual
nature of the situation for him? Can you suppose he could
have remained master of himself? So much the master of
himself, in fact, as to carry out a series of amazing actions?

"Look! First, he would have had to notice a weapon
under his daughter, one that must have been so well covered
by her body that the robots never noticed it. Secondly, from

whatever small scrap of object he noted, he must have deduced the presence of the weapon and seen at once that if he could but sneak off with that weapon, unseen, a murder accusation against his daughter would be hard to substantiate. That's pretty subtle thinking for an old man in a panic. Then, thirdly, he would have had to carry the plan through, also tough for an old man in a panic. And now lastly, he would have to dare to compound the felony further by sticking to his lie. It all may be the result of logical thinking, but none of it is reasonable."

Daneel said, "Do you have an alternate solution to the crime, Partner Elijah?"

Baley had sat down during the course of his last speech and now he tried to rise again, but a combination of weariness and the depth of the chair defeated him. He held out his hand petulantly. "Give me a hand, will you, Daneel?"

Daneel stared at his own hand. "I beg your pardon, Partner Elijah?"

Baley silently swore at the other's literal mind and said, "Help me out of the chair."

Daneel's strong arm lifted him out of the chair effortlessly.

Baley said, "Thanks. No, I haven't an alternate solution. At least, I have, but the whole thing hinges on the location of the weapon."

He walked impatiently to the heavy curtains that lined most of one wall and lifted a corner without quite realizing what he was doing. He stared at the black patch of glass until he became aware of the fact that he was looking out into the early night, and then dropped the curtain just as Daneel, approaching quietly, took it out of his fingers.

In the split fraction of a moment in which Baley watched the robot's hand take the curtain away from him with the loving caution of a mother protecting her child from the fire, a revolution took place within him.

He snatched the curtain back, yanking it out of Daneel's grasp. Throwing his full weight against it, he tore it away from the window, leaving shreds behind.

"Partner Elijah!" said Daneel softly. "Surely you know now what the open will do to you."

"I know," said Baley, "what it will do *for* me."

He stared out the window. There was nothing to see, only blackness, but that blackness was open air. It was unbroken, unobstructed space, even if unlit, and he was facing it.

And for the first time he faced it freely. It was no longer bravado, or perverse curiosity, or the pathway to a solution of a murder. He faced it because he knew he wanted to and because he needed to. That made all the difference.

Walls were crutches! Darkness and crowds were crutches! He must have thought them so, unconsciously, and hated them even when he most thought he loved and needed them. Why else had he so resented Gladia's gray enclosure of his portrait?

He felt himself filling with a sense of victory, and, as though victory were contagious, a new thought came, bursting like an inner shout.

Baley turned dizzily to Daneel. "I know," he whispered. "Jehoshaphat! I know!"

"Know what, Partner Elijah?"

"I know what happened to the weapon; I know who is responsible. All at once, everything falls into place."

17. A MEETING IS HELD

Daneel would allow no immediate action.

"Tomorrow!" he had said with respectful firmness. "That is my suggestion, Partner Elijah. It is late and you are in need of rest."

Baley had to admit the truth of it, and besides there was the need of preparation; a considerable quantity of it. He had the solution of the murder, he felt sure of that, but it rested on deduction, as much as had Daneel's theory, and it was worth as little as evidence. Solarians would have to help him.

And if he were to face them, one Earthman against half a dozen Spacers, he would have to be in full control. That meant rest and preparation.

Yet he would not sleep. He was certain he would not sleep. Not all the softness of the special bed set up for him by smoothly functioning robots nor all the soft perfume and softer music in the special room of Gladia's mansion would help. He was sure of it.

Daneel sat unobtrusively in one darkened corner.

Baley said, "Are you still afraid of Gladia?"

The robot said, "I do not think it wise to allow you to sleep alone and unprotected."

"Well, have your way. Are you clear as to what I want you to do, Daneel?"

"I am, Partner Elijah."

"You have no reservations under the First Law, I hope."

"I have some with respect to the conference you wish arranged. Will you be armed and careful of your own safety?"

"I assure you, I will."

Daneel delivered himself of a sigh that was somehow so human that for a moment Baley found himself trying to penetrate the darkness that he might study the machine-perfect face of the other.

Daneel said, "I have not always found human behavior logical."

"We need Three Laws of our own," said Baley, "but I'm glad we don't have them."

He stared at the ceiling. A great deal depended on Daneel and yet he could tell him very little of the whole truth. Robots were too involved. The planet, Aurora, had its reasons for sending a robot as representative of their interests, but it was a mistake. Robots had their limitations.

Still, if all went right, this could all be over in twelve hours. He could be heading back to Earth in twenty-four, bearing hope. A strange kind of hope. A kind he could scarcely believe himself, yet it was Earth's way out. It must be Earth's way out.

Earth! New York! Jessie and Ben! The comfort and familiarity and dearness of home!

He dwelled on it, half asleep, and the thought of Earth failed to conjure the comfort he expected. There was an estrangement between himself and the Cities.

And at some unknown point in time it all faded and he slept.

Baley, having slept and then wakened, showered and dressed. Physically he was quite prepared. Yet he was unsure. It was not that his reasoning seemed any less cogent to himself in the pallor of morning. It was rather the necessity of facing Solarians.

Could he be sure of their reactions after all? Or would he still be working blind?

Gladia was the first to appear. It was simple for her, of course. She was on an intramural circuit, since she was in the mansion itself. She was pale and expressionless, in a white gown that draped her into a cold statue.

She stared helplessly at Baley. Baley smiled back gently and she seemed to take comfort from that.

One by one, they appeared now. Attlebish, the Acting Head of Security, appeared next after Gladia, lean and haughty, his large chin set in disapproval. Then Leebig, the roboticist, impatient and angry, his weak eyelid fluttering periodically. Quemot, the sociologist, a little tired, but smiling at Baley out of deep-set eyes in a condescending way, as though to say: We have seen one another, we have been intimate.

Klorissa Cantoro, when she appeared, seemed uneasy in the presence of the others. She glanced at Gladia for a moment with an audible sniff, then stared at the floor. Dr. Thool, the physician, appeared last. He looked haggard, almost sick.

They were all there, all but Gruer, who was slowly recovering and for whom attendance was physically impossible. (Well, thought Baley, we'll do without him.) All were dressed formally; all sat in rooms that were well curtained into enclosure.

Daneel had arranged matters well. Baley hoped fervently that what remained for Daneel to do would work as well.

Baley looked from one Spacer to the other. His heart thudded. Each figure viewed him out of a different room and the clash of lighting, furniture, and wall decoration was dizzying.

Baley said, "I want to discuss the matter of the killing of Dr. Rikaine Delmarre under the heading of motive, opportunity, and means, in that order——"

Attlebish interrupted. "Will this be a long speech?"

Baley said sharply, "It may be. I have been called here to investigate a murder and such a job is my specialty and my profession. I know best how to go about it." (Take nothing from them now, he thought, or this whole thing won't work. Dominate! Dominate!)

He went on, making his words as sharp and incisive as he could. "Motive first. In a way, motive is the most unsatisfactory of the three items. Opportunity and means are objective. They can be investigated factually. Motive is subjective. It may be something that can be observed by others; revenge for a known humiliation, for instance. But it may also be completely unobservable; an irrational, homicidal hate on the part of a well-disciplined person who never lets it show.

"Now almost all of you have told me at one time or another that you believed Gladia Delmarre to have committed the crime. Certainly, no one has suggested an alternate suspect. Has Gladia a motive? Dr. Leebig suggested one. He said that Gladia quarreled frequently with her husband and Gladia later admitted this to me. The rage that can arise out of a quarrel can, conceivably, move a person to murder. Very well.

"The question remains, though, whether she is the only one with a motive. I wonder. Dr. Leebig, himself——"

The roboticist almost jumped. His hand extended rigidly in the direction of Baley. "Watch what you say, Earthman."

"I am only theorizing," said Baley coldly. "You, Dr. Leebig, were working with Dr. Delmarre on new robot models. You are the best man in Solaria as far as robotics is concerned. You say so and I believe it."

Leebig smiled with open condescension.

Baley went on. "But I have heard that Dr. Delmarre was about to break off relations with you for matters concerning yourself of which he disapproved."

"False! False!"

"Perhaps. But what if it were true? Wouldn't you have a motive to get rid of him before he humiliated you publicly by breaking with you? I have a feeling you could not easily bear such humiliation."

Baley went on rapidly to give Leebig no chance to retort. "And you, Mrs. Cantoro. Dr. Delmarre's death leaves you in charge of fetal engineering, a responsible position."

"Skies above, we talked about that before," cried Klorissa in anguish.

"I know we did, but it's a point that must be considered, anyway. As for Dr. Quemot, he played chess with Dr. Delmarre regularly. Perhaps he grew annoyed at losing too many games."

The sociologist interposed quietly. "Losing a chess game is insufficient motive surely, Plainclothesman."

"It depends on how seriously you take your chess. Motives can seem all the world to the murderer and completely insignificant to everyone else. Well, it doesn't matter. My point is that motive alone is insufficient. Anyone can have a motive, particularly for the murder of a man such as Dr. Delmarre."

"What do you mean by that remark," demanded Quemot in indignation.

"Why, only that Dr. Delmarre was a 'good Solarian.' You all described him as such. He rigidly fulfilled all the requirements of Solarian custom. He was an ideal man, almost an abstraction. Who could feel love, or even liking, for such a man? A man without weaknesses serves only to make everyone else conscious of his own imperfections. A primitive poet named Tennyson once wrote: 'He is all fault who has no fault at all.'"

"No one would kill a man for being too good," said Klorissa, frowning.

"You little know," said Baley, and went on without amplification. "Dr. Delmarre was aware of a conspiracy on Solaria, or thought he was; a conspiracy that was preparing an assault on the rest of the Galaxy for purposes of conquest. He was interested in preventing that. For that reason, those concerned in the conspiracy might find it necessary to do away with him. Anyone here could be a member of the conspiracy, including, to be sure, Mrs. Delmarre, but including even the Acting Head of Security, Corwin Attlebish."

"I?" said Attlebish, unmoved.

"You certainly attempted to end the investigation as soon as Gruer's mishap put you in charge."

Baley took a few slow sips at his drink (straight from its original container, untouched by human hands other than his own, or robotic hands, either) and gathered his strength. So far, this was a waiting game, and he was thankful the Solarians were sitting still for it. They hadn't the Earthman's experience of dealing with people at close quarters. They weren't in-fighters.

He said, "Opportunity next. It is the general opinion that only Mrs. Delmarre had opportunity since only she could approach her husband in actual personal presence.

"Are we sure of that? Suppose someone other than Mrs. Delmarre had made up his or her mind to kill Dr. Delmarre? Would not such a desperate resolution make the discomfort of personal presence secondary? If any of you were set on murder, wouldn't you bear personal presence just long enough to do the job? Couldn't you sneak into the Delmarre mansion——"

Attlebish interposed frigidly. "You are ignorant of the

matter, Earthman. Whether we would or would not doesn't matter. The fact is that Dr. Delmarre himself would not allow seeing, I assure you. If anyone came into his personal presence, regardless of how valued and long-standing a friendship there was between them, Dr. Delmarre would order him away and, if necessary, call robots to help with the ejection."

"True," said Baley, "*if* Dr. Delmarre were aware that personal presence was involved."

"What do you mean by that?" demanded Dr. Thool in surprise, his voice quavering.

"When you treated Mrs. Delmarre at the scene of the murder," replied Baley, looking full at his questioner, "she assumed you were viewing her, until you actually touched her. So she told me and so I believe. I am, myself, accustomed only to seeing. When I arrived at Solaria and met Security Head Gruer, I assumed I was seeing him. When at the end of our interview, Gruer disappeared, I was taken completely by surprise.

"Now assume the reverse. Suppose that for all a man's adult life, he had been viewing only; never seeing anyone, except on rare occasions his wife. Now suppose someone other than his wife walked up to him in personal presence. Would he not automatically assume that it was a matter of viewing, particularly if a robot had been instructed to advise Delmarre that viewing contact was being set up?"

"Not for a minute," said Quemot. "The sameness of background would give it away."

"Maybe, but how many of you are aware of background now? There would be a minute or so, at least, before Dr. Delmarre would grow aware that something was wrong and in that time, his friend, whoever he was, could walk up to him, raise a club, and bring it down."

"Impossible," said Quemot stubbornly.

"I think not," said Baley. "I think opportunity must be canceled out as absolute proof that Mrs. Delmarre is the murderess. She had opportunity, but so might others."

Baley waited again. He felt perspiration on his forehead, but wiping it away would have made him look weak. He must maintain absolute charge of the proceedings. The person at whom he was aiming must be placed in self-convinced inferiority. It was hard for an Earthman to do that to a Spacer.

Baley looked from face to face and decided that matters were at least progressing satisfactorily. Even Attlebish looked quite humanly concerned.

"And so we come," he said, "to means, and that is the most puzzling factor of all. The weapon with which the murder was committed was never found."

"We know that," said Attlebish. "If it were not for that point, we would have considered the case against Mrs. Delmarre conclusive. We would never have required an investigation."

"Perhaps," said Baley. "Let's analyze the matter of means, then. There are two possibilities. Either Mrs. Delmarre committed the murder, or someone else did. If Mrs. Delmarre committed the murder, the weapon would have had to remain at the scene of the crime, unless it were removed later. It has been suggested by my partner, Mr. Olivaw of Aurora, who is not present at the moment, that Dr. Thool had the opportunity to remove the weapon. I ask Dr. Thool now, in the presence of all of us, if he did this, if he removed a weapon while examining the unconscious Mrs. Delmarre?"

Dr. Thool was shaking. "No, no. I swear it. I'll abide any questioning. I swear I removed nothing."

Baley said, "Is there anyone who wishes to suggest at this point that Dr. Thool is lying?"

There was a silence, during which Leebig looked at an object outside of Baley's field of vision and muttered something about the time.

Baley said, "The second possibility is that someone else committed the crime and carried the weapon off with him. But if that were so, one must ask why. Carrying the weapon away is an advertisement of the fact that Mrs. Delmarre was not the murderess. If an outsider were the murderer, he would have to be a complete imbecile not to leave the weapon with the corpse to convict Mrs. Delmarre. Either way, then, *the weapon must be there*! Yet it was not seen."

Attlebish said, "Do you take us for fools or for blind men?"

"I take you for Solarians," said Baley calmly, "and therefore incapable of recognizing the particular weapon that was left at the scene of the crime as a weapon."

"I don't understand a word," muttered Klorissa in distress.

Even Gladia, who had scarcely moved a muscle during the course of the meeting, was staring at Baley in surprise.

Baley said, "Dead husband and unconscious wife were not the only individuals on the scene. There was also a disorganized robot."

"Well?" said Leebig angrily.

"Isn't it obvious, then, that, in having eliminated the impossible, what remains, however improbable, is the truth. The robot at the scene of the crime was the murder weapon, a murder weapon none of you could recognize by force of your training."

They all talked at once; all but Gladia, who simply stared.

Baley raised his arms. "Hold it. Quiet! Let me explain!" And once again he told the story of the attempt on Gruer's life and the method by which it could have been accomplished. This time he added the attempt on his own life at the baby farm.

Leebig said impatiently, "I suppose that was managed by having one robot poison an arrow without knowing it was using poison, and having a second robot hand the poisoned arrow to the boy after telling him that you were an Earthman, without its knowing that the arrow was poisoned."

"Something like that. Both robots would be completely instructed."

"Very farfetched," said Leebig.

Quemot was pale and looked as though he might be sick at any moment. "No Solarian could possibly use robots to harm a human."

"Maybe so," said Baley with a shrug, "but the point is that robots can be so manipulated. Ask Dr. Leebig. He is the roboticist."

Leebig said, "It does not apply to the murder of Dr. Delmarre. I told you that yesterday. How can anyone arrange to have a robot smash a man's skull?"

"Shall I explain how?"

"Do so if you can."

Baley said, "It was a new-model robot that Dr. Delmarre was testing. The significance of that wasn't plain to me until last evening, when I had occasion to say to a robot, in asking for his help in rising out of a chair, 'Give me a hand!' The robot looked at his own hand in confusion as though he thought he was expected to detach it and give it to me. I had to repeat my order less idiomatically. But it reminded me of something Dr. Leebig had told me earlier that day. There was experimentaion among robots with replaceable limbs.

"Suppose this robot that Dr. Delmarre had been testing was one such, capable of using any of a number of interchangeable limbs of various shapes for different kinds of specialized tasks. Suppose the murderer knew this and suddenly said to the robot, 'Give me your arm.' The robot would detach its arm and give it to him. The detached arm would make a splendid weapon. With Dr. Delmarre dead, it could be snapped back into place."

Stunned horror gave way to a babble of objection as Baley talked. His last sentence had to be shouted, and, even so, was all but drowned out.

Attlebish, face flushed, raised himself from his chair and stepped forward. "Even if what you say is so, then Mrs. Delmarre is the murderess. She was there, she quarreled with him, she would be watching her husband working with the robot, and would know of the replaceable-limb situation—which I don't believe, by the way. No matter what you do, Earthman, everything points to her."

Gladia began to weep softly.

Baley did not look at her. He said, "On the contrary, it is easy to show that, whoever committed the murder, Mrs. Delmarre did not."

Jothan Leebig suddenly folded his arms and allowed an expression of contempt to settle on his face.

Baley caught that and said, "You'll help me do so, Dr. Leebig. As a roboticist, you know that maneuvering robots into action such as indirect murder takes enormous skill. I had occasion yesterday to try to put an individual under house arrest. I gave three robots detailed instructions intended to keep this individual safe. It was a simple thing, but I am a clumsy man with robots. There were loopholes in my instructions and my prisoner escaped."

"Who was the prisoner?" demanded Attlebish.

"Beside the point," said Baley impatiently. "What *is* the point is the fact that amateurs can't handle robots well. And some Solarians may be pretty amateurish as Solarians go. For instance, what does Gladia Delmarre know about robotics? . . . Well, Dr. Leebig?"

"What?" The roboticist stared.

"You tried to teach Mrs. Delmarre robotics. What kind of a pupil was she? Did she learn anything?"

Leebig looked about uneasily. "She didn't . . ." and stalled.

"She was completely hopeless, wasn't she? Or would you prefer not to answer?"

Leebig said stiffly, "She might have pretended ignorance."

"Are you prepared to say, as a roboticist, that you think Mrs. Delmarre is sufficiently skilled to drive robots to indirect murder?"

"How can I answer that?"

"Let me put it another way. Whoever tried to have me killed at the baby farm must have had to locate me by using interrobot communications. After all, I told no human where I was going and only the robots who conveyed me from point to point knew of my whereabouts. My partner, Daneel Olivaw, managed to trace me later in the day, but only with considerable difficulty. The murderer, on the other hand, must have done it easily, since, in addition to locating me, he had to arrange for arrow poisoning and arrow shooting, all before I left the farm and moved on. Would Mrs. Delmarre have the skill to do that?"

Corwin Attlebish leaned forward. "Who do you suggest would have the necessary skill, Earthman?"

Baley said, "Dr. Jothan Leebig is self-admittedly the best robot man on the planet."

"Is that an accusation?" cried Leebig.

"Yes!" shouted Baley.

* * *

The fury in Leebig's eyes faded slowly. It was replaced not by calm, exactly, but by a kind of clamped-down tension. He said, "I studied the Delmarre robot after the murder. It had no detachable limbs. At least, they were detachable only in the usual sense of requiring special tools and expert handling. So the robot wasn't the weapon used in killing Delmarre and you have no argument."

Baley said, "Who else can vouch for the truth of your statement?"

"My word is not to be questioned."

"It is here. I'm accusing you, and your unsupported word concerning the robot is valueless. If someone else will bear you out, that would be different. Incidentally, you disposed of that robot quickly. Why?"

"There was no reason to keep it. It was completely disorganized. It was useless."

"Why?"

Leebig shook his finger at Baley and said violently, "You asked me that once before, Earthman, and I told you why. It had witnessed a murder which it had been powerless to stop."

"And you told me that that always brought about complete collapse; that that was a universal rule. Yet when Gruer was poisoned, the robot that had presented him with the poisoned drink was harmed only to the extent of a limp and a lisp. It had actually itself been the agent of what looked like murder at that moment, and not merely a witness, and yet it retained enough sanity to be questioned.

"This robot, the robot in the Delmarre case, must therefore have been still more intimately concerned with murder than the Gruer robot. This Delmarre robot must have had its own arm used as the murder weapon."

"All nonsense," gasped out Leebig. "You know nothing about robotics."

Baley said, "That's as may be. But I will suggest that Security Head Attlebish impound the records of your robot factory and maintenance shop. Perhaps we can find out whether you have built robots with detachable limbs and, if so, whether any were sent to Dr. Delmarre, and, if so, when."

"No one will tamper with my records," cried Leebig.

"Why? If you have nothing to hide, why?"

"But why on Solaria should I want to kill Delmarre? Tell me that. What's my motive?"

"I can think of two," said Baley. "You were friendly with Mrs. Delmarre. Overly friendly. Solarians are human, after a fashion. You never consorted with women, but that didn't keep you immune from, shall we say, animal urges. You saw Mrs. Delmarre—I beg your pardon, you viewed her—when whe was dressed rather informally and——"

"No," cried Leebig in agony.

And Gladia whispered energetically, "No."

"Perhaps you didn't recognize the nature of your feelings yourself," said Baley, "or if you had a dim notion of it, you despised yourself for your weakness, and hated Mrs. Delmarre for inspiring it. And yet you might have hated Delmarre, too, for having her. You did ask Mrs. Delmarre to be your assistant. You compromised with your libido that far. She refused and your hatred was the keener for that. By killing Dr. Delmarre in such a way as to throw suspicion on Mrs. Delmarre, you could be avenged on both at once."

"Who would believe that cheap, melodramatic filth?" demanded Leebig in a hoarse whisper. "Another Earthman, another animal, maybe. No Solarian."

"I don't depend on that motive," said Baley. "I think it was there, unconsciously, but you had a plainer motive, too. Dr. Rikaine Delmarre was in the way of your plans, and had to be removed."

"What plans?" demanded Leebig.

"Your plans aiming at the conquest of the Galaxy, Dr. Leebig," said Baley.

18. A QUESTION IS ANSWERED

"The Earthman is mad," cried Leebig, turning to the others. "Isn't that obvious?"

Some stared at Leebig wordlessly, some at Baley.

Baley gave them no chance to come to decisions. He said, "You know better, Dr. Leebig. Dr. Delmarre was going to break off with you. Mrs. Delmarre thought it was because you wouldn't marry. I don't think so. Dr. Delmarre himself was planning a future in which ectogenesis would be possible and marriage unnecessary. But Dr. Delmarre was working with you; he would know, and guess, more about your work than anyone else. He would know if you were attempting dangerous experiments and he would try to stop you. He hinted about such matters to Agent Gruer, but gave no details, because he was not yet certain of the details. Obviously, you discovered his suspicions and killed him."

"Mad!" said Leebig again. "I will have nothing more to do with this."

But Attlebish interrupted. "Hear him out, Leebig!"

Baley bit his lip to keep from a premature display of satisfaction at the obvious lack of sympathy in the Security Head's voice. He said, "In the same discussion with me in which you mentioned robots with detachable limbs, Dr. Leebig, you mentioned spaceships with built-in positronic brains. You were definitely talking too much then. Was it that you thought I was only an Earthman and incapable of understanding the implications of robotics? Or was it that you had just been threatened with personal presence, had the threat lifted, and were a little delirious with relief? In any case, Dr. Quemot had already told me that the secret

weapon of Solaria against the Outer Worlds was the positronic robot."

Quemot, thus unexpectedly referred to, started violently,
and cried, "I meant——"

"You meant it sociologically, I know. But it gives rise
to thoughts. Consider a spaceship with a built-in positronic
brain as compared to a manned spaceship. A manned spaceship could not use robots in active warfare. A robot could
not destroy humans on enemy spaceships or on enemy worlds.
It would not grasp the distinction between friendly humans
and enemy humans.

"Of course, a robot could be told that the opposing spaceship had no humans aboard. It could be told that it was an
uninhabited planet that was being bombarded. That would
be difficult to manage. A robot could see that its own ship
carried humans; it would know its own world held humans.
It would assume that the same was true of enemy ships and
worlds. It would take a real expert in robotics, such as you,
Dr. Leebig, to handle them properly in that case, and there
are very few such experts.

"But a spaceship that was equipped with its own positronic brain would cheerfully attack any ship it was directed
to attack, it seems to me. It would naturally assume all other
ships were unmanned. A positronic-brained ship could easily be made incapable of receiving messages from enemy
ships that might undeceive it. With its weapons and defenses
under the immediate control of a positronic brain, it would
be more maneuverable than any manned ship. With no room
necessary for crewmen, for supplies, for water or air pur-
ifiers, it could carry more armor, more weapons and be
more invulnerable than any ordinary ship. One ship with a
positronic brain could defeat fleets of ordinary ships. Am I
wrong?"

The last question was shot at Dr. Leebig, who had risen
from his seat and was standing, rigid, almost cataleptic
with—what? Anger? Horror?

There was no answer. No answer could have been heard.
Something tore loose and the others were yelling madly.
Klorissa had the face of a Fury and even Gladia was on her
feet, her small fist beating the air threateningly.

And all had turned on Leebig.

Baley relaxed and closed his eyes. He tried for just a few moments to unknot his muscles, unfreeze his tendons.

It had worked. He had pressed the right button at last. Quemot had made an analogy between the Solarian robots and the Spartan Helots. He said the robots could not revolt so that the Solarians could relax.

But what if some humans threatened to teach the robots how to harm humans; to make them, in other words, capable of revolting?

Would that not be the ultimate crime? On a world such as Solaria would not every last inhabitant turn fiercely against anyone even suspected of making a robot capable of harming a human; on Solaria, where robots outnumbered humans by twenty thousand to one?

Attlebish cried, "You are under arrest. You are absolutely forbidden to touch your books or records until the government has a chance to inspect them——" He went on, almost incoherent, scarcely heard in the pandemonium.

A robot approached Baley. "A message, master, from the master Olivaw."

Baley took the message gravely, turned, and cried, "One moment."

His voice had an almost magical effect. All turned to look at him solemnly and in no face (outside Leebig's frozen glare) was there any sign of anything but the most painful attention to the Earthman.

Baley said, "It is foolish to expect Dr. Leebig to leave his records untouched while waiting for some official to reach them. So even before this interview began, my partner, Daneel Olivaw, left for Dr. Leebig's estate. I have just heard from him. He is on the grounds now and will be with Dr. Leebig in a moment in order that he may be put under restraint."

"*Restraint!*" howled Leebig in an almost animal terror. His eyes widened into staring holes in his head. "Someone coming here?" Personal presence? No! No!" The second "No" was a shriek.

"You will not be harmed," said Baley coldly, "if you co-operate."

"But I won't see him. I can't see him." The roboticist

fell to his knees without seeming aware of the motion. He put his hands together in a desperate clasped gesture of appeal. "What do you want? Do you want a confession? Delmarre's robot had detachable limbs. Yes. Yes. Yes. I arranged Gruer's poisoning. I arranged the arrow meant for you. I even planned the spaceships as you said. I haven't succeeded, but, yes, I planned it. Only keep the man away. Don't let him come. Keep him away!"

He was babbling.

Baley nodded. Another right button. The threat of personal presence would do more to induce confession than any physical torture.

But then, at some noise or movement outside the field of sound or vision of any of the others, Leebig's head twisted and his mouth opened. He lifted a pair of hands, holding something off.

"Away," he begged. "Go away. Don't come. Please don't come. Please——"

He scrambled away on hands and knees, then his hand went suddenly to a pocket in his jacket. It came out with something and moved rapidly to his mouth. Swaying twice, he fell prone.

Baley wanted to cry: You fool, it isn't a human that's approaching; only one of the robots you love.

Daneel Olivaw darted into the field of vision and for a moment stared down at the crumpled figure.

Baley held his breath. If Daneel should realize it was his own pseudo humanity that had killed Leebig, the effect on his First Law-enslaved brain might be drastic.

But Daneel only knelt and his delicate fingers touched Leebig here and there. Then he lifted Leebig's head as though it were infinitely precious to him, cradling it, caressing it.

His beautifully chiseled face stared out at the others and he whispered, "A human is dead!"

Baley was expecting her; she had asked for a last interview; but his eyes widened when she appeared.

He said, "I'm seeing you."

"Yes," said Gladia, "how can you tell?"

"You're wearing gloves."

"Oh." She looked at her hands in confusion. Then, softly, "Do you mind?"

"No, of course not. But why have you decided to see, rather than view?"

"Well"—she smiled weakly—"I've got to get used to it, don't I, Elijah? I mean, if I'm going to Aurora."

"Then it's all arranged?"

"Mr. Olivaw seems to have influence. It's all arranged. I'll never come back."

"Good. You'll be happier, Gladia. I know you will."

"I'm a little afraid."

"I know. It will mean seeing all the time and you won't have all the comforts you had on Solaria. But you'll get used to it and, what's more, you'll forget all the terror you've been through."

"I don't want to forget everything," said Gladia softly.

"You will." Baley looked at the slim girl who stood before him and said, not without a momentary pang, "And you will be married someday, too. Really married, I mean."

"Somehow," she said mournfully, "that doesn't seem so attractive to me—right now."

"You'll change your mind."

And they stood there, looking at each other for a wordless moment.

Gladia said, "I've never thanked you."

Baley said, "It was only my job."

"You'll be going back to Earth now, won't you?"

"Yes."

"I'll never see you again."

"Probably not. But don't feel badly about that. In forty years at most, I'll be dead and you won't look a bit different from the way you do now."

Her face twisted. "Don't say that."

"It's true."

She said rapidly, as though forced to change the subject, "It's all true about Jothan Leebig, you know."

"I know. Other roboticists went over his records and found experiments toward unmanned intelligent spaceships. They also found other robots with replaceable limbs."

Gladia shuddered, "Why did he do such a horrible thing, do you suppose?"

"He was afraid of people. He killed himself to avoid personal presence and he was ready to kill other worlds to make sure that Solaria and its personal-presence taboo would never be touched."

"How could he feel so," she murmured, "when personal presence can be so very——"

Again a silent moment while they faced each other at ten paces.

Then Gladia cried suddenly, "Oh, Elijah, you'll think it abandoned of me."

"Think what abandoned?"

"May I touch you? I'll never see you again, Elijah."

"If you want to."

Step by step, she came closer, her eyes glowing, yet looking apprehensive, too. She stopped three feet away, then slowly, as though in a trance, she began to remove the glove on her right hand.

Baley started a restraining gesture. "Don't be foolish, Gladia."

"I'm not afraid," said Gladia.

Her hand was bare. It trembled as she extended it.

And so did Baley's as he took her hand in his. They remained so for one moment, her hand a shy thing, frightened as it rested in his. He opened his hand and hers escaped, darted suddenly and without warning toward his face until her fingertips rested feather-light upon his cheek for the barest moment.

She said, "Thank you, Elijah. Good-by."

He said, "Good-by, Gladia," and watched her leave.

Even the thought that a ship was waiting to take him back to Earth did not wipe out the sense of loss he felt at that moment.

Undersecretary Albert Minnim's look was intended to be one of prim welcome. "I am glad to see you back on Earth. Your report, of course, arrived before you did and is being studied. You did a good job. The matter will look well in your record."

"Thank you," said Baley. There was no room for further elation in him. Being back on Earth; being safe in the Caves; being in hearing of Jessie's voice (he had spoken to her already) had left him strangely empty.

"However," said Minnim, "your report concerned only the murder investigation. There was another matter we were interested in. May I have a report on that, verbally?"

Baley hesitated and his hand moved automatically toward the inner pocket where the warm comfort of his pipe could once more be found.

Minnim said at once, "You may smoke, Baley."

Baley made of the lighting process a rather drawn-out ritual. He said, "I am not a sociologist."

"Aren't you?" Minnim smiled briefly. "It seems to me we discussed that once. A successful detective must be a good rule-of-thumb sociologist even if he never heard of Hackett's Equation. I think, from your discomfort at the moment, that you have notions concerning the Outer Worlds but aren't sure how it will sound to me?"

"If you put it that way, sir . . . When you ordered me to Solaria, you asked a question; you asked what the weaknesses of the Outer Worlds were. Their strengths were their robots, their low population, their long lives, but what were their weaknesses?"

"Well?"

"I believe I know the weaknesses of the Solarians, sir."

"You can answer my question? Good. Go ahead."

"Their weaknesses, sir, are their robots, their low population, their long lives."

Minnim stared at Baley without any change of expression. His hands worked in jerky finger-drawn designs along the papers on his desk.

He said, "Why do you say that?"

Baley had spent hours organizing his thoughts on the way back from Solaria; had confronted officialdom, in imagination, with balanced, well-reasoned arguments. Now he felt at a loss.

He said, "I'm not sure I can put them clearly."

"No matter. Let me hear. This is first approximation only."

Baley said, "The Solarians have given up something

mankind has had for a million years; something worth more than atomic power, cities, agriculture, tools, fire, everything; because it's something that made everything else possible."

"I don't want to guess, Baley. What is it?"

"The tribe, sir. Co-operation between individuals. Solaria has given it up entirely. It is a world of isolated individuals and the planet's only sociologist is delighted that this is so. That sociologist, by the way, never heard of sociomathematics, because he is inventing his own science. There is no one to teach him, no one to help him, no one to think of something he himself might miss. The only science that really flourishes on Solaria is robotics and there are only a handful of men involved in that, and when it came to an analysis of the interaction of robots and men, they had to call in an Earthman to help.

"Solarian art, sir, is abstract. We have abstract art on Earth as *one* form of art; but on Solaria it is the *only* form. The human touch is gone. The looked-for future is one of ectogenesis and complete isolation from birth."

Minnim said, "It all sounds horrible. But is it harmful?"

"I think so. Without the interplay of human against human, the chief interest in life is gone; most of the intellectual values are gone; most of the reason for living is gone. Viewing is no substitute for seeing. The Solarians, themselves, are conscious that viewing is a long-distance sense.

"And if isolation isn't enough to induce stagnation, there is the matter of their long lives. On Earth, we have a continuous influx of young people who are willing to change because they haven't had time to grow hard-set in their ways. I suppose there's some optimum. A life long enough for real accomplishment and short enough to make way for youth at a rate that's not too slow. On Solaria, the rate *is* too slow."

Minnim still drew patterns with his finger. "Interesting! Interesting!" He looked up, and it was as though a mask had fallen away. There was glee in his eyes. "Plainclothesman, you're a man of penetration."

"Thank you," said Baley stiffly.

"Do you know why I encouraged you to describe your views to me?" He was almost like a little boy, hugging his pleasure. He went on without waiting for an answer. "Your report has already undergone preliminary analysis by our sociologists and I was wondering if you had any idea yourself as to the excellent news for Earth you had brought with you. I see you have."

"But wait," said Baley. "There's more to this."

"There is, indeed," agreed Minnim jubilantly. "Solaria cannot possibly correct its stagnation. It has passed a critical point and their dependence on robots has gone too far. Individual robots can't discipline an individual child, even though discipline may do the child eventual good. The robot can't see past the immediate pain. And robots collectively cannot discipline a planet by allowing its institutions to collapse when the institutions have grown harmful. They can't see past the immediate chaos. So the only end for the Outer Worlds is perpetual stagnation and Earth will be freed of their domination. This new data changes everything. Physical revolt will not even be necessary. Freedom will come of itself."

"Wait," said Baley again, more loudly. "It's only Solaria we're discussing, not any other Outer World."

"It's the same thing. Your Solaria sociologist—Kimot——"

"Quemot, sir."

"Quemot, then. He said, did he not, that the other Outer Worlds were moving in the direction of Solaria?"

"He did, but he knew nothing about the other Outer Worlds first-hand, and he was no sociologist. Not really. I thought I made that clear."

"Our own men will check."

"They'll lack data too. We know nothing about the really big Outer Worlds. Aurora, for instance; Daneel's world. To me, it doesn't seem reasonable to expect them to be anything like Solaria. In fact, there's only one world in the Galaxy which resembles Solaria——"

Minnim was dismissing the subject with a small, happy wave of his neat hand. "Our men will check. I'm sure they will agree with Quemot."

Baley's stare grew somber. If Earth's sociologists were anxious enough for happy news, they would find themselves agreeing with Quemot, at that. Anything could be found in figures if the search were long enough and hard enough and if the proper pieces of information were ignored or over-looked.

He hesitated. Was it best now to speak while he had the ear of a man high in the government or——

He hesitated a trifle too long. Minnim was speaking again, shuffling a few papers and growing more matter-of-fact. "A few minor matters, Plainclothesman, concerning the Delmarre case itself and then you will be free to go. Did you intend to have Leebig commit suicide?"

"I intended to force a confession, sir. I had not anticipated suicide at the approach, ironically, of someone who was only a robot and who would not really be violating the taboo against personal presence. But, frankly, I don't regret his death. He was a dangerous man. It will be a long time before there will be another man who will combine his sickness and his brilliance."

"I agree with that," said Minnim dryly, "and consider his death fortunate, but didn't you consider your danger if the Solarians had stopped to realize that Leebig couldn't possibly have murdered Delmarre?"

Baley took his pipe out of his mouth and said nothing.

"Come, Plainclothesman," said Minnim. "You know he didn't. The murder required personal presence and Leebig would die rather than allow that. He *did* die rather than allow it."

Baley said, "You're right, sir. I counted on the Solarians being too horrified at his misuse of robots to stop to think of that."

"Then who did kill Delmarre?"

Baley said slowly, "If you mean who struck the actual blow, it was the person everyone knew had done so. Gladia Delmarre, the man's wife."

"And you let her go?"

Baley said, "Morally, the responsibility wasn't hers. Leebig knew Gladia quarreled bitterly with her husband, and often. He must have known how furious she could grow in moments of anger. Leebig wanted the death of the husband under circumstances that would incriminate the wife. So he supplied Delmarre with a robot and, I imagine, instructed it with all the skill he possessed to hand Gladia one of its

detachable limbs at the moment of her full fury. With a
weapon on her hand at the crucial moment, she acted in a
temporary black-out before either Delmarre or the robot
could stop her. Gladia was as much Leebig's unwitting
instrument as the robot itself."

Minnim said, "The robot's arm must have been smeared
with blood and matted hair."

"It probably was," said Baley. "but it was Leebig who
took the murder robot in charge. He could easily have instructed any other robots who might have noticed the fact
to forget it. Dr. Thool might have noticed it, but he inspected
only the dead man and the unconscious woman. Leebig's
mistake was to think that guilt would rest so obviously on
Gladia that the matter of the absence of an obvious weapon
at the scene wouldn't save her. Nor could he anticipate that
an Earthman would be called in to help with the investigation."

"So with Leebig dead, you arranged to have Gladia leave
Solaria. Was that to save her in case any Solarians began
thinking about the case?"

Baley shrugged. "She had suffered enough. She had been
victimized by everyone; by her husband, by Leebig, by the
world of Solaria."

Minnim said, "Weren't you bending the law to suit a
personal whim?"

Baley's craggy face grew hard. "It was not a whim. I
was not bound by Solarian law. Earth's interests were par-
amount, and for the sake of those interests, I had to see that
Leebig, the dangerous one, was dealt with. As for Mrs.
Delmarre." He faced Minnim now, and felt himself taking
a crucial step. He *had* to say this. "As for Mrs. Delmarre,
I made her the basis of an experiment."

"What experiment?"

"I wanted to know if she would consent to face a world
where personal presence was permitted and expected. I was
curious to know if she had the courage to face disruption
of habits so deeply settled in her. I was afraid she might
refuse to go; that she might insist on remaining on Solaria,
which was purgatory to her, rather than bring herself to
abandon her distorted Solarian way of life. But she chose

change and I was glad she did, because to me it seemed symbolic. It seemed to open the gates of salvation for *us*."

"For *us*?" said Minnim with energy. "What the devil do you mean?"

"Not for you and me, particularly, sir," said Baley gravely, "but for all mankind. You're wrong about the other Outer Worlds. They have few robots; they permit personal presence; and they have been investigating Solaria. R. Daneel Olivaw was there with me, you know, and he'll bring back a report. There is a danger they may become Solarias someday, but they will probably recognize that danger and work to keep themselves in a reasonable balance and in that way remain the leaders of mankind."

"That is your opinion," said Minnim testily.

"And there's more to it. There *is* one world like Solaria and that's Earth."

Plainclothesman Baley!"

"It's so, sir. We're Solaria inside out. They retreated into isolation from one another. We retreated into isolation from the Galaxy. They are at the dead end of their inviolable estates. We are at the dead end of underground Cities. They're leaders without followers, only robots who can't talk back. We're followers without leaders, only enclosing Cities to keep us safe." Baley's fists clenched.

Minnim disapproved. "Plainclothesman, you have been through an ordeal. You need a rest and you will have one. A month's vacation, full pay, and a promotion at the end of it."

"Thank you, but that's not all I want. I want you to listen. There's only one direction out of our dead end and that's outward, toward Space. There are a million worlds out there and the Spacers own only fifty. They are few and long-lived. We are many and short-lived. We are better suited than they for exploration and colonization. We have population pressure to push us and a rapid turn-over of generation to keep us supplied with the young and reckless. It was our ancestors who colonized the Outer Worlds in the first place."

"Yes, I see—but I'm afraid our time is up."

Baley could feel the other's anxiety to be rid of him and

he remained stolidly in place. He said, "When the original colonization established worlds superior to our own in technology, we escaped by building wombs beneath the ground for ourselves. The Spacers made us feel inferior and we hid from them. That's no answer. To avoid the destructive rhythm of rebellion and suppression, we must *compete* with them, follow them, if we must, lead them, if we can. To do that, we must face the open; we must teach ourselves to face the open. If it is too late to teach ourselves, then we must teach our children. It's vital!"

"You need a rest, Plainclothesman."

Baley said violently, "Listen to me, sir. If the Spacers are strong and we remain as we are, then Earth will be destroyed within a century. That has been computed, as you yourself told me. If the Spacers are really weak and are growing weaker, then we may escape, but who says the Spacers are weak? The Solarians, yes, but that's all we know."

"But——"

"I'm not through. One thing we *can* change, whether the Spacers are weak or strong. We can change the way we are. Let us face the open and we'll never need rebellion. We can spread out into our own crowd of worlds and become Spacers ourselves. If we stay here on Earth, cooped up, then useless and fatal rebellion can't be stopped. It will be all the worse if the people build any false hopes because of supposed Spacer weakness. Go ahead, ask the sociologists. Put my argument to them. And if they're still in doubt, find a way to send me to Aurora. Let me bring back a report on the *real* Spacers, and you'll see what Earth must do."

Minnim nodded. "Yes, yes. Good day, now, Plainclothesman Baley."

Baley left with a feeling of exaltation. He had not expected an open victory over Minnim. Victories over ingrained patterns of thought are not won in a day or a year. But he had seen the look of pensive uncertainty that had crossed Minnim's face and had blotted out, at least for a while, the earlier uncritical joy.

He felt he could see into the future. Minnim would ask the sociologists and one or two of them would be uncertain. They would wonder. They would consult Baley.

Give it one year, thought Baley, one year, and I'll be on my way to Aurora. One generation, and we'll be out in space once more.

Baley stepped onto the northbound Expressway. Soon he would see Jessie. Would *she* understand? And his son, Bentley, now seventeen. When Ben had a seventeen-year-old of his own, would he be standing on some empty world, building a spacious life?

It was a frightening thought. Baley still feared the open. But he no longer feared the fear! It was not something to run from, that fear, but something to fight.

Baley felt as though a touch of madness had come over him. From the very first the open had had its weird attraction over him; from the time in the ground-car when he had tricked Daneel in order to have the top lowered so that he might stand up in the open air.

He had failed to understand then. Daneel thought he was being perverse. Baley himself thought he was facing the open out of professional necessity, to solve a crime. Only on that last evening on Solaria, with the curtain tearing away from the window, did he realize his need to face the open for the open's own sake; for its attraction and its promise of freedom.

There must be millions on Earth who would feel that same urge, if the open were only brought to their attention, if they could be made to take the first step.

He looked about.

The Expressway was speeding on. All about him was artificial light and huge banks of apartments gliding backward and flashing signs and store windows and factories and lights and noise and crowds and more noise and people and people and people...

It was all he had loved, all he had hated and feared to leave, all he had thought he longed for on Solaria.

And it was all strange to him.

He couldn't make himself fit back in.

He had gone out to solve a murder and something had happened to him.

He had told Minnim the Cities were wombs, and so they were. And what was the first thing a man must do before he can be a man? He must be born. He must leave the womb. And once left, it could not be re-entered.

Baley had left the City and could not re-enter. The City was no longer his; the Caves of Steel were alien. This *had* to be. And it would be so for others and Earth would be born again and reach outward.

His heart beat madly and the noise of life about him sank to an unheard murmur.

He remembered his dream on Solaria and he understood it at last. He lifted his head and he could see through all the steel and concrete and humanity above him. He could see the beacon set in space to lure men outward. He could see it shining down. The naked sun!

ABOUT THE AUTHOR

Isaac Asimov was born in the Soviet Union to his great surprise. He moved quickly to correct the situation. When his parents emigrated to the United States, Isaac (three years old at the time) stowed away in their baggage. He has been an American citizen since the age of eight.

Brought up in Brooklyn, and educated in its public schools, he eventually found his way to Columbia University and, over the protests of the school administration, managed to annex a series of degrees in chemistry, up to and including a Ph.D. He then infiltrated Boston University and climbed the academic ladder, ignoring all cries of outrage, until he found himself Professor of Biochemistry.

Meanwhile, at the age of nine, he found the love of his life (in the inanimate sense) when he discovered his first science-fiction magazine. By the time he was eleven, he began to write stories, and at eighteen, he actually worked up the nerve to submit one. It was rejected. After four long months of tribulation and suffering, he sold his first story and, thereafter, he never looked back.

In 1941, when he was twenty-one years old, he wrote the classic short story "Nightfall" and his future was assured. Shortly before that he had begun writing his robot stories, and shortly after that he had begun his Foundation series.

What was left except quantity? At the present time, he has published over 260 books, distributed through every major division of the Dewey system of library classification, and shows no signs of slowing up. He remains as youthful, as lively, and as lovable as ever, and grows more handsome with each year. You can be sure that this is so since he has written this little essay himself and his devotion to absolute objectivity is notorious.

He is married to Janet Jeppson, psychiatrist and writer, has two children by a previous marriage, and lives in New York City.

Always *My* Girl

SAMANTHA CHASE

sourcebooks
casablanca

Published by Sourcebooks Casablanca, an imprint of Sourcebooks, Inc.
P.O. Box 4410, Naperville, Illinois 60567-4410
(630) 961-3900
Fax: (630) 961-2168
www.sourcebooks.com

Printed and bound in Canada.
MBP 10 9 8 7 6 5 4 3 2 1

Also by Samantha Chase

Meet the
Shaughnessy Brothers

Made for Us

"Chase grabs readers by the heartstrings and reels them right into the antics of the lively Shaughnessy family... gratifying and realistic; it's an uncluttered, perfectly paced look at two individuals trying to move forward after tragedy."

—*Publishers Weekly*

"Delightful...heartfelt...classic romance."

—*RT Book Reviews*, 4.5 Stars

"Elegant prose and honest dialogue...a heartwarming story that sizzles with passion."

—*Fresh Fiction*

"A classically styled romance...filled with sweetness, humor, and heartfelt emotion. *Made For Us* is a winner."

—*Long and Short Reviews*

"A beautiful perfection of a read...I will treasure the first Shaughnessy brother forever and can't wait to be a part of the rest of this dynamic family and their love stories."

—*Romancing Life*

Prologue

Twenty-four years ago…

FASTER. *I NEED TO GO FASTER.* THE WORDS WERE A SIMPLE chant in six-year-old Quinn Shaughnessy's mind. Whether it was running, swimming, or riding his bike, nothing felt good unless it was done really fast.

"Quinn Darragh Shaughnessy! You slow that bike down right this minute!" Lillian Shaughnessy watched with a hand over her heart as her young son raced down the block in front of their house. Why couldn't the boy simply do anything at a normal pace?

A minute later, Quinn skidded to a halt in front of his mother. He saw the look on her face and had the good sense to look ashamed. "Sorry, Mom," he said quietly.

"What have I told you about riding so fast?" she prodded gently.

Quinn sighed. He hated when she made him repeat the rules to her. "It's not safe and you won't stand for it."

"And?"

He looked up at her, his blue eyes wide and on the verge of filling with tears. This wasn't a new discussion, and he knew he had been warned that if she caught him riding recklessly again, he'd lose his biking privileges. "But…it wasn't that fast, Mom. Honest."

Looking down at him, she smiled sadly. "You know

the rules, Quinn. You were told to slow it down and you didn't. Now go and put your bike away."

She was about to say more, he noticed, but her focus was on something behind him. Turning around, he saw some people walking toward them from the house next door. They had just moved in and he guessed they were coming over to say hello.

"Hi!" the woman of the family said as she approached Lillian with her hand held out. "I'm Mary Hannigan." They shook hands and then Mary turned to introduce her children. "This is my son, Bobby, and my daughter, Anna."

"It's a pleasure to meet you," Lillian said and then introduced herself. "This is my son Quinn."

"Is he your only one?" Mary asked.

"Oh, heavens no. I have a ten-year-old son, Aidan, and an eight-year-old, Hugh. Quinn here is six, and then I have four-year-old twin boys—Riley and Owen."

"My! That's quite impressive!" Mary said. "Bobby is eight and Anna is six." She smiled at Quinn. "She's the same age as you!"

Quinn had no idea what the lady was smiling about. What difference did it make that some girl was his age? He looked over at Anna and saw she was staring at him with as much disinterest as he was showing her. Whatever. There was no way he was going to play with a girl anyway. Maybe Bobby would want to play.

"Why don't you come inside?" Lillian asked. "I'll introduce Bobby to the older boys. The twins are napping, but they're going to be up soon and I need to get back inside." She started to take a step away before turning back to her young son. "Why don't you put your bike away, Quinn, and show Anna the jungle gym? I bet she'd like to see it."

And with that, he was stuck alone with Anna. She wasn't really dressed like a girly-girl. Her blond hair was in pigtails and she wore a pair of jeans and a T-shirt. Most girls he knew wore dresses and bows in their hair. What was wrong with her? Without a word, he pushed his bike along the driveway and walked toward the house.

"Where are you going?" she asked.

He sighed loudly. "Didn't you hear my mom? I have to put my bike away."

"Oh," she said. "Where's the jungle gym?"

"In the backyard, dummy. Where else?" Girls were dumb. No boy would ever ask such a stupid question.

"Why can't we ride our bikes? My bike is over in our garage. I saw you riding yours up and down the street. You were going really fast."

Quinn stopped in his tracks. "That's why I can't ride my bike. My mom got mad because she says I was riding too fast. But I wasn't."

"Yes you were," Anna corrected. "Really, really fast."

Yeah, girls were dumb. "Look, do you want to see the jungle gym or not?" he snapped.

"I guess." She quietly followed him up the driveway and watched as he put the bike away in the garage and then as he dragged his feet on the way out. "Are you sad 'cause you can't ride your bike anymore?"

"Well…yeah," he said sarcastically. "What's the point in riding a bike if you can't go fast? Now I'm in trouble and I can't ride my bike and my mom will probably stay mad and not let me have any of the cookies she baked today. That's gonna be my punishment."

"What kind of cookies?" Anna asked, her head tilting slightly as she studied him.

"Oatmeal raisin. They're my favorite."

"Oh. We made chocolate chip cookies today. We were going to bring some over but my mom said she wanted to bake a cake for you guys instead."

Quinn's head popped up. "Chocolate chip is my second favorite cookie."

A small smile played across Anna's lips. She looked around as if making sure they were alone before stepping in close and whispering, "We could sneak over to my house and you can have some. You know, since you're going to be punished and not get to have any from your mom."

Maybe girls weren't so dumb. "Really? Won't your mom get mad you went home without her?"

Anna shook her head. "It's only right next door, and we'll be superfast. She won't even know I'm gone. If you want, we can even grab some juice boxes. Then we'll eat out on the jungle gym, okay?"

"But…" Why was he arguing this? Free cookies! "Won't she notice some cookies are missing?"

"Nah, she made, like, a hundred of them. We'll just take a couple each."

For a moment, Quinn wasn't so sure it was a good idea. His mom was already mad at him for racing his bike up and down the street. She'd probably be even madder if she caught him sneaking a snack when he wasn't supposed to.

"C'mon," Anna said excitedly. "I'll race you!"

And in that moment, Quinn Shaughnessy decided girls weren't dumb at all. Especially Anna Hannigan.

Chapter 1

ONE LOOK AT THE MASSIVE BEACH HOUSE HAD QUINN Shaughnessy shaking his head. Why this wedding couldn't just be a normal event—at a hotel—he couldn't understand. It would be easier. It would be more practical.

And it would mean there was a bar on the premises for him to go to and get away from his family for a little while and maybe pick up an attractive woman.

Not that he didn't love his family—he did. But three days with everyone back under one roof was a little more togetherness than he was in the mood for. No matter what the occasion.

Ever since moving out of the family home at eighteen and going to college, Quinn had never looked back. There were the occasional trips home for school breaks, when he was forced to go home and share a room with one of his brothers, but for the most part, he found excuses to stay other places. He enjoyed his space, his freedom, and he'd never felt the need to make excuses about it.

Being one of six kids in a four-bedroom house growing up had been less than a dream. When he went to college—even though he shared a room there with one other guy—living in the dorm felt different. No one was looking over his shoulder or trying to get him into trouble or trying to tell him what to do.

It was like nirvana.

After graduation, he'd lived on his own while on the race-car circuit. When his career came to an end—sooner than he'd anticipated—Quinn still managed to land on his feet. And with a place of his own...rather than having to move back home.

The large house loomed in front of him.

Aidan and Zoe were getting married this weekend, and because Zoe didn't have any family left and Aidan was a private kind of guy, they'd opted for a small, intimate wedding. On the beach. With only the family and a few friends in attendance.

All under one roof.

He cursed under his breath and sighed. It was only one weekend. It was the chant he kept repeating in his brain as he climbed from the car and stretched. Why they had to choose a beach four hours from home when they lived at the beach in North Carolina was beyond him. And to make it worse, they'd chosen a location that wasn't all that far from Hugh's Hilton Head Island resort! They could all have their own rooms at a luxury resort right now, having drinks served to them by the pool instead of...this.

"Clearly, being in love makes you an idiot," he muttered and opened the trunk to grab his luggage.

"You've been here less than five minutes and you're already calling people idiots?" a voice said from behind him. Turning, he saw his brother—the groom—walking toward him with a big, sappy grin on his face.

Quinn straightened. "Not people, just you," he teased.

"Aww...you say the sweetest things," Aidan teased right back before grabbing Quinn in a bear hug. "Glad you made it."

"Like I had a choice."

Aidan sighed good-naturedly. "This makes Zoe happy. So I'm happy."

"You could have picked a place closer to home. Or Hugh's place."

Aidan shook his head. "The resort was beautiful and everything would have been taken care of, but Zoe and I aren't like that. We wanted a place where—"

"You can be in control?" Quinn interjected with a laugh.

Aidan couldn't help but laugh with him. "Something like that. Either way, the house is great—six bedrooms—and we snagged the place next door for the rest of the guests."

"How many people are coming? I thought it was just us."

"No, we couldn't do that. We do have friends we wanted to have here, you know. Some of them had to travel a lot farther than you, so we wanted to have them close by and give them a place to stay."

"Makes sense. So who's on the guest list? Any single friends of Zoe's?" he asked with a lecherous eyebrow waggle.

"Keep your hands to yourself," Aidan chided. "Three of her friends from Arizona are flying in for the weekend. They'll get one of the bedrooms next door. Then Aunt Rose and Uncle Ryan will have one, Uncle John and Aunt JoAnn will have one, the Hannigans will be over there, and Bobby snagged the last bedroom. It's a kiddie space and we've all gotten a good laugh at that one. Can't wait for him to get here and see his reaction."

"Man, that's going to be good," Quinn laughed. "So everyone else is over here? In this house?"

"Yup. It will be like old times."

Quinn groaned. "Oh…good."

"What? What's wrong with that?"

"I'm sure it's not a big deal for you—you get to share a room with Zoe. But I'm going to have to share a room with Riley and Owen. It's like I'm twelve again."

"Actually, you're sharing a room with Dad."

His eyes went wide. "Why?"

"Riley's people didn't want him traveling alone— he's made the news lately with his plans to take an extended break from singing and the press is hounding him. They're sending a bodyguard with him."

"So the bodyguard gets my space in the room?"

Aidan nodded. "So you'll be spooning with Dad."

Quinn groaned even louder. "Oh man, come on! Why me?"

"Because you've always bitched about sharing a room with the twins. Your entire life! So I figured you and Dad would be a better fit. It's only for a couple of nights. You can handle it."

"Dad snores."

"Trust me, bro, so do you. It's like a match made in heaven."

Turning, Quinn picked up his suitcase and slammed the trunk shut. "Screw you. This sucks. Please tell me there's at least some beer in the fridge."

Aidan nodded. "Go around back. Zoe's out by the pool, and she'll give you the grand tour and show you your room—and where the beer is."

"Where are you going?"

"I'm picking up Riley, Owen, and the bodyguard from the airport. They're landing at one of the smaller ones to try and avoid some of the drama and bypass the press."

"Well, just give me a few and I'll go with you."

Aidan shook his head. "It's going to be tight in my car as it is and I have no idea what kind of luggage any of them are bringing. You hang out here and get settled in. Hugh and Aubrey should be arriving in about an hour, and Dad and Darcy shouldn't be too far behind."

"Fine," Quinn grumbled. "I'll stay and be the welcoming committee. Thanks."

"It's that sparkling personality of yours that helped me make the decision." He gave Quinn a friendly pat on the back. "Keep on smiling, sunshine."

Quinn cursed a little more colorfully this time and gave his brother the one-finger salute before turning and heading for the house.

"If this whole situation didn't suck before, it certainly does now." He made his way toward the gate at the side of the house. Aidan said he'd find Zoe back there. Maybe he could convince her to give him a sofa to sleep on rather than sharing a room with his dad.

That held little to no appeal.

Okay, fine, he'd share the room with his father and smile when he was supposed to and be nice to people. It was only three days and there were going to be three single, out-of-town girls here for him to entertain.

Maybe it wasn't going to be such a bad weekend after all.

~~~

"This is how life was meant to be lived."

"You got that right."

"Why don't we live this way?"

"Because we're poor and have to work."

"Oh yeah. I temporarily forgot about that. Thanks for the reality check." Anna Hannigan stretched out on her belly on the chaise lounge by the pool and sighed with happiness. Her best friend was getting married, she had the weekend off, and the sun was shining. Life didn't get much better than this.

"It's what I do," Zoe said from her chaise beside her. "Although, all this sun is going to give me a very freckly look soon."

Anna raised her head and looked at her friend. "You've got on a hat with a brim as wide as a UFO, and we've coated you with enough SPF one million to keep you safe. And, might I add, you're practically in the shade thanks to that giant umbrella."

Zoe sighed. "You have no idea what it's like to be a fair-skinned redhead. I just want to look perfect for tomorrow."

"Zoe, you could be freckly, blotchy, and have no makeup on, and you'd still be stunning."

"Ha! Clearly you have not seen that look on me before. Trust me. It's not pretty. And honestly, neither has Aidan. I'm saving it until after the wedding, when it's too late for him to turn tail and run."

"Good plan." They sat in companionable silence for a few minutes. "I love this."

"The beach?"

"The peace. It's so quiet and relaxing. I just feel all of the tension of the workweek rolling away."

"I thought things would be a little less intense for you since quitting the pub. Real estate isn't quite the same frantic pace."

"No, but it's a different kind of tension. It's all on me now, you know? Before, I collected a paycheck whether the pub was busy or dead. Now, I have to earn a commission and that means getting sales. I'm still settling in to the whole thing."

"Yeah, I know the feeling. Working essentially for yourself is never easy. But you had saved up enough to carry you through all this in the beginning, right? We went over your budget."

"I know and I appreciate you helping me with it." She paused and then looked at Zoe. "Can you keep a secret?"

Zoe nodded.

"Part of me really misses the pub. Maybe…maybe I made a mistake."

"Why would you say that? You just got started. It could just be nerves."

Anna shook her head. "No, it's more than that. You see…I didn't really make the career change for the right reasons."

"Uh-oh…"

"Yeah," Anna sighed. "I…I wasn't getting anywhere. I was meeting the same people and doing the same thing day in and day out. I want what you and Aidan have—to be in a relationship, to be in love, to know that the rest of my life is just getting started and there's a future to it that includes a husband and kids and a happily ever after."

Zoe was quiet for a moment. "Why didn't you tell me any of this before? And you think leaving the pub and going into real estate is going to help you achieve that dream?"

"I don't know." Anna shrugged. "But at least I'm getting out and meeting new people. Everyone who came into the pub has pretty much known me my entire life. I was never going to find my future husband there."

"Maybe you already know him and you just haven't realized it yet."

Anna made a face. "Please. I think I would know by now. It's the same old crowd in there, and they all still look at me like I'm the tomboy they knew in high school. They come in and talk sports with me and want to relive a little of their glory days. It's kind of sad."

"Quinn doesn't do that."

"Yeah, well...maybe not to all of it. Quinn likes to talk about himself, mostly. But at the end of the day, he still sees me as Anna, the girl he grew up with and played baseball with and who kicks his ass at basketball. I'm one of the guys to him."

"Maybe because it's all you let him see."

Anna put her head back down and sighed. "There isn't much more to see. This is who I am."

Zoe started to say something but cut herself off. "I'm going to get something to drink. You want something?"

"Some water would be great."

Standing, Zoe took her oversized hat off and placed it on the back of Anna's head. "Watch this for me, will you?"

Anna laughed. "Sure. Whatever." She wasn't sure why Zoe tossed the hat on her, but it didn't matter—she was too relaxed. Wiggling slightly, she got more comfortable and sighed. This was good.

"Hey, you made it," Zoe said quietly to Quinn as she approached him. "I didn't expect you here so early. I figured we'd have to send out the search party to get you."

"Yeah, well...I decided to skip work today and head down here and see if you needed help with anything."

He looked past Zoe's shoulder and spotted someone lying on one of the chaises.

Zoe followed his gaze. "Well, why don't you come inside? I was just about to grab a couple of bottles of water and then I can show you your room."

Quinn shrugged. "Sure, yeah. Um…is that one of your friends from Arizona? Aidan didn't mention anyone being here yet." He took a couple of steps past Zoe, a grin slowly appearing on his face as he appreciated the curvy, half-naked woman on the chaise. She was wearing a tiny blue bikini and was all tanned limbs.

"Uh…Quinn?" Zoe began.

"You go and grab the drinks. I'll go and introduce myself." He continued to walk.

Rather than do as he suggested, Zoe followed slowly behind him, anxious to watch what was about to unfold.

Quinn sat down on the chaise Zoe had vacated and cleared his throat. "Hey," he said smoothly. "I'm Quinn, Aidan's brother. Zoe's going inside to grab some drinks and I thought I'd come over and—"

Anna turned over, the large, floppy hat falling behind her.

Quinn quickly stood and stumbled and fell backward over Zoe's chaise. "Holy shit! *Anna?*" He slowly came to his feet. "What the hell?"

She shaded her eyes and gave him a sour look before looking over at Zoe. When Zoe started to come forward, Anna held up a hand to stop her. "I got this." Once her friend was gone, she returned her focus to Quinn. "Is there a problem?"

Quinn helplessly looked around and grabbed the

towel from Zoe's chaise and threw it at Anna. "For crying out loud, what are you doing?"

"Um…sunbathing? Lying out? Getting a tan? Really, take your pick."

He straightened the chaise and sat down, but his eyes stayed focused on the ground. "Well, maybe you've had enough sun for today and should…you know…put some clothes on."

A small laugh escaped before she could help it. It would seem she had finally managed to get Quinn Shaughnessy to notice she was a girl. Well…a woman. Great. It only took her being practically naked for it to happen.

When she stayed silent, Quinn lifted his head but kept his eyes firmly on hers. "I'm serious, Anna. You need to go and get dressed."

It was the tone that did it. Anna was used to him being bossy and condescending most of the time—it was who he was—but right now, all of her good humor and thoughts of teasing him went right out the window. "No," she said firmly and made herself more comfortable by rolling over onto her back.

He said her name again. This time it was nearly a growl.

She turned her head and looked at him. "If you have a problem, maybe *you* should go inside. I'm staying right here."

A stream of curses was his immediate response. "Any minute, my brothers are going to be showing up here. Is this how you want them to see you?"

Now she reached for her sunglasses that were tucked away under the chaise and put them on. "They've all seen me in a bathing suit before, Quinn. Why is this such a big deal?"

He stood angrily. "Because it is! This…this isn't a bathing suit," he stammered, waving his arms over her. "This is indecent!"

Zoe came sauntering back over with a huge grin on her face. "I know, isn't it fantastic? Who knew Anna was hiding such a rocking figure under those T-shirts and jeans?" She handed Anna a bottle of water and then a beer to Quinn. "I figured you might appreciate one of these."

Quinn took it from her and opened it, muttering the whole time under his breath about people being stubborn. He took a long pull of his beer before turning to Zoe. "Would you please tell her to go and put something on before everyone gets here? I mean, she's being stubborn."

"Aidan was here with her earlier and everything was fine. I don't think anyone's going to have a problem with her," Zoe said evenly and gently moved Quinn out of her way so she could resume her position on her own chaise. "Can you hand me my hat, Anna?"

"No problem," Anna said sweetly and smiled at Quinn as she picked up the hat and handed it over to Zoe.

Quinn rolled his eyes and looked around for a place to sit. "At least roll back over. Or put on more sunscreen or…something!"

"I just got comfortable, Quinn. Now either be quiet, or go away. Go unpack or watch TV or just…stop being annoying."

"*I'm* annoying?" he asked sarcastically. "I ask for one simple request and I'm the one being annoying." He huffed. "When does your brother get here? I bet he'll back me up on this."

Anna lifted her sunglasses and glared at him. "I wore this exact bathing suit to the beach with Bobby last week. No issues. So why don't you unclench and… again…go away." Putting her sunglasses back in place, she wiggled a little—unnecessarily—and got comfortable. Was that a groan she heard coming from Quinn? She smiled to herself.

"You know, Anna," Zoe began, "it really has been a while since you've put on some sunscreen. You're probably due." Then she picked up her phone and began to furiously type something.

Anna looked at her quizzically.

Zoe nodded while Quinn wasn't looking and then nudged her head in his direction with a thumbs-up. "Yeah. I definitely think it's time. Especially on your back. Your shoulders are getting a little red." More typing.

Anna still wasn't sure what Zoe was up to. "Oh…um. Okay. Can you help me?"

"Sure, let me just grab…" And then her phone rang. "I really need to get this. Quinn? Can you help Anna? I need to take this inside. Wedding stuff." And then she was on her feet and walking away.

If Anna wasn't mistaken, Quinn was actually blushing. "You don't have to help me," she said quickly.

"No, no," he grumbled. "It was my suggestion, so…" He came and stood beside her. "I don't know…roll over or something."

She rolled her eyes and did as he requested. Why was he being such a jerk? And why did it only seem to make him more appealing? Clearly she needed to get her head examined. Or get a boyfriend. Or just get some relief from the sexual frustration that was dominating her life right now.

She'd always been in love with Quinn. Ever since they were kids. She just...*knew*. He was the one for her. Her soul mate. The only problem was Quinn didn't feel the same way. She was his pal. His buddy. There'd never once been anything romantic between them, and if he even suspected how she felt, he'd never let on.

With a sigh, she relaxed back on her belly with her arms folded under her head. And now, even if he did suddenly notice she was a woman, it still didn't make a difference. He was still surly and difficult and not impressed. Rather than making him act a little more charming—like he always was with other girls—her lying there in next to nothing was making him angry, and he tried to clover her up.

Quite the ego boost. *Not*.

And then his hands were on her and...*oh*. Slowly, those big, work-roughened hands started at her ankles and began a journey upward. *Oh my...*

She almost wanted to turn and watch him work. With his sandy-blond hair, blue eyes, and rough hands, he was her every dream. All the Shaughnessys had dark hair except for Quinn. It used to bother him, and by the way he normally wore some sort of hat or beanie, Anna could tell it still did. But he wasn't wearing one now, and with all the sensations he was creating in her, she wanted to roll over and rake her hands through his hair and pull him down toward her.

It was never going to happen, but the imagery kept her smiling while he touched her.

Quinn was completely silent and Anna seemed unable to breathe. She couldn't move, couldn't breathe...she could only feel. And, boy oh boy, was Quinn making her feel. His hands skimmed the backs of her knees, and when they hit her thighs and one finger came close to her bottom, she had to stifle a moan of pleasure.

His hands stopped for a moment as if he realized what he was doing. Anna almost lifted her head to look at him but thought better of it. And then his hands were on her again—this time on the small of her back. And then upward—circling, rubbing, massaging. She wanted to purr.

When they hit her shoulders, his motions seemed to slow as he went into what could only be described as a deep tissue massage. All of the tension from a few minutes ago completely faded away as his hands—those magnificent hands—worked on her. On any given day, Anna was all for a good massage, but this was beyond good. It was almost a religious experience. And this time she couldn't stop herself from purring.

His hands instantly were gone.

She didn't bother to look up. Didn't bother to question it. No good would come of turning around and seeing the look of horror on his face at her reacting the way she just had to him.

Idiot.

Beside her, Quinn cleared his throat and stood, the bottle of sunscreen hitting the ground. "Um…yeah, so… that should do it," he croaked. "You should be good for now. I'm going to go and find Zoe and get settled in. I'll see you later."

Again, Anna didn't bother to respond. The man was clearly running away because she had been foolish enough to let her guard down for a minute. She waited until she heard the sliding doors to the house open and then close before she allowed herself to lift her head and look around.

Out of the corner of her eye, she saw Zoe stepping back outside shaking her head. When she got closer, she said, "What did you do to him?"

"*Me?* Nothing! I just laid here and let him put sunscreen on me. Why?"

Zoe laughed as she sat back down. "He ran in the house as if he were on fire and demanded to know which room was his. I offered to show him, but he was already halfway up the stairs yelling for me to just tell him which one!"

"So weird."

"Tell me about it." Zoe relaxed back in her spot. "So…he didn't say anything to you? Not even while he had his hands all over you?"

Anna glared at her. "Yeah, thanks for that. The only time Quinn ever touches me is to give me a high-five or to punch me in the arm when I beat him at something."

"Ah…so this was the first time he, like…*really* touched you."

"What are you doing, Zoe?" Anna asked wearily. "Why are you stirring up trouble?"

"Because it's so obvious you're into him."

"Well, duh! It's no surprise. We've talked about this. A lot."

"Yeah, we have, but you never do anything about it. I was merely…prodding things along."

"Yeah, well, keep your prodding to yourself. In case you didn't notice, your little attempt failed. Big time. Now I know what it feels like to have his hands all over me, and while I'm sitting here in a puddle of my own drool, he's running and hiding in his room to escape. He couldn't get away fast enough."

"Oh, I don't think I'd count this as a fail, my friend," Zoe said sweetly. "I think you made him nervous. I think we prodded him just enough for the blinders to finally come off."

"What are you talking about? He was horrified. He was massaging my shoulders and I…" Anna paused and cringed. "I moaned."

"Like a sex noise?"

Anna shot her a look. "Yes, like a sex noise. Like a big, loud 'I'm on the verge of an orgasm' sex noise. There. Are you happy?"

Zoe threw he head back and laughed. "Oh my gosh! That's awesome!"

This time Anna twisted and sat up. "How is it awesome? He's going to avoid me like the plague from now on! It's bad enough he only sees me as a friend and now I'll lose that! Dammit, Zoe."

"Okay, hold on. You're freaking out over nothing. I'm telling you, that man just got the shock of his life. When he spotted you over here, he didn't realize it was you, and he was practically salivating."

"Yeah, and it all stopped as soon as he got a look at my face and saw it was me."

"Anna—"

"Forget it," she said and got to her feet. "I can't talk about this anymore. I'm going for a quick dip and then I'm going inside. Maybe *I* need to hide out in my room for a while." And then she took the few steps to the side of the pool and swiftly dived in.

—◦◦◦—

Quinn slammed the door behind him, threw his suitcase on the bed, and then cursed a blue streak. Raking his hands through his hair, he paced the room from one side to the other, unable to see anything except Anna in her tiny bikini. Where did she get off having a body like that?

He cursed again.

Why had he never noticed that about her? He saw her almost every day. Okay, maybe not *every* day, but he'd seen her enough over the course of his life that he should have noticed she had…curves. Lots of them. Stopping, he racked his brain for what he normally saw when he looked at her.

Short blond hair. Brown eyes.

Jeans. T-shirts.

No curves.

"Man, was I way off base there," he muttered. Even now, he could close his eyes and see them, feel them.

Finally taking a moment to look at the room, he groaned. Twin beds, dresser, nightstands, closet. Small. The walls were closing in on him already. At least the beds were long twins. There was no way he and his father would be able to fit in anything smaller and even that was going to be pushing it.

Eyeing his suitcase, he contemplated unpacking but couldn't summon the will to do it. Instead he flopped down on the mattress and closed his eyes.

Big mistake because there she was again. Except now he was horrified to find his hands twitched with the need to touch her again. Her legs had been firm and soft at the same time. He knew Anna had always been athletic—hell, she competed with him in almost every activity and most of the time could kick his ass.

But the things he normally loved on a woman—the small of her back, her grab-able ass—now he noticed on Anna, and it felt...different. Not wrong, exactly, but definitely different. Thank God Zoe was going to have her single friends here this weekend. Quinn had a feeling he was going to need a distraction or he'd end up pouncing on Anna, and he couldn't allow himself to do that. They were friends—*best* friends—and there was no way he was going to ruin that over a great ass.

Or long, tanned legs.

Or... He groaned. The list was now endless. How the hell was he supposed to survive the weekend like this? They were going to be together the entire time and Quinn had no doubt Anna was going to be in his face if he ignored her. No doubt she'd call him out on being a jackass and tell him to grow up. And in any other situation, he'd gladly take it and admit she was right. But now? He had no idea how he was going to look her in the eye without letting his eyes wander and wondering what she was wearing underneath her jeans and T-shirts.

Damn wedding.

Why couldn't he be at work right now? If he were working on a classic car, everything would be right with his world. When he was working on a project, it held his attention from start to finish—no distractions. Sure, he went out and socialized. Hell, he even dated. He was a guy, after all. But it was all superficial—a quick stop at the pub, a quick bite to eat, and some hot sex. But for the next three days, there was nothing but family and...Anna.

He seriously hoped Zoe's friends were hot. It would be a welcome distraction. It would quite possibly be the only thing that would save him from any awkward interactions with Anna. Then at night, he'd have to deal with the other awkward situation—sharing a room with his dad.

A shudder wracked through his body. He knew it was only for three nights, but the only person Quinn wanted to share a room with was Anna. *NO!* Wait… Oh hell. A woman. He only wanted to share a room with a *woman!* Damn Anna and her bikini. Now he was going to have to be even more careful for the rest of the weekend, or it wouldn't only be Anna getting in his face about his behavior. Soon his brothers would be in on it and eventually…Bobby.

Crap. It was no secret there was no love lost between Quinn and Bobby. He wasn't even sure when it started. They were all friends when they were kids, but somewhere along the way—probably around high school or maybe even as early as middle school—Bobby had taken a disliking to Quinn, and that, in turn, had made Quinn dislike Bobby. They'd had more than their share of brawls, but whenever Quinn would come out and say, "What is your problem?" Bobby would just throw his hands up in disgust and walk away.

And it got worse when Bobby became a cop. Not to say he was harassing Quinn, but Quinn knew he got more tickets than the average citizen and it was usually over nothing. You'd think Quinn would just pack it in and set up his business's home base someplace else. But no. Not only did he set up one of his shops in his hometown, but he'd seriously expanded and made it his crowning location.

Idiot.

Okay, so now he was up to three awkward situations on tap for the weekend. Maybe he should just stay in his room and fake being sick or something. Luckily there weren't any medical professionals in the bunch. Riley wouldn't come near him for fear of getting sick and missing out on being with the public. Owen was a bit of a germophobe and would definitely stay away. Darcy would poke her head in just to be nosy, while Hugh wouldn't want to risk getting Aubrey sick. And Aidan…well, it was his wedding, there was no way he'd risk getting sick for his wedding day.

But could he really do it? Just to get a room to himself and not have to face Anna or Bobby? Was he really so completely selfish that he'd risk ruining Aidan and Zoe's weekend?

Maybe.

"No," he growled and sat up. He wasn't a coward. And hiding out implied he was. "I can face all of them and tell them each to go to hell if they have a problem with me." Well, except his dad. There was no way he'd say that to his dad. Ian Shaughnessy was the best dad a guy could ever ask for, and even though Quinn wasn't looking forward to bunking with him, it wasn't an attack on his father.

Just his snoring.

Outside, he heard a couple of car doors slamming. Walking over to the window, he saw Hugh and Aubrey had arrived. Another car pulled in behind them but Quinn didn't recognize it. It wasn't particularly unusual—there were guests coming that he didn't see on a regular basis. For all he knew, it was one of his aunts or uncles, the Hannigans, or even Zoe's friends. It could be…

Wait a minute…

Squinting a little, Quinn leaned closer to the glass and felt an impending sense of doom. Rising from the driver's side door of the second car was Martha Tate. Nothing wrong with that; she was Zoe's boss. She was laughing and smiling, and she waved at Hugh and Aubrey like they were old friends. But she wasn't alone. Stepping out from the passenger side was… Oh dear Lord.

Ian Shaughnessy.

Chapter 2

"No, no, no, no, no, no," Quinn grumbled as he stalked across the room. This was the icing on the cake of a really crappy day. His father didn't drive anywhere with anyone. Hell, only recently had he started socializing with his old friends again, and the only people Quinn ever saw him driving around with were his own kids. Mainly Darcy. But Martha Tate? What the hell?

He took off down the stairs and nearly collided with Anna at the bottom. She had a towel wrapped around her, thankfully. "Whoa, where's the fire?" she said with a nervous laugh.

Quinn was sorely tempted just to step around her and keep going, but he figured Anna might be a little more in the know on this situation than he was because she was so close with Zoe. "Why is my father arriving here in Martha Tate's car?" he asked suspiciously.

Anna instantly looked uncomfortable. "Are they here already? I didn't think—"

"So you knew about this? And you didn't tell me?"

"There really isn't anything to tell. They've had dinner a couple of times, and I knew Martha was coming for the wedding. I guess—"

"When did they have dinner?" he snapped and then took a step away and raked a hand through his already-disheveled hair. "This is crazy!"

"It's really not that big a deal, Quinn," she said evenly. When he finally went to move around her, she placed a firm hand on his arm and stopped him. "What are you doing? You can't go out there like this."

"And why the hell not?"

"Because you're freaking out over nothing. So they drove here together. You're going to look like a crazy person going out there like this."

He seemed to consider what she said. "He was supposed to drive here with Darcy. So…where the hell is Darcy? And why is Martha here now instead?"

At that moment, Zoe walked down the hallway toward them. "Everything okay?"

Anna looked at Quinn and then back to Zoe. "Ian just pulled up with Martha," she said and silently motioned to the look on Quinn's face from behind him. "Quinn wasn't aware of the situation."

"So there is a situation," Quinn interrupted, turning toward Anna.

She rolled her eyes. "Fine. Quinn wasn't aware they were arriving together."

"Oh no," Zoe said. "Neither was I. Martha said she couldn't make it here today. I don't have a room for her. All the bedrooms are taken."

"Maybe Hugh can get her a room at the resort. It's only thirty minutes away and—"

"No. I can't do that to her. We'll have to reconsider everything. Damn it. I hate when people don't follow the plan." And then she was gone, walking away and talking to herself about bedroom assignments.

Anna glared at Quinn. "There. Happy now?"

"Me? What did I do?"

"You upset the bride! Like she doesn't have enough to worry about without you freaking her out!"

"Hey!" he snapped. "In case you haven't noticed, I'm the one who's upset here! Why aren't you going out there and yelling at my dad and Martha for making me upset?"

The laugh came out before she could stop it. "Oh my God. Do you even hear yourself? You're a grown man, Quinn. This isn't a big deal. Now take a deep breath and maybe go out back for a few minutes until everyone comes in. And for the love of it, keep your mouth shut for as long as possible."

"Why—?"

Anna held up a hand to silence him as everyone started to file in. She could feel him bristling beside her and finally leaned back and elbowed him in the ribs. His muffled "*oof*" almost made her smile. Before she could do more than blink, everyone was talking and saying hello and she went from person to person hugging and greeting them.

"I can't believe you beat us here, bro," Hugh said as he shook Quinn's hand. "I thought for sure you'd be one of the last to arrive."

Quinn took the good-natured ribbing with a smile. Hopefully Anna was the only one to notice it was forced and that his eyes kept darting over to his father and Martha.

Deciding to keep things light for a little bit longer, Anna said, "Quinn? Why don't you take Hugh and Aubrey out back and show them the pool and get them a drink?"

He eyed her suspiciously. "I'm sure they can—"

"And see if Zoe needs anything," she quickly added to cut him off. "You know she's feeling a little *frazzled* right now." Anna gave him a stern glare that warned him not to argue, and breathed a sigh of relief when he just nodded and led his brother and his brother's wife through the house.

When she heard the sliding glass doors open and close, she turned to Ian and Martha, who were looking at her oddly. "Okay, here's the thing," she began, her heart racing a little at having to have an awkward discussion with the man who had always been like a second father to her. "Quinn is a little freaked out that the two of you are here together."

Ian's brows rose. "Why?"

"Well…he was expecting you to arrive with Darcy." And then she looked apologetically at Martha. "And I'm afraid Zoe didn't know you were coming today. So she's panicking about where to put you. Room-wise."

The older couple looked at one another nervously and then back at Anna and her stomach sank. *Oh. My. God.* She said a silent prayer she was not going to be forced to stand here and listen to them talk about the new turn in their relationship and how they were hoping to share a room.

So not the discussion she ever wanted to have.

"Actually—" Ian began, unable to look Anna in the eye.

She cut him off before he could go any further. "It's okay. Really. You were supposed to room with Quinn, but I'm sure Zoe can find another spot for him."

"Why was I rooming with Quinn?"

Anna gave him the short version of Riley's situation with the bodyguard and how all of the rooms were filled. "I'm sure Quinn can sleep on one of the sofas or the floor somewhere or maybe with Bobby."

Ian laughed. "Let's hope it doesn't come to that.

Those two will probably try to kill each other by the end of the first night."

The laugh came automatically, but Anna wasn't really feeling it. No doubt she was now going to have to be the bearer of this awkward news.

"Maybe I should find a hotel," Martha said after a long silence.

Ian looked at her apologetically. "I hate to see you do that. Why don't we wait and see how things unfold here?"

"Tell you what," Anna said, interrupting them again, "let me go and talk to Zoe and then we'll deal with Quinn. I'm not sure which room you're in, so just leave your luggage here and go on out back and grab a drink."

"Anna," Ian said, "I appreciate what you're doing, but maybe it would be better if I was the one to deal with Quinn."

It would have been easy to agree, but she had a feeling things would go a lot easier this weekend if she was the one dealing with Quinn's wrath rather than his father. "Let me at least try first. If I need to, I'll let you take over." She walked away before he could stop her.

When Anna was out of sight, Martha turned to Ian. "How long has she been in love with him?"

Ian sighed. "Since forever."

"Any chance of him feeling the same way?"

"I wish I knew."

Quinn's eyes kept darting toward the sliding doors to see if his father was coming outside. He had no idea what he was going to say to him, but he knew he had to say something. What the hell was he doing here with Martha

Tate? Like a couple! And why hadn't he given any of them a heads-up? A warning? Something? Anything?

Beside him, Hugh and Aubrey were talking about how their neighbor was dog-sitting for them. Crap. Who cares? Didn't they realize there were bigger issues to be dealt with than making sure the dogs didn't shit in the house? It was on the tip of his tongue to say something when a movement caught his attention.

Anna.

She stepped out onto the patio—alone—and Quinn knew immediately she was gunning for him. Great. As if he needed her in his face any more today. And why wasn't she dressed yet? The towel was replaced with some sort of white, gauzy cover-up kind of thing and if anything, it was sexier than her just being in the damn bikini.

Closing his eyes, he shook his head. When he opened them, Anna was standing in front of him. "Are you okay?"

All he could do was nod. Quinn was certain if he opened his mouth to speak, he wouldn't be able to control himself and he'd end up not only ranting—loudly—about his father and Martha, but also about Anna and her current wardrobe. Or lack thereof.

"Everything okay?" Hugh asked. He looked at his brother and then at Anna and then back again. Aubrey stepped in close to them as well.

"Quinn's a little upset about your dad and Martha," Anna said quietly.

Hugh sighed. "Yeah. I have to admit it was a bit of a shock, but…" He stopped and shrugged. "He's entitled to have a life too."

"Does he have to have one now?" Quinn hissed. "I

mean…this is a family event! He couldn't find a better time to break the news to us all?"

Hugh looked at him oddly. "Dude, where have you been? They've been dating for a while now. This is hardly news."

Quinn shot an accusing look at Anna. "So everybody knew except me?"

"Well," Hugh began, "I can't say with any great certainty, but—"

"What about Darcy? Does she know? Is she okay with it?" he snapped.

Anna looked between the brothers and stepped in. "Hugh, can you take Aubrey and check out the area we have set up for the dinner tonight and make sure it's all right? I know Zoe would appreciate it."

The couple took their cue and excused themselves, leaving Quinn alone with Anna. She glared at him before taking his hand and dragging him down to the beach. The sand was hot and he was all but fuming by the time they stopped.

"Okay look," she began, "I know you're upset—"

"You don't know the half of it," he countered.

"But," she continued, "you need to understand several things."

"Anna, please don't pretend you understand or that you've got it all figured out, because you don't. This was a crappy time for him to bring Martha around."

"Honestly, it wasn't," she argued. "If you had been paying attention lately—"

"I've been busy!" he yelled. "I've got a new phase of the business going on and that's where my time has been spent. Had I known I was supposed to be sitting around like a gossipy teenager watching my dad, someone should have told me. *You* should have told me," he accused.

"Oh, for crying out loud," she huffed and took several steps away before coming back to him. "It's not my job to keep you up-to-date on your family, Quinn!"

"And yet here you are doing just that."

She gasped and moved away again. It took a moment for Anna to find her voice. "Look, I'm not going to stand here and argue with you. All I'm saying is you need to calm down. This is your brother's wedding. Zoe's stressed out enough, and she and Aidan don't need you starting a fight."

"Oh, I'm not the one who's going to start the fight. I can guarantee when Darcy gets here, she'll—"

"She won't do anything," Anna said bluntly.

Quinn could only stare.

"Who do you think encouraged him to start dating? Who do you think orchestrated their first date? Who do you think is the most excited about maybe having more women in her life?"

"But…no," he said adamantly. "Darcy wouldn't do that. She and my mom…"

Anna's shoulders sagged, her expression growing sad. "Quinn, Darcy doesn't remember your mom," she said softly. "I know we all like to think differently, but the reality is she was a baby when Lillian died. She has no memory of her and it's hard for her to pretend otherwise. It's hard for her to have a connection to someone she doesn't remember." She paused. "It doesn't mean she doesn't love your mom—she does. But it's not the same as the connection you and your brothers had to your mother."

It had been a long time since Quinn had felt over-whelmed with memories of his mother, but right now that was exactly how he felt. He swallowed hard and walked toward the water, not wanting Anna—or any-one—to see him like this.

Sometimes it was easy just to pretend everything was okay, that there wasn't this massive void in his life. And other times—like now—it was hard to ignore. With the scent and sound of the surf all around him, it was as if he were a kid again, on vacation with his family. It had always been their thing—they'd go to Myrtle Beach and spend the week just playing in the sand and the water.

Anna came to stand beside him, and suddenly he was back in the present. His mother wasn't here; they weren't on vacation. And the reality hit him like a punch in the gut.

"I wish Darcy remembered her," he said quietly. "I know Mom loved us all, but she was just over the moon when she had Darcy—finally had a little girl." He took a steadying breath. "I wish Darcy remembered some of Mom's joy."

"So does she," Anna replied before she turned and faced him. "It's not easy for her, Quinn, but you have to know that just because she encourages your father to date, it doesn't lessen her feelings for Lillian."

"I know."

"And you need to realize that just because he is dating, it doesn't mean he doesn't still love your mom. Or that he's forgotten her."

Quinn swallowed hard, his eyes still focused on the waves crashing over the sand. He felt Anna's hand slip into his and he grasped it hard. It was reassuring, soft, comforting. Everything he needed in that moment. They stood like that for several silent minutes before Anna simply leaned in and hugged him.

"You going to be okay?" she asked.

"I don't really have a choice, do I?" The anger from earlier was gone and in its place was quiet acceptance. It wasn't unusual for him to hug Anna, but it was normally in a playful manner. This quiet, intimate embrace was new. Different.

And yet not in a bad way.

"Come on. We should get back up to the house. The rehearsal for the ceremony is in a couple of hours, and then we have the dinner with everyone."

He sighed and released her reluctantly. "I guess I'm going to be relegated to sleeping on the couch now, aren't I?"

Anna chuckled. "I'm sure you can share a room with Bobby."

His laughter matched hers. "Thanks, but I think I'll take my chances with the couch. Your brother would probably smother me in my sleep."

"He's not quite that bad."

Quinn knew a token defense when he heard one. "You have to say that. He's your brother."

"It's only for a couple of nights. It won't be so bad."

"Yeah, yeah, yeah," he said and took her hand in his and together they walked back up to the house.

~~~

The sun was setting, and everyone was milling about, laughing and smiling. The rehearsal had gone smoothly, and now everyone was enjoying an amazing seafood buffet Hugh's resort had catered. Anna couldn't remember the last time she had seen such an incredible display of food.

As she mingled with everyone, her eyes kept straying to Quinn. At that moment, he was standing and talking with Zoe's friend Kathy. Anna had met all the girls earlier, and Kathy had shared that she was three months pregnant. Her husband hadn't come with her, though, due to a work conflict. Pausing, she discreetly watched as Quinn's smile faltered slightly; no doubt he was now finding out all his flirting was for nothing—married woman, baby on the way. He said something and smiled before walking away.

"If you don't watch where you're walking, you'll end up in the pool."

She looked up and found her brother frowning at her. "I was watching where I was going," she said pleasantly even though she was annoyed Bobby had clearly caught her watching Quinn.

"Seriously, Anna, move on. The guy is not worth it."

"I don't know what you're talking about."

Bobby sighed loudly. "Okay, you're far too intelligent to pretend you're not. You were staring at Shaughnessy, and if I noticed it, I'm sure everyone else did too. You need to stop."

Anna felt tension and anger begin to rise in her but she managed to hold her tongue.

"Look, I'm not saying this to be a jerk or anything. I'm saying it because I love you and I don't like seeing you get hurt. Quinn's not the kind of guy you want to get involved with, and trust me when I say he's not the right guy for you."

"And you know this how?" she asked, hoping she sounded bored rather than defensive.

"You've known him almost your entire life. Has he ever even hinted he's interested in you?" He paused but didn't let her answer. "He's a serial dater, Anna. He goes out with a girl once or twice, sleeps with her, and then moves on. You wouldn't be any different. You'd just be one of many. I don't want to see that happen to you. You deserve better."

She rolled her eyes. "Look, let's not go there tonight, okay? It's Aidan and Zoe's party and I don't want to ruin it. Stop hovering and go socialize a little bit."

"Yeah, well…if any of Zoe's friends were single, it would be a lot more fun to socialize. This is basically just a family event." He sighed dramatically. "So my options were either come over here and play the big-brother card or go and kick Quinn's ass."

"Bobby—"

"I know, I know. Hugh already talked to me."

"About what?"

"It's nothing." He grabbed Anna and pulled her into his embrace and gave her a loud, smacking kiss on her head. "Behave yourself and go find someone else to get all moon-eyed over."

"Yikes," she chuckled. "Leave me alone."

"No can do. You're my baby sister and this is my job."

"You're killing me."

"Like I said…my job."

"You need to find something else to do, or I'll tell Mom you're bothering me."

He laughed a little harder. "Eventually you'll have to stop using that as your go-to defense. You're getting too old for it."

"And yet it works like a charm," she teased and gave him a wink before walking away.

Bobby was right—about all of it. She was getting too old to play the tattletale card, and she really did need to get over her stupid crush on Quinn. It wasn't healthy and it wasn't getting her anywhere. Looking around the yard, she saw everything she wanted: love, happiness, and a family. She envied what Aidan and Zoe had— more than she cared to admit. And if she kept on pining away for a man who was never going to be anything more than a friend to her, she was never going to have this for herself.

"A girl can dream," she said softly before walking over and joining her parents who were sitting with Ian and Martha.

———

"It's been very entertaining watching you," Riley Shaughnessy said with a cocky grin.

Quinn glared at him over his beer. "And why is that?"

"Well, it was impressive watching you strike out with all the bridesmaids. Really. I think it has to be some sort of Shaughnessy record. Epic, really."

"Shut up."

"I guess you missed the memo saying they were all married," Riley said with a wicked grin.

"Oh, and you knew this ahead of time?" Quinn snapped.

Riley nodded. "Oh yeah. I got the low-down from Aidan weeks ago. I'm surprised you didn't bother to inquire about it."

"Yeah, well…some of us genuinely have real work to

do and don't have time to think about asking in advance if there are any potential hookups."

Riley's smile faltered a little. "So now I don't work?"

"Shit, Ry, don't start this again."

"No, come on. Tell me how it is I don't have a real job. Please," he said sarcastically.

Quinn sighed loudly. "I'm not doing this here, okay? I don't know what your deal's been for the last six months or so, but trust me when I say we all wish you'd get over it. No one's doubting you or your job or your career, talent, or whatever."

"Your comment a minute ago says otherwise."

"Look, you come over here and start mocking me and I'm not supposed to mock back? Seriously? What the hell?"

"Okay, fine. Let's just drop it." Riley looked around the yard and then gave a low wolf whistle. "Look at little Anna Hannigan. She's grown up all kinds of nice, hasn't she?" he said with a grin. "Hard to believe she's the same tomboy who used to come around and play ball with you."

If Quinn had thought he was angry with his brother a minute ago, it was nothing compared to now.

"I know I saw her at Dad's birthday party, but I don't remember her looking so…hot," Riley said. "And when did she get so curvy?"

It wasn't until Riley went to step toward Anna that Quinn reached out and grabbed him. "Stay away from Anna," he said, his tone so low it was a near growl.

Riley arched a brow at him. "Is there a problem?"

"Right now? Specifically? You."

Riley chuckled. "I don't think so. I find it interesting

how you've spent a large portion of the night hitting on married women—"

"I didn't know they were married!"

"Whatever. But you spent a large portion of the night hitting on them when you've clearly got a thing for our little Anna."

Quinn released him immediately. "I don't have a thing for her...or anyone. You don't know what the hell you're talking about."

"Um, I think I do," Riley teased. "Wow, I can't believe I didn't put it together sooner. Dad's birthday party, tonight... It all makes sense now."

"Ry," Quinn warned.

"So what's the problem? Why are you wasting your time hitting on married bridesmaids?"

"I already told you, I didn't know—"

"No one cares," Riley interrupted. "Why waste your time when you've got a thing for Anna? She's had a crush on you since forever."

"What? What the hell are you talking about?"

"Oh, dude, come on! How could you not know?"

"Anna and I are friends. That's it," Quinn said defensively.

Riley shook his head. "So delusional. Seriously, we all know it. She's been crushing hard on you for years. How could you not have noticed? You can't possibly be that oblivious."

Quinn didn't know what to say. Hadn't Anna accused him of the same thing a few hours ago where his father and his family were concerned? Was it possible he had missed out on the fact that Anna had feelings for him too?

He shook his head. No. It was impossible. If Anna

had feelings for him that were beyond friendship, he would have known. They spent too much time together and he knew everything about her; he knew what she was thinking even before she did. There was no way Anna saw him as anything more than a friend.

Looking across the yard, he spotted her. She was wearing a nearly nude-colored dress that hugged her like a second skin. He couldn't help but frown. For years, Anna had favored jeans and T-shirts. Ever since she left the pub and started working in real estate, she was changing. And he didn't like it. Her clothes…her hair… Clearly he hadn't been paying attention because the woman walking around the yard right now bore little resemblance to the girl he'd grown up with.

In some ways she was the same, but he was beginning to feel like he was losing her—like she was slipping away. And he wouldn't be able to tolerate that.

Anna Hannigan was beginning to make him crazy in ways he'd never fully imagined, and if he didn't get a grip on it soon, Quinn wasn't sure what would happen.

"From the look on your face, I can see this may be brand-new information to you," Riley said from beside him, humor lacing his tone. He clapped a hand on Quinn's shoulder. "Just remember this, big brother—she's a beautiful woman and she's only going to sit around and wait for your dumb ass for so long."

Quinn wanted to argue, but he didn't know what to say. Up until today, he had never even imagined the possibility of him and Anna being anything more than friends. But after the whole bikini incident and now seeing her in that dress…well, he wasn't so sure he'd be able to think of anything but.

But the thought of losing her as his best friend? He wasn't sure he could handle it.

"Fine, stay there and think, Romeo," Riley said with a smile. "I'm going to go over and get reacquainted with the lovely Anna."

It would have been easy to grab his brother by the scruff of his neck and haul him back, but what was the use? There was no way he was going to make a scene in the middle of the party. And knowing Riley, his body-guard would be all over Quinn in the blink of an eye and that would really ruin the party.

With nothing else to do, Quinn walked over and got himself another beer and sat in the corner.

Anna couldn't sleep. The whole night had been a bit weird. Everything suddenly felt different, and for the life of her, she couldn't figure out why. Well, that wasn't completely true—Quinn's behavior was the real reason why. She just wasn't sure what to do about it.

Watching him flirt with Zoe's friends bothered her. But then again, it always bothered her to watch him hit on anything in a skirt. It was almost comical when he realized none of them were single. It seemed like he didn't know what to do with himself—other than glare at Anna.

She was getting pretty tired of Quinn's glare. Like it wasn't bad enough he didn't want her, was never going to see her as anything other than a friend…did he have to give her the kind of look that was pretty much killing her self-confidence too?

It was late and everyone had already gone to bed, but

Anna knew she would only make herself crazy if she tried to force herself to go to sleep. Kicking the blankets off, she stood and decided to go and get some fresh air. Deciding to forgo a change of clothes, she quietly padded out of her room in her oversized T-shirt, down the stairs, and out to the back patio and the pool.

It was so peaceful and the sky was full of stars. There were a couple of small lights on around the pool to help her keep from tripping. At the water's edge, Anna crouched down until she was sitting on the concrete and then lowered her feet into the water. The pool was heated and the water felt good and she let out a small hum of delight. With her palms flat on the ground and her feet slowly swaying in the water, Anna threw her head back and sighed, finally feeling the tension leaving her body.

"It's a little late for a swim, isn't it?"

Dammit. Refusing to move or open her eyes, Anna forced herself to stay put. "I don't plan on swimming. I'm just dunking my feet." Even without looking, she could feel Quinn lowering himself down beside her. The slight splash as his own feet hit the water confirmed it.

"Fine. It's a little late for dunking your feet, isn't it?" he asked and then added, "Why aren't you asleep? It's late."

Anna shrugged, her head still thrown back, eyes closed. "Just couldn't sleep."

Quinn made a noncommittal sound beside her.

"What about you? What are you still doing up?"

"The couch isn't very comfortable," he said, and Anna could tell without even looking that he was pouting.

This time, she did open her eyes to look at him. "So that really happened, huh? I thought maybe you were still going to be sharing the room with your dad."

Now it was his turn to shrug. "Somehow, Zoe managed to move people around, and now Martha's sharing a room with Darcy," he muttered.

"I didn't think... I mean... I just thought..."

"Yeah, yeah, yeah, we all did. Shit." He raked a hand through his hair. "It sort of took us all by surprise. I can't believe he chose this weekend of all times to throw that bit of news at us."

"Maybe he thought it was safer this way."

"What do you mean?" he asked, brows furrowed.

"You know, less chance of anyone arguing with him about it. No one's going to pick a fight if Aidan and Zoe's wedding is tomorrow." She tilted her head back and sighed. "Although it might have been a whole lot less awkward if he and Martha had just stayed at Hugh's resort or something."

"It would be awkward no matter what. I sure as hell don't want to think about my father and Martha sleeping together. Even now it makes me want to stab pointy things into my brain."

Anna chuckled. "Don't be such a baby."

"I'm not," he snapped. "All I'm saying is maybe he could have waited for another time to drop his bombshell. You know, maybe have a little respect for the rest of us."

With a slight turn of her head, Anna gave him a stare. "Do you even hear yourself when you talk?"

Quinn looked at her with utter confusion. "Of course I do. Why?"

She rolled her eyes. "Quinn, your father is a grown man. He has the right to do what he wants—with whomever he wants. He's been alone for a long time. Cut him some slack."

"Slack? *Slack?* What about me? Maybe if he had talked to me—or Aidan or Hugh or…anyone—things wouldn't have been so weird earlier! We had to try and maneuver everyone around, and now I'm sleeping on the damn couch without a room of my own! Everyone else here has a bed to sleep in but me!"

"But you… Wait. I'm confused. If your dad and Martha aren't sharing a room, why are you sleeping on the couch?"

"He pulled me aside earlier and wanted to talk to me about how I reacted when he and Martha arrived," he said with a huff. "I'm pretty sure it would have ended with a birds-and-bees talk and I just couldn't handle it. Plus, he snores." He shook his head slowly. "And now I'm stuck in the living room, with no privacy, sleeping on a couch."

"I thought the couch pulled out into a sofa bed."

"Yeah, it does. And the mattress is about two inches thick and painful as hell to sleep on!"

It was on the tip of her tongue to offer to switch places with him—it was the sort of thing she normally did—but she quickly opted not to. So she shrugged. "It's only for the weekend. Maybe you should just sleep on the floor. You know, grab a sleeping bag and camp out sort of thing."

"What am I? Twelve?"

"Sometimes."

"Ha-ha," he deadpanned and then sighed loudly. "Seriously, Anna, the whole thing is just… I don't know. It feels weird."

And right then and there, the old sympathy was back. Unable to help herself, she reached out and put a hand on his shoulder and gave a small, reassuring squeeze. "Of course it does. And you're not wrong for the way you feel. It was always going to feel weird, Quinn. No matter when Ian started dating again, you and your siblings were always going to feel strange about it. It's been a long time. You've only ever seen your father with your mom. But he's finally getting out and socializing and having a life again. Don't make him feel bad about it."

Quinn was silent for several minutes. "I know you're right," he said quietly. "I just don't know how I'm supposed to act. I'm just… I feel…" He turned and looked at her. "Restless."

Boy oh boy, did she know that feeling well. It was exactly how she'd felt just thirty minutes earlier. A slight breeze blew and she shivered. Quinn moved closer and put his arm around her, and everything inside of Anna melted. If only he were hugging her as a lover rather than a friend. But that wasn't going to change and she had to accept it. Maybe she even needed a reminder of it. So she did the one thing that would certainly do the trick.

"Come on," she said, pulling away and rising to her feet. "I think I saw that *The Fast and the Furious* is on. We can watch it together if you want."

Quinn jumped to his feet. He towered over Anna by a good six to eight inches and he gave her a lopsided grin. "You'd stay up and watch a racing movie with me?"

God, what his grin did to her insides. Her stomach was doing little flips and her pulse kicked up. She willed them both to calm down. "I'm not tired," she said. "And if I get tired, I'll go to bed."

"Yeah, but…you don't really like the whole franchise. You say it all the time," he reminded her.

"I'm figuring it will put me to sleep."

Quinn laughed out loud and pulled her into his arms and gave her a quick hug. "Oh, the sacrifices you're willing to make for a friend," he teased.

Anna held in the sigh that longed to get out. If only he knew the sacrifices she was genuinely making on a daily basis where he was concerned. "And don't you forget it," she said and moved out of his embrace. Stepping around him, she straightened her nightshirt and made sure it was covering her completely before she made her way back toward the house.

"Jesus, Anna…"

She stopped and turned around and noticed Quinn hadn't moved. "What? What's the matter?"

He swallowed hard, his expression unreadable in the dim light.

Anna waited a full minute, and when Quinn didn't answer, she turned and walked into the house, suddenly unsure if staying up and watching a movie with him was really the smartest thing to do.

~~~

It normally took a lot to throw Quinn, but today he had hit his limit. As much as he wanted to keep blaming it on his father and Martha, the fact was that Anna and her curves were wreaking far more havoc on him than anything else.

Just thinking about it made him feel like a colossal jerk. If he'd caught other guys ogling her, he would have kicked their asses. But if he was being honest, he had ogled her a time or two himself. Great, now he was going to have to kick his own ass.

"Quinn? You coming?" Anna called from the doorway.

Shit. With the light from the house shining behind her, he could practically see through the white T-shirt she was wearing. Was she trying to kill him? She probably would if she knew he was checking her out.

It didn't matter what Riley had said earlier. She couldn't think of him as anything more. And really, he couldn't think of her as more either.

Or could he?

Anna called his name again and snapped him out of his wayward thoughts, and Quinn knew he'd have to keep his eyes above her shoulders if he was going to survive watching a movie with her. Like a man walking to his execution, he made his way into the house, locking the sliding doors behind him and shutting off the outside lights.

"Oh no," Anna muttered from the living room.

"What's up?"

"This has got to be the smallest television in the house, and you were right about the bed."

He almost swallowed his own tongue. "Bed?" he croaked.

"Well, yeah. You've got it opened up, so I just figured we were going to sit on it to watch TV, but it really is uncomfortable." She stopped and chewed on her full bottom lip for a minute. "Maybe I can find an extra blanket or two to pad it with." And before he could stop her and say maybe they should just skip the movie, she was on the move and out of sight.

"Damn it," he mumbled. He had completely forgotten about the open bed. It was one thing to sit on the couch and watch a movie; it was another to be on the bed. Looking around, Quinn made a snap decision and quickly folded up the bed and put the sofa back together.

"Hey," Anna said, confusion written all over her face, an extra blanket in her hands as she looked at the now-closed sofa. "Why'd you close it up? I just went to get stuff to make it more comfortable."

Heat crept up his cheeks. "Oh, um…well, I don't think there's enough extra blankets to make this thing even remotely comfortable. At least this way we can sit with the cushions and have real padding."

"Oh. Okay." She looked at the sofa and then at the blanket in her hands. "I'll just leave this out here for you to use later, I guess."

"Yeah. Thanks." Damn. When were things ever this awkward? Oh, that's right. A lot. Especially lately.

They'd missed the first thirty minutes of the movie but it didn't matter; they'd seen it several times already. Quinn did his best to focus on the film, but out of the corner of his eye, he saw Anna slowly slouching down. Her legs—those gloriously bare, silky looking legs—were curled on the couch, her feet almost touching his thighs. He had to fight the urge to reach out and touch her.

"You don't have to stay up, Anna," he said softly.

With her head resting on the armrest, she kept her eyes on the TV. "It's okay. I'm good."

But Quinn knew her. Anna liked to have her head on a pillow. She was a bit fanatical about feeling comfortable, really. Reaching over to the chair beside him, he grabbed a throw pillow and put it on his lap before reaching for her hand.

"What? What's the matter?" she asked, raising her head.

"Come on. I know you're not comfortable." With a little tug, he had her sitting up. Why he didn't just give her the pillow, he couldn't say for certain. It would have been easier—on him at least—if she kept her distance, but right now it was the last thing he wanted.

"It's not a big deal," she protested and then yawned. "I can just—"

He didn't let her finish. He tugged again until she was leaning against him. "Just, you know, get comfortable. We're missing the movie," he added lamely.

Anna's look was hesitant, but she finally shifted and lay down—stretching out beside him with her head on the pillow in his lap. One hand rested on his knee. It felt…right, Quinn thought. Forcing himself to go back to watching the movie, it wasn't until sometime later that he realized Anna was asleep and he was gently playing with her hair.

"I'm totally losing it," he muttered but didn't pull his hand away. The movie was almost over, and once it ended, he'd wake her up. But for now he was going to enjoy how soft her hair was. She was growing it longer—something she hadn't done in a long time. He wasn't sure how he felt about it, but for right now he liked it.

Fifteen minutes later, the movie was over. It was after two in the morning, and he finally felt like he could sleep. His hand drifted from Anna's hair to her shoulder. It felt small under his palm. He gave her a gentle shake. "Anna?" he whispered.

"Mmm," she hummed.

"The movie's over," he said softly. "Come on. You need to go up to bed."

She snuggled up closer, her hand on his knee gently squeezing. "Too comfortable."

He couldn't help but chuckle. It never occurred to him how by making her comfortable, he wouldn't be able to wake her up. Shifting slightly, he maneuvered himself until he could stand up. Anna didn't stir. The first order of business was to stretch. He had been sitting for so long he felt a little stiff and achy. Gazing down at Anna, Quinn forced himself to really look at her.

Her dark blond hair was getting longer and he realized now he preferred it short. The sun had given her skin a golden glow today, and she had a band of freckles across her nose. He knew her face as well as his own. He couldn't remember a time when she hadn't been there with him, for him. Just the thought of her not being his friend caused a tightening in his chest he'd never felt. He'd never had to consider it before.

She was the one constant in his life. Sure, he had his brothers and Darcy, but it was different with Anna. They had simply clicked as kids, and she was the only person he felt truly comfortable around. She didn't judge him— at least not that he was aware of. If she did, she kept it to herself.

Unlike his siblings.

In all honesty, she was his safe spot. His home.

And it killed him how even looking at her now had him thinking about sex rather than getting the comfort he normally did.

"Okay, that's enough," he mumbled and leaned forward to gently shake Anna again. She still didn't stir, so Quinn cursed and then reached for her to pick her up.

Bad idea, he immediately thought. Now he could feel

the silky skin of her legs, and as the T-shirt rode up her body, he saw her plain white cotton panties. And damn if they didn't look sexy as hell too. Images of Anna in her bikini immediately came to mind, and Quinn knew he was going to have to practically sprint to the bedroom and drop her on her bed and run if he was going to survive.

And that's pretty much what he did. Walking quickly up the stairs to Anna's bedroom, he simply deposited her on the bed and pulled the blankets over her before he walked from the room, quietly closing the door behind him.

And then breathed a sigh of relief.

It was going to be a long weekend.

Anna woke up slowly and for a moment forgot where she was or how she'd gotten there. The last thing she remembered was Quinn getting a pillow for her and then tugging her down beside him. They'd never done that before—the whole closeness on the couch thing. So many changes in the last twenty-four hours. It made her head hurt and made her want to pull the blankets over her head and go back to sleep.

The knock on her door was the only thing stopping her.

"Are you awake?" Zoe asked, peeking her head in the doorway.

"Barely."

Stepping inside, Zoe closed the door behind her and sat down on the corner of the bed. "Well, you need to work on it because we have a lot to do and not a lot of time to do it in."

Anna looked at the clock and then back at Zoe. "You realize it's only seven a.m., right?"

Zoe nodded. "Exactly. We should have been up an hour ago. We have the hair and makeup girls coming soon." Then she paused and grinned broadly. "It's my wedding day! Can you believe it?"

Forcing herself to sit up, Anna couldn't help but smile back. "I can totally believe it. What I can't believe is how bad you are at math."

Zoe frowned at her.

"The girls aren't coming until eleven. That's four hours from now. We have plenty of time. What you need is to relax."

"Oh, I'm relaxed. Completely and utterly relaxed," she said, still grinning.

"Yeah, yeah, yeah. You had sex this morning and you're all glowy. Good for you," Anna said as she slumped back against her pillows. "There's no need to brag about it and make the rest of us jealous."

"Rest of you?"

"Okay, fine. Me. No need to make *me* jealous. There. Happy?"

"You're awful grumpy this morning. Didn't you sleep well?"

Anna wanted to argue that she had slept fine—and it was probably because she had fallen asleep against Quinn—but she decided to keep quiet. "It's seven in the morning, Zoe. No one's cheery at this hour."

"I am."

"Yeah, well, it's because you're getting married today. You should be cheery."

And then Zoe's smile fell a little.

"What? What's the matter?" Sitting back up, she reached up and placed a hand on Zoe's arm.

"I just… I wish…"

"Your mom was here," Anna finished for her, and Zoe nodded. "I know, sweetie. And I'm sorry. You know we're all here and we're all your family, but I know it's not quite the same."

"I know I'm so lucky," Zoe began, "and so blessed to have gained such a big family between you and the Shaughnessys, but I can't help but feel a little outnumbered here today."

"You know she's watching over you and smiling down on you today, right?"

Zoe nodded again. "I think she would have loved everyone. I know she would have loved Aidan."

Anna squeezed her arm reassuringly. "Of course she would. He's an easy man to love. You're very lucky."

And then her smile was back. "I am, aren't I?"

It was Anna's turn to nod. "And you're going to make a beautiful bride."

Zoe leaned over and hugged her. "And you're going to make a beautiful maid of honor. Thank you for being here for me."

"I wouldn't have missed it for the world."

They slowly moved apart and got comfortable again. "So," Zoe began, "last night was interesting, don't you think?"

"You mean the whole Ian and Martha thing? Yeah, it was kind of funny watching everyone's reaction."

"Um, no, clueless one," Zoe teased. "I'm talking about Quinn."

"Oh no," Anna mumbled under her breath.

"Come on. You know what I'm talking about. He was trying so hard to stay away from you and make it seem like he was interested in my friends, but he didn't take his eyes off you all night. Hugh had to keep Bobby from going over and punching him!"

"Not again…"

"We were starting to take bets on how long it would take before Bobby snapped, but Hugh put a stop to it. He said it wasn't the time or place for a fight."

"Thank God someone was thinking clearly. I know my brother can be a bit of a hothead where Quinn is concerned."

"Again, clueless." Zoe sighed. "Anna, your brother isn't a hothead simply where Quinn is concerned. He's a hothead where Quinn and *you* are concerned. He doesn't like the way Quinn treats you."

This wasn't new information. Anna just didn't like to think about it. "Well, it really doesn't matter. I'm just glad someone had the good sense to keep things from getting out of hand."

"I know it was a good thing, but still, it's going to happen eventually. You know that, right?"

Unfortunately, she did. No matter how much she tried to pretend it wouldn't, Anna knew her brother too well. He'd always been protective of her—particularly where guys were concerned—but his feelings toward Quinn were completely different. There was rage there, and it really was only a matter of time before he let loose.

With a nod, Anna sighed. "As long as it's not today, I'll be happy."

"You and me both, girl. You and me both."

Chapter 3

"YOU KNOW THIS IS A HAPPY OCCASION, RIGHT?"

Anna's reaction was a simple look of annoyance.

Quinn and Anna were dancing together along with the rest of the family at the reception, and Quinn noticed the teary look on Anna's face. "Look around," he said cheerfully. "Nothing but smiles and happy people. What gives?"

"It was all just so beautiful, and I know Zoe was feeling a bit overwhelmed earlier—missing her mom and all—but watching her now, you'd never know it. She's positively glowing."

"So then why do you look like…?"

"Like what?" she asked defensively.

He shrugged. "I don't know—like you're ready to cry." And then he silently prayed she wasn't going to.

"People cry at weddings all the time."

"Um…yeah. And they also cry at funerals."

Anna rolled her eyes. "Oh, shut up," she sniffed.

This was another new layer—Anna acting all…feminine. She used to laugh and make fun of the kind of girls who cried at movies or just in general. She was tough. She was edgy. The woman in his arms was softer, and it was freaking him out. It was suddenly too much. He had to say something or the dialogue in his head was going to make him crazy.

"You're acting weird lately. What's going on?"

Her gaze immediately snapped to his. "Weird? What are you talking about?"

Great. Why couldn't she just agree with him and read his mind like she normally did? "I don't know…the job, the wardrobe, and now you're all crying and acting like, all girlish."

"In case you haven't noticed, Einstein, I am a girl."

Yeah, he'd noticed. "I get it, Anna, but all these changes, it isn't you. So again, what's going on?"

She sighed, and he knew the sound well. Her posture relaxed slightly as she looked away. "It was just time for a change. I didn't want to work at the pub for the rest of my life, and believe it or not, this is how most women dress and look. I can't sell houses wearing jeans and sneakers, you know," she said.

"Okay, okay, no need to get all snippy. It's just… you're making a lot of changes and I'm not used to it."

"Yeah, well…*get* used to it," she said, but there was little strength behind it.

"Hey," he said softly and waited until she looked at him. "If this is what you want to do with your life, then I'm right there with you. I'll get used to the changes and whatnot. And I'll support whatever it is you want to take on next. You've always been there for me. It's what friends do, right?"

Maybe he was testing her. Maybe he wanted to see if she would react in some way to his reminding her of their status as friends.

Anna smiled. "Yes. It's what friends do."

And dammit, he couldn't read anything in her reaction. It was all just…Anna.

"I'm serious, Anna. I mean, I don't understand why

you feel the need to make all these changes. There wasn't anything wrong with you. But if quitting the pub and selling real estate makes you happy, then…I'm happy."

Was it his imagination, or did she just blush? Or maybe it was wishful thinking.

The music ended, then they were getting corralled for pictures and the moment was gone. And Quinn was left possibly more confused than he already was.

They posed for pictures and everyone ate and danced and celebrated. When the time came for Quinn to give his best man toast, he found, for the first time, he was possibly at a loss for words. He had a basic outline written down for what he wanted to say, but when it was his turn to stand, suddenly none of it seemed right.

"I didn't meet Zoe under the best of circumstances," he began. "She and Aidan weren't speaking. I had to get Darcy home from a job site, and then I needed to get back to work. It was one of those times when there was just way too much going on." There were smiles and nods all around the room. "Anyway, I was kind of proud of myself that I threw the poor girl back into Aidan's path. You see…my brother can be a bit difficult, and he was off pouting, so I threw Zoe right into the lion's den with him." Quinn chuckled. "So I guess you can say they owe their reconciliation and now their marriage to me!"

Everyone laughed and Quinn looked at his brother with a big grin before winking at Zoe. When everyone quieted down, he continued. "When he brought her home for one of our traditional Friday night pizza nights, it was amazing how she instantly fit in. Considering we never really invite anyone to join us for that kind of thing, it was really cool how it just seemed as if Zoe was meant to be there." He paused. "And she was. I'm a firm believer that things happen for a reason, and knowing what I know now about Zoe, there isn't a doubt in my mind that our mom chose her specifically for Aidan and sent her our way."

There was the familiar pang in his heart at thinking of his mom. When he looked over at his brother and his brother's bride, he couldn't help but feel a little bit envious. Maybe someday he'd have what they did. But not right now. He wasn't looking for the whole love, marriage, and all that went with it. There were still so many things Quinn wanted to accomplish with his life and his business, and he didn't want a serious relationship getting in his way.

It was why he had to stop thinking about what Riley had said last night. Anna was his friend and that was the way it should be. Quinn knew he needed Anna to keep his life on an even keel. It wasn't worth losing their friendship—no matter how attractive he suddenly found her or what his family thought about her feelings for him.

The room was fairly silent, and that's when he realized he needed to finish his toast.

Zoe was resting her head on Aidan's shoulder, tears glistening in her eyes. "I wish the two of you a lifetime of happiness." He raised his glass and everyone joined in. Quinn took a long drink of his champagne before setting it back down.

Music started up again and after several songs, he found himself paired back up with Anna. Funny how it kept happening.

"What happened to you up there?" she asked.

"When?"

"During your toast. You sort of zoned out for a minute."

Crap. He wondered if anyone else had noticed. It would be easy to pretend he didn't know what she was talking about, but knowing Anna, she would call bullshit on it. Might as well be honest. Or…almost honest.

"I was thinking about the sudden change in my family."

"What? You mean with Aidan and Hugh both married? And having more women as part of your family?"

He nodded. "Yeah. I mean, I get it with Aidan. He's the homebody type. If ever there was a guy who was the poster child for marriage and kids and the white picket fence, it's him. But Hugh? That one still stumps me."

"Why?"

"He travels all over the world. He was a major player. He had all kinds of beautiful women at his beck and call. The fact that he chose to settle down with just one? It just boggles my mind."

She stiffened in his arms. "Jeez…what in the world, Quinn?"

"What? What did I say?"

"You're a pig, you realize that, right?"

"Me? Why am I a pig?"

"Did it ever occur to you that not everyone wants to just sleep around? That maybe the thought of random hookups isn't appealing?"

"No, actually, it didn't." He smirked.

She made a sound of disgust and almost pulled out of his embrace.

"Anna," he said with just a hint of a whine as he pulled her back in close, "you know me. I never saw the appeal of marriage and kids and mortgages and all that crap. Especially when there are so many options out there."

For a minute, all she could do was stare at him. "So you subscribe to the theory of plenty of fish in the sea, life is like a smorgasbord, blah, blah, blah. Is that what you're saying?"

He nodded. "Sure am. How can you possibly know you've picked the right person to settle down with when there are so many to choose from? I just don't think Hugh should have given up so quickly."

"He didn't give up, you moron! He fell in love! People do it all the time, you know!" She was clearly pissed off and was pulling away again. Quinn knew he needed to calm her down before she started talking any louder and drew attention to them.

He tugged her in close. "Okay, okay, calm down. No need to get all huffy."

"Huffy!" she cried. "What is wrong with you? You can't possibly stand here and tell me you don't see how Hugh and Aubrey are completely in love. You just can't!"

"Sure…for now. What's gonna happen when Hugh goes back to traveling and Aubrey's left behind and some hot chick hits on him, huh? You don't think he's going to wonder about all he's missing?"

"No, I don't! When did you become so cynical? When you fall in love, you don't sit around thinking about what you're missing!"

"Says you."

"Says anyone who's ever been in love! You mean to tell me that in all of the relationships you've had, you've never been in love?" Then she stopped and shook her head. "What am I saying? Of course you haven't."

"No, I haven't, and it's not a crime."

She studied him for a long moment before a small smile played across her face. Quinn knew that look and it kind of freaked him out.

"What are you thinking?" he forced himself to ask.

"I think it would be kind of fun to watch all of those things happen to you."

"All of what?"

The song ended and Anna stepped away from him and started walking back toward her table. Quinn was hot on her heels, and just as she was about to sit down, he placed a hand on her arm and gently spun her around. "All of what? What the hell are you talking about?" he demanded.

"Tell me something…describe your perfect woman."

He swallowed hard because right now the only woman he could picture was her. Needing a moment, he tried to come off as being bored. "Why?"

"Just humor me. Please." She crossed her arms over her coral bridesmaid gown.

With a sigh, he mimicked her pose. "Okay, the perfect woman… She'd be tall, skinny but curvy." He stopped and thought a little more. "Big boobs, the kind of ass that—"

"Okay, stop describing the latest *Playboy* centerfold, perv," she interrupted. "Personality. Let's focus on the kind of personality you look for in a woman."

"I don't look at personality," he said, his tone challenging.

"Fine," she said with a huff. "Here's the thing, Quinn, sooner or later you're going to find a woman who is your ideal—in looks and personality. She'll be someone you're going to want to stick around for more than a night or two, and when it happens, you'll have to eat those words."

"What words?"

"You're such a douche sometimes," she said, shaking her head. "You're going to realize you're no different from your brothers. They found the perfect woman for them."

"Not gonna happen, Anna. There is no perfect woman out there—for me or otherwise."

"So cynical."

"I'm a realist. There is no such thing as perfect," he said with a shrug.

"So if you met a woman who...let's just say... enjoyed racing. It wouldn't mean anything to you?"

He shook his head. "Not particularly."

"What if she enjoyed other sports too—particularly baseball. Then what?"

He thought about it for a minute. "Well, it would be cool, sure. But it wouldn't make her perfect."

"And she could cook."

"Lots of women can cook."

"And she knew how to fix cars."

"Keep talking..."

"And she was independent—not clingy—and preferred burgers and pizza to steak and lobster."

"Does she have a nice ass?" he asked, a smirk on his face.

"Naturally."

"And is she good in bed?"

"Like a goddess," Anna instantly replied.

Quinn took a moment to process it all. "Okay, you

find me *that* woman, and I'll eat my words about Hugh and Aidan and let you do the 'I told you so' dance."

Anna's smile grew. "You're on."

———

For the remainder of the weekend, Anna had to wonder what in the world had gotten into her. Why had she even made that bet with Quinn? She didn't want him to find the perfect woman; she wanted him to find…*her*!

It wasn't until she was driving home that the idea came to her—she was already in the process of making herself over. Why not make herself over into the woman she described to Quinn? She almost squealed with joy. It wouldn't take much. Most of the things she described already fit her to a T. Well, except the car fixing and goddess in bed things, but hey, a girl could learn, right?

For the first time in…forever…Anna honestly felt hope for her and Quinn.

The key to it was not making it too obvious or too easy. No. She needed to become a little less accessible and make him come to her. But how? There were the obvious methods—simply not being available for him like she normally was. That made her laugh. She'd need a backup for the plan. It didn't seem to matter when he called or what he wanted, she usually went running. She was going to need someone who was in on her plan to make sure she stayed strong and in control.

The obvious choice was Zoe. Although she had just left on her honeymoon, Anna made a mental note to get together with her for lunch as soon as she got back. That would give her time to really formulate her plan of action.

"Operation Get Quinn." She chuckled to herself as she drove through town, thankful to almost be home. "Oh, it's going to be perfect!"

Zoe would be the only one who could know what she was doing. To the rest of her friends and family, it would look like she was finally moving on—she'd go on dates that would hopefully make Quinn jealous, and take some classes to make it look as if she was just broadening her horizons. She thought of her brother and their conversation back at the wedding and knew he'd probably be the most excited at her new pastimes.

Then he'd be pissed when he found out she was doing it all to get Quinn.

"Then he won't find out why I'm doing it," she quipped with another laugh and felt as if everything was already falling into place.

When she pulled into her driveway and got out of the car, Anna had a little spring in her step that hadn't been there before.

And it felt pretty damn good.

For the next week, Anna did her research. Community college courses, YouTube videos—you name it, she was using it. Of course, there were some things you couldn't take a class for. Like the sex goddess thing.

I draw the line at taking a class on how to be like that in bed, she told herself. More than once.

The Internet was really quite handy, and she hadn't appreciated all you could learn on it up until now. Over the last several days, Anna had learned to change a flat tire and to do minor maintenance on her car, like changing out windshield wipers and several filters.

It was Saturday, and today's project was learning how to change a spark plug. The first thing she was trying it on was her lawn mower. It was an old one—her father had given it to her when he'd upgraded—and she figured it was a good place to start. Five minutes later, she was done.

"Well, that was a little anticlimactic," she muttered, sitting on the floor of her garage.

The car was a different matter. Unwilling to spend a fortune on a set of tools, Anna had had no choice but to call Bobby and ask to borrow some of his. Luckily, his timing was perfect, and when she looked over her shoulder, he was already pulling into the driveway.

"What's going on, squirt?" he asked as he strolled her way.

"I told you," she began, rising to her feet, "this old car is starting to show its age, and in order for me to be responsible, I need to learn how to do some basic stuff to it."

Bobby rolled his eyes. "That's what you pay a mechanic for."

She rolled her eyes right back at him. "And that's not being very responsible. Come on, Bobby, you know I'm trying to be financially responsible. Some of the stuff this car needs I can probably do myself." Then she showed him the new wiper blades. "And…" she said, popping the hood, "new air filters! Look at me! I'm practically a mechanic!"

Bobby leaned over the engine and looked around. "Not bad. Not bad at all." Then he straightened. "Why the sudden interest in car repair? I mean, I know what you just told me, but this car's been a bit of a nightmare for a while."

She shrugged. "With the new career and all, my schedule isn't what it used to be. I've got student loans to pay off and I'm just trying to save money where I can."

"Dammit, Anna, do you need money? I knew when I moved out things were going to be harder on you and… shit…I should have offered to keep helping you out with some of the bills."

"Oh, for crying out loud," she huffed. "No, I don't need money. Why is it so wrong for me to just want to learn something new that will help me? I can't keep running to you or Quinn whenever I have car trouble."

"You certainly can keep running to Shaughnessy. With everything you do for him, he should be putting a whole new engine in this thing for you! With all the food and the running around for him and—"

"I'm not doing this with you!" she cried in exasperation. "Seriously, I am so tired of having this conversation with you over and over. Quinn is my friend! You have got to get over this…thing you have where he's concerned! I don't get on you about your friends!"

"That's because my friends don't take advantage of me like he does you!" Bobby fired back. "You keep chasing after him, hoping he'll fall in love with you or something. You can stand here all day long and play the 'he's just my friend' card, but you're not only lying to me, you're lying to yourself!"

It really sucked when she was so transparent.

"Look, are you going to help me or not?" Anna said, crossing her arms over her chest.

"Anna, all I'm saying is—"

"Enough with the lectures, Bobby! I'm a grown woman! Jeez, I just need a little help from my brother, so I can be a little more independent. I didn't think it was a bad thing!"

Bobby had the good sense to know when to quit arguing. "You're right. I'm sorry. I really do think it's a good thing for you to know how to take care of yourself and your car. I'd hate to think of you broken down someplace and not knowing what to do."

"Believe me, if I'm broken down someplace, I'll definitely call for help. But the maintenance stuff just seems like a smart place to start."

He stepped closer and wrapped her in a brotherly embrace, kissing her on the forehead. "I'm proud of you, Anna. I know I don't say it enough, but I really am proud of all you're doing with yourself."

She beamed at his praise. "Thank you," she said. "Now, show me what kind of thingamajig helps me get a spark plug out of a fifteen-year-old Honda."

Business was booming for Quinn. The new auto shop had a waiting list of people wanting their cars looked at, and the custom restoration part of the shop was finally coming together. Standing back and looking at the two cars currently sitting in the bays was almost enough to make him giggle like a schoolgirl.

Cars had always been his passion—he loved to drive them; he loved to take them apart and put them back together. His years on the racing circuit with NASCAR had been like a damn dream come true—the cars, the speed, the women. When one of his best friends was killed in a crash, Quinn had walked away from the circuit. Watching Todd's family in the days and weeks following the accident had been a real eye-opener. There was no way he wanted his family to go through something like that—and watching footage of the crash every time they turned on the TV.

Crashes had been an everyday occurrence for so long that Quinn had thought himself desensitized to it. That had changed in the blink of an eye.

Once he retired, he was thankful for having the business sense to have invested his money during his career. True, he'd thought he'd have at least another ten years to keep putting money into it, but it was still enough for him to move on to the next phase of his life in automotive repair and restoration.

His brothers had thought he was crazy. His father had simply asked if he needed a hand getting started. And Anna? Well, she had brought him food at all hours of the day and night because he had refused to stop working in those first few months, and she had always made sure he was taken care of.

Shit. He hadn't allowed himself to think about her much since the wedding. The entire weekend had pretty much messed with him on multiple levels. The whole thing with his dad and Martha still made Quinn want to shudder, but he knew it wasn't something that was going to go away. His father deserved to be happy, and if right now that meant dating Martha Tate, then who was Quinn to try and stop it?

But the whole revelation thing with Anna? It was something that was going to stick for a while. Besides the whole crazy bikini body thing, having his brother tell him Anna had been crushing on him for years? Hell, he still couldn't wrap his brain around it.

The sound of approaching footprints had Quinn looking over his shoulder. A smile soon followed. "Hey! Wasn't expecting to see you around so soon," he said as Aidan walked up and gave him a hug.

"We got back last night, and I was driving through town and saw your car outside and figured I'd stop by and see the new shop. I haven't been in here since before you opened."

"Yeah, I know, and it was really starting to piss me off," Quinn teased.

Aidan looked around the shop and then spotted the two cars, his eyes going wide. "Holy crap," he said with a hint of awe. "Is that…? Are those…?"

Quinn stepped up beside him and placed an arm around his brother's shoulder with a friendly pat. "Yup. You are looking at a 1969 Chevy Camaro and an amazing 1960 Corvette."

Aidan simply stared at the cars for a long moment before turning toward Quinn. "Am I allowed to touch them?"

A loud laugh escaped before Quinn could help himself. "Dude, you can even sit in them."

"Seriously? That's allowed?" he asked even as he walked toward the Corvette. "I don't think I've ever seen one of these up close. How'd you get your hands on one?"

"They belong to a buddy of mine I used to race with. He's a collector, and he's had these two cars in storage for a while and finally decided he wanted to go ahead and restore them."

Aidan gingerly opened the car door and sat down. And sighed. "Oh man...this is incredible. It almost seems a shame to do anything to it."

Quinn chuckled. "Yeah, I used to think of it like that too, but Jake wants to be able to take them out once in a while. Personally, I'm all for it. Cars are meant to be driven and enjoyed—not just looked at."

"So what are you going to do to them?"

Walking around each of the cars, Quinn allowed himself to get a little lost in the details. "Both of their engines are in fair condition, so we're going to take them out, clean them, and replace whatever needs replacing. The Camaro has a fair amount of rust, so we're going to be sanding the body down and setting it right and then repainting. New tires for each of them. Replacing the vinyl on the interior of the Corvette and the entire backseat in the Camaro."

"Damn. That's a lot of work, Quinn."

"And that's only the half of it."

"No!" Aidan cried, climbing from the car and walking over to the other.

Quinn nodded. "There's a lot to it. Each car will almost be completely pulled apart then and put back together to make sure everything is pristine—the wiring, the fuel system, the exhaust...everything."

"What's your timeline on something like this?"

"It's not a quick turnaround if that's what you're thinking."

Aidan shook his head. "No, I'm serious. You've never done the restoration around here, close to home, so I have no idea."

"At minimum? You're looking at a thousand hours

per car at least. And that's if there aren't any surprises, complications, or mishaps. The average car collector—if he was doing it on his own—could take up to two years to complete a job like this on one car."

"Holy crap."

Quinn nodded again. "Exactly. I'm going to go a little in between and figure about fifteen hundred man hours per car."

Aidan chuckled. "Good thing your friend isn't in a rush."

"That's the beauty of working with a fellow car enthusiast. They know the importance of doing things right. If he gives me the time now, he'll get all the time he wants out of the car when I'm done."

Aidan stopped and thought for a moment. "You said this guy's name is Jake?"

"Yeah."

"You mean Jake Tanner? *The* Jake Tanner?"

Quinn rolled his eyes. "Yes, Jake Tanner. Why? Got a man crush on him?"

Aidan let out a bark of laughter. "Cute, but no. I just remember he was an amazing driver. I used to follow him when you were racing."

"Oh yeah? Then you know that I ranked higher," Quinn said a bit defensively.

"Easy there, baby girl. No one's saying he was better than you. I was merely pointing out that I was a fan."

"Yeah, well…you were supposed to be cheering for me. Not following and cheering other racers."

Aidan ran a hand gently over the Camaro's hood. "Insecure much? What's going on in this family? First Riley, now you?"

"I'm not insecure. I just didn't realize you followed anyone else in racing other than me. And as for Riley, who knows? I'm sure it's hard for him. There are new bands coming out every day. There's constant competition and he's having to prove himself on a daily basis. Anyone would get freaked out from time to time if they had to live like that."

"I guess." Stepping away from the car, Aidan sighed. "Where were cars like this when we were kids?"

"Out of our price range."

"Oh yeah. That's right." Aidan laughed and then straightened and looked at his brother. "So things are going well?"

"Absolutely. I didn't think I'd enjoy sticking around town for so long, but it's really not so bad."

"I never understood your need to move around so much."

"Yeah, well, you're a homebody. No one else in the family is, other than Dad."

A small shrug was Aidan's only reply.

"And now that I've got these babies here, I'll be around even longer," Quinn continued. "I promised Jake I'd be the one to do the bulk of the work."

"Is that smart for you? I mean, you have other shops to manage."

"It's not a big deal. I have a great team of mechanics and managers. I'll still go and spend some time at each of them, just not the extended amount I was doing before."

"You've done other restorations before. Why is this one such a big deal?"

"The other cars weren't nearly as impressive as these—at least not to me. I've done cars from the thirties

and onward, but the muscle cars? Those are my favor-
ites. And to have two of them here?" He sighed dramatically. "It's almost enough to give me a hard-on."

"Grow up."

Then Quinn's teasing grin faded. "If I get these cars
right, besides making a boatload of money on them, it
will go a long way in cementing my name in the industry. There are still a lot of people who think this is just
a hobby for me and that I don't take it seriously. I really
need to get everyone to see how I love what I do and
I'm good at it."

Aidan nodded. "I get it. And you'll get there, Quinn.
You do great work and it's going to speak volumes."

"I don't know. So many things have come easily to
me, and this is the first time in my life I'm having to
really prove myself. Car restoration isn't a quick turnaround. It's not like racing or baseball, where I could
have a good season and make the news. I just...I didn't
think it would be so hard."

"It's not a bad thing, you know. Having to work a
little harder. Makes you appreciate it all the more."

"Yeah, well, I'm not getting any younger."

Aidan laughed. "Or prettier."

"Shut up," Quinn said and walked over to the cooler
he kept in the corner and grabbed a couple bottles of
soda, handing one to Aidan. "Anyway...what about
you? How's married life?"

Aidan broke out in a sappy grin. "Loving it."

"Figures." He was about to say more when his cell
phone rang. He motioned to his brother to give him a
minute before answering it. He listened intently and then
said, "Sounds good. See you in a few minutes."

"Everything okay?" Aidan asked.

"Yeah, but you may want to take a minute and prepare yourself."

"Oh, really? Why is that?"

"Because that was Jake and he's on his way here."

"What?" Aidan cried. "Now?"

Quinn rolled his eyes. "Yup, so you better go fix your hair and make yourself pretty."

"Screw you."

But as Aidan walked off, all Quinn could do was laugh.

—⁓—

Clearly, Anna was a glutton for punishment. She had just finished showing a house and was on her way home. This particular route took her past Quinn's shop. She hadn't seen or talked to him since the wedding and… well…she missed him. It wasn't unusual for them to go a week without seeing or talking to one another, but right now she just really wanted to see him.

Pulling into the parking lot, she noticed Aidan's car and smiled. It was on her mind to give Zoe a call and now she knew for certain they were back from their honeymoon.

Waving to one of the mechanics, she was immediately told—without asking—that Quinn was over in the restoration building. It was separate from the main shop, out back with its own office and setup. She knew why Quinn set it up that way, and she was excited because if he was back there, it meant he had some new cars to restore. She was almost giddy at the thought of what kind they might be.

Letting herself in, she immediately heard the loud

male laughter and knew both Quinn and Aidan were there. A minute later, she heard a voice she'd never heard before. As she stepped into the bay area, Aidan spotted her first.

"Anna!" He walked toward her, his arms open wide. "How are you?" He hugged her and kissed her on the cheek. "Have you spoken to Zoe yet? I know she was dying to tell you all about the trip."

She hugged him back. "As soon as I saw your car, I made a mental note to give her a call when I get home." She stepped back and smiled. "Was it wonderful?"

His grin was the only answer she needed.

"So what brings you here?" he asked.

"I was driving by and thought I'd stop in and say hello." Aidan was looking at her a little funny until Anna started to squirm. "What? What's wrong?" She looked down at her outfit and wondered if she'd spilled something on herself.

"I still can't get used to seeing you in career-woman mode. I miss the girl in the blue jeans who makes the world's greatest burgers."

Anna blushed. "I'm still the same girl, Aidan," she said shyly. "But sometimes a girl has to grow up." She was saved from saying anything else when Quinn walked over with a guy she didn't recognize.

"Hey, Anna," Quinn said with a smile that didn't quite reach his eyes.

"Hey," she said, forcing her own smile while checking out the attractive guy standing beside him. Without waiting for an introduction, she held her hand out. "Hi, I'm Anna. I'm a friend of Aidan and Quinn's."

Mr. Tall, Dark, and Muscular gave her a sexy smile

and took her hand in his. "Nice to meet you. I'm Jake. Also a friend of Quinn's."

"Really?" she said, her smile growing until her cheeks hurt. "Then how come we haven't met before?"

Jake stepped in closer, shouldering Quinn out of the way. "I have no idea. I used to race cars with Quinn. We met on the circuit." He still hadn't let go of her hand. "Do you follow racing, Anna?"

For a minute she almost wanted to pinch herself. Here was an incredibly attractive man—almost too good-looking for his own good—practically flirting with her, and she hadn't had to lift a finger. Aidan was grinning and Quinn looked ready to spit nails. It was almost as if she had scripted the moment herself!

"Oh, I follow all kinds of sports, Jake." She quickly racked her brain for racing stats until she remembered something about Jake's. "You used to drive a Chevy, right? Number thirty-four?"

His smile grew and his grip on her hand tightened before his thumb began to stroke her wrist. "That's right, darlin'," he drawled. "I had a lot of good luck with that car." Then he leaned in close. "And in Quinn's last season, I beat him by twenty points."

"It was *two*, Jake," Quinn corrected. "Two. Not twenty. Every time you tell that story, you embellish."

Jake stepped back and finally released Anna's hand. "So what is a lovely woman like you doing in a dirty garage like this?" he asked.

Before she could answer, Quinn spoke. "Dude, what the hell? It's a brand-new shop and it's just Anna. She's been in my shops before."

Anna shot him an annoyed look. "Oh, I don't mind

coming to the shop. It's not a big deal. A little engine grease and some exhaust fumes don't bother me. I actually do some work on my own car."

"Since when?" Quinn demanded.

She ignored him and focused on Jake. "Of course, I don't drive anything like these cars." Looking over at the classic cars, she sighed. "Those are real beauties. Whoever owns them is really lucky."

Quinn groaned, Aidan chuckled, and Jake stepped forward and wrapped his arm around Anna's shoulders. "It just so happens I own them."

"No!" she cried.

He nodded. "I sure do." Then he led her over to them, leaving Quinn and Aidan behind.

It took a full minute before Quinn could find his voice. "What the hell just happened here?"

Aidan was practically wiping tears from his eyes from laughter. "I think your friend just swooped in here and swept Anna off her feet."

"No," Quinn said firmly, defiantly. "No way. Anna doesn't go for that type."

"What? The tall, dark, good-looking, and successful type?" Aidan teased.

Quinn glared at him. "Are we talking her type or yours?" He shook his head in disgust. "Anna is not impressed with that kind of stuff. She's been around drivers before and it never made a difference."

"I'm sure there's a big difference between the way they treat someone they meet while on the track and off." He nodded in Jake and Anna's direction. "There's no distractions here, and if you ask me, she definitely seemed...impressed."

Quinn shook his head. "Uh-uh. No way. She's just being nice. There's no way Anna would go out with a guy like Jake."

"How much you wanna bet?"

Just then, Anna let out a very feminine giggle that echoed off the shop's walls. And suddenly, Quinn wasn't so sure about anything.

Chapter 4

"LOOK AT YOU...ALL GLOWY."

"I know."

"How were the Mayan ruins?"

"I have no idea."

"How were the beaches?"

"Not a clue."

Anna sighed and threw her head back in disgust. "You know, it's as if this were the first time you and Aidan had sex! You went to Mexico for a week, and you're telling me you didn't leave the room?"

Zoe giggled. "I know it sounds crazy, but...we had our own little villa and just enjoyed staying in our cocoon."

"Unbelievable."

"Don't be hatin'," Zoe said, standing and going to the kitchen to get them each another drink. "The thought of playing tourist just wasn't appealing."

"Okay, let's just leave it at that. I don't need to know all the details of what the two of you were doing in your cocoon."

"Don't worry. I wasn't going to share."

"Thank you."

Sitting back down on the sofa, Zoe curled her legs up under her. "So what about you? What's been going on this last week? Aidan said he saw you yesterday at Quinn's shop."

"Yeah, I was just driving by and decided to stop and say hello."

"Uh-huh. Right."

"What? I did!"

Zoe gave an exaggerated wink. "Okay. I also heard there was a very good-looking race-car driver there who seemed a little smitten with you."

"Did Aidan honestly describe Jake as good-looking and use the word *smitten*?"

"Okay, maybe I'm putting my own spin on it but the results are the same. So? Spill it! Did he ask you out?"

Anna nodded. "Well, he wanted to take me to dinner last night but I turned him down."

"But…why? Did you already have plans?"

"No…not exactly."

"Okay, now you really have to spill it. I know that look on your face. You're up to something."

Anna explained her plan to get Quinn to notice her. "So you see, it's perfect. Here's this amazing guy and I didn't have to do a thing!"

"Um, I hate to point out the obvious, but the only way to make Quinn jealous because you're out with some guy is to actually go *out* with said guy. You just said you didn't."

"No, but I will. He called me last night just to talk, and then again today."

Zoe let out a little squeal. "Anna, that's great! So when are you going out? Tonight? Where is he taking you?"

"Yeah…um…no. We're not going out tonight either."

Zoe sagged in her seat. "Okay, you've lost me. Why aren't you going out with him?"

"I don't know. I can't seem to get excited about

saying yes. I figure with a guy like him, it's all about the ego. He's going to keep calling until I say yes. So maybe by next weekend, I'll finally be able to make myself go."

"Maybe this isn't such a good idea. Why would you want to go out with someone you clearly don't have any interest in?"

"No one else is asking me out!" she cried. "Do you think I like this? Do you think I like sitting around pining for a guy who has zero interest in me?"

"Oh, sweetie," Zoe began, "I know it's hard and I'm sorry. I just don't want to see you do something you really don't want to just because you think it *might* make Quinn sit up and take notice. You know there's no guarantee of that, right?"

Unfortunately, Anna refused to think that way. At least she had until just that minute. "I guess I thought if I made myself into his perfect woman…"

Reaching out, Zoe put her hand on top of Anna's and squeezed. "If he doesn't love you for who you are, then you need to move on. It will never work if you're trying to be someone you're not."

"I have to admit, I started doing the online stuff and researching car repairs as a way to impress Quinn, but as it turns out, it's not so bad." She shrugged. "It's a lot like cooking—with the right tools, you can do almost anything."

Zoe gave her a small smile. "You need to be doing these things for you. You should be choosing classes and hobbies based on your interests, not Quinn's."

"I have another two weeks of the auto-mechanic thing, so—"

"Anna."

The reality of the whole situation was finally starting to sink in. Zoe wasn't saying anything Anna hadn't heard before—from her parents, her brother, and, if she were honest, herself. Looking up at Zoe, tears filled her eyes. "I just don't know how to move on. He's been such a huge part of my life for so damn long and I've been in love with him almost since the beginning. How do I just stop?"

"I wish I knew, Anna. I really do. Maybe you need to, you know, step away from the situation for a while and try dating."

"I guess I can still go out with Jake."

Zoe shook her head. "I don't think it's a good idea."

"Why not?"

"It's still too close. No doubt Quinn's name will come up in conversation, and that's just going to keep you in this place. That's the last thing you need."

"I don't know. Maybe. But I have a feeling I'm not going to quit hearing from him until I at least meet him for a drink or dinner."

Zoe frowned. "Okay. So go for something short, like a drink, and then tell him you're not interested. Hopefully he'll take you at your word and move on."

Now Anna sagged down on the sofa. "Why does this have to be so damn hard? Why can't I just meet someone and fall in love and be happy?"

Once again, Zoe squeezed her hand. "Because you keep putting yourself in Quinn's path. You need to make a clean break—no stopping by the shop, no baking cookies or bringing him food…none of it."

"Damn. How am I supposed to do that?"

"Cold turkey. Trust me. I think it's the only way."

"But—"

"Go on the date with Jake. Maybe go out with your new coworkers and see if you like anyone there. Just… no Shaughnessys."

"But you're a Shaughnessy," Anna said with a slight pout.

"Okay, let me clarify—no *Quinn* Shaughnessy. Deal?"

It pained her to do it, but she agreed. "Deal."

—⁘—

Ten minutes into her date with Jake, Anna was already regretting it. On the surface, Jake Tanner was the complete package. After a little while, however, she began to realize he was also a complete tool.

The man talked about nothing but himself. His career. His cars. His conquests—yes, the man even talked about all the women who threw themselves at him. Anna knew she certainly wasn't going to be one of them. Jake had pursued her. Relentlessly. Since she'd talked to Zoe, he'd continued to call every day until she said yes.

It wasn't as if Anna was a stranger to dating. She had an okay dating life, even with her stupid crush on Quinn, but this date was definitely one of her worst. Looking around the bar he had suggested they meet at, Anna wondered if the bathroom window was big enough for her to climb out of.

Jake had gone to the bar to get their drinks, and when Anna saw him heading back toward her, she thought she was going to be sick.

Placing the drink down in front of her, Jake sat down

and smiled. "So tell me, Anna, how do you like selling real estate?"

Wow. A question about her. Color her surprised. "You know, it's not so bad. I've only been doing it for about six months."

"And what did you do before that?"

"I managed a pub in town," she said and noticed the bored look on Jake's face. "I started out waitressing and tending bar every now and again, but then took over managing it and even did most of the cooking."

"Great," he said, but his eyes didn't meet hers. He nodded toward her drink. "You should try it. See if you like it."

She looked at him oddly. "It's just a Malibu and pineapple. They're pretty hard to screw up."

He gave her a weak smile. "Is there a big housing market here? I mean, it's a pretty small town. Do you have to travel a lot to get listings?"

And we're back to me. Impressive. "I do have several listings in surrounding towns, but there are plenty of vacation rentals here that keep me busy, and I'm branching out into the commercial sector."

"Really? Like what? Shopping centers?"

She shook her head. "Right now I'm working on a project for a large resort. The property was originally zoned for a subdivision, but it fell through—before I started working in the industry—and now we're looking to build a luxury resort on the land."

"Very nice."

They were quiet for a minute and Anna realized she should probably ask something about his life. Again. Not that she really wanted to know, but clearly he didn't engage in conversation unless it was about him.

"So…what have you been doing since you retired from racing?" Clearly it was the right thing to ask because he immediately started talking. Taking a sip of her drink, Anna looked around the bar and wished someone she knew would come in and save her. It would be rude of her to just get up and say she wanted to leave and that she had no interest in seeing him again. One drink. She'd have this one drink and then tell him.

"…I have a vacation home in Maui I love to visit…"

Her head felt funny. She looked at Jake and could see his lips moving but couldn't quite focus on what he was saying. The music and voices around her suddenly seemed like one long hum.

"…my private jet can get us there in a couple of hours if you'd like…"

"Excuse me," Anna forced herself to say, and before Jake could say another word, she ran for the ladies' room, certain she was going to be sick.

Once she was safely ensconced in a stall, she fished in her purse for her phone. The screen was blurry, and she did her best to get her eyes to focus and find Bobby's number. She hit "call," and it went directly to voice mail. "Damn," she muttered and scrolled again, hitting "call" and praying someone would answer.

———~~~———

"I'm telling you, Zoe, if my brother hadn't found you first, I would have married you."

Zoe laughed out loud. "Good one, Quinn, but I highly doubt it."

"It's true!" he said, slapping his hand on the dining

room table for emphasis. "Your cooking is amazing. Can I have dinner with you guys every night?"

"See?" Aidan said. "The way to a man's heart truly is through his stomach."

"Leave my brother," Quinn said, his blue eyes big and pleading. "We can run away together. I'll get us a house with the world's biggest kitchen."

Tears of laughter streamed down Zoe's cheeks. "As flattering as it is that you only want me for my mastery of Irish cuisine, I'm afraid I'll have to pass"—she walked over and kissed Aidan soundly on the lips—"because your brother here owns my heart."

"Well damn," Quinn said with a pout. "All of the good ones are taken."

Zoe was just about to speak when her cell phone rang. "Excuse me," she said with a smile as she picked up the phone.

"Uh-oh, this can't be good if you're calling me already," she said as a greeting. "Are you home or on your way there?"

"Z...Zoe?" Anna's voice was small and weak.

"Anna? Sweetie, what's the matter? Are you all right?" Both Aidan and Quinn stopped talking and turned toward Zoe.

"I...I don't feel right."

"Did you eat something bad? Are you sick?"

"Drink," she said. "Only one sip."

"Did you watch the bartender? Do you think something's wrong with the drink?"

"Jake...gone for a while. He got the drinks."

"Okay, okay. Tell me where you are, Anna. Tell me and I'll be right there to get you."

"I'm in the bathroom. Don't want to go back out there."

"Good. That's good. Stay in there until I get there. But I need to know the name of the restaurant you're at."

"Tavern…something tavern."

Zoe placed her hand over the phone and looked at Aidan frantically. "Where is the tavern? Some place around here with the word *tavern* in it."

Both brothers jumped up. Quinn demanded, "What's going on?"

"Something's wrong with Anna. I need to go pick her up."

"No," Anna mumbled. "Don't send Aidan. Don't tell anyone. Just you. You come and get me. I'm so embarrassed, Zoe. Please."

"Okay, don't worry. I'm on my way. Stay on the phone with me, Anna."

"Can't," she said. "I…I think I'm going to be sick." And then the phone went dead.

"Damn it," Zoe said as she ran across the room and grabbed her purse.

"What's going on?" Aidan asked.

"Anna…" she began and then looked at Quinn and hesitated. And then it didn't matter. "She's out with Jake Tanner and…I don't know. She said she took a sip of her drink and now she doesn't feel right. She's in a bathroom stall at this tavern place and I need to go get her."

"Son of a *bitch*," Quinn cursed as he kicked his chair out from behind him. "Not again."

"What?" Zoe asked. "What do you mean by that?" She grabbed Quinn's arm as he walked out of the kitchen but he didn't stop.

"We're going with you," Aidan said, opening the front door.

"She's scared and sick and embarrassed, Aidan. She doesn't want an audience."

Quinn called over his shoulder as he went right out to his car, "Well, that's too damn bad."

His car was out of the driveway by the time Aidan and Zoe got into theirs.

———

Anna's head was spinning. Someone knocked on the stall door and asked if she was okay, and she merely mumbled her response. A few minutes later, someone else came and said her date was worried about her.

"I want to go home," she whispered and wished Zoe would get there and help her leave.

After a few minutes, she forced herself to do the one thing she hated more than anything—throw up. If there was something bad in her system, she wanted it gone. Once she was done, she slowly got to her feet, and when the room stopped spinning, she left the stall.

Her reflection nearly made her scream. She rinsed out her mouth and was about to leave the ladies' room when two women walked in.

"Don't go out there!" one of them cried. "There's a fight going on."

"Did you see him? I mean, he just came into the bar and walked right up to that guy and punched him in the face!"

"I think I recognized the guy in the booth. He's a race-car driver. You know…from NASCAR."

Oh no. Anna quickly made her away around the two

women and pulled the door open—and ran directly into Zoe.

"Oh thank God," Zoe cried, pulling Anna into her arms. "Are you okay?"

"I...I don't know. I think so," Anna said. The sound of a loud crash had her looking over Zoe's shoulder. "What's going on?"

"I'm sorry. I really tried to stop him, but—"

"Oh my God...is that Quinn?" Anna tried to step around Zoe, but she held her firm. "Zoe?"

"Sweetie, don't, okay?"

"Why is he here? And why is he beating up Jake?"

"We'll talk about it later. Let's get you home."

Anna's head was starting to clear. She managed to outmaneuver Zoe and headed toward where Jake and Quinn were pounding on one another.

"You son of a bitch!" Quinn snarled. "Is this the only way you can get women to go home with you?"

"Screw you," Jake spat.

"I will end you," Quinn said and got in one more punch before Aidan pulled him off.

"That's enough!" Aidan said, yanking his brother back. "The last thing you want is to make this worse."

Quinn broke free and turned on him. "*Worse?* This asshole drugged Anna!"

"You don't know that," Aidan said, trying to be the voice of reason.

"He's done it before," Quinn said, his breathing ragged. "Granted, it was years ago, but...it's why she's sick right now."

Neither of them noticed Anna's approach. "You knew he drugged girls?" she asked, her voice small and shaky as she came to stand in front of Quinn. "You knew and you didn't tell me?"

"Anna, that's not... I didn't think... I had no idea you would actually go out with him."

She slapped him hard across the face.

The room went silent.

She looked over to where Jake was sprawled out on the floor and felt her insides lurch again. Placing a hand on her stomach, she forced herself to breathe through it. Then she returned her focus to Quinn and almost smiled at the red handprint on his cheek. "Honestly, the *one time* you don't warn me off a guy."

Quinn reached for her, but she stepped away. "Anna...I'm sorry. Please. Let me explain."

She turned and spotted Zoe, who was now standing next to Aidan. "I'd really like to go home now."

Without a word, Zoe took Anna's hand and together they walked out of the bar.

Five minutes later, Aidan and Quinn came out, their expressions grim. "You should have taken her home," Aidan said softly to Zoe when they got close enough.

"We needed to make sure the cops weren't coming and that you were okay," Zoe replied. "Everything okay in there?"

"We just wanted to talk to the manager and apologize for what happened. Sort of." Aidan turned and took Anna in his arms. "You okay, kiddo?"

She nodded and let out a shaky breath. "Yeah. I'm going to be okay. The fresh air is really helping."

"Come on, we'll take you home," Aidan said and turned them toward his car. "We'll pick up your car in the morning."

"No," Quinn said. "I'll take her home."

"Quinn," Aidan warned. "This isn't the time. Let it go for tonight."

"No," he repeated, more firmly this time. "Please."

Aidan looked at Zoe and then Anna. When she nodded silently, Aidan kissed her on the top of the head and stepped away. "Call us if you need anything," he said as he put his arm around Zoe, watching as Quinn stepped forward and put his own arm around Anna. She immediately moved away and Aidan and Zoe couldn't help but smile.

"I think she's going to be okay," Zoe said quietly.

"Are you kidding me? She's going to be great. I just wish we could be flies on the wall to watch her do to him what he just did to Jake."

⁓⁓⁓

The entire ride was spent in silence.

Anna couldn't wait to just get home, take a shower, and put the whole night behind her. It probably wasn't the smartest idea, letting Quinn be the one to take her home, but she knew him well enough to know that if she hadn't let him, he would have shown up eventually to check on her. Maybe now she could just get it out of the way and be done with him for tonight.

"Thanks for the ride," she said as soon as the car came to a stop in her driveway and reached to open the door. When Quinn shut the car off and she heard the jingle of keys, Anna turned and faced him with disbelief. "What are you doing?"

"I'm coming in with you," he said gruffly, his expression tinged with anger.

"Um…no, you're not. It's been a bad night and I didn't invite you in." Quickly, she climbed from the car and walked up to her front door. Quinn was beside her in an instant.

"Seriously?" she said over her shoulder. He didn't budge or even react, so she opened the door and stepped inside.

Quinn shut the door behind him and watched her move around the house. "What's going on, Anna?"

Without looking at him, she nervously fluttered around, hoping he'd take the hint and just leave. "It's been a long night. I've got a headache and I just want to go to bed."

"Do you feel all right? I mean…do you still feel sick from—?"

"From the drug your friend slipped me?" she asked sarcastically.

Quinn cursed. "Damn it, Anna, I swear it never occurred to me he'd do something like that again. It was years ago and it was never proven, but he'd been accused of it."

"You should have told me," she said defensively. "You heard him ask me out in your shop that day and you didn't think to warn me? I mean, what the hell, Quinn? You warn me off guys all the damn time! You once told me not to go out with a guy because he liked to listen to jazz music, and you didn't think telling me Jake had a history of drugging women was important enough to mention?"

"Okay, I'll admit it, I screwed up! You can't possibly know how sorry I am, but…come on. I've apologized. What more do you want from me?"

She stared at him hard. "I want you to leave."

"No."

Her brown eyes widened with disbelief. "Excuse me?"

"I'm not leaving. I think it's time you and I sat down and talked."

"I don't want to sit and talk, Quinn. I'm fine. I just want to go to bed."

He stepped farther into the room. "Quit shoveling, Anna."

"Shoveling? What the heck does that even mean?" she asked, looking up at him from across the room.

"I know when you're lying and when you're just shoveling bullshit around. So spill it. I know you're dying to light into me about tonight. And normally you wouldn't have held back this long. You haven't been acting like yourself lately and you've been blowing me off and I want to know why."

Anna rolled her eyes. "Okay, for starters, yes, I would like to light into you, but in case you haven't noticed, I'm not quite feeling like myself. I had to stick my finger down my throat to get whatever was in that drink out of me. Excuse me if my feeling like hammered shit hasn't allowed me to put all my attention on you."

"Anna—"

"And for the record, I haven't been blowing you off, Quinn. Sheesh. Has it ever occurred to you that I have a life and I have better things to do than wait on you?"

"You've been there for every move and every store opening I've done in the tri-state area. It's a whole new phase for me starting now and you've hardly come by. And the one time you do come by, you spend the entire time flirting with Jake. And look how that worked out for you."

"You bastard," she hissed, ready to smack him again. "You're seriously going to stand here and lecture me? Now? Do you have any idea how scared I was tonight?"

He immediately apologized. "I...I am so sorry. You're right. That was a low blow. I don't know what I was thinking." They stood in silence, facing one another. "You're just never around anymore."

A million retorts were on the tip of her tongue—most were childish—so she went for the basics. "I have a new job, a new career. I don't have time to play cheerleader for you and bake cookies. Besides, you have more than enough people around you helping out." Turning her back to him, she put her purse on the kitchen table and then walked in the direction of her bedroom. "Be sure to lock up on your way out."

Closing her bedroom door, she silently prayed she'd ticked him off enough to make him leave. Maybe something would go her way tonight. With a sigh, Anna kicked off her shoes, walked over to her dresser, and pulled out her pajamas. Without a thought to keeping her room neat, she stripped right there on the spot and walked to the en-suite shower, turned the hot water on full blast, and stepped in. It wasn't about relaxing or luxuriating; it was simply about washing the night off of her.

It would have been easy to just stand there and cry, but she didn't even have the energy for that. With swift efficiency, she shampooed her hair and soaped her body from head to toe. She stood under the spray until the water cooled.

Stepping out, she dried off and pulled on her flannel pajama pants and slipped the cami over her head.

A quick glance in the mirror showed a very tired, very defeated woman. After taking a minute to towel-dry her hair and brush her teeth, she sighed.

"It figures the only kind of guy I'd attract with any ease is a psychopath," she muttered. Kicking her discarded towel aside, she shuffled back into the bedroom, and when she had nothing left to do, she contemplated going back out to the living room.

She no longer had a headache.

And she wasn't tired.

She could only hope Quinn was gone.

Off in the distance, she heard the ding of the microwave and sighed with defeat. Not only had the jerk not left, but he was clearly making himself at home. She pulled the door open and spotted Quinn walking across the room with a large bowl in his hands. "What do you think you're doing?"

"I made us some popcorn. I haven't had any time to just chill in a while, so I thought we'd watch a movie."

"Didn't you hear me? I'm tired. I want to be alone." She said the words, but there was little force behind them.

"I'm not going anywhere," he said defiantly. If it were anyone else, she would have thrown him out on the spot. But this was Quinn, the one guy she could talk to about anything.

"Quinn," she whined. "I think I've earned the right to be alone after the night I've had. Can't you just for once deal with not getting your own way?"

"This isn't about getting my own way," he said quietly, his voice thick. "This is about making sure you're okay."

"Well, I'm not, okay?" she cried. "I went out on a date I really didn't want to go on and the guy was a freak! Even if it weren't for the fact that he slipped something into my drink, he was a complete ass! He only talked about himself!"

"Then why'd you go out with him?"

"Why not?" she said, self-loathing lacing her tone. "He was a good-looking, successful man and he wanted to go out with me. He called me every day for a week. I figured what harm could one date do?" She gave a mirthless laugh. "Well, now I know, don't I?"

"Anna—"

"No, it's the truth. Clearly, the only guys who want to go out with me are freaks. Banner day for Anna Hannigan!"

"That's not true and you know it." His expression softened. "I'm so sorry. I really don't even know what to say. It's not like Jake and I are really good friends. We're just doing business together. It wasn't until you called Zoe that I even remembered the incident when he...you know...years ago. Please tell me you forgive me, Anna. Please."

She was completely torn. It would have been so easy to just say yes and forgive him, but she also knew that if she did, it would just take her back to where she had been before.

It was a no-win situation no matter what she did.

"Come on, Anna. Just come and sit on the couch. You can have the sectional and relax." He put the bowl down on the coffee table and turned back toward the kitchen to grab some drinks. "And besides, *Monty Python and the Holy Grail* is on."

Dammit. That movie was one of her weaknesses and judging by the smirk on Quinn's face, he knew it.

Jerk.

"Fine. Whatever," she muttered and walked over and flopped down on the couch.

With a full-blown grin, Quinn sat down and picked up the bowl of popcorn and put it between them before reaching for the remote and turning to the movie.

As much as she wanted to be pissed, the scene was oddly comforting—probably because it was something they'd done since they were kids. It just sucked that she wanted more—wanted Quinn to see her as a woman instead of a buddy. A lover instead of a friend.

It didn't take long for them to settle into the movie and soon they were laughing and quoting lines right along with the actors. Anna snuggled with her favorite throw and found that the more comfortable she got, the heavier her eyelids felt. She thought she could hold out until the end of the movie, but the reality was she was practically asleep.

Quinn looked over at Anna and smiled. He didn't know what had been going on with her lately, but he missed her. There were a ton of questions he'd wanted to ask her tonight, but he had decided to just let them go and do what he could to get her to relax around him and to try and erase the thought of what could have happened to her.

Beside him, Anna sighed and began to lean toward him. If he didn't do something, she was going to fall face-first into the popcorn bowl. He quickly scooped it up and put it on the coffee table—and froze with shock when Anna shifted and lay down with her head in his lap. It took a moment for the shock to wear off, and then he slowly let himself relax. The last time they had been like this had been the night before Aidan and Zoe's wedding and at least he had had a pillow acting as a buffer then.

"Not a big deal," he muttered and shifted to get them both a little more comfortable. The movie was almost over, and it didn't take long for him to get pulled back into the plot while he mindlessly played with Anna's hair. When the movie ended and he realized what he'd been doing—again—he pulled back like he'd been burned. He cursed. "I have *got* to stop doing that!"

"Anna?" he whispered, but she didn't move. He muttered under his breath and tried to think of what he should do. He knew he needed to leave—it was late and he had a lot to do at the new shop early in the morning—but he didn't want to disturb her.

The scene was eerily familiar and was seemingly becoming a habit for them.

While he continued to study her face, he finally let the guilt wash over him. He'd heard Jake ask her out and it had pissed him the hell off. He knew Jake was a player, but when Anna had turned him down, he'd thought that was the end of it. Quinn had been so wrapped up in— *hell, just call it what it is*—jealousy that he hadn't really thought about all the reasons why Anna shouldn't go out with Jake.

Because she's mine.

Yeah, that was becoming more and more apparent, but for the life of him, he didn't know what to do about it. And now, because of his own stupid pride and childish behavior, Anna could have been seriously hurt.

It wasn't something he was likely to forget anytime soon—or be able to forgive himself for.

Carefully, he slid out from under her head. Standing,

he walked into her bedroom and pulled the comforter and sheet back and then looked around and chuckled. The room was a bit of a mess, but then again, he knew Anna wasn't the prissy type who obsessed about everything needing to be in its place. If anything, it comforted him to see her room in slight disarray.

He walked around and really looked at the space. The light-colored furniture and the pastel-blue walls gave the room a beachy vibe he knew Anna tended to favor. On her shelves were books and knickknacks and pictures. He chuckled at how many different types of frames she had—another quirk of hers. But as he took a minute to look at the actual pictures, he noticed one thing—he was in most of them.

Pictures from her childhood, holidays, parties, and just…life. And he was there for all of them. They were laughing and smiling, and in some of them, Quinn could actually remember what it was they were joking about. A soft chuckle slipped out as he found a picture from Anna's sixteenth birthday. Her parents had gotten her a car. It was a used Mustang, and they had parked it in the driveway with a big red bow on it. In the picture, she was smiling so brightly, and he was standing right beside her.

Quinn ran a finger over the picture. It was her special day, and she had begged him to be in the picture with her. She did that a lot. Hell, he didn't think his own father had as many pictures of him as the Hannigans did.

He put the picture back down on the shelf and moved over toward the lone framed picture on her nightstand. For some reason, his heart began to race as he reached for it. It was a fancy silver-and-crystal frame. In it was a picture taken about a year ago of the two of them. It wasn't a special occasion; it was just a family day at the beach. They were sitting side by side in the sand, and he remembered Darcy coming over and snapping the picture. Anna's head was on his shoulder and they were smiling and looking so happy and relaxed and… He swallowed a lump in his throat. Being with Anna was normally the only time he felt happy and relaxed.

At least until recently.

Or maybe some time after this picture was taken.

Could he have known even then that things were changing? Was he subconsciously already noticing Anna wasn't just his pal but a woman?

Carefully, he put the picture back down and sighed. Tonight wasn't the night to figure it all out. Too much had happened, and his mind was spinning with it all. It was late, and he needed to help Anna get to bed and then go home himself. He was suddenly very tired—exhausted, really—and knew it would be better for both of them if he just gave her a little space.

Once back in the living room, he stood over her and studied her for a minute. She was out cold. They were going to have to talk. Really talk. Soon. They'd been friends for too long to just…stop. He needed Anna in his life—couldn't imagine a life without her in it. Eventually he'd wear her down and get her to tell him how he'd screwed up and then they could move on. He was just impatient, and wished she'd tell him now.

"Problem for another day," he whispered. "Anna? Anna, come on. You need to go to bed."

"Too tired," she murmured as she shifted on the couch.

Quinn sighed and reached down to gently scoop her

up into his arms. He straightened and stiffened when Anna snuggled closer and seemed to hum her approval. He took a step but instantly stopped when he felt her breath on his neck. And then her tongue. And then her lips. *What the…?*

"What are you doing?" she whispered sleepily.

"Taking you to bed," he said gruffly.

"Mmm…finally," she purred.

This was Anna. *Anna*, for crying out loud! He chanted to himself to just keep walking, and almost made it to the bed when once again her breath was replaced by her lips. Quinn froze as Anna slowly kissed and licked her way up the column of his throat and then nipped at the line of his jaw. He jerked back and looked down at her face as he continued to hold her in his arms. Her eyes were closed, but there was a very sexy smile on her face. "Anna," he whispered.

In a flash, her hands raked up into his hair and pulled his face closer to hers, and then Quinn was lost. He closed the distance between them and tentatively touched his lips to hers.

And then all rational thought left him.

Her lips were softer than he'd ever let himself imagine, and when she purred into his mouth and opened for him, he felt a sense of completion he'd never felt before. Slowly, he lowered Anna to the bed as her arms wound around him, holding him close. Quinn stretched out on top of her and smiled at Anna's whispered yes.

It was instantaneous, the surge of arousal and excitement he felt. He kissed her, as ravenous as a starving man at a feast, as her legs came up and lazily wrapped around his waist. He wanted to touch her, taste her everywhere, while at the same time he was questioning his own actions and sanity.

This was Anna. His best friend.

And clearly she didn't know what she was doing.

Cursing, he forced himself to move away from her and rose from the bed. She moaned her disapproval and whispered his name again before her head rested to the side and she sighed.

"Don't go," she said softly, but her words sort of trailed off, and then she rolled over and didn't say another word.

Shit. She was dreaming.

And he felt like a complete jerk for giving in to the temptation. He knew she was tired—clearly more tired than he'd realized—and he should have just put her down and left.

If she didn't hate him before, she'd certainly hate him now. Forcing himself to look away, he slowly backed out of her room and shut the door before making a hasty retreat from her house.

Cursing himself and his lack of control the entire time.

Chapter 5

THE NEXT MORNING, ANNA FELT MARGINALLY BETTER. Not great, but better. Other than being angry at Jake and what he had tried to do, she was embarrassed that she was so stupid and had so many witnesses to her rotten luck. After a cup of strong coffee, she reached for her phone and called Zoe.

"How are you feeling? Any better?"

"You mean other than like a giant idiot?" Anna asked, sitting on her sofa and putting her feet up on the coffee table.

"You're not an idiot, Anna. God, when I think about what could have happened to you, I'm so glad you had the good sense to get away from the table and call me!"

"I don't know how much of it was good sense. I never should have gone on the stupid date to begin with. I should have listened to you in the first place."

"Look, no one knew Jake was going to be such a freak."

"Quinn knew."

Zoe sighed. "Yeah, but...I don't know. I don't think he really expected something like that to happen. When he heard me on the phone with you, he really freaked out. I thought he was going to kill Jake."

"Right."

"No, I'm serious, Anna. I don't think I've ever seen Quinn so angry. The whole time we were driving over there and Aidan was trying to keep up, even he was saying how out of character it was for Quinn. We were seriously worried things were going to get a whole lot worse."

"Well, I do appreciate the fact that you all came down there to help me. I wasn't at the time—mainly because I was so out of it—but the more I thought about it, the more I realized how blessed I am to have such good friends. So...thank you."

"You never have to thank me. I'm just glad we were able to get there and help you."

"I guess it's a good thing Jake didn't press charges against Quinn."

Zoe snorted with disbelief. "Are you kidding? If he had tried to do it, the cops would have arrested him too for slipping something into your drink."

"We don't know that for sure—"

"Anna, stop!" Zoe cried. "Stop defending people! Stop always making excuses for them! Bobby's going down to talk to the bartender—"

"*What?* How does Bobby know what happened?"

Zoe hesitated. "Well, you know...small town and all."

"Zoe..."

"All right, all right. Aidan called him. But don't be mad! He was seriously just looking out for you!"

"Great, now on top of everything else, I'll—"

As if on cue, her front door opened and her brother walked in.

"And here he is," Anna said. "I have to go. I'll call you later."

"Don't be mad at him, Anna. He's just doing his job."

Anna wasn't so sure, but she didn't mention it. Once she hung up the phone, she faced her brother. "What brings you here today, Officer Hannigan?"

Bobby was dressed in his full police uniform and had a murderous look on his face. "I had to find out from Aidan Shaughnessy that some guy slipped you a roofie? Are you kidding me, Anna? Why the hell didn't you call me?"

"I did!" she cried, jumping to her feet. "You were the first person I called, but it went right to voice mail!"

"So call the station! They would have found me!"

"Bobby, I barely knew my own name at the time. After I couldn't get through to you, it was pure luck I managed to hit Zoe's number!"

He began to pace. "I'm going to the tavern as soon as it opens and looking at security footage and talking to the staff. I want you to press charges against this guy."

Without a word, Anna walked to the kitchen and poured Bobby a cup of coffee. He followed her and sat down at the breakfast nook. When she put the mug down in front of him, he looked up at her sadly. "Are you all right? I mean…do you feel okay?"

She shrugged. "I don't feel great. I forced myself to get sick to get it out of me, but…I'm more embarrassed than anything."

"Damn it, Anna, I can't believe something like this happened. Nothing like that has ever happened around here."

"Well, Jake isn't from around here."

Bobby frowned. "No, he's not. Leave it to Quinn to bring that sort of element into our lives."

"Oh, for the love of it… Please don't make this about Quinn."

"But it is!" Bobby yelled. "It was *his* friend who did this to you, and from what Aidan told me, the guy has a history of doing this! What the hell was Quinn thinking, letting you go out with a guy like that?"

"It wasn't his call to make!"

"Bullshit! Quinn Shaughnessy has had something to say about the guys you date for years! All of a sudden he chooses to keep his big mouth shut? When I get my hands on him—"

"That's enough!" she shouted, and Bobby instantly stilled. Anna never raised her voice to him, but she had hit her limit. "I am so sick and tired of this! If you are here as an officer or my brother, your rage should be on one person and one person only—Jake Tanner!"

Bobby stared at her with disbelief that quickly turned to shame. "You're right. I'm sorry, Anna. I just…I hate that I wasn't there for you."

"You can't be there all the time," she said softly, resting her elbows on the counter and facing him. "What happened last night was really scary, and like I was just telling Zoe on the phone, I feel incredibly blessed I have such good friends who were able to come and help me."

"Including Quinn," Bobby muttered and then flinched when Anna slapped him upside the head. "Ow! What'd you do that for?"

"Because you're still being an idiot!"

He took a drink of his coffee and waited a minute before speaking again. "Okay, I'm going to stop being your brother for now and be here in official police capacity."

"Bobby?"

He looked up at her.

Anna's eyes suddenly filled with tears. "Don't ever stop being my brother." And then she walked around the counter and let him hold her while she cried.

─⁓─

Quinn couldn't focus on anything.

Standing in the shop that housed Jake Tanner's two classic cars, he wasn't sure what he was supposed to do. He'd beaten the crap out of Jake last night. There was no way the two were going to work together, and as much as he was fine with never seeing the smarmy bastard again, he kind of hated the idea of losing the cars.

Which pretty much made him an equally smarmy bastard.

The door to the shop opened, and his main shop manager, Troy, stepped in. "Hey, Quinn. Jake Tanner's here to see you."

Son of a—

Quinn couldn't believe the guy was stupid enough to come around, but since he himself had just been thinking about the situation with the cars, it wasn't really surprising Jake was too. "Show him in, but I want you to stay close by, okay?"

Troy didn't question it; he simply nodded and walked out.

When Jake walked in, Quinn felt a real sense of satisfaction at the amount of bruising on the guy's face. Even though Jake was wearing sunglasses, Quinn could see enough of the bruising to know he'd done some damage.

"You've got a hell of a nerve coming here," Quinn said, standing with his feet planted firmly and his arms crossed.

"We need to make arrangements for the cars," Jake said, his speech a little slow—no doubt thanks to his split lip.

"You could have had someone call."

Jake shrugged and then winced. "Look, you can tell me to go to hell, and after last night I wouldn't blame you, but…" He stopped and sighed. "I'd still like you to do the work on the cars."

Quinn was shocked. It was the last thing he'd expected to hear. His eyes narrowed. "Why? Why would you even trust me to work on them? Who's to say I won't mess them up on purpose?"

"You wouldn't do that. You're an arrogant pain in the ass and have a colossal ego. There's no way you'd damage your reputation by messing with cars of this magnitude."

Damn it, he was right.

"You've got a gift for this sort of thing, man. Like I said, you can throw me out of here and tell me to go to hell, but last night—"

Quinn moved before Jake could blink and had him by the throat, his back slammed against the wall. "You're just lucky you didn't get the chance to put a hand on her or you wouldn't be breathing right now." The hand on Jake's throat tightened just for good measure.

Jake squirmed and managed to shake Quinn off. He was gasping for air as he held up a hand to ward Quinn off. "Just…hear me out."

"I don't think so. You need to leave," Quinn said through clenched teeth.

"Think about it. It's all I'm asking. You won't have to deal with me personally. I'll have my manager take care of everything. I've already got several publications interested in doing stories on the cars. You'd be getting all kinds of free publicity for you and the business."

Bile rose in Quinn's throat. Was this bastard seriously trying to negotiate a business deal after what he'd done?

"You're out of your mind, Tanner. You picked the wrong girl to mess with. Anna is—"

"Yeah, yeah, I get it. I don't know why." He paused and cleared his throat before straightening. "Call it ego. It pissed me off how she kept turning me down. Now that I know about you and her…"

Quinn could only stare. "Be very careful what you say because I'm not afraid to finish what I started last night."

"That won't be necessary."

Quinn and Jake both turned to find Bobby Hannigan and another police officer standing in the doorway. For once, Quinn was genuinely relieved to see Bobby. Taking a step back, he simply motioned for the officers to come in and do their job.

Once Jake had been read his rights and was being led out, Bobby turned to Quinn, his expression fierce. "The only reason I'm not pounding on you the way you pounded on Tanner is because I promised Anna I wouldn't."

Quinn nodded.

Bobby nodded once and started to turn away but stopped and faced Quinn again. "Thank you. For being there for her when I couldn't be."

"I'd die before I let anything happen to her," Quinn said solemnly.

Another nod and then Bobby strode out of the garage.

Two days later, Anna stared at her reflection in the mirror for a solid ten minutes before she finally decided it was the best she could do. This whole dressing-up thing was really starting to get old. While she knew it went with the job and the whole life-change thing, she couldn't help but let her gaze linger longingly on her old jeans and sneakers.

Checking herself from every angle, she knew she looked professional. The muted-mint-green sundress was simple, with wide shoulder straps, a gentle curve-hugging bodice, and skirt cut to the knee. Paired with a little white cardigan and a casual strand of pearls, she felt ready to go.

Her client today was an important one—Dan Michaels, an old high school classmate who had done very well for himself and now was looking for a beach-front home. When he had specifically asked for Anna, she had been excited to see him. When she found out how much he was looking to spend on a property, she was damn near ecstatic.

Real estate was challenging, and there were things Anna really wanted to accomplish with her life. She had dreams and goals, and her commissions weren't making them happen just yet. But if she could find Dan the perfect property, the commission would help her a lot. Student loans would start to get paid off and she might even be able to get a decent car.

Plastering a smile on her face, she checked her reflection one last time before grabbing her purse and heading out the door. The high wedges she was wearing were already annoying her, and she stopped and looked back at her house and wondered if she should grab a pair of flats just in case.

"No," she told herself as she unlocked her car door. "You're an adult. Act like one. Dress like one." Once inside, she started the car and kicked on the air conditioning and thought about how she wished her mom had warned her of how uncomfortable adults had to be in the real world.

Fifteen minutes later, she pulled up in front of the house she prayed would impress Dan. Beachfront, three-car garage, four stories. It had six bedrooms, eight bathrooms, a theater room, a game room, an elevator, plus an outdoor entertaining area that included a multi-level deck, a heated pool, outdoor kitchen as well as an outdoor shower. Hell, if it was missing anything, she'd be completely surprised.

Grabbing her purse, she got out of the car and went into the house. It was currently vacant but fully furnished. Walking through the main floor, Anna fluffed pillows and opened the sliding doors that led out to one of the decks before making sure everything looked dust free. By the time Dan pulled up, she was almost out of breath from going up and down the stairs.

"Anna Hannigan," he said with a smile when she opened the door. "You look amazing." Reaching for her hands, he squeezed them and leaned in to place a kiss on her cheek. "How are you doing?"

For a minute, Anna was speechless. Dan Michaels had been cute in high school. He was out-and-out gorgeous now. She had to stop and swallow before she could speak. "I'm good," she said and then cleared her throat. "I'm good. How about you?"

She motioned for him to come inside and managed to get one of her hands free of his. Dan held on to the other. Amazingly enough, she didn't mind.

"I'm doing well," he said. He was six feet tall with dark brown hair and eyes. With an easy grin that showcased his dimples, she couldn't help but smile back. Stepping into the main living area, he let out a low whistle of approval. "Wow. When you said you knew of the perfect place, you weren't kidding."

This time when he moved, he did release Anna's hand. She read off the list of all the house had to offer as she followed behind him. "With a little over six thousand square feet, you won't have any privacy issues when you have your family here with you."

He chuckled. "That's definitely a good thing. I know my brother and sister and their families are going to want to come and visit for extended weekend trips. I love my family, but with all their kids, it's nice to know I can hide out if I want to."

So he isn't married, she thought to herself. *Interesting.*

They slowly toured the entire house from top to bottom, talking the entire time not only about the property, but also about high school and mutual acquaintances and just getting caught up on each other's lives. All in all, Anna found him to be incredibly charming. And if it hadn't been for her unfortunate incident with Jake, she would probably have been angling for a chance to go out with Dan for a drink.

Not yet. She wasn't ready to trust anyone just quite yet.

When they found themselves back on the main floor and looking out at the ocean, Anna looked down at her watch. Two hours! They had been walking around and talking for two hours already! Not that she had anything to do, but she just couldn't believe how fast the time had flown by.

"So...what do you think, Dan?" she finally asked.

"Is this one a contender, or do you want to look at a few more properties?"

He took a deep breath and smiled. "I love the smell of the ocean, don't you?"

Anna smiled. "Absolutely. I can't imagine living anywhere else but near the coast. I would miss it too much."

He nodded. "I moved away when I left for college and stayed away all this time. Now that my life has calmed down a bit, I know what I want. If I'm going to invest in a home, I want it to be here. We never lived right on the beach, but I always dreamed of it." He looked at her with a lopsided grin. "And now I can do it."

"You're very lucky."

They stared at one another for a minute before Dan looked back at the ocean. "This one is definitely a contender, but I'd like to look at maybe a few more properties just to be sure. Do you have anything else available?"

Pulling her tablet out of her purse, Anna pulled up one of the other listings she had considered. "This one here is similar in square footage but has a few more updates. I can see if we can look at it now, if you have the time? It's only about a mile up the road."

"That sounds great," he said and stepped away while Anna made the call. When she was done and told him they were welcome to go and see the house, he added, "I'll follow in my car. I have a dinner appointment in town I'll need to get to."

"If you'd prefer to go another day…?"

He shook his head. "No, today is fine. I'd really like to see it, but I probably won't linger as long as we did here, if that's okay."

It was said with a smile, but Anna made a mental note

to stick to business and ease up on the personal chitchat. "Not a problem. I just need to close everything up here." She wrote down the address on the back of her business card and handed it to him. "Why don't you head down there and at least get a look at the outside? I'll be five minutes behind you."

"Sounds good, Anna. Thanks for understanding."

She watched him walk out the door and sighed. Here was a perfectly nice man, and if she were a normal woman, she'd be attracted to him and flirting with him. But between Quinn and the Jake incident, the idea of dating wasn't appealing at the moment.

Walking around and double-checking all the doors and windows, she quickly scooped up her purse and made her way out the front door.

In a perfect world, she would make this sale, get her finances in order, and find the man of her dreams.

Instead, she walked down the front steps, climbed into her old Honda, and faced the reality of having to put her dreams on hold for a little while longer.

—⁓—

It was another two hours before she watched Dan drive away. After another lengthy house tour, he told her he loved both houses but needed to think about it. Of course she understood—it was a pretty massive purchase.

Still…it would have been nice if he had wanted to sign a contract today.

With the house locked up, Anna climbed back into her car and headed toward home. It was dinnertime, and she was hungry but didn't feel like cooking. Takeout was looking more and more appealing. Maybe some

Chinese food, or maybe she'd stop at the pub and grab a burger, or—

The check engine light came on.

Again.

"Dammit," she muttered. Quinn had been after her about it for a long time, and Anna had a feeling she couldn't ignore it much longer. The drive through town to her house would take her right by the new shop, and if she just didn't let herself worry about getting a lecture about car maintenance or about the incident with Jake, she could actually stop in and ask Quinn to look at her car without feeling like an idiot.

Or maybe she could wait another day.

As if on cue, the car started to sputter a bit, and Anna knew she had pushed her luck as far as she could. The car definitely needed to be looked at.

Another sputter.

There went her hopes of getting takeout.

At this point, she'd be lucky to make it to the shop without having to push the damn car.

Anna turned the corner and pulled into the parking lot of Shaughnessy Automotive and Restoration. The parking lot was empty, and Anna worried that it was after hours. Quinn's car was there, however, so there was no avoiding him. Taking a deep breath, she climbed from the car and went in search of him.

It didn't take long—he walked out of the open garage bay as she was approaching. "Hey," he said and Anna thought his tone was a bit…cautious.

"Hi," she said, forcing a smile.

He looked her over and frowned. "What are you so dressed up for?"

Anna looked down at herself and then back at him. "Dressed up? Quinn, you've seen me in this dress about a dozen times before. I had a house to show."

He grunted and shrugged. "You never wore it with high heels before."

Rolling her eyes, she got to the purpose of her visit. "The, um…the engine light came on again. And it's sputtering."

Quinn's eyes never left hers. "And isn't it a little late in the day for a showing?"

"For crying out loud, can you please look at the car? I really think it's bad this time. I'm afraid to drive it home!" she said with exasperation.

"I thought you knew all about car maintenance now," he said with a hint of sarcasm. "Isn't that what you said the other day?"

Doing her best to remain calm, she met his gaze. "I can change a tire, replace an air filter, change a spark plug, and even replace my windshield wipers. Whatever's going on this time is way beyond that. Can you please just not be a jerk for five minutes and cut me some slack?"

Without a word, Quinn walked over to the car and popped the hood. Anna couldn't help but stand back and admire his physique from behind. Faded blue jeans hugged him, and his gray T-shirt—even though it was stained—just accented how muscular he was. And then there was the cap. Today it was one of his old baseball caps worn backward. Somehow he managed to even make it look sexy. The man seemed to only get better with age. A small sigh escaped before she forced herself to walk over to the car.

"Jeez, Anna. I told you this piece of junk was gonna crap out on you. I mean, until I get it on the lift, I can't say for certain, but knowing its history, it could be about a half a dozen different things. You need a new car."

Her spine stiffened. She hated that superior tone he used. "Oh, really? Gee, Quinn, I didn't know that," she retorted. "Tell you what, let me go and rub my magic lamp and see if my genie will grant me a new car."

Quinn stood and wiped his hands on the rag he had hooked in his back pocket while giving her a sour look. "This isn't news, Anna. And you have a job. It's not like you can't get a new car."

They'd had this discussion before and it always ended like this—with an argument. "I told you I don't want a car payment right now. Getting my real estate license wasn't free, you know!" She huffed and paced away and then back again. "Can't you just…do something with it? You know, to tide me over?"

"What, again?" he asked, crossing his arms over his chest.

That was it. It was all too much, and she finally hit her limit. Tears were starting to build, and there was no way she was going to let Quinn see her cry. She'd take the risk and drive the damn hunk of junk home and find another mechanic tomorrow. Maybe Bobby could help her with getting around and to and from work for a little while.

Without looking at him, Anna stepped forward and slammed the hood closed before opening the car door.

"What are you doing?" he asked.

"Leaving."

"Why? Because I asked you an honest question?"

Anna threw her purse back into the car before facing

him again. "No, because you're a jackass." She growled with frustration. "If I can convince Dan to buy the house I showed him today, I'll make enough commission to make a reasonable down payment on a used car. But for now, I just needed a little help, not a lecture. Obviously it was too much to ask!"

Quinn reached out and tugged her away from the car before she could sit. "Dan who?"

"Dan Michaels. From high school. Remember him?"

Quinn thought for a moment. "Pretty boy. Played baseball with me junior year. When did you see him?"

"Today. That's who I was with earlier. He's looking at the Stanleys' place on the beach. The house is like a damn showplace, like something out of a magazine, and if I can convince him to buy it, the commission will go a long way toward giving me some breathing space. With this car thing now, I need it more than ever."

"So you dressed up for him in hopes of enticing him to buy?"

"What?" she cried with disbelief. This time she shoved at his chest with both hands. "What is the matter with you? What the hell have I ever done to you to make you be such a complete ass to me?" They were both breathing hard as they glared at one another.

Quinn cursed under his breath and stormed back into the shop through the garage. Anna quickly followed. It wasn't an easy task in the dress and heels—which she cursed the entire time. She found him in his office, throwing the rag down on the desk.

"Hey," she snapped, slamming the office door closed behind her. "I asked you a question." Quinn's blue eyes flashed with fire as he looked at her. Anna had seen that look before, normally directed at other people. It was the first time she had been on the receiving end of it, and she wasn't sure if it scared her or just served to make her madder.

"Oh yeah? Well, I asked *you* one earlier and you didn't answer. I guess we're even." Crossing his arms over his chest, he waited her out—a smug expression on his face.

"Seriously? Are we really going there? The whole 'I'm rubber, you're glue' thing? Aren't we getting too old for this crap?" And then the fight started to leave her. This wasn't getting her anywhere. The man clearly had an issue with her that he wasn't going to share and she was just tired of the whole thing. "You know what? Never mind. Just…never mind," she said wearily and turned to open the office door and leave.

"Did you kiss him?" he called after her and waited until she turned around and looked at him. "Did you kiss him too?"

Slowly Anna stepped back into the office and looked at Quinn as if he'd lost his mind. "Are you high or something? Kiss him? Kiss who? Could you please explain to me what the heck you're talking about?" She was completely confused by the turn in the conversation. Did he think she'd kissed Jake? Other than Jake, she hadn't even been out on a date in what felt like forever, so what was he even referring to?

He moved in close and kept going until Anna's back was against the wall. "Is that your new thing? Just kissing guys to pass the time?" Quinn's breathing was ragged as he looked down into Anna's wide eyes.

"I don't know what you're talking about. I haven't

kissed anyone," she said shakily as her tongue came out to moisten her suddenly dry lips.

"You kissed me."

Those brown eyes got impossibly wider as she softly gasped. "No, I didn't."

Wait…did I? Was that not a dream the other night?

"Yeah, you did," he said in a low voice. "You fell asleep on the couch, and then I carried you to bed and you kissed me."

She shook her head, unable to find her voice. But even as she tried to deny it, the image came to her mind that she would have sworn had just been a dream—not that she was going to share that bit of information with Quinn.

He continued to watch her, his eyes never leaving hers. "Yes. You. Did."

"I…I don't believe you," she stammered, wishing like hell she could just escape and die of embarrassment.

"Let me remind you," he growled fiercely as he closed the distance between them so they were pressed together from head to toe. His hand reached up and anchored itself around her nape as his mouth crashed down on hers.

Shock held Anna still for only a few seconds before she gave in and kissed him back. It was better than the dream! Well, clearly not a dream, but reality. Unable to help herself, she sighed and completely melted against him. His lips were softer than she'd imagined, and when his tongue reached out and teased hers, she thought she'd melt in a puddle at his feet.

Quinn changed the angle of his head and his lips gentled against hers. Suddenly, neither of them was quite so frantic. Now they were sipping at each other and getting acquainted with the feel, the taste of each other. Anna sighed into his mouth as her arms wrapped around him—knowing that she was really doing it and was allowed to touch him was a complete turn-on.

Quinn must have felt the same way because he suddenly crowded her in and then his hands started to wander—first to her shoulders, then slowly downward as he skimmed his hands along her sides to her waist, her hips. They gripped there as they gently kneaded and rocked her against him.

Yes, yes, yes! her brain cried, and then she got in on more of the touching too. For so many years, she'd thought about it—fantasized about it—about touching Quinn at her leisure and she was finally allowed! Her hands moved up and down his muscled arms first and gently squeezed his biceps.

They were hard and huge, and he flexed them beneath her hands.

Then they wandered up the column of his neck and up into his thick, silky hair—knocking his hat off—and gripped it. It made him growl, and she held on a moment longer just because she could.

Distantly, she realized his hands had continued downward and were now at the hem of her skirt and he was slowly raising it. Should she protest? Help? Hell if she knew. For now she'd go with enjoying it. When he had it up to an obscene height, Anna shamelessly hooked one leg up around Quinn to hold him even closer.

Another masculine growl.

"Damn, Anna," he panted, kissing and licking his way across her cheek, her throat, her collarbone.

It was on the tip of her tongue to beg him not to stop,

to take her right there, but clearly he was one step ahead of her. His hand came up and firmly cupped her cheek, forcing her to look at him, his eyes glazed with desire.

"How…how did this happen?" he whispered, his eyes scanning her face.

"I don't know." She almost cursed her honesty. Now wasn't the time for her to come off as being unsure of anything! What if he pulled back? What if the fog of lust suddenly cleared and—

"I want you," he said thickly, hotly.

"I'm yours," she whispered, and then his lips were back on hers as he clasped her waist and lifted her until both her legs wrapped around his waist. The sensations were glorious. The feeling of Quinn—*aroused* Quinn—between her legs was every fantasy come to life. Anna had never found the appeal in wearing dresses before.

She did now.

One of Quinn's hands moved from her waist to her hip and then to cup her bottom. Her panties were of the barely there variety and clearly he approved. She felt him wrap the fabric in his fist as he began to tug.

And then the phone rang.

"Quinn," she whispered.

"Ignore it," he said and immediately went back to kissing her and adjusting his grip on her panties.

While the phone on his desk continued to ring, his cell phone began to go off with what sounded like a dozen text messages arriving at once.

This time, she didn't have to say his name; they were on the same page. Something was up and needed his attention. As much as Anna wanted to argue how much *she* needed his attention, it was obvious something was wrong. Quinn gently lowered her to the floor, and Anna silently fixed her dress while he picked up his cell phone in one hand and the office phone in the other.

"*What?*" he barked into the office phone. He raked a hand through his hair as he listened then cursed. "I'm on my way." Then he slammed the phone back down and focused on his cell phone before shoving it into his pocket and turning toward Anna.

"What is it?" she asked nervously. "Is everything okay?"

He shook his head. "Aubrey's in the hospital."

Without a word, Quinn picked his hat up off the floor and searched for his car keys. Anna didn't ask; she simply followed him outside as he locked up before running to her car and grabbing her purse. When she turned around, Quinn had already pulled his truck up behind her and was waiting.

She found comfort in the fact that they were in sync. Climbing into the truck, all she said was, "Let's go," and Quinn immediately put the truck in drive and took off.

~~~

They had barely left the parking lot when Anna pulled her phone out. "Okay, what's going on? Who called? Who texted?"

"It was my dad on the office phone. Aidan texted."

"What do we know? What happened?"

"Hugh's away on business. Aubrey was supposed to go with him, but they didn't have anyone to watch the dogs," he said with exasperation. "Owen was driving through on his way to some seminar, and he stopped by, not knowing Hugh wasn't home, and found her passed out on the floor."

Anna gasped. "Oh no!" They all knew of Aubrey's history with cancer as a teen, so any mystery illness was cause for alarm. "Where is Hugh?"

"He's on a flight home right now from New York." Quinn cursed. "I'm sure he's freaking out."

"Of course he is," she said. "So is everyone on their way to the hospital?"

He nodded. "Aidan and Zoe probably got a thirty-minute start on us, and Dad's ahead of them. Owen called him first after he got Aubrey to the hospital."

"He didn't drive her himself, did he?"

"I don't even know. Once Dad said what was going on, I just sprang into action. Why don't you call Zoe and see if you can get more details and if she knows how Hugh is getting to the hospital from the airport? We can meet him if we need to."

Nodding, Anna dialed Zoe's phone and was relieved when she answered. "Hey, where are you guys?"

"We're about thirty miles out from the hospital," Zoe said. "What about you?"

"I'm with Quinn and we just left the shop. Who's getting Hugh from the airport?"

"Ian is going to pick him up. So we'll all meet up at the hospital."

"What happened? Do you know?"

"All I know is Owen stopped by and found her on the floor. I can't… I don't even know what to think. I mean, did she fall? Was she sick? We don't know!"

Anna sighed. "Poor Hugh. Has anyone talked to him?"

"Just Ian. We didn't want to add to his stress—plus

he's on a plane right now, so we probably wouldn't get through to him."

"Did Owen drive her to the hospital? Did she wake up?"

"No," Zoe said. "He called 9-1-1 and rode in the ambulance with her. He's a wreck."

"I'm sure. It had to be pretty scary finding her that way."

"I think he was more upset he couldn't help diagnose what was wrong. He told Aidan he'd never felt so help-less in his life."

It was exactly how Anna felt at that moment—it was good to know she wasn't alone. "Okay, so Ian's getting Hugh, Owen's with Aubrey…are we missing anything? What about the dogs? They're going to need someone to go in and let them out, I would imagine. Right?"

"I didn't even think of that. Damn it."

"Okay, you guys go on to the hospital, and Quinn and I will swing by the house and check on them. Aubrey's mentioned her next-door neighbors have helped her out with the dogs before, so we'll check in with them."

"Sounds good. If I hear anything, I'll let you know, okay?"

"Thanks, Zoe. We'll talk to you soon."

After she hung up, Anna looked over at Quinn. "I hope you don't mind. I volunteered us to check on the dogs."

He shook his head. "No, it was a good idea. Since Aubrey didn't go on this trip with Hugh because of the dogs, we may not be able to find anyone else. The more we can do to help, the better. Did she tell you anything different or have any updates?"

"Nothing yet. Your dad's going to pick up Hugh. Owen's at the hospital."

"He's a mess, isn't he?"

"Who? Owen?"

Quinn nodded.

"You know he's not good in situations like this," Anna said softly. "His bedside manner isn't exactly warm and fuzzy. He's going to get all clinical."

Quinn chuckled. "He can't help it. It's how his brain works. But I'm sure he's also nervous because he's not comfortable with Aubrey yet."

"It's not like she's new to the family," Anna pointed out. "She and Hugh have been together for almost a year."

"Yeah, but he hasn't been around much, so he's only met her a handful of times. He was the same way with Zoe."

Anna nodded. "Hell, I grew up with you guys and it took Owen until I was almost fifteen before he would say more than two words to me."

"Yeah, well…you intimidated him."

"What? Me? How?" she asked, laughing a little.

"You held your own with all of us—you played ball and ran around and climbed trees. You didn't fit his perception of a typical girl."

Anna wasn't sure how to take that, so she let it be. "Well, he didn't fit my perception of a typical boy either, you know. I don't think I've ever met anyone as smart as Owen. He still has a way of intimidating me by making me feel like a moron."

"Join the club. He does it to all of us. The key is to just remind him he's talking Klingon and he'll stop." Chuckling, he shook his head. "Although he may take that as a compliment. Then we'd have to be the ones explaining to him how it's not."

That made Anna laugh. "I don't want him to get a complex. There's nothing wrong with how he speaks or the things he says. He just needs to…"

"Dumb it down?" Quinn suggested with a grin.

"Exactly!"

The drove without talking for a while, the radio playing softly in the background. For the first time possibly ever, Anna was grateful for Quinn's driving skills. She was certain they'd get pulled over due to the way he was speeding, but he drove with confidence into the night. She'd deal with the white-knuckle grip she had to take a time or two if it meant getting to Hugh and Aubrey faster.

"I hate to ask," Anna finally said, "but I was on my way to get some dinner when the car started doing its thing. Do you think we can go through a drive-through and grab something? I don't want to hold us up but I'm starving."

"Oh thank God," Quinn said with relief. "I was thinking the same thing but I figured you'd yell at me for stopping when we needed to get to the dogs and then to the hospital."

"You will never get yelled at by me where food is concerned."

A bark of laughter was his first response. "That is not true!" He looked over at Anna. "You yell at me all the time about food!"

"That's because you're normally calling me at some crazy hour wanting cookies or burgers or something ridiculous!" she replied with a laugh.

"Oh, I see. So as long as you're getting fed too, it's okay. Is that it?"

Anna pretended to think about it. "Hmm…maybe."

Quinn pulled in to the first burger place they came to and ordered enough food for six people.

"Are we bringing food to the hospital?" she asked.

"No. Why?"

"You cannot possibly be that hungry! The amount of food you just ordered is way too much for one person."

"You're eating too," he reminded her.

"Um…one burger, one order of fries, buddy. The rest is all you."

"So you're saying you don't want one of the milk shakes I ordered."

Dammit. She did enjoy a good milk shake. "Okay, fine. I'll take one of the milk shakes."

"And onion rings. You're not gonna have any?"

Anna sighed loudly. "You know I will. They're just so crispy and good!"

"And the freshly baked cookies," he said, shaking his head. "I guess I'll have to eat them all." He turned and winked at her. "And I do enjoy a good chocolate chip cookie."

"You're the devil, you know that, right?"

His smile grew and became just a bit wicked. "You know it, sweetheart."

By the time they reached the hospital, it was after nine. Quinn knew they weren't going to be able to get in and see Aubrey, but he wanted to be there for Hugh. The dogs had been let out and fed, and the neighbors had promised to go over again before midnight if no one had come home.

Sitting in the waiting room with his family, Quinn

felt restless. Uneasy. The last time he had sat like this was after the crash that had taken his friend Todd's life. He had sat in the waiting room with Todd's family and what seemed like a hundred members of the NASCAR family. He could still see the look on the doctor's face when he came out to talk to Todd's wife. His stomach sank.

It was the same look they had all seen the night his mother had died. Taking a shaky breath, Quinn wiped at his eyes, certain he felt tears welling there.

And then Anna's hand was on his arm, her head on his shoulder. He couldn't move, didn't want to draw attention to the fact that he was overwhelmed emotionally. That was the last thing anyone needed right now. So he sat and drew comfort from her until he could get himself under control.

Just think of something else. Anything. Just move on from all thoughts of doctors and hospitals and focus on something else.

He thought about what had happened earlier at the shop, and it brought up an entirely different emotion. Anna had been so hot in his arms, and he couldn't believe how incredible it had been.

Kissing her, touching her, was not part of the plan. Any plan. Especially after the other night at her house; but once he saw her in that dress, it reminded him of the curves she had beneath it. And then when she mentioned being with another guy? Well, something had simply snapped. He didn't want her with another guy—for business or otherwise—and now that he had experienced what it was like to kiss her when she was completely into it too?

"*I'm yours.*"

Anna's words played in his head over and over. It was inevitable. She *was* his. It was still hard to wrap his brain around it, and they were going to have to talk about it. No doubt it would be awkward. He hated the thought of doing anything to jeopardize their friendship, but they'd crossed that line together and there was no way he could just forget it happened. Hell no. He'd been replaying the kiss they'd shared at her house almost nonstop since it had happened. Add tonight's escapade to it, and he had his own X-rated movie going on in his head.

Tilting his head, he rested it on Anna's. Quinn heard her sigh. It was weird how he kept thinking about Anna in this new light—this new sexy light—and it wasn't… weird. He would have thought going from thinking of her as a buddy to thinking of her as a lover would have been difficult, but it wasn't. If anything, the thought of it was an incredible turn-on. His fingers almost twitched with the need to touch her and find out what she liked, what turned her on. He was almost desperate with his need to discover her.

"*I'm yours.*"

Yeah. She was.

And it scared the shit out of him.

Chapter 6

"WELL? ANY NEWS?"

Hugh Shaughnessy walked into the waiting room looking as if he hadn't slept in a week. It was after midnight, and he had been back with Aubrey and the doctors ever since he'd arrived. He sat down in a chair next to his father as the entire family leaned forward and waited for the update.

"She's awake," he said and then yawned broadly. "She didn't fall, so there's no injury or concussion from that." He shifted in the seat to get more comfortable. "They did find she was mildly dehydrated and right now we're just waiting for some test results. Because of the late hour, we'll probably have to wait until morning for them to do the more…you know…invasive tests."

Quinn silently cursed. It wasn't fair. Even though they all knew there was a possibility of Aubrey's cancer coming back, no one expected it to happen so soon. "What are they thinking?" he asked.

Hugh wiped a weary hand across his face. "Honestly, they're stumped. Aubrey goes for exams twice a year and hasn't presented any symptoms that raised red flags. When the doctor asked how she felt before she fainted, all she could say was she was hungry and was going to get something to eat and then she felt dizzy and…" He shrugged. "It could be something really simple or it could be—" He stopped and hung his head.

"How is she doing now?" Anna asked softly.

Lifting his head, it was easy to see the tears. Hugh didn't bother to wipe them away. "She feels fine. She's tired, so the doctors said the best thing was to let her sleep and they'll come in and see her first thing in the morning."

"Are you going to stay the night?" Ian asked, his hand firmly on his son's shoulder. "Or do you want me to take you home?"

"I honestly don't know. I hate the thought of leaving Aubrey alone here, but…there's nothing else I can do tonight. I'm not going to be any use to her tomorrow if I've been up all night watching her sleep."

They all nodded. "Then let's go back to your place," Ian suggested. "You may not get a lot of sleep, but it will be more than you'll get here sitting in a chair. We'll get up early so you can shower and change your clothes, and we'll have you back here first thing."

Wordlessly, Hugh nodded and then stood. He looked around at his family. "What about the rest of you? You'll all come back to the house for the night, won't you? It's too late to drive home."

"You sure you want us all camping out at the house?" Aidan asked. "We can go to a hotel if it would be easier on you."

Hugh shook his head. "We'll make it work. There's only three bedrooms including mine, so…"

"We'll make it work," Zoe said. "Don't worry."

But Hugh was a planner at heart. It was something that came naturally to him and helped relax him. "No…no…we'll put Dad and Owen in one room." He turned to his younger brother. "You're staying, right? Or do you need to get going to your seminar?"

Owen shook his head, his jet-black hair in disarray, his glasses slightly crooked. "I gave myself extra time so I could visit with you. I've got a couple of days."

Hugh smiled. "Good. You and Dad will room together. Aidan and Zoe will take the other room and"—he looked over at Quinn and Anna—"you guys can camp out in the den. Will that be okay?"

"Absolutely," Anna said with a warm smile while Quinn nodded.

"Zoe, Anna, you guys can borrow something to sleep in. Aubrey's got a pretty extensive wardrobe, and I know she won't mind."

"Hugh?" Zoe interjected. "Stop talking. You're exhausted. It's late. Let's just go home," she said as she walked over and hugged him. "We'll worry about the little things when we get there, okay?"

He nodded and yawned. "Okay."

—⁓—

It was two in the morning and Anna was wide-awake. They were all back at Hugh and Aubrey's home, and it had taken a little while to get everyone situated and settled. She was standing in the doorway to the den looking at Quinn, who was shirtless in his well-worn jeans. Memories of what had happened between them earlier in the shop flooded her, and she wondered what was going to happen now that they were alone.

"This opens up into a bed," Quinn said when he saw her standing there. "Or we can use the blankets and pillows and camp out on the floor. What do you think?"

What did she think? Um…bed please! She searched for a way to say it without it sounding as if she was nervous—like it was the most natural thing in the world for them to be talking about sharing a bed or camping out on the floor together. Well, camping out on the floor kind of wasn't a big deal. They'd done it a ton of times while growing up.

"The bed should be fine—just as long as it's not like the one at the beach from Aidan and Zoe's wedding."

Quinn chuckled and began to pull the cushions from the couch. In minutes, he had it all unfolded and was sitting on the bed. "This is a pretty good mattress. You can't even feel the bars." He lay down and moved around a bit. "Nope. It's definitely better than the other one."

He jumped up and began making the bed. Anna walked over and helped him. It didn't take long to do, and once all the sheets and blankets were on and the pillows back in place, there didn't seem like there was much to do except…get in the bed.

Looking around, Anna saw a pile of blankets and some pillows still on the floor. She looked at them and then back at Quinn. He shrugged. "You take the bed. I'll camp on the floor."

Disappointment swamped her. So they weren't picking up where they left off earlier. Well…damn. Of course it made sense. The den in Hugh and Aubrey's house was certainly not the place she wanted to get intimate with Quinn for the first time. But still.

"Unless…" he began, and Anna's gaze instantly went to his.

"Unless?"

Quinn cleared his throat and looked at the floor—very insecure and very unlike the confident man she knew him to normally be.

"Unless you wouldn't mind…sharing." He looked up at her, his blue eyes uncertain as his gaze held hers.

This was it. This was her chance to finally live at least part of the fantasy. "I wouldn't mind," she said softly and smiled when she saw his shoulders relax, as if he was relieved.

Suddenly shy, Anna looked down at the oversized T-shirt she was wearing. She was comfortable in it, and knew Quinn had seen her in one just like it not too long ago, but suddenly she wished she were wearing something sexier. Her hand smoothed over the fabric, and when she looked up, Quinn was standing right beside her.

His hand came up and caressed her cheek. "You're beautiful," he murmured, but he didn't do anything else—didn't touch her anywhere else, didn't attempt to kiss her. Instead, he stepped back, pulled the blankets down, and motioned for Anna to lie down. Then he walked over and closed the door to the den and turned out the light.

Anna's heart was racing. All of her senses were on high alert. She heard him walking back over to the bed, where he stopped. The sound of the zipper on his jeans going down seemed unusually loud, and she found her breath coming in little gasps. Was he going to completely undress? She heard the jeans hit the floor and then felt him climbing into the bed beside her.

She went perfectly still—afraid to move, afraid to breathe. Quinn moved closer and she almost let out a loud *whoosh* of air when she realized he still had his boxers on. There was just a sliver of light shining into the room through the blinds, enough for her to see him lying on his side looking at her.

"Are you okay?" he asked quietly.

"Uh-huh."

He chuckled. "It's just me, Anna," he said, and then he did reach out and touch her—just on her arm, but even that light touch was enough to make her skin tingle.

"I know," she said, finally letting herself relax. "This is just…new."

"But it's not bad, right?"

Was it? Right then she'd have had to say no, but the timing was less than ideal. "No, it's not bad. A little confusing, but not bad."

Beside her, he shifted so his head was resting on his pillow, but his eyes never left hers. "This wasn't the way I pictured the night ending. What happened in my office…well… If the phone hadn't rung—"

"I know," she whispered.

"You're trembling. I can feel it."

She let out a low, nervous laugh. "It's just…I never thought… I mean, it's you and me. I always wanted—"

"You did?" he interrupted.

Uh-oh. It was too late to take it back. Thank God for the lack of real lighting. Maybe Quinn wouldn't be able to see how embarrassed she really was. She nodded and then realized he probably couldn't see that either. "Yes."

"Jesus, Anna. I never knew. How come you never said anything?"

"Seriously?"

"Yeah. We tell each other everything."

"Quinn, you never once looked at me as anything other than a friend. We've been hanging out together since we were kids. You tell me about the girls you date and the hookups you've had. I figured if I told you how

I felt, you'd—" She stopped and tried to keep her voice steady even though her heart was ready to beat right out of her chest. "I figured you wouldn't want to be around me anymore."

"Anna…"

"I'd rather have you as my friend than lose you."

Quinn reached and took one of her hands in his. "You're never going to lose me."

"How can you be so sure? What if…what if we… change things and it doesn't work out? Are you honestly telling me things would go back to the way they were before? That it wouldn't be weird to hang out together?"

"I honestly don't know," he said, his voice calm and soothing. "But…I'm also not afraid to try." He raised her hand to his lips and kissed it. "All I know is that for a long time now, things have been…different between us. It bothers me to see you with other guys, and I miss you when you aren't there. I didn't understand what I was feeling. Or at least I didn't until the last couple of days."

"Oh," she said on a breathy sigh.

"Yeah," he said, his own voice sounding a bit breathless. "I want to kiss you again, Anna." He leaned closer until his lips touched her cheek, her jaw. "I know nothing is going to happen here tonight, but I'd really like to kiss you and hold you. Can I? Would that be all right?"

If she hadn't been in love with him before, she certainly was now. This was a side of Quinn she hadn't really thought existed. She knew the cocky and arrogant side of him. She knew the loud and boisterous side. Hell, she even knew the condescending and jackass side. But this considerate one? This was brand-new, and she really liked it.

"Yes. I'd like that a lot." And then she held her breath as one arm moved across her and his weight shifted so his body covered half of hers. It felt better than she'd fantasized. He was large and warm and so damn muscular she almost purred.

Then his lips were on hers—softly exploring, familiarizing himself. Anna was doing the same with him. They shared lazy kisses and sweet, slow caresses, and rather than being awkward, to Anna it felt like coming home. Like this was what had been missing from her life.

She lost track of time and let herself just get lost in Quinn and all he was doing to her—which was mild in terms of anything sexual but it was arousing nonetheless. When he finally lifted his head, he placed one last kiss on her forehead before wrapping an arm around her shoulder and tucking her in beside him.

"We need to be up early for Hugh. I think we should try and grab a couple of hours of sleep."

Anna nodded and couldn't help but place her hand on the middle of Quinn's chest and then place a kiss there as well. He hissed in a breath.

"Careful, Anna. I'm trying to behave here tonight."

She giggled. "Sorry. I just always wanted to do that."

He hugged her to him. "Well, when we're someplace other than my brother's den, I'll let you do that all you want."

"Promise?"

He chuckled. "Definitely."

Anna sighed beside him and fell asleep with a smile on her face.

⁓

It was almost lunchtime and they were all sitting in another waiting room. Hugh had gone to the hospital before the rest of the family that morning, but they weren't too far behind him. Now, as they sat silently drinking coffee, reading newspapers, and watching the muted television, they were anxious for an update.

Quinn took the last sip of his coffee and grimaced. It was cold and completely disgusting. Beside him, Anna sat flipping through a magazine.

Last night had been amazing. For the first time in his life, Quinn had simply enjoyed the act of kissing a woman. He hadn't done that since he was fifteen. He had been filled with awe every time he touched Anna. She was a mystery and yet still familiar to him, and it was an incredibly heady experience learning this side of her.

Being here for his brother and Aubrey was his first priority, but he couldn't help but feel a little impatient to get Anna home and be alone with her. He looked at his watch and sighed with frustration—not just for himself but for Hugh. It had been hours, and as far as he knew, there hadn't been any updates on Aubrey.

"Maybe we should go down to the cafeteria and get some lunch?" Anna said to him as she put the magazine down beside her.

"I don't know. What if the doctors come out and we're not here?"

She bit her lip while she thought about it. "Perhaps Hugh will want to stay here and we can bring something back for him. What do you think?"

Zoe looked over and smiled. "What's going on?"

"We're thinking about lunch," Anna said.

Aidan perked up and looked over at them. "I could eat."

They all stood and walked over to where Hugh, Ian, and Owen were sitting. Quinn told them what they were planning and asked if they wanted to join them. Hugh refused, not wanting to take the risk of missing the doctor. Ian opted to stay with Hugh. Owen stood and said he'd go along.

The five of them walked to the cafeteria in silence. They grabbed their food and found a table, and there was a collective sigh as they sat down. Quinn knew they were all worried about the same thing—what if the doctors came out and said Aubrey's cancer was back? How would Hugh survive, and how could they all be there to help? It was too much to think about, so Quinn did his best to find another topic.

"So, Owen, where were you heading to? Some big seminar or something?"

Owen slowly unwrapped his sandwich before answering. "I've been down in Atlanta for a couple of weeks and was heading up to Washington, DC, to the Albert Einstein Planetarium. I'm going there to teach a couple of classes."

"Well, that's exciting," Zoe said. "I've never been to that one. I've gone to the Moorehead Planetarium in Chapel Hill, but never thought to go to another one. Do you like the Albert Einstein? Have you been there before?"

This time Owen took a bite of his sandwich and chewed slowly and took a sip from his bottle of water before answering. "It's one of the top ten planetariums in the United States. Some people find it a bit intimidating, but it's really quite fascinating."

"Why is that?" Anna asked.

"Well, for starters, it's part of the Smithsonian Air and Space Museum and is the largest of the Smithsonian's nineteen museums. Its Center for Earth and Planetary studies is one of the institution's nine research centers."

There was a collective "wow" around the table before Owen continued. "The museum's collection encompasses some sixty thousand objects ranging in size from Saturn V rockets to jetliners to gliders to space helmets to microchips. Fully one-third of the museum's aircraft and spacecraft are one of a kind or associated with a major milestone." He paused and took another bite of his sandwich and another drink.

"Plus, more than twelve thousand cubic feet of documents recording the history, science, and technology of flight are housed in the museum's archives. The facility also holds the most complete collection of aviation and space images—more than 1.75 million photographs and fourteen thousand film and video titles. All of which I'll have access to. It will aid in teaching my classes."

Quinn couldn't help but smile. He may not have a bit of interest in what Owen was talking about—or understand it half the time—but it still gave him a sense of pride to see how his little brother was doing what he loved. "I'm sure you'll kick ass, Owen," he said and then noticed the look of horror and confusion on Owen's face. "It means you'll do great."

Everyone chuckled and eventually Owen joined in.

"You really need to brush up on these phrases, bro," Aidan said before reaching over and patting Owen on the back. "The younger generation is going to confuse the hell out of you if you don't keep up with the lingo."

"Scientists don't really use lingo. We use scientific facts and phrases. You'd be surprised at how intense it can be. If you came and sat in on one of my classes or seminars, you'd find you'd be in the minority."

"Owen," Aidan began apologetically, "I wasn't judging. I just meant—"

"I know," Owen said quickly. "You're not the first person to mention it and you won't be the last." He sighed. "More times than not, I'm around other scientists and it's not an issue. But I know eventually that's not going to be the case. It's not easy to change the way I think and act and speak. Sometimes I wish I could."

It was probably the longest speech Owen had ever given that didn't include some sort of statistic or fact, and Quinn felt bad for him. Reaching over, Quinn put his arm around him and gave him a brotherly hug. "It's not all it's cracked up to be, Owen. Don't worry about it. You're fine just the way you are."

"Absolutely," Anna chimed in, and that made Owen blush before he ducked his head down and finished his lunch.

The rest of the meal was eaten in relative silence until Aidan's phone buzzed. He looked down at the screen and his shoulders sagged.

"What?" Zoe asked. "What is it?"

"The doctor just called Hugh back. Dad said he looked pretty grim."

"Shit," Quinn muttered, and they all stood and quickly began clearing the table. It didn't take long for them to head back up to the waiting area, Quinn and Anna bringing up the rear.

Anna gripped his hand. "I'm afraid to go back up there."

He nodded. "I know. Me too. But we have to be brave for Hugh. And for Aubrey. We can yell and scream and cry when we get home, but we have to make sure we hold it together up there."

They were all standing waiting for the elevator and nodded at Quinn's words.

"Do you really think it's going to be bad?" Zoe asked no one in particular.

"Unfortunately, it's hard to think otherwise. And the fact it wasn't something that was easily diagnosed makes me think it has to be something more serious than the flu or an ear infection," Aidan said solemnly.

They rode up to the fifth floor in silence and found Ian sitting by himself, praying. They each took a seat around him and bowed their heads and silently joined him. When Ian said "Amen," it wasn't long until each of them raised their heads too.

"Any word yet?" Quinn asked.

Ian shook his head. "This is the hardest part. The waiting. I'm sure Hugh is feeling some relief because they're finally telling him something. I just pray it's not as bad as we're all thinking."

There was another round of nods, and just when they were all settling back in and relaxing, Hugh came out, his face wet with tears.

Anna gripped Quinn's hand tightly in hers as he cursed under his breath again. He had really hoped the news would be good, that they'd be sending Aubrey home and it was all going to be all right.

The last time Quinn had seen his brother cry was when their mother had died, and in that instant, he felt as if he had traveled back in time and they were standing in

the waiting room that cold October day hearing that she
was gone. It was Anna's hand stroking his that brought
him back to the present and kept him from staying
locked in the memory.

"Well?" Ian said, standing up and going to his second
oldest child.

Hugh didn't speak. He sat down and seemed to crumple into a chair as he openly wept. Ian, Aidan, and Quinn
were instantly beside him, each with a hand on him.
Owen got up and went to grab a cup of water. Anna and
Zoe clung to each other, tears welling up in their eyes.

"It's going to be all right, Son," Ian said. "Whatever
it is, we're all here for you. Whatever you and Aubrey
need, we're here, you understand?"

Hugh nodded but still didn't look up. Owen came
back and knelt in front of Hugh, the cup of water in his
hand. They all stayed like that—the four Shaughnessy
men huddled together as if trying to give Hugh their
strength. Anna and Zoe stood up and joined the huddle,
where they stayed for another few minutes before Hugh
cleared his throat and straightened.

Wiping his tears away, he took a minute to compose
himself. "I'm sorry I fell apart like that," he finally said.
"It's… I just never…"

"It's all right, Hugh," Aidan said. "Take your time."

Everyone stepped back and took a seat, giving Hugh
the time he needed. Owen handed him the drink, and
when Hugh drank it all, he looked at everyone and gave
a weak smile.

"What did the doctor say?" Ian finally asked. "And
how is Aubrey?"

"She's great," Hugh said and they all looked at one

another with mild shock. "She's feeling much better today. And surprisingly enough, she got a good night's sleep and that helped."

Everyone started to speak at once, but Ian held up a hand to stop them. "I don't understand. What did they find, Hugh? What caused her to faint in the first place?"

Hugh straightened in his seat and took a steadying breath. "She's pregnant."

And then everyone really was talking at once, but this time joyfully. They stood and took turns hugging Hugh and asking when they could see Aubrey.

"I don't understand," Quinn said when things calmed down. "I thought you said…you know…it wasn't possible."

Hugh shrugged. "That's what Aubrey had been told years ago and she never questioned it. And to be honest with you, as much as I was disappointed at the thought of never having kids of our own, in the end it didn't matter. I was in love with Aubrey and wanted to spend my life with her." Then he blushed. "So we haven't taken any precautions because we didn't think…"

"This is incredible news!" Ian cried. "A miracle, really!"

Hugh nodded enthusiastically. "I'm in shock! Aubrey's in shock! We were preparing ourselves for bad news. We never expected something like this."

"So when can she go home?" Anna asked.

"They're going to keep her one more night for observation. This is still going to be considered a high-risk pregnancy, and she'll probably spend a lot of time being poked and prodded by doctors, but we'll gladly deal with it."

"We're so happy for you," Aidan said as he pulled Hugh in for a hug. "Seriously, we're so happy and so relieved."

"You and me both," Hugh replied.

"Can we see her?" Zoe asked.

"Absolutely. Come on. She's in room five seven-teen." Hugh motioned for everyone to follow him but held back and waited for Anna. "Can I talk to you alone for a minute?"

"Sure," she said. Quinn was beside her and he looked at his brother quizzically.

"You don't mind, do you?" Hugh asked with a know-ing grin.

"I'll see you guys inside," Quinn said and walked away, giving Anna's hand one last squeeze.

Hugh led Anna back to the sofas and sat down. She sat down beside him. "What's going on?"

"I know this may seem like odd timing, but... remember the property you showed me a couple of months back?"

Anna nodded.

"Is it still available?"

Again, she nodded.

"You up to writing up some contracts?"

"Are you kidding?" she cried, a smile spreading across her face. "Why? How? When?"

"Exactly!" Hugh said with a laugh. "It's been on my mind for a while, and it was something I had planned on pursuing a little further down the road, but with this news about Aubrey and the baby, I don't want to be trav-eling. I want to stay close to home. Getting this property and starting the plan-and-design phase of it will keep me here and give me something to do other than hovering over my wife—something I'm sure she'll appreciate."

"Hugh, are you sure? It's a really big investment. I know we've done the research but—"

"Anna, one of the most important rules of business—don't talk the customer out of making a purchase, okay?" he said with a wink.

"I'm just so surprised!" she said. "I would have thought this would be the last thing on your mind right now."

"Like I said, I've been thinking about it for a while, and Aubrey and I knew it was something we wanted to do. It's something we can work on together from start to finish, and I'm really excited about it. So what do you say? Are you ready to make some serious money?"

"Um…are you kidding? Hell yes!" she said with a laugh.

"All right then," he said and held a hand out for her to shake. Once she did, he pulled her in for a hug. "Come on, we can celebrate after we sign everything."

"You're on!"

They rose and he put an arm around her shoulders as they headed down the hall toward Aubrey's room. "So…you and Quinn, huh?" When Anna's eyes went wide, Hugh simply laughed. "Second-best news I've heard today!"

—⁓—

It was late in the afternoon when Quinn and Anna were back in Quinn's truck, heading home. The family had all stayed at the hospital long enough to visit with Aubrey and make sure she was okay before leaving.

"Do you think we should have stayed another night?" Anna asked as they pulled out of the hospital parking lot.

Quinn shook his head. "I think my brother is going to go home and get a good night's sleep—after he makes seventeen to-do lists about what he'll need to do to the house to prepare for the baby, and then he'll make spreadsheets to plan out the baby's life."

Anna laughed, mainly because she knew he wasn't exaggerating. "Eventually he'll learn to calm down a little with the planning. He's already gotten better."

"I know he has. Aubrey's been good for him, and I think the curveballs he's been thrown since meeting her have made a big difference too."

Anna relaxed against the seat. "Pregnant. I can't even imagine how shocked and relieved they must have felt when the doctor gave them the news. I'm sure my shock was nothing compared to theirs."

"I know. I was sitting there in the waiting room and when Hugh came out… Damn. I was certain it was bad news, and I felt sick for him. I hated even thinking of the two of them facing something so harsh."

"You know he's going to make her crazy, right?"

Quinn chuckled. "No doubt. He's going to want to put her in bubble wrap and not let her do a thing." Then he laughed harder. "She'll want to strangle him by the time the baby comes!"

They drove in companionable silence. Anna watched the scenery go by, her mind wandering to all of the events of the last several days, when she sighed.

"What?" he asked softly. "What's the matter?"

She turned to him and smiled. "A baby. A Shaughnessy baby," she said with wonder. "This is going to be the first baby since…Darcy. The first grandchild for your father. It's all just so…so…" She was at a loss for words.

"I know," he said and reached over and took one of

her hands in his. And they drove like that until they hit the outskirts of town. "You hungry?"

She nodded. The lunch at the hospital cafeteria had left a lot to be desired, and even though it was earlier than when she normally ate dinner, she was definitely ready to eat. "You know what? I kind of am. What do you have in mind?"

"We can stop at the pub and grab a burger," he suggested. "I know it's not the same since you're not there making them, but I think it will be okay." He winked at her.

"That sounds pretty good. Plus, you may not agree, but it's always better when someone else does the cooking."

"I don't know about that. I think it's better when *you* do the cooking rather than me," he teased.

She couldn't help but laugh. Why had she thought he wouldn't agree? "Well, they're not as good as mine, but Johnny still does a pretty good job with them."

"Why didn't you just give him your recipe?"

Anna looked at Quinn with mock horror. "Give him my recipe? Are you crazy? It's a secret family recipe!"

Quinn rolled his eyes. "Anna, I've been going to barbecues at your parents' house since I was six. Their burgers have never tasted like yours. Clearly you created the recipe. Why does it have to be a secret?"

"Maybe I enjoy all the attention," she said saucily and winked at him, and they both laughed.

"Sweetheart, I will gladly give you all the attention you want as long as you feed me."

Instantly, sexy images of doing just that played in Anna's mind. Sleeping with Quinn last night had been wonderful. Waking up in his arms had been like a dream come true. It was sweet. It was innocent. And it was completely comfortable. It was almost as if they were an old married couple.

No! she corrected herself. *Don't think like that. It implies boredom.* She most certainly did not want Quinn to be bored with her already. Maybe…

"Maybe we should just stop at the supermarket and get some groceries and I can make burgers back at my place. I wouldn't mind some clean clothes, and you could run home too if you want, while I cook."

"You just don't want me to see what you do to the burgers," he said suspiciously.

"Good grief! I was just saying—"

He chuckled. "I know, I know. You are just way too easy to tease." He picked up her hand again and kissed it. "I like your plan. I could definitely go for changing out of yesterday's clothes. I know we got to shower this morning and all, but a fresh set of clothes would have felt even better."

"Okay, so it's a plan. We'll stop at the store and then you can drop me off at home and—" She stopped and cursed.

"What's wrong?"

"My car! I totally forgot that my car is still crapped out at your shop!"

"Don't worry about it," he said. "I've got a loaner car you can use until we get yours taken care of."

She sagged with relief but frowned.

"Now what?" he asked.

"I just hate having to do that."

"It's not a big deal, Anna. You need a car and I have one you can use. Don't worry about it, okay?"

She nodded but still wasn't happy about it. They pulled up to the supermarket, went in, and grabbed all the ingredients they needed for dinner.

"Do you have beer at your place?" he asked.

"I do."

"How about ice cream?"

"Beer and ice cream? It just sounds wrong. And a little disgusting." She shuddered at the thought.

He laughed again. "Well, not at the same time."

By the time they were back in the truck, Anna was feeling the first tingles of excitement. Cooking a meal for Quinn and eating together were no big deal. They did that at least once a week. But she couldn't help wondering how it was all going to be different this time. After all, they had kissed, they had spent the night together, and, if she was really lucky, they were going to again.

"You're quiet," he said as they drove through town.

"Just thinking." She kept her gaze focused on the passing scenery because she was certain her blush would give her away.

"Anna," he said, and when she didn't look at him, he said it again. His smile was comforting. "Let's just focus on dinner for right now, okay?"

Right then, Anna wasn't sure if it was a blessing or a curse how he knew her so well. As friends, it was definitely a good thing, but in this new relationship—as lovers—it could get her into a lot of trouble.

In the past, they would talk about the relationships they were in. Quinn tended to overshare, but she wasn't going to think about it. Who was she going to talk to now? What if they had a fight or a problem or if things just didn't go the way she thought they would? He was her best friend and the one she turned to no matter what the problem was. Was she foolish for being willing to throw it all away on a relationship that may not work?

"You're doing it again," he said, pulling into her driveway.

"Get out of my head," she snipped, but there was no real heat behind the words. Anna was surprised when Quinn climbed out of the car with her and carried the groceries into the house. The house was dimly lit, as the sun was starting to go down, and Anna didn't turn on any lights and neither did he.

She turned to grab one of the bags and found Quinn right behind her. "Oh!" she softly cried. "I didn't expect you to be right there."

His blue eyes darkened as he looked at her upturned face and slowly walked her backward until her back gently bumped the countertop. He placed the bags on the counter. Strong arms came around either side of her, boxing her in.

"I should go home," he said, his voice a low rumble.

Anna could only nod, but her eyes never left his.

"I need to get changed and make some calls." He was listing all the reasons for him to leave, but all Anna could think about were ways to make him stay.

"You could make your calls from here," she said, her voice a breathy whisper. "And Bobby keeps some clothes here. I'm sure you could find something to—"

It was all she could get out before Quinn swooped down and kissed her. Where last night's kisses had been slow and sweet, this time it was back to the fast and frantic kind they'd shared in his shop. Was it only twenty-four hours ago? she wondered.

Who cares? a little inner voice cried out. And that's when Anna's mind just shut off as she let the sensations take over. Quinn's body pressed against hers. The feel of his lips on hers. The way his tongue slowly reached out and teased hers. It was sensory overload, and if they never got around to eating dinner, she'd be perfectly okay with that. Starvation was completely worth it.

Her hands roamed the muscled expanse of his chest, up over his stubbled jaw, and into the thick, blondish hair she loved. She could feel his body vibrating as he growled into her mouth, and that's when she knew they weren't waiting. They weren't going to talk or take it slow. Hell, they weren't even going to barbecue.

She'd be lucky if they made it to the bedroom.

Just then, Quinn lifted his head and took a minute to catch his breath. "I'm not leaving."

Anna couldn't help but smile. "Good."

One of his hands caressed her cheek, and his eyes followed its path downward—her jaw, her shoulder, before finally stopping and gently cupping her breast. He inhaled deeply while Anna almost melted on the spot. She sighed his name as her eyes fluttered closed.

"Look at me, Anna," he said gently, and she had to force herself to comply. "Are you sure about this? If you're not, I'll go. I don't want to, but I'll go."

She said his name again, and his hand moved back up to cup her jaw.

"This is different. You're not a casual hookup. You're not a one-night stand. I'm not just here for tonight, Anna."

Relief flooded her because on some level, she had worried about that. She knew the kind of relationships

Quinn usually had. She'd been warned by more than one person that it was a good enough reason not to get involved with him. And yet, hearing him put her fears to rest was as much of a turn-on as his kisses were.

"I want you to stay," she said, her voice barely audible.

And before she could say another word, Quinn scooped her up in his arms and carried her to her bedroom. Excitement warred with disappointment. Part of her had been hoping they'd stay in the kitchen. She wanted to be the type of woman who caused a man to lose control—to the point where he had to have her right there, right now.

A goddess.

But this was good too, she thought as he placed her down on the bed. He straightened and pulled his T-shirt up and over his head, tossing it on the floor. His body was absolute perfection. For all the times she'd seen him shirtless, it was quite another experience to know he was doing it specifically for her.

And in a matter of minutes, she'd be able to touch it, feel it.

Quinn kicked off his shoes and socks, but when his hands went to the button on his jeans, he stopped and looked down at her, a bashful grin on his face. "Is it weird how I'm nervous all of a sudden?"

Anna couldn't help the nervous bubble of laughter that came out. "Thank God you said it! I thought it was just me!"

He hung his head and chuckled. "Damn, Anna. I know this is what I want, and I…I just don't know what to do."

She pushed up on her elbows and looked at him,

a smile of understanding on her face. And then she decided to have a little fun with him. "You mean you're a virgin?" she teased.

And that broke the tension. A bark of laughter was his first response, but he was able to reel it in quickly. "Why don't I prove to you how unvirginal I am?"

"Bring it."

Quinn shucked his jeans but left his boxers on as he crawled on the bed and covered her body—kissing her along the way. "I think one of us is still overdressed," he murmured.

She couldn't help but tease him. "I was wondering why you left your boxers on."

And then he rested his forehead against hers, closed his eyes, and smiled. "You're not going to make this easy, are you?"

She shook her head. "I was hoping to make it…hard. Very, very hard."

Slowly, Quinn lifted his head, his expression dark, serious. No more teasing. No more smiles. "Bring it."

And she did.

Chapter 7

QUINN WAS STANDING ON ANNA'S BACK DECK AFTER midnight, manning the grill. If anyone had told him he'd be doing this—or how he'd be doing it wearing nothing more than his boxers and a grin—he'd have told them they were crazy.

And yet, there he was.

He stretched and flexed his shoulders, happy to be a little sore. The last few hours had been the best kind of workout he'd ever had.

Anna Hannigan.

He still couldn't wrap his brain around it. His best friend, the girl he'd grown up with, had completely rocked his world. Quinn found he was suddenly jealous of every guy she had ever dated, any guy who'd ever touched her. She was beautiful and sexy and, he thought with an even bigger grin, a goddess in bed.

Yeah, he'd said it—he'd actually spoken those words to her while they were in bed, and she had blushed and then given him a sexy grin that had him getting hard all over again. He was hard now just thinking of it.

Damn burgers. He flipped them and made sure they were done before plating them and shutting off the grill. Walking back into the house, he found Anna wearing the T-shirt he had discarded earlier and nothing else. She was putting the rest of their meal together and hadn't noticed him yet.

How the hell had he been so blind for so long? When

had he simply stopped paying attention to the woman she was becoming in favor of only seeing her as the girl she had once been? And how was it he was lucky enough that she wanted him?

Quietly, he stepped farther into the room and watched her. She spun around and moved with such grace that it left him mesmerized. And then she bent over to get something and…

Holy hell!

Stalking across the room, he put the plate down on the counter and came up behind her. Anna let out a little squeal of surprise. "I didn't even—"

Spinning her around, his mouth crashed down on hers as his hands went to her waist and lifted her until she was seated on the counter. Then she squealed again as the cold surface hit her bare skin.

"Quinn? What…?"

"No talking," he said between kisses. "Just let me… I need…"

And then he was done talking for several long, breathless minutes.

Cold burgers certainly weren't a favorite, but knowing she was the kind of woman who made a man completely lose control certainly was!

Anna quickly heated up the patties before putting them on the buns and making up their plates. Quinn was sitting on the couch, flipping through the TV channels like she had asked him to. Not that she really wanted him to, but she needed a few minutes to pull herself together after their impromptu romp.

The look in Quinn's eyes as he'd made love to her had been better than anything she'd ever fantasized. *He* was better than anything she'd ever fantasized.

Picking up the plates, she thought of how this scene was so familiar and yet now so different. Quinn smiled at her when she stepped around and put their plates on the coffee table.

"There isn't a whole lot on right now, unless you want me to find something on Netflix," he said and then reached for one of her hands and pulled her down on the couch beside him.

"It doesn't really matter to me. Any one of the late night shows is fine."

Quinn nodded, flipped to one of them, tossed the TV remote aside, and immediately picked up his burger. Before he took his first bite, he turned toward Anna. "I'm just warning you, this isn't going to be pretty. I'm starving."

"Ditto," she said, and then they each dug into their meals. They ate in silence for the most part, stopping to laugh or comment on what they were watching on television. When Anna was done, she slouched back on the couch. "Too. Much. Food."

He chuckled. "No such thing." Wiping his mouth, Quinn looked toward the kitchen. "You bought ice cream, right?"

She waved her hand toward the kitchen. "Help yourself. I'm too tired to move."

Standing, he stepped over her outstretched legs and then bent over and kissed the top of her head. "Rest up while you can. This is simply refueling!" Then he winked at her and walked to the kitchen.

Anna wasn't sure if he was serious or not, and as

much as she really wanted sleep, her body was already humming and more than willing to stay up and play. "Traitor," she mumbled.

"Did you say something?" Quinn called out from the kitchen.

"Nope," she replied. "Just talking to the TV."

—∕∕∕—

The next morning, Quinn took Anna to his shop and gave her the keys to his truck.

Anna looked at the keys and then at Quinn like he was crazy. "I don't understand. Why am I taking your truck? I thought you said you had a loaner for me to use."

He shrugged, but his gaze didn't meet her eyes. "It's no big deal. I want to make sure you're safe driving around."

She couldn't help but grin. "And the loaner isn't safe?" she asked playfully, nudging him with her shoulder. "Are your customers aware of this?"

"It's fine, but…this is better."

Leaning in, she kissed him on the cheek. "You're very sweet. Thank you." Then she looked around the parking lot. "What are you going to drive?"

"I'll probably use the Corvette," he said blandly.

Anna's jaw dropped. "*The Corvette*? You're seriously going to drive the Corvette? You never take it out!" She took the keys to the truck and put them back in his hands. "I can't. I can't take the truck. I'll take the loaner or I'll call Bobby."

Quinn took her hands in his. He was momentarily distracted at how soft they were and remembered how incredible they'd felt roaming all over his body. Shaking his head free of the erotic images, he focused on Anna.

"It's not a big deal. We'll look at your car today and hopefully have it back to you tomorrow. I can handle driving the Vette for a day or two."

"But you baby that thing," she reminded him anxiously. "You treat that car better than some people treat a real baby. I don't want you doing this on my account. Really. It's not a big deal. Please."

He pulled her into his arms and kissed her soundly. "No arguing. Take the truck and get going. I want to get your car up on the lift, and I'm sure you have calls to get caught up on since you were out of the office yesterday."

"Oh!" she cried. "That reminds me. I can't believe I forgot to tell you! Hugh decided to buy the property I showed him! Can you believe it?"

"Are you serious? That's great!" And then he pulled her back into his arms and spun her around excitedly before kissing her again. "I knew you could do it!"

"This is huge," she said when he put her back on her feet. "Because it's a commercial property deal, the paperwork is a little bit more of a nightmare, but once everything is signed, sealed, and delivered, I can finally think about a new car. Just think—this will be the last time you have to patch the Honda up!"

"I just want you to be safe, Anna," he said, his expression going serious. "I'm sorry if I made you feel bad the other night. I was…" He shook his head. "It wasn't right. You know I'll do whatever I can to fix the car and make sure it's safe for you, and if I can't, I'll help you get another car."

She pulled back. "Quinn, I appreciate your helping me with the loaner for a couple of days, but if the Honda can't be fixed, I'll take care of it."

He threw his head back and let out a growl of frustration. "Why do you argue everything with me?"

"I do not argue everything," she said defensively and then frowned when Quinn gave her a pointed look. "Okay, fine. I argue some stuff, but this time it's legit. I don't expect anyone to help me get another car. I'll make do until my commission on the property comes through. It's not a big deal."

As much as Quinn wanted to argue with her, he decided to bide his time. The car was a complete disaster, and he'd patched it up far too many times. Every time he gave her the keys back, he begged her to just sell it for scrap and get another car, but Anna held firm. He understood her reasoning—sort of. She didn't want to take on the financial burden of a car payment, but she wasn't thinking about her own safety.

He was.

And whether she liked it or not, Anna Hannigan wasn't going to get the last word this time.

A week later, Anna was still driving Quinn's truck. He wouldn't tell her exactly what was wrong with her car, just that he was waiting on parts. It all seemed logical, but she couldn't help but feel bad about it.

Quinn, on the other hand, was having a good time driving his beloved Corvette. He thanked her every time he saw her for forcing him to drive it. They would laugh about it, but deep down, Anna still felt guilty. Worse, she felt like a charity case and she hated it.

They had spent every night together and each one had been hotter, sweeter, and sexier than the night before.

Anna couldn't believe how easily they had transitioned from friends to lovers. She kept waiting for something to happen—for something to go wrong where they'd both look at one another and be like, "Well, we tried," and call it a day.

Not that she wanted to. Hell no. Quinn Shaughnessy had always had a knack for making her heart race, but now? She had to fan herself. The man was an incredible lover—not that she'd tell him so just yet; he had a huge ego as it was. No need to add to it. They were able to sit and talk about their days and joke and laugh one minute and then be tearing at each other's clothes the next. It was never boring and she was loving every minute of it.

Standing in her living room, she looked at her overnight bag that was waiting by the door. Quinn was due to pick her up any minute. They were heading to Hugh and Aubrey's for the weekend, so she and Hugh could go over the contracts for the sale of the property. They'd been emailing and talking on the phone, but when he asked if they could get together and talk, Anna was more than willing to do so. He extended the invitation to Quinn as well, so they were making a weekend of it.

Their first official outing as a couple.

It scared the hell out of her.

Not that she had any real reason to be scared or nervous. All the Shaughnessys had known about her feelings for Quinn for a long time. Hugh had even laughed about it when they had last seen him. But now that it was real? She just hoped Quinn was going to be able to handle the good-natured ribbing she was certain Hugh was going to throw his way.

Only time would tell.

The knock at the door made her jump, but she didn't have to walk over to open it—Quinn let himself in. "Hey, gorgeous," he said, sauntering over to her. "You all ready?" Without waiting for her answer, he leaned down and kissed her.

She loved that about him. It usually took less than ten seconds for him to take her in his arms and kiss her. Like he couldn't wait any longer to do it. She sighed against him. How had she survived all this time without being loved like this by him? When he lifted his head and smiled, her heart raced.

"Are you all packed?" he asked.

Anna nodded. "Sure am. I really didn't need much— Hugh said we were staying in. I don't think he wants to take Aubrey out just yet."

"Tell her to give us a safe word," he said with a chuckle as he stepped away and went to grab her bag, "and we'll break her out of there."

"A safe word?"

"Yeah, you know, like a code word to let us know she needs to escape."

Anna laughed. "You may need to take your brother out someplace so I can get Aubrey out of the house for a little while. Even if it's just to go and grab some groceries, I'm sure she'll appreciate it."

"No doubt."

"Although your brother just may surprise us. Maybe he's not being overprotective or hovering. Maybe—"

"You've met Hugh, right?"

Anna rolled her eyes. "Stop. He's been getting better!"

"Not that much better," Quinn replied. "Trust me. For all the progress he's made since meeting Aubrey, this whole situation has more than likely set him ten steps back." He looked around the house. "Is everything locked up?"

She grabbed her purse and her keys. "Yup." Turning off the kitchen light, Anna turned and followed Quinn out the door. "We're taking the truck, right?"

Quinn shook his head. "Nah. I figured we'd take the Corvette."

She stopped dead in her tracks. When Quinn got to the car and put her luggage in the trunk, he turned and noticed her standing there. "What?"

"You are freaking me out!" she said with a nervous laugh. "Who are you, and what have you done with Quinn Shaughnessy?"

He walked back over to her. "What's the big deal?"

"You've had this car for a year, and you drove it home from the dealership and that was it. Then you decided you could drive it to and from work until my car was ready—which, by the way, do you have any idea when that will be?"

He shook his head. "Still waiting on some parts."

She looked at him oddly. "It's taking an awful long time for them to come in. What's the hold up?"

Quinn took her hand and led her over to the car. "It happens sometimes, especially with older cars. Don't worry. We'll get it taken care of."

He was being evasive, of that she was certain. But why? He opened the car door for her and then she remembered her original question. "Oh yeah…so after a year of not driving this car, now you want to take it on a road trip?"

"It's not really a road trip. They only live an hour away."

"But still—"

"Anna?"

"Hmm?"

"Get in the car," he said lightly before placing a light kiss on her nose and walking around to his side of the car.

—⁓—

"Blink twice if you want me to slip a Valium in Hugh's tea," Quinn whispered loudly to Aubrey, and they all broke out in laughter.

Except Hugh.

"Not funny, bro. Seriously."

Quinn just laughed harder. "Dude, the doctors all said Aubrey is fine and you're treating her like an invalid!"

"It's not quite that bad," Aubrey said lightly, in defense of her husband.

"Don't let him keep going with this," Quinn said, leaning back in his chair and reaching for his drink. "You're going to start to go crazy before too long."

"I don't see anything wrong with pampering my wife," Hugh said as he smiled at Aubrey. "She deserves it."

"Oh my God, give me a break," Quinn whined. "You're making me lose my appetite." Then he looked down at his plate of grilled steak tacos. "And these are too good to skip out on."

Hugh grinned. "My baby wanted steak tacos, so I made steak tacos."

Quinn dramatically rolled his eyes and groaned.

"Oh, stop," Anna finally interjected. "I think it's sweet he's taking such good care of Aubrey, and look at her—she looks fabulous. Pampering obviously agrees with her."

Aubrey smiled and blushed. "I have to admit, it's not hard to get used to."

Quinn leaned over in his brother's direction. "You're creating a monster, that's what you're doing. You'll do this for nine months and then when the baby comes, you'll have two of them to take care of."

Hugh's smile broadened. "Can't wait."

"Fine," Quinn mumbled. "But don't come crying to me when you're feeling all left out and neglected, because I'm not going to be sympathetic."

"Like you ever are!" Hugh said with a loud bark of laughter. "You are the least sympathetic person I know!" Then he turned to Anna. "Seriously, what do you see in him? He's cranky, completely unsympathetic, and I'd bet you a month's salary he hasn't the first clue how to pamper you properly!"

It was all said in jest, but Quinn's spine stiffened a bit.

"Hey!" Quinn snapped.

"Don't even," Hugh countered. "Tell me I'm wrong! Tell me you've done anything that was solely for Anna and I'll apologize."

"Hugh," Anna warned playfully, "come on. Let's change the subject. Let's talk about your plans for the property and the new resort. Have you gotten any drawings on the design yet?"

"Wait, wait, wait," Quinn said, holding up a hand. He looked at Anna first and then his brother. "It's not a competition, bro," he said defensively. "All I'm saying is Aubrey isn't made of china, and it's okay for her to have a little time to herself doing the things she wants to do without you hovering over her. If the doctor said it's okay, then it's okay."

Hugh's grin faded. "I agree. But it doesn't mean I *can't* take care of her, either. If I want to cook her a meal or let her relax and rest, then I'll do it. Just because it's never once occurred to you to take care of someone other than yourself, it doesn't mean the rest of us have to be so selfish."

Seriously? This is what his family thought of him? Quinn silently fumed.

"Hugh," Anna said quickly, "what did you use on the steak for these tacos? They're fabulous."

Quinn glared at her. "You agree with him, don't you?" he asked Anna harshly.

"What? What do you mean?"

He threw his napkin down on the table and stood up. "I can't believe this. You agree with him. You think I'm some sort of selfish jerk!"

"Quinn, that's not what I think," Anna pleaded with him.

"No, no, it's okay. It's fine," he said and took a step away from the table. "Clearly I'm the jackass of the family."

Now it was Hugh's turn to roll his eyes. "Quinn, knock it off and sit back down. Come on. I'm sorry. I was just kidding around. Let it go."

"No, I don't think you were kidding. You really think those things. You wouldn't have said them otherwise. You're the most honest one in the family," he mocked.

"Oh, for crying out loud," Hugh huffed. "Stop being such a drama queen and sit down."

"Come on," Anna said in a tone she always used when she was trying to tell him he was wrong. "Let's finish this delicious lunch and tonight I'll cook for us and we can eat out on the deck looking at the ocean. Won't that be nice?"

He wanted to argue; he really did. But then he'd be accused of being the guy who ruined lunch. *Fabulous*. Grabbing the back of his chair, he yanked it away from the table and then sat back down.

They all ate in silence for about a minute until he couldn't take it anymore. He would show them all he wasn't the jerk they all thought him to be.

"For your information," he said, looking at his brother, "I bought Anna a car! Hers crapped out and I bought her a new one because she didn't want a car payment. So now she'll have one free and clear. Tell me again how selfish I am!" Then he sat back smugly, crossing his arms over his chest.

"You did what?" Anna cried.

Uh-oh…

He turned to her, his arms dropping. He smiled at her reassuringly. "It was supposed to be a surprise. When we got home tomorrow night, it was going to be waiting for you in your driveway. One of my guys was going to deliver it and take the truck back." He noticed she wasn't smiling. If anything, her face was flushed with anger and embarrassment.

"And you didn't think to ask me before you did something like this? I told you how I felt about the whole car situation, Quinn!" she said and then jumped to her feet. "I'm not a charity case!"

She fled from the room and Quinn immediately jumped up to go after her, but Aubrey stopped him. "Let *me* go," she said, coming to her feet. "I have a feeling she's going to need a few minutes to herself. You two stay here and try not to start any more arguments." She walked away, leaving the brothers alone.

Quinn looked over at Hugh. "What did I do? Tell me what I did that was so horrible?"

Hugh chuckled. "Dude…sometimes I can't even believe we're related."

"What?" Quinn snapped. "Seriously, what did I do that was so wrong? Anna's car was on its last legs and she couldn't afford a new one yet. I'm just helping her out."

Leaning forward on the table, Hugh turned serious. "Did she ask you or even imply she needed help buying a car?"

He thought about it for a minute. "Not exactly."

"How long have you known Anna?"

Quinn looked at him dryly. "You know the answer to that."

"I do. And I was going for irony. You've known Anna almost your whole life. She's very independent and doesn't like anyone helping her—no matter how much she may need it. It's a pride thing. Hell, even I know that about her! How did you think she was going to react?"

"I don't know…grateful?"

"Your lack of common sense is astounding," Hugh said, taking another drink of his tea. "If you had presented it to her as some sort of business deal or that you found a great deal on a car and managed to secure reasonable payments for her, she might not have gotten so angry." He paused. "She was going to be pissed off initially, but she would have eventually cooled off and gone for it. But what you did? Taking the matter out of her hands completely? It's going to take her a little while to get over that."

Damn it, his brother was right. Why hadn't he thought of it that way? And then it hit him. "I wanted to take care of her," he mumbled. "I really... I just..." He shrugged. "For once, I wanted to do something for her."

And then Hugh relaxed back in his chair and smiled. "Finally."

Quinn's head snapped up. "What?"

"I knew you had it in you somewhere."

"Had what?"

"The ability to put someone else first." He held up his hand when Quinn started to argue. "Before you get all pissy again, hear me out." He paused again. "You've always been strong-willed and a bit self-centered. It's not always a bad thing, but sometimes...it's a little hard to take. Anna's been putting you first practically since the first time you met. And you know what? You always took."

"That's not—"

"Yeah, yeah, yeah...you helped her with her car or you beat up anyone who bothered her, but it wasn't a completely selfless act. I know your heart was in the right place with this car thing, and I'm sure she'll calm down about it, but you have to be able to explain to her why you did it."

"I would think it's obvious," Quinn said. "She needed a car and couldn't afford one. I could. End of story."

Hugh sighed and ran a weary hand over his face. "How it is that she fell in love with you and stayed there is absolutely astounding."

"Now what?" Quinn cried.

"How about explaining it to her as her boyfriend and not as her buddy? How about making her feel like she's special rather than some sort of burden? Maybe make it like a romantic gesture rather than a tax write-off?"

"Is that all? Maybe I should fill the damn car with roses while a full orchestra plays for her under a starry sky? Or maybe—"

"Just shut up," Hugh said. "You're killing me."

They sat in silence and picked at what was left of their lunches. "Okay, so what do I do?" Quinn finally asked. "How do I get her to…you know…not hate me?"

"Are you sure you want to ask me? After all, it was only a few minutes ago you were attacking the way I treat my wife."

"Well, I still think it's a bit much, but at least Aubrey's still talking to you."

Hugh laughed. "You may want to take notes on this because I have a feeling Anna's not going to be quite as easygoing."

"I know you're really angry right now, and rightfully so, but can I just say thank you for giving me an excuse to come down here and put my toes in the sand?"

Anna looked over at Aubrey and smiled. She had pretty much stormed out the back door of the house and down the deck steps that led to a path through the dunes to the beach. It left her breathless, but Aubrey looked completely at peace.

"It's beautiful down here," Anna said. "You and Hugh picked a great house."

"I'll admit, when we first found it, I was a little

disappointed it was set so far back from the actual sand, but then after hearing about Zoe's first beach house, I'm kind of glad."

Anna nodded. "That was a nightmare. She had already been through so much with losing her mom and relocating, then to lose her house like that? In all the years I lived close to the beach, I never saw a house just fall into the ocean like that during a storm. It was horrible. I still can't imagine how she felt watching it happen on the news! Thank God Aidan had convinced her to leave." She looked around. "No, what you have here is perfect. You're set far enough back that you should be good in a storm."

Aubrey sat in the sand and tilted her head back so the sun could shine on her face. "I know it's the same sun I get up on the deck, but when you combine it with the feel of the sand between your toes, it's just better."

"I agree." She sat down beside her. "Am I being stupid? Did I overreact?"

Keeping her head back and eyes closed, Aubrey let out a sigh of contentment. "How bad was your car?"

"Really bad."

"How many times have you had to get it fixed?"

"Too many to count."

"Did you have plans to buy a new car?"

Now Anna sighed. "Yes. No. Kind of."

"Yeah, okay. That was clear."

"Fine. I knew I had to buy a car, but…I just kept putting it off. I don't want a car payment right now, and I figured once we closed the deal on the property, I'd be able to do something."

"That could still take some time, Anna. Are you sure the car would have held out that long?"

"Probably not. It's just…I wish he would have talked to me about it! He gets so high-handed and acts like some superior know-it-all." She fell back on the sand. "I swear he must think I'm some kind of idiot who can't take care of herself."

"Or maybe he really cares about you and your safety and wanted to make sure you would be okay," Aubrey said quietly. "Knowing what I do about Quinn, he acts first, thinks later. In this case, he saw you had a need and took care of it. It wasn't about proving you can't take care of yourself. It was about…maybe…him doing something nice for you."

"Well, crap," Anna muttered. "That does sound like him."

"I'm not saying you can't be annoyed at him for not talking to you first, but maybe try and see his side of it." She lay back and turned her face toward Anna. "So now that that's out of the way…you and Quinn, huh? Is it awesome? Is it everything you dreamed it would be?"

Anna laughed out loud. "Oh God." She put her hands over her face in embarrassment.

"Come on, you've been wanting this since forever. Don't get shy on me now! Come on! Spill it! I want details!"

"You are so *not* getting details!" Anna said, forcing herself to sit back up and focus on the waves crashing on the beach.

"Okay, you can leave some things out. I don't need to think that way about my brother-in-law," she laughed. "Or you."

"Let's just say it's all good. Really good." Anna blushed. "Better than I ever really thought it could be."

"Yeah!" Aubrey squealed, waving her hands in the

air. "I'm so happy for you guys! So what has everyone else had to say about it?"

Anna shrugged. "You guys are really the first to know. Or at least, you're the first ones we've been around since things started."

"Really? Wow. So when did things...start?"

Anna told her about the way things were before Aidan and Zoe's wedding and then about the incident with Jake.

"Oh my gosh, Anna! That's horrible! I can't believe nobody told me about this. Are you okay?"

"I'm fine. Luckily I only had a little bit to drink and was able to call Zoe to come and get me. She showed up with Aidan and Quinn. And, well...let's just say things got messy."

"I'm sure."

"When Quinn took me home afterward, we hung out until I fell asleep. He claims I kissed him."

"And did you?"

"I kind of thought I was dreaming."

"But you weren't," Aubrey said with a big grin.

"No, I wasn't. But he still left."

"Damn."

"Tell me about it." She sighed. "So a few days later, I was driving home after showing a house when my car started acting funky, and luckily I was near the shop, so I stopped in. Quinn was acting all weird, and next thing I knew, we were kissing."

"No!"

"Yes," Anna said, unable to stop her own grin. "And it was so hot and so amazing, and I couldn't believe it was happening."

"And then what? Did you guys do it right there in his office?" Aubrey asked giddily.

"Um...no."

She frowned. "Well, why not?"

Anna looked at her with a lopsided smile. "That's when we got the call about you. So we hopped in the truck and drove down here."

"Yikes...so I'm the reason you guys didn't get a hot and heavy first time. Damn. Sorry."

Anna chuckled. "Don't be. The actual first time was very hot and heavy and...perfect. And that's all I'm going to say about it."

"Good for you." Aubrey relaxed back in the sand again. "This really does feel good. Can you stay mad at Quinn for a little bit longer? Hugh thinks the walk to the sand is too much for me and makes me stay on the deck. I just need about fifteen more minutes of this bliss and then I'll be ready to go back inside."

"No problem. I'm just disappointed I didn't get to finish my lunch. Those tacos were awesome. I may have to ask Hugh for the recipe."

"We can reheat them when we get back inside," Aubrey said. "Or I can tell Hugh I want fresh ones." She looked at Anna with a wicked grin. "Don't believe for one minute I don't find ways to take advantage of all his hovering."

"You're an evil genius. I love it!"

⁓⁓⁓

No one mentioned the car—or the subsequent argument—again for the rest of the day. When Anna and Aubrey had gone back up to the house, Hugh offered to make them some fresh plates. The women looked at each other and giggled but refused to say why.

After lunch, they all sat out on the deck and talked about Hugh's plans for the property and the resort. There wasn't much Quinn could contribute to the discussion, but he loved watching how happy his brother was and how pleased Anna seemed to be.

Deep down, he knew real estate wasn't her dream. He understood—sort of—why she felt like she had to find a different career, but he knew that if she had her way, this wouldn't be what she was doing. So maybe she'd make enough money to get her to the point where she felt a little financially secure and then she could do what she loved.

Which was cooking.

She'd deny it till her last breath, but like he said, he knew her. She enjoyed the praise she received whenever she cooked, and she had loved running the kitchen at the pub. Hell, she should own the damn place! She had a head for business and the customers loved her. But for some reason, she didn't think it was something she should do. Something about breaking out of a rut, and not working in jeans…he wasn't sure, but he remembered all those things as parts of multiple conversations.

She made dinner for all of them, and they ate it out on the deck. Aubrey looked very relaxed and, for the first time since they'd arrived, so did Hugh. And Anna was positively glowing. That's how he knew he was right. If something as simple as making a meal for her friends put that look on her face, why was she wasting her time in real estate?

After the way he'd screwed up with the whole car

thing earlier, Quinn knew tonight wasn't the time to bring it up, but he made a mental note to talk to her about it a little more. Soon. There was no reason for her to be miserable. Ever. He wanted to make sure she was happy—and that she stayed happy.

That made him stop and think. When had he ever been that considerate? No doubt he'd dated more than his share of women, but he had never been overly concerned about their happiness. Well, their future happiness. He was all about making them happy while they dated, but once they were done, he didn't give them another thought.

He was far from done with Anna. Wasn't sure he'd ever be. And not just because of their friendship, but because of the way he was beginning to feel. He'd always loved Anna—as a friend. He'd always been protective of her and loved spending time with her, just hanging out. But now it was different, in a good way. There was genuine affection. His need to protect her went deeper, and the need to spend time with her? Well, he almost wished he didn't have to go to work most days because he just wanted to stay in bed with her, holding her, touching her…just being with her.

By the time they said good night to Hugh and Aubrey, Quinn realized he and Anna hadn't really talked to one another since lunch. They'd talked as a group all day, but they hadn't had any one-on-one conversation all day. And it bothered him. A lot.

Closing their bedroom door, he leaned against it and watched her move around the room. She was taking all the decorative pillows off the bed and pulling down the comforter. Then she went to her overnight bag and pulled out a T-shirt and the little bag that probably held her makeup and whatnot. Without a glance in his direction, she walked toward the attached bathroom. He reached out and placed a hand on her arm to stop her.

"Hey," he said softly and waited until her brown eyes looked up at him. They weren't twinkling like they normally did when she looked at him. Carefully, he maneuvered the two of them until she was in his arms. She held herself stiff, and he knew this wasn't going to be easy. "Dinner was excellent tonight. You didn't have to do that. It's good for Hugh to have to work a little," he teased, hoping to get a smile out of her.

He didn't.

Okay, new approach. "Aubrey looked great after you guys came back in. This pregnancy is really agreeing with her so far."

Nothing.

Not knowing what else to do, he released her and took a step back. "I'm sorry."

Anna eyed him warily. "For what?"

She knew him too well, knew he had a tendency to throw a blanket apology out there just to make a situation go away.

"For not talking to you about the car. I should have. I didn't mean for it to be a bad thing, Anna, I swear. I just..." He sighed. "For years, you've been the one taking care of me, and I let you. Hell, I even took advantage of it. And I finally found a way I could take care of you. I wanted...I wanted to do something that would make your life a little bit easier—to take at least one burden away from you. I know I didn't handle it right and—"

She immediately dropped her things on the floor and went up on her tiptoes and kissed him soundly on the lips. Quinn wasn't going to question it; he was just happy she was forgiving him. And she was kissing him. Anna was a spectacular kisser. One hand cupped her bottom while the other reached up to curl around the nape of her neck. God, she felt so good. All soft and warm and…everything.

Not wanting to break the kiss, he scooped her up in his arms and walked them over to the bed. Thankful the blankets were turned down, he immediately stretched out on top of her, kissing her, touching her, loving her.

Anna sighed his name when his mouth moved from hers. Quinn lifted his head and looked down at her. Her skin was flushed, her lips red from his kisses. "I want to take care of you, Anna," he said, his voice soft and low. "Let me."

A slow smile spread across her face as she relaxed beneath him. "I'm all yours," she said.

They were the three sweetest words Quinn had ever heard.

Chapter 8

"OH, QUINN," ANNA SAID THE NEXT DAY AS THEY DROVE up to her house. "What did you do?"

"What? We already covered this."

She leaned forward in her seat as they pulled into the driveway. "I wasn't... I didn't think... Oh my God." She sighed as he parked.

Yes, she knew there was a car waiting for her, and yes, she knew it wasn't going to be something old like her Honda, but...

Quinn climbed from the car and walked around to the passenger side to help her out. He opened the door and held out a hand to her. "You promised not to be mad. Remember that."

Anna took his hand and stood. His name came out on another sigh. "I can't believe..."

"You seemed to have some sort of weird connection with your old Honda, so I figured I couldn't go wrong with a newer one." He let go of her hand as she began to walk around the new car. "It's not brand-new, but it's only two years old and has under five thousand miles on it. My guys checked it out, and it's in perfect condition. I tried—"

But he never got to finish because Anna launched herself into his arms and kissed him. This was a much better reaction than what he had been expecting, so he readily jumped on board, banded his arms around her, and held her close. When she lifted her head, her smile was dazzling. "So…you like it?" he asked, gently lowering her to her feet.

"It's perfect. It looks like it just rolled off the showroom floor! And I love the color! That blue is just so beautiful!" She gave a little squeal of delight. "Where are the keys? Can I look inside? Can I drive it?"

Quinn nearly sagged with relief and laughed as he reached into his pocket. "Here you go. The second set should be in the car, under the driver's seat. It's where I told Tommy to leave it."

But Anna wasn't listening. She had the car door open and was sitting in the driver's seat and starting the car. "Ooo…power windows! I almost forgot what those were! Mine stopped working last year."

"I remember," Quinn mumbled, shaking his head.

"And power seats and mirrors!" She pushed buttons until the seat was in the perfect position for her and then worked on getting the mirrors just right. "This stereo is better than the one I have in my house!"

Quinn walked over to the passenger side and climbed in. "You've got every option available—cruise control, back-up camera, the radio has satellite, there's a USB port here for your phone, and there's Bluetooth—"

"This is amazing! I never thought I'd have a car this new." Turning toward Quinn, she smiled, leaned in, and kissed him on the cheek. "I'm sorry I was a bit of a brat the other day about this. This is incredibly generous of you, and I…well…I want to say it's too much but I love it already!"

"I figured we've got about twenty-plus years of you feeding me and helping me out," he teased. "Now we're kind of even."

She shook her head and reached out and cupped his face in her hands. "It was never a competition. I wasn't keeping track. I enjoy taking care of you and helping you."

"Oh yeah?" he asked quietly. "I have to be honest, Anna. I really enjoy taking care of you too. I just wish I had been smart enough to start doing it sooner." Then his expression turned serious, somber. "I should have paid more attention and not been so selfish. I don't deserve you."

A slow, sweet smile crossed her face as her thumbs skimmed over his cheeks. "Don't talk like that. I don't see it that way at all."

"Then you're the only one," he said.

"Why would you even say that?"

"Trust me. I've heard it a lot over the years."

"From whom?" she asked, pulling back slightly.

Quinn took one of her hands from his face and pulled it around so he could kiss her palm. "It doesn't matter."

"Damn right it doesn't," she said firmly.

"You sound pretty fierce there, Anna Hannigan," he said with a grin.

She nodded. "It's true. You're stuck with me and there's nothing you or anyone can do about it."

Quinn wasn't sure what to say to that. He kissed her and was about to go for something light and funny but she cut him off.

"Now close the door so we can take this baby out for a ride!"

For another week, they managed to stay somewhat cocooned in their own little world. While Hugh and

Aubrey knew about the change in their relationship—
and Anna was certain the rest of the Shaughnessys had
an idea—Anna had managed to avoid her own family.

It was early on Saturday morning, and they were lying
side by side in her bed catching their breath. "This is the
best way to wake up," Quinn said, turning his head and
kissing her bare shoulder. "Let's throw out our alarm
clocks and stick with this."

Anna playfully swatted him away. "We'd never get
up if that were the case."

Quinn sat up. "Nonsense. I'm energized and ready to
go." He looked over at the clock. "Holy shit…it's after
nine already?"

She chuckled. "See? I told you."

He stood up and reached for his jeans. "How
about some breakfast? I happen to make some great
French toast."

"You're on," she said and snuggled back under
the blankets.

"Oh no," he said, reaching for her hand and forcing
her to sit up. "No going back to sleep. You've got about
fifteen minutes and then breakfast will be on the table."

"What? Not in bed?" She pouted. "Seems to me the
least you could do is bring me breakfast in bed."

"And I promise I will—another time," he added.
"I've got to go in to the shop today. Those two classic
cars are supposed to get picked up at noon and I need to
be there to sign some papers."

Anna stared at him for a minute. "You mean Jake
Tanner's cars?"

Quinn nodded.

Guilt washed over her. She hated that she had

managed to cost Quinn some very lucrative business. She reached for the hand that had just let hers go. "Quinn, I…" She sighed. "I'm really sorry. I didn't expect you to lose such an important job because of me."

His gaze hardened as he looked at her. "You're kidding, right? Did you honestly think I'd still want to do business with that guy after—?"

"Look, what happened with Jake was awful and horrible and I hate it, but the bottom line is I'm okay. I was lucky. Nothing happened to me other than getting sick and feeling embarrassed."

"Anna, what the hell are you saying?"

She shrugged. "I just think you should, you know, still do the work. I'd double the price if I were you," she said in an attempt at humor, "but I'd still do the restorations. It would be great for your business. You know it, and I know it."

"I don't know," he said hesitantly. "The thought of ever dealing with Jake Tanner again—"

"I know," Anna interrupted. "Believe me, I know. But…just think about it, okay? I know how much you were looking forward to working on those cars. It meant a lot to you and the business."

"You mean more to me than that, Anna," he said fiercely, leaning on the bed toward her. "I can always find other restoration jobs, but if anything happened to you?" He stopped when Anna placed a finger over his lips.

"Don't, okay?" she whispered. "Don't think like that." She kissed him and then smiled. "Now go and make me some breakfast. I'm starving."

Quinn stood and still looked a bit unsure of himself,

but he watched as Anna rose from the bed—naked and beautiful—and walked to the bathroom.

He was shirtless, his hair was a mess, and his pants weren't buttoned. He raked a hand through his hair and walked out to the kitchen. He was pulling eggs and butter from the refrigerator when a sound by the front door caught his attention.

"Hey, Anna! What's with the—" Bobby Hannigan stopped dead in his tracks at the sight of Quinn in his sister's kitchen. "What the hell are you doing here?" he snarled, slamming the door closed.

For his part, Quinn did his best to remain calm. He had known they were going to have to deal with Bobby eventually—and Bobby's intense dislike of him—but he had been really hoping it wasn't going to happen quite like this.

"Hey, Bobby," he said casually. "I'm making French toast. You want some?"

"You son of a bitch," Bobby hissed as he stalked across the room, tossing his keys on the ground as he went. When he got close enough, he lunged at Quinn.

Quinn managed to dodge him, but a plate crashed to the floor in the move. "Look, let's just talk for a minute, okay?" he said, trying to reason with Bobby.

"Are you sleeping with my sister? Is that why you're here?" he growled, doing his best to back Quinn into a corner.

"Seriously, just calm down. I don't want to fight with you."

"Too bad," Bobby snapped. "You couldn't just leave her alone, could you? It's not enough you've been taking advantage of her for years, or that your friend drugged her. No. You had to just swoop in and do this now!"

"It wasn't like that!" Quinn yelled. "And it's really none of your damn business what's going on between me and Anna."

"She's my sister. That makes it my business." He shook his head in disgust. "I really hoped she'd outgrow the stupid crush she had on you, but you just kept dragging her along."

"No one was getting dragged! We were friends! Shit, Anna's the best friend I've ever had! I would never hurt her, and as for what's going on right now—"

"Shut up!" Bobby interrupted. "You just shut the hell up. I've been waiting a long time for this. I've been waiting for the opportunity to punch you in your damn smug face."

Quinn stopped. His hands dropped to his sides. "You want to hit me? Would that make you feel better? Then go ahead. I'll stand here and I'll take it. If that's what it takes for you to realize I'm not just fooling around with your sister, that she means something to me, then go ahead. Take your best shot."

Bobby's eyes narrowed.

"So help me, Bobby, if you do it, you'll have me to deal with," Anna yelled from the bedroom doorway. Slowly, she walked into the room. "What in the world is going on here?"

Bobby turned and looked at her. "I've been driving by your house for the last couple of days and haven't seen your car. Finally I decided to stop in and see what was going on. Where's your car? Did it break down again?"

"Actually," she said hesitantly, "that's my new car out in the driveway."

"New? How?" Bobby stammered. "I thought you said you couldn't afford a new car right now?"

She shrugged. "I couldn't. But my old one crapped out, and Quinn helped me out and—"

"You bought her a car?" He cursed under his breath and took a few steps away. "You seriously bought her a freaking car?"

"Um…help me out here," Quinn said quietly to Anna. "I can't tell if he's angry or impressed right now."

"Yes, he bought me a car," Anna answered instead. "I didn't ask him to, and at first, I was really annoyed he did it, but…" She looked at Quinn and smiled. "But he knew I needed the help."

"I knew you needed the help too!" Bobby said defensively. "I would have helped you get a car, Anna! You don't need him doing it for you! You don't have to sleep with him because he bought you a car!"

"Okay, that's enough," she said and walked over and gave her brother a shove until he fell back on the couch. "You need to understand and accept that Quinn and I are together. I don't know what your deal is with him, but it's got to stop."

"You're too good for him, Anna," Bobby said through clenched teeth. "All these years you've waited on him hand and foot and he never gave you a second thought."

"That's not true," Quinn protested. "I've always been there for Anna! We've been friends our whole lives!"

"That's not what I'm talking about, jackass," Bobby snapped at him. "She's been pining after you since you were teenagers and you never noticed. Do you have any idea how many times she cried after you started dating someone new?" He didn't wait for an answer. Slowly, he stood up and began stalking Quinn again. "Or how many times she would come home brokenhearted and disappointed because you didn't thank her or appreciate the things she did for you?"

"Bobby," Anna warned.

"No! It's time he knew just how awful he was!" Slowly, he walked around Quinn. "How many times did you call her and ask her to make you food or bake you cookies, and she did it only to find you with another girl when she arrived?"

Quinn watched him warily at first and then with defeat. "If I could go back and change any of it, I would," he said quietly. "I know I can't and it kills me. I had no idea Anna felt that way about me."

"Yeah, well…maybe if you paid attention to someone other than yourself—"

"Look, I get it!" Quinn finally snapped. "Do you think I like knowing how much I hurt her? Do you think it's easy for me to stand here and listen to this?"

"You're not good enough for her," Bobby snarled. "You're having fun right now and everyone's happy, but I know you, Quinn. You don't stick around. You don't have staying power. Eventually, you're going to get bored, and you'll start treating her exactly like you used to. And I'll be the one whose shoulder she'll cry on."

"It's not like that," Quinn said.

"We'll see."

Anna stepped in between the two of them, facing her

brother. "Thanks for the vote of confidence, Bobby," she said sadly. "Thanks for believing I'm the type of girl who isn't enough for someone to stay with."

And then she stormed from the room, slamming the bedroom door behind her.

"Way to go, genius," Quinn said, raking a hand through his hair.

"*Me?* This is all your fault!"

Quinn shook his head. "Uh-uh. No way. You came in here and started this. And by the way, why not try knocking next time instead of just barging in?"

"Barging…?" Bobby let out a growl of frustration. "You do realize I used to live here too, right?"

"Whatever. That was like…two years ago. This is Anna's house now, and you have no right just letting yourself in. She's entitled to her privacy."

"Don't you dare lecture me about my sister."

Quinn threw up his hands in defeat and frustration. "You know what? We're done. You need to leave so I can go and make sure Anna's okay."

"I'll go and see—"

"No, you won't," Quinn said firmly. "You need to leave." Then he sighed. "Honestly, Bobby, let me go and take care of her."

"I don't trust you, Shaughnessy."

"That's fine. I don't really care what you think of me, but you'll respect your sister. Just go. I'll make sure she calls you later."

Bobby hesitated for a full minute before he simply nodded and bent to pick up his keys on his way out the door.

Once it was shut and Quinn heard Bobby's car pull

way, he walked over to the bedroom door and lightly knocked. "Anna? Can I come in?"

"Sure."

He opened the door and found her lying on the bed, one arm flung over her face, covering her eyes. "You okay?"

"Oh, yeah. Just great," she mumbled.

Quinn sat down beside her. "You know he's just looking out for you."

"It didn't feel that way."

"Yeah, well, trust me. I think if I walked in on Darcy and found some guy in her place, I'd probably kick his ass first and ask questions later."

She moved her arm away from her face. "It's not like that at all. Bobby knows you. He's known you as long as I have. What he said out there—and what he implied— was pretty insulting." She sat up. "And Darcy's still a child. Any guy you found with her would be a complete stranger to you, so you'd better punch first and talk later."

He loved how she was just as protective of his little sister as he was. "I'll remember to tell her it was your idea, should it ever happen." He pulled her into his arms and kissed the top of her head.

"And I'll completely deny it. No one would believe you over me. Your family thinks I'm very sweet."

Quinn tucked a finger under her chin. "I think you're very sweet too." He kissed her nose, her cheek, and then her lips. "Everything about you," he murmured before kissing her again.

Soon they were lying down on the bed and he was rolling her beneath him. It would have been easy to distract her—and him. With very little effort, Quinn knew he could have them both naked and lost to the world outside. But he knew it wasn't the way to really make her feel better.

Instead, he lifted his head and looked down at her solemnly. "I really am sorry, Anna. All this time I thought I was a good friend to you, but I wasn't. I hurt you and I didn't even realize I was doing it."

One of her hands came up and caressed the side of his face. "It wasn't your fault, Quinn. I could have handled things differently too. I should have said something a long time ago."

"No. I hate that you got hurt because of me, but I think where we are now, here like this, it wouldn't have happened unless we went through all we went through. Does that make sense?"

She nodded.

Rising from the bed, he pulled her up with him. "Now come on. It's your turn to sit and watch me do all the cooking." He took her by the hand and led her from the bedroom.

Of course, once the cat was out of the bag—compliments of Bobby—the phone started ringing. First it was her parents, and then some of their friends, and eventually the Shaughnessys chimed in. But in their defense, it was a family dinner invitation, and Anna never turned one of those down. This would be the first one—kind of—that she and Quinn would be going to as a couple.

Ian Shaughnessy was hosting a barbecue because all of the restoration and remodeling on his home was officially done. At one point or another, each of his six children had come home and helped with the work, but this was the first time everyone was going to be there to see the finished product.

Quinn had to work that morning, so Anna told him she'd meet him at his father's. It wasn't unusual for her to go there on her own, and if anything, it was no different from going home to her parents'. Well, it could also be because her parents lived right next door to Ian, and if they were in town, she had no doubt they'd be joining the family for the festivities.

Ian greeted her at the door with a big smile and a kiss on the cheek. "There's my girl," he said and took the large bowl from her hands. "What have you made for us?"

"This is some potato salad," she said with a proud grin—it was one of her specialties and she knew the Shaughnessys all enjoyed it. "And I happen to have several trays of brownies out in the car. I just need to—"

"Did someone say brownies?" Riley asked as he came over and kissed her on the cheek too. "I'll just go and grab them from your car."

"It's the blue Honda," she yelled over her shoulder as Riley walked out the door.

She made her way into the house, saying hello to everyone as she went until she was in the kitchen. Zoe and Darcy were in there slicing vegetables and talking. "Hey, girls! How are you both doing?"

Zoe looked up and smiled while Darcy continued to look down at the tomato she was slicing. Anna walked over and hugged Zoe and looked at her questioningly. Then she turned to Darcy. "Hey, kiddo. What's going on?"

Darcy shrugged and Anna looked back at Zoe. "Am I missing something?"

There was a moment's hesitation before Zoe sighed. "Darcy asked if she could go on a trip to Florida for spring break and Ian said no."

Darcy looked up at Anna. "Honestly? *Everyone* said no." She glared at Zoe.

"O-kay," Anna said and put her purse down on the kitchen table. "So who's going on this trip?"

Slamming down the knife she was using, Darcy huffed. "Everyone! All of my friends are going— Michelle, Diana, Amy, Jennifer, Mike, Rob—"

"So it's a coed trip?" Anna asked, grabbing a celery stalk and munching on it as she leaned a hip against the counter.

"Well, yeah…it's college. Of course it's a coed trip."

Anna chuckled. Oh, to be young and think everyone around you was a moron. "Were you planning on flying or driving?"

"Driving. Why?"

"And where were you going to stay?"

"We were going to rent a house in Daytona," Darcy replied.

"Hmm…and how much was it going to cost?"

A shrug was her only response.

"Come on, Darce," Anna said. "Out with it."

"Okay, so I was going to need about fifteen hundred dollars for everything. But it would cover everything! Gas, food, the house—all of it!"

"And do you have that much money saved?" Anna asked.

Darcy looked at her like she was crazy. "No, why?"

"So basically you not only asked your dad for permission to go, but you wanted him to finance it too?" She didn't wait for Darcy to answer. "And you were foolish enough to ask for way more than you could possibly need for the trip. That's a huge red flag to me."

"What are you talking about?" Darcy asked defensively. "We worked out the budget. That's how much it's going to cost."

Anna finished her piece of celery, rested her elbows on the counter, and looked at Darcy with a mixture of sympathy and condescension. "Sweetheart, I hate to break it to you, but whoever worked that budget up probably failed fifth-grade math."

"What do you mean?"

"The cost of driving from here to Florida—in one car—would maybe be a hundred bucks tops. Split that between however many are in the car and you're maybe at twenty dollars a person." She paused. "Then if seven of you are going in on a house and are splitting the cost of the house—a three-bedroom one would be completely sufficient—you're looking at about three hundred per person."

Darcy sputtered a little bit but couldn't seem to get a word out.

"Then food and whatnot for one person, you're looking at maybe—at most—about two hundred. And that's only if you are eating out every day. Renting a house means you can stock the fridge to cut costs." She straightened. "Sorry, baby girl, but honestly, had you said six hundred dollars, you might have had a chance."

"No," Darcy said. "They all said no because of the guys. If it were all girls, I'm sure Dad would have said yes."

"Dad would have said yes to what?" Ian asked as he strolled into his newly designed kitchen.

Anna didn't have a problem dealing with family matters head-on, and this family was like her own, so she knew it wouldn't be a big deal to throw herself into the middle of this mess. "What was your biggest issue with the spring break thing, Ian? The cost or the boys?"

Ian looked at Anna for a minute and then glanced at his daughter. "Honestly? The cost. I'm not an idiot, Anna. She goes to school and lives on campus and is even in a coed dorm. The cost of that trip was just excessive." He looked at Darcy again. "Sorry, sweet pea." Then he kissed her on the head, grabbed a beer from the refrigerator, and walked back out to the living room.

"Holy cow." Darcy sighed and then stared at Anna. "How did you do that? How did you know?"

Anna walked over and put her arm around Darcy. "Believe it or not, kiddo, you're not the first college girl to try and con her way into a sweet spring break. Mine was Hawaii. I thought my dad was going to have a heart attack. Had I aimed small—like Florida—he might have gone for it. But I got greedy." She ruffled Darcy's hair. "Lesson learned."

"Well, shit," Darcy said and pushed the plate of tomatoes away.

"Language," Aidan said as he strolled into the room.

"Oh, for crying out loud," Darcy muttered. "Unclench."

He went to Zoe and kissed her soundly on the lips. "And here I thought a big family get-together wasn't going to be any fun. Who knew my baby sister would be so entertaining?" He turned and grinned at Darcy and almost choked when she flipped him the bird and stormed from the room.

"Aidan," Zoe admonished. "That wasn't very nice. You know she's already upset."

"And it's all her own doing. She still hasn't outgrown the need to make a scene when there's an audience. She chose today to ask about that ridiculous trip because she figured Dad would be too distracted to question it. We're all here for a nice day and to see the house as a finished product, and she had to ruin it."

"I wouldn't say she ruined it," Anna chimed in.

Aidan gave her a bland look. "Anna, come on. As much as Darcy has grown up, she's still very immature." He shrugged. "Hell, we all were at her age, and it just sucks for her that there are so many of us who've been there before her." He reached over and grabbed a beer. "We should be thankful Quinn wasn't here to witness the whole thing. There would have been a lot more screaming and crying."

"Yikes," Anna said and walked over to grab herself a bottle of water.

"Speaking of which—when is he supposed to get here? I figured he'd be here by now."

Anna looked at her watch. "Yeah, I thought so too, but he probably lost track of time. He had to go into the shop this morning to do some work on a car he's restoring."

"Not Jake Tanner's, I hope," Aidan said and then shook his head. "If it were me, I would have put those cars out in the middle of the road with the keys in them after what happened." Zoe elbowed him in the ribs. "Sorry. Didn't mean to bring that up."

"It's okay, Aidan. Really. I told Quinn he should do the work on the cars."

"*What?*" Aidan and Zoe cried at the same time.

Anna nodded.

"Sweetie, are you crazy?" Zoe asked. "Why would you want him to work for that jackass? After what he did, I'd think you wouldn't want Quinn to have anything to do with him!"

"I thought about it, but it's a really big opportunity for his business. It isn't like Jake's going to be working beside him." She shrugged again. "It's really not a big deal. Quinn's business is more important."

"Um…no," Aidan said. "*You're* more important." He stopped and cursed under his breath. "So is that why he's not here? Because he's working on one of Jake's cars?"

At this point, Anna was afraid to confirm or deny it.

Riley walked into the kitchen with the trays from her car. "I'm not going to lie to you," he said with a grin, "I ate two of them before I closed the car door."

Anna chuckled. "You didn't need to confess. The chocolate crumbs on your shirt gave you away. You're forgiven."

"Excellent." He put the trays down and walked over to hug her and then kept his arm around her shoulders. "My brother's a lucky man." Then he looked around a bit. "Come to think of it, it looks like most of my brothers are lucky men."

"And don't you forget it," Zoe said.

Riley looked from person to person and noticed the conversation had stopped. "Okay, what's going on? Why'd everyone clam up when I came into the room?" He paused. "It's the new song I sent, isn't it? You guys hate the new music." He stepped away from Anna and cursed. "Just come out and say it. I can take it."

Anna immediately reached out and touched his arm. "No one hates your music, Riley. Relax."

"Then why is everyone so damn quiet?"

"It's…it's nothing," Anna said.

"I'll tell you what it is," Aidan began. "Quinn kept those classic cars that belong to Jake Tanner. He's still going to do the work on them!"

Riley's eyes went wide. "Wait…Jake Tanner? The guy who…" He looked at Anna and then back to his brother. "Are you kidding me?"

"It's really not a big deal," Anna murmured, but no one seemed to be listening.

"I have no idea what's wrong with him," Aidan said, shaking his head with disgust.

"Why would he do that?" Riley asked, brows furrowed.

Before anyone could reply, Anna stepped in between the two brothers and held up her hands to stop them. "Look, I told Quinn he should keep the cars and work on them. The publicity he's going to get once the cars are done will be a real boost to his business. So if I'm okay with it, then you all should be too. I don't want anyone giving him any grief when he gets here." Her voice was firm, as was her expression.

Wordlessly, Riley held up his hands in defeat. Reaching over, he grabbed one more brownie, and with the grin he was famous for, he left the kitchen.

Anna turned to Aidan and Zoe. "Promise me," she said. "Promise me you're not going to say anything to him." She paused. "Today is about your dad and the house. I don't know if any of you noticed, but he didn't invite Martha, so that should tell you how important it is that the family is here. I'm sure it would be helpful if everyone got along. Darcy already got everyone riled up. Let's not add to it, okay?"

Zoe nodded, and when Aidan didn't say or do anything, she elbowed him in the ribs. "Fine," he finally said. "But I'm still annoyed—"

"I get it," Anna interrupted. "Just let it go for today. Please. For me."

He nodded and kissed his wife on the cheek, and then kissed Anna on the cheek as well before walking from the kitchen to join the rest of his family in the living room.

"You won't be able to keep them quiet forever, you know," Zoe said when they were alone.

"I know. But for today I just want everyone to get along."

Zoe laughed. "You know that's not very realistic. Whenever you get more than two Shaughnessys in the room, they're bound to disagree about something. It's just the way it is."

"Oh, you don't have to tell me. I know it's the norm, but maybe they'll find something else to argue about."

Zoe sighed. "I wouldn't hold my breath if I were you."

"Hey, a girl can dream."

He could barely hear himself think, the room was so noisy. It was full of conversation and laughter and, yes, arguments. With ten people around the table, dinner was boisterous to say the least.

There was steak and chicken Ian had grilled on the barbecue, salads, corn on the cob, dinner rolls, and baked potatoes. There was enough food for a small army—which they kind of were. Plates and bowls were passed around almost continuously.

Aubrey updated everyone on her health and how she was feeling with her pregnancy. Hugh grinned as he watched his wife, making sure she had everything she could possibly want to eat. Darcy talked about school, Riley talked about the possibility of a tour to promote his new album—if he ever finished it—and Owen shared how he had been offered the opportunity to teach at UC Berkeley at the Lawrence Hall of Science.

The only problem with all of this was everyone was talking at once.

Quinn looked around the table and caught a couple of words of each conversation. He thought about talking about how business was going, but he kind of felt like flying under the radar right then. Not about work, but he had a feeling he and Anna were under the microscope. It was their first time with everyone, and he suddenly felt uncomfortable in his own skin.

"So, Anna," Ian said loudly to be heard over all his kids, "I hear you and Hugh are working on the contracts for the coastal property here. It's very exciting!"

She nodded. "Things are moving along and my bosses are very pleased."

"I'm sure. I know we're all looking forward to having him work close to home for a while. So thank you for helping to make it possible."

"Hey," Hugh protested with a laugh, "I would have come around eventually."

Ian laughed and shook his head. "Not soon enough."

"Yeah, we'll see how you feel when I'm around all the time," Hugh challenged.

"I still think I'll be okay with it," Ian replied.

"Well, I can't take all the credit," Anna said. "I wasn't really the one to approach him with the potential property. Quinn presented it to him first."

"Dude," Riley said with a grin, shaking his head. "Not cool. You totally stole Anna's thunder."

Quinn looked around and found the conversation had calmed down and everyone was looking his way. "What?"

"That was totally Anna's place to present the property deal to Hugh. Why'd you interfere?" Riley asked. His tone was light, but it still rubbed Quinn the wrong way. Then he added, "Seriously, Anna, what do you see in this guy?"

Everyone laughed. "I always pictured you with a guy in a suit," Hugh said with a playful grin. "You know, a businessman."

"I agree," Aidan chimed in. "You can do way better than our resident grease monkey here." He looked over at Quinn and saw the tension there and then winked at Anna. "I bet a businessman wouldn't horn in on your job."

"I did not horn in!" Quinn snapped, slamming a hand down on the table. "I was simply trying to move things along to help her!"

"Call it what you want, Quinn," Riley said. "But you still stole her thunder." He shook his head and made a tsk-ing sound before focusing on Anna again. "I wouldn't tolerate it if I were you."

"It really wasn't a big deal," Anna said quietly, looking down at her plate.

And it hit Quinn for the first time—had he really done that? Had he stolen her thunder? Had he interfered when he shouldn't have? He thought about it for a minute and shook his head. *Hell no!* This was the dynamic of his and Anna's relationship—they helped one another out. They always had. That's what friends did. And technically, when he had called Hugh, he and Anna had still been just friends.

Did she resent him for interfering?

Would she even tell him if she did?

No. Anna had a way of keeping certain things to herself—especially when it applied to things he did that upset her.

Which, apparently, was a lot over the years.

Knowing he wasn't capable of participating in any more conversation, he ducked his head and focused on his meal, thankful the conversation turned to Hugh and his plans for the new resort.

Out of the corner of his eye, he could see Anna was eating and she was even participating in the discussion, but Quinn couldn't bring himself to. Right then, his head was messed up.

What if everyone was right? What if he wasn't right for Anna? What if she did deserve to be with someone else? Instantly, an image of some corporate guy in a suit sprang to mind and it made him angry. The guy was faceless and yet Quinn could feel the rage building.

What was so wrong with him that made everyone so damn certain he was wrong for her? Granted, he hadn't been the most observant guy over the years, but he was working on it! Why wasn't he getting any credit for trying to be a better person?

He was so lost in thought that he didn't notice everyone standing up and starting to clear the table. In the Shaughnessy house, it was a group effort. No one person had dish duty; everyone did. For once, Quinn was glad to get lost in the shuffle. Conversation flowed around him, and when things were almost done, he ducked out and went to the backyard. The sun had gone down, and for a minute, all he could do was stand there and breathe, his head thrown back.

"I wish I had my telescope with me."

Quinn didn't need to turn his head to know Owen was coming up beside him.

"The sky on a clear night offers an ever-changing display of fascinating objects you can see, from stars and constellations to bright planets, the moon." He sighed wistfully. "If you want, I can point out some of the things you're seeing."

Shaking his head, Quinn straightened and looked at his brother. "Thanks, but…not tonight."

"They're all wrong, you know."

"About what?"

"You," Owen said simply. He wasn't looking at Quinn; his attention was still on the sky.

"Oh yeah? What makes you so sure about that?" Quinn asked, curious to get his brainiac brother's spin on the whole thing.

"For starters, there's more to you than just being— what did they call you? A grease monkey?" He looked at Quinn with confusion. "I'm guessing it's a play on words because you work on cars."

Quinn couldn't help but chuckle and nod.

"Anyway, I don't understand why they say it like it's a bad thing. Aidan builds houses, Hugh builds resorts, and Riley builds songs." He shrugged. "You build cars—and not just one kind of car, every kind.

You need to have a working knowledge of how every kind of car works. Most people don't understand how an internal combustion engine operates. You do." Then he turned and looked at Quinn. "Seems to me that makes you smarter than they are."

Well, hell. "You think I'm smart?" Quinn asked quietly.

Owen nodded. "You're one of the smartest guys I know. You've mastered so many different things already—and you didn't go to school for any of them. I mean, I know you had to get certified to be a mechanic, but for you, that was just a technicality. You already knew how to do everything. You put your mind to something, and you make it happen. It's impressive."

Wow. His genius brother was seriously standing there telling him he was impressed. Damn. "Yeah, well…no one else sees that."

"Does Anna think that?"

"What?"

"That you're just a grease monkey?"

Quinn chuckled. "No," he said, smiling. "She's never thought that. It doesn't matter what I'm doing or what I'm trying, she makes me feel…hell…she makes me feel like I'm the best at it."

"It's because you usually are," Owen said simply.

"Dude, knock it off. I'm blushing."

Owen looked at him oddly. "I wouldn't really know. It's dark out here."

Leave it to Owen to take him literally. "Can I ask you something?"

"Sure."

"Do you think I'm wrong for Anna?"

"No."

"Care to elaborate?"

With a sigh, Owen faced him. "People like to argue how opposites attract. And in some ways, it's true. But it seems to me what you and Anna have is something most people only hope to attain."

"And what's that?"

"You genuinely like each other."

Quinn's eyes went a little wide. "That's it? No scientific facts or figures?"

Owen shrugged. "From the first time the two of you met, you clicked. You were instant friends and you've stayed that way. Why? Because you have a love and respect for one another. Granted, it didn't turn into a romantic love until recently, but I think it's always been there. It just needed time to be nurtured."

"I wish I could believe that. My track record is really working against me here—at least where everyone else is concerned."

"It shouldn't matter what everyone else thinks. What do you think? Do you think you're the right man for Anna? Do you believe you have staying power even if you don't wear a suit to work?"

Quinn didn't know what to say.

His confidence was slightly rattled after dinner, and he wasn't so sure of anything right then.

Chapter 9

SOMETHING WAS BECOMING BLAZINGLY OBVIOUS TO Anna—she and Quinn spent most of their time alone at her place.

After the dinner at Ian's, Quinn had been a little sullen and withdrawn, and she normally had to work at getting him to relax. They spent almost every night together, but she was beginning to realize they had gone out more when they were just friends than they had since they'd started dating.

Not that she was complaining—not really. The time they spent alone after work was her favorite part of the day. They'd share dinner, watch movies, and make love. The man was insatiable, and she was finding her inner goddess was too! But there was going to come a time when they both needed something more. Neither of them was antisocial, and next week they had their monthly softball game. They'd been on the local league together for years, and it was something they'd always enjoyed. She could only wonder how Quinn was going to handle it. Maybe she needed to nudge him out of their routine and see how it went.

It was after six on a Thursday night when he showed up. He looked exhausted and sexy as hell. Anna's original plan had been to grill a couple of steaks and watch the Yankees game, but after her realization earlier, she changed it.

Quinn kissed her thoroughly before walking over to the refrigerator and grabbing a beer. It was a very domestic scene—including the "Hi, honey! How was your day?" and it normally made Anna smile. Unfortunately, she didn't feel much like smiling. She felt like shaking things up.

"I don't feel like cooking tonight," she said casually, grabbing a bottle of water for herself out of the refrigerator. "I was thinking we'd go into town and grab something to eat, maybe some pizza or something."

Placing his beer down on the counter, Quinn looked at her. "You should have called me. I would have picked one up on the way home."

She shrugged. "Nah. I really want to get out and eat someplace. Come on. We'll keep it casual. Just go and get changed, and we'll go."

He looked completely uncomfortable. "Seriously, Anna? It's been a crappy day. The Camaro is giving me fits, and we have cars parked all over the property waiting to be worked on and not enough space or manpower to get to them all. I was really just looking forward to staying in tonight."

"We stay in every night," she reminded him. "We went out more before we started dating." Then she chuckled. "Although I don't really think we can call this dating since we haven't gone out on any dates, so I guess I should rephrase and say we used to go out more before we started sleeping together."

His anger was apparent. "What the hell's gotten into you?" he demanded. "So we haven't gone out much. I didn't think you minded."

She shrugged. "Normally, I don't. But tonight I'd like

to go out. I didn't think it was a big deal. Obviously I was wrong."

He huffed and raked a hand through his hair, sending his hat flying. "Look, if you had mentioned it earlier, I would have been a little more mentally prepared for it, that's all."

"Since when do you need to be mentally prepared to go for pizza? For crying out loud, Quinn, I'm not asking you to take me to the Four Seasons; it's just a quick dinner so I don't have to cook!"

He studied her hard for a minute and then seemed to relax. "You're right, you're right. I'm sorry. Like I said, it was a crappy day. Give me a few minutes to wash up and change." He walked back to her bedroom and she heard the bathroom door close.

For a minute, she almost felt bad. Almost felt the need to go and tell him to forget about it and she'd cook for them instead, but she had a feeling that's what he was hoping for. The old Anna would have done it, and she was done being that girl. Why, all of a sudden, she didn't know. But right then, the only thing she was certain of was that she was tired of being kept locked up and not seeing anyone.

Well, anyone other than the Shaughnessys.

Fifteen minutes later, they were in his truck heading into town. "So…pizza?" he asked.

"Sure. Unless there's someplace else you'd like to go."

When they drove past Main Street, Anna questioned it.

"There's a really good seafood place I've been wanting to try," Quinn answered. "We can get pizza anytime. What do you say?"

She wouldn't have minded if he'd asked before they'd passed the pizza place, but whatever. "Sure. That sounds good."

Thirty minutes later, Anna was a little suspicious. "This is kind of far, don't you think?"

Quinn shrugged and parked the truck. "Yeah, but sometimes the good places are worth it. Come on. All the guys at the shop have been talking about this place and telling me how good it is."

She supposed it made sense. It was a small place — barely more than a shack — and she could only hope the inside was more appealing than the outside.

Quinn took her by the hand and pulled her in close, kissing her deeply. "Maybe after dinner we can go for a walk on the beach. There's supposed to be outside seating in the back that overlooks the sand."

And then she relaxed. She was being suspicious for nothing. Maybe he really did just want to take her someplace different and have a date that wouldn't include a dozen interruptions from everyone in town.

"I think it sounds absolutely perfect."

And it was. She was completely dazzled by this side of Quinn. They talked all through dinner, and she was pleasantly surprised at how amazing the food was. The place certainly didn't look like much, but it more than made up for it with its meals.

After dinner, they walked along the beach hand in hand. The sky was clear and the breeze coming off the water was refreshing. They'd kicked off their shoes, and to Anna, it could quite possibly have been the most perfect date.

"I'm glad we did this," he said after a few minutes.

"Me too."

"I know you may not believe this, but…I really just don't think of things like this. I'm not usually that kind of guy." He shrugged.

"I don't know about that. In the past you've told me—"

He cut her off. "I don't want to talk about my past. I was a completely selfish jackass, Anna. I never should have talked to you about my dates, and I certainly don't want to be reminded of them."

She looked at him and smiled softly. "I don't think you were a selfish jackass, Quinn. I just miss going out places with you. We used to go to the movies or bowling or…anyplace. I'm beginning to feel like you're embarrassed to be seen with me."

That stopped him in his tracks. "*What?!* Why would you even say such a thing? I would never…could never—"

"You have to admit it seems pretty suspicious," she interrupted with a nervous chuckle. "You never want to go anywhere anymore."

He reached up and cupped her face in his hands. "Did it ever occur to you that I don't want to share you with anyone else? That maybe now that I've realized how much you mean to me, I want to show you as much as I can? Or maybe because you're so damn sexy and my every freaking fantasy that I can't wait to get you alone, so I can touch you, kiss you, and love you from head to toe?"

His words made her weak. "Oh my…"

"Even standing here right now, all I can think about is getting you home, undressing you, and making love to you until neither of us can move." He leaned in and kissed her cheek. "All day long, I think about you." He kissed her forehead. "The drive home seems to take forever because all I can think about is being with you." Another kiss on the tip of her nose. "And it's not just the sex. I just want to be with you. You're my home. My heart. I love you."

And then she couldn't breathe. It was everything she had ever dreamed of—only it was better because it was real. She sighed his name as she reached up and touched his face. Tears swam in her eyes. "I…I never thought… I just…"

"Shh… I know. I don't deserve you. I know that. But you're everything, Anna. Everything."

She shook her head. "I feel the same way about you. I always have. I love you too."

And then, finally, his lips claimed hers, consumed her. They stood locked together with the waves crashing on the shore and stars shining in the sky, and Anna lost all track of time. When Quinn raised his head, the look of pure need there almost brought her to her knees.

"Let's go home," he said huskily, taking her hand in his again as he began to lead her back to the truck.

She could only nod.

The entire drive home, Quinn kept her tucked close to his side, his hand playing with her hair and skimming up and down her neck. Anna had to fight the need to climb into his lap and beg him to pull over and have his way with her right then.

As if reading her mind, he turned and gave her a sexy grin. "Patience. I promise you we'll be home soon."

"Not soon enough," she said, snuggling closer.

By the time they pulled into the driveway, she was ready to explode. She needed to touch him, to have his hands on her, and it didn't matter if they made it to a bed or not. A slow smile crept across her face.

Reaching over, she ran a hand up his denim-clad thigh. She loved the way his eyes closed as he sighed. "So...I've always had this...fantasy," she said softly, her hand roaming up and down his leg and up his stomach and chest.

"Really?" he said in a low voice.

"Mm-hmm," she purred. "I always thought you looked very sexy driving this truck. I remember you had another one in high school, and I used to imagine what it would be like if it were me you were fooling around with in it."

Quinn opened his eyes and scanned her face. "You wanted to fool around in my truck?" He looked toward the house and then back at Anna. "There's a bed just a few feet away."

"Yeah, but..." she began, "we can finish up in there. I think it would be really hot if we got things started right here." Shifting, she got up on her knees and started kissing his neck. "You don't even have to do much. This is more about me...and what I always wanted to do."

"Anna," he sighed. "Baby, you're killing me."

"I'm just getting started." She gently bit him and then ran her tongue over the same spot. Quinn hissed in a breath, and in the blink of an eye, she was sprawled out across the seat with him stretched out on top of her.

"Now you're just teasing," he growled before kissing her roughly, his tongue dueling with hers until she began to whimper beneath him. He raised his head. "Tell me what you want, Anna—anything, and it's yours."

"I want you to make love to me right here, right now."

Her eyes never left his as she issued her sexy challenge. She waited for him to argue. She waited for him to try and change her mind.

Then she squealed with delight as he quickly began to work on the button of her jeans.

"Your wish is my command," he said before his lips claimed hers again and made one of her long-time fantasies come true.

—ᴡᴡ—

A week later, her suspicions were not only back, but they were pretty much like a giant neon sign she couldn't turn off. Since their dinner and walk on the beach—and subsequent hot sex in his truck—they'd gone out four more times, each place farther from home than the last. She was seriously beginning to get a complex.

Anna tried to remember all the things Quinn had said to her about why he enjoyed being alone with her, and sometimes it was enough. But she couldn't help but be a little annoyed by some of it. She was all for being alone with him and not wanting to share him with anyone— particularly the little fan club of women who seemed to flock to him whenever they used to go anyplace local— but she was still willing to try. It would mean so much to her to see him willingly ignore the women and claim her as his in front of people they knew.

After each date, they'd come back to her house, and just when she was ready to comment on where they'd been and how far away it was, he'd seduce her to the point where she barely knew her own name.

It was a gift he had.

But one she was starting to really resent.

"I thought you had a house to show tonight?" Quinn said, coming out of the bedroom dressed to play softball.

Anna had done the same while he was in the shower. She shook her head. "Nope."

"Are you sure?" he asked, grabbing a couple of bottles of water from the pantry. "I thought you said something about showing the two-bedroom place over on Billings."

"Quinn, I think I would know if I had an appointment. If you don't believe me, look at my calendar." She took her phone out and slid it over to him and then walked over and found her day planner and did the same. "No showings."

"Oh."

"Besides, I wouldn't miss a game. I've never missed a game." She chuckled. "And I think the team would miss me if I wasn't there. I'm the queen of first base. You guys would lose without me." She said it with a smile but noticed he didn't seem amused. Sighing, she leaned against the countertop. "Okay, spill it. What's wrong?"

"What? Nothing. Nothing's wrong. Why would you even say that?"

"Um…maybe because you're acting like a complete tool. You're making it seem like you don't want me at the game tonight and I want to know why."

"You're imagining things, Anna. That's not it at all. I'm just… I guess my head's just not in the game, that's all. These restorations are harder than I thought. Maybe I shouldn't play."

Yeah, her suspicions were almost blinding her now. "Don't be ridiculous. You've never missed a game no matter what was going on in your life." She reached for her duffel bag and slung it over her shoulder. "Come on. Let's get going or we'll be late."

"I left my mitt at home. Why don't you go ahead and I'll meet you there?" he suggested.

Anna wanted to argue but found she couldn't. All she could do was sigh. "Just make sure you're there in time for the first pitch," she said wearily and walked out the door. Quinn followed silently behind her.

He gave her a distracted kiss on the cheek.

And he didn't respond to her statement.

Anna sat in her car and watched him drive away, wondering what in the world she was going to do. There was a time when they'd told each other everything—even if it wasn't comfortable. But for some reason, Quinn was keeping this to himself. It was obvious he was uncomfortable with the game tonight, and she couldn't understand why. Did he think she was going to demand sex in front of everyone?

These were their friends! There wasn't anything for them to worry about. No one was going to make any snarky remarks like his brothers had, and no one was going to say anything stupid.

At least…she hoped they wouldn't.

———

The mitt was in his truck and Quinn had no place to go. He just needed to get his head on straight. Normally the thought of going out on the field and playing the game was exciting, something he looked forward to.

And right now, he didn't.

This was going to be one of those moments that was

a game changer—no pun intended. Taking Anna to his father's house for dinner and getting ribbed by his brothers was one thing. It was what they all did and it was normally done in good fun. But to face a bunch of their friends tonight and have everyone witness the change in his relationship with Anna scared the hell out of him. Why? Because he had a feeling he'd get a lot of the same comments and it wouldn't all be said in fun.

It would be the truth.

He wasn't good enough for Anna and she deserved better.

Slamming his hand on the steering wheel, he cursed. He was the most confident member of his entire family. Hell, he was probably one of the most confident people he even knew. Why was it then that this situation had him feeling so insecure?

Because Anna does deserve better.

Better than what? He was truly committed to her—and not just as her boyfriend, but as her best friend. Her happiness meant everything to him, and now that he knew all the ways he'd hurt her in the past, he was doing his damnedest to make up for it. Wasn't everyone entitled to a second chance?

Yeah, but you're pushing, like, your thirtieth chance where she's concerned.

Okay, fine. This was still all kind of new to him. He didn't do long-term relationships. He'd never seen the appeal of it, but now…now he did. Being with Anna had him thinking of his life differently. He used to enjoy his freedom, his independence. Now the thought of being alone wasn't all that appealing. He liked going to sleep beside her and waking up with her in his arms.

He loved her.

And even saying the words to her hadn't scared him. He'd never said them to anyone before—shouldn't that count for something? And she'd said it back! So they were solid on that front, but…why couldn't they just be…them? Just the two of them? Why did everyone else get to have an opinion and butt in?

He thought of how sad she looked when he'd suggested they take separate cars to the game. Yeah, he was pretty much scum. *You can't be in love one minute and push her away the next,* he chided himself. A little too late for that now.

The field came into view, and he pulled into the parking lot. There weren't any open spots near Anna's car, and Quinn had no choice but to park on the other side of the lot. He climbed out and slowly made his way toward the dugout. Everyone was there already and talking strategy.

"Nice of you to join us," Billy Harper called out. He was the team captain and could be a real pain in the ass, but the man had a pitching arm that was a thing of beauty.

Looking around, he saw Anna standing in the back of the group with a couple of people—mostly guys—and frowned. There were three other women on the team. Why did she have to be surrounded by men? Then he thought about it and realized she normally did hang out more with the guys and knew he was going to have to deal with it, no matter how much it peeved him.

When Billy finished his lengthy spiel about teamwork and kicking ass, the group broke apart and everyone finished getting their gear ready. Quinn walked over to Anna and felt a pang of regret when she merely gave him a cursory glance and went about her business.

"Hey," he said softly.

"Did you get your mitt?" she asked, not even bothering to look at him.

"Uh…yeah. Look, I'm sorry. I was a jerk and—"

"Anna!" someone yelled. "Come and toss a few with me!" Quinn looked over and saw Mark Brady standing on the first base line grinning. Quinn normally liked the guy, but right then, Mark's grin was pissing him off.

"In a minute!" Quinn yelled back and then saw the look of irritation on Anna's face. "What? What did I do?"

"I can answer for myself," she said tartly as she straightened and faced him. "Say what you have to say because I have things to do."

He sighed with frustration. There was no way he wanted to create a scene here. "I'm sorry, all right?" he snapped. "Sometimes this shit freaks me out. I'm not perfect, Anna, and you of all people should know that. So…are we good?"

She eyed him warily. And it seemed like there was a war going on inside of her. When her shoulders relaxed, his did too.

"Neither of us is perfect, Quinn," she said quietly, "but at least we used to talk to each other when there was a problem. You know damn well I didn't have a showing tonight, and I can guarantee you your mitt was in your truck." She let out a growl of frustration. "Not so long ago, you accused me of shoveling bullshit, and that's what I'm saying right now to you. You're shoveling it. So when you can be honest with me and tell me the truth about what's freaking you out, I'll listen. Until then, just…leave me alone."

And then she walked out of the dugout, and Quinn had a feeling that if he didn't get his shit together, she'd walk out of his life just as easily.

It was the bottom of the ninth, and their team needed one more run to win. Anna was on third base and knew she could do it—she'd be the one to get the win. Suzi Hall was up at bat, and the woman was one of their best hitters.

With her heart threatening to pound out of her chest, Anna began to slowly inch off the base as the first pitch was thrown.

Strike one!

Inching back, her toe on the base, she waited for the second pitch.

Strike two!

Dammit. She was so close to making this happen. Anna was never the one in this position, and it felt pretty freaking fantastic. If Suzi could just hit the ball out of the park, Anna could fly across home plate, and their team could officially claim the victory.

Another pitch and…

A hit!

At the crack of the bat, Anna took off and didn't even bother to look and see where the ball went. All she knew was she had to run and run fast. People were cheering her on and as her foot touched home plate, she was immediately whisked up in Billy's arms.

"You did it! You did it!" Everyone crowded around her as the rest of the team rounded the plates. When Suzi ran over home plate, she was hailed for her spectacular hit. Everyone was cheering and high-fiving one another.

Anna made her way through the crowd, and when she spotted Quinn, her smile grew. They lived for games like this. The victory, the celebrating. She was about to launch herself into his arms when he stopped her, his hands on her shoulders.

Then he high-fived her.

"Good job!" he said and then blended into the crowd, leaving her standing there dumbfounded.

Good job? Good freaking job? That was it? It wasn't as if Anna was expecting a make-out session, but seriously, a high five? With a snort of disgust, she allowed herself to get caught back up in the excitement of the win before she ended up punching Quinn in the face. *Jerk*.

The usual routine after a win consisted of everyone going to the pub to celebrate, and while normally that was extremely appealing, Anna couldn't help but feel a sudden lack of enthusiasm. Everyone started walking toward their cars, and she spotted Quinn standing near the dugout alone. She was tempted to just ignore him and keep walking, but that wasn't their thing—sex or no sex. Anna wasn't one to shy away from a fight with him.

"You going to the pub?" Quinn asked when she approached.

She noted that almost everyone was out of earshot and that made her frown. "I don't think so. I'm probably just going to head home."

"Why? You had the winning run. I would have thought you'd want to go and celebrate."

She shrugged. "Yeah, it wasn't as exciting as I

thought it would be." They stood there in awkward silence for a few moments before she couldn't take it anymore. "What about you? Are you going?"

"I was thinking about it…"

She knew what he was doing and couldn't decide if it was sweet or annoying. "You don't need my permission to go to the damn pub, Quinn. If you want to go, then go. We don't have to go everywhere together."

"That wasn't what I was saying—"

"No," she interrupted. "You were probably making sure we both weren't going to be there at the same time. We don't want our friends to actually know we're involved, right?"

"Anna, it's not—"

"Hey!" Mark Brady came walking over with a big grin on his face. "Great game, Anna." He looked between the two of them. "Am I interrupting a lovers' spat or something?" Then he broke out laughing. "Sorry, couldn't help that one."

"What the hell is that supposed to mean?" Quinn snapped.

"The two of you looked like you were fighting, and I was being sarcastic about the lovers thing." He laughed again. "As if the two of you would ever hook up."

Anna felt her skin heat with embarrassment.

"And why the hell not?" Quinn demanded.

"Look, no offense, Anna," he began, and then focused on Quinn, "but you're more of the blond-bimbo type, and Anna's…well…not." He shrugged. "You guys coming?"

"Not me," Anna mumbled, and reached for her duffel bag and slung it over her shoulder.

"Anna," Mark said, "I didn't mean it as an insult to you. Quite the opposite, really. You're better than those girls. I know you wouldn't be crazy enough to get involved with our resident playboy here. You're smarter than that." He pulled her into a bear hug and kissed her on the head. "I hope you change your mind and come to the pub. Drinks are on me!" Then he jogged away.

Well, if the silence was awkward before, it was downright painful now.

Anna couldn't help but think of the way Quinn's brothers had teased him at the family dinner, and now with the things Mark said…she suddenly understood some of his reluctance to go out places with her.

"Quinn—"

He held up his hands. "You know what? You should go to the pub with everyone. I think I'll be the one to skip it." He collected his gear and walked away.

Her first impulse was to go after him, but she didn't have the first clue as to what to say. She knew the real Quinn—and that was really all that mattered. Unfortunately, she also knew what it was like to live with people's preconceived impressions and opinions. Wasn't that one of the reasons she had started to make changes in her own life, so other people would stop seeing her as nothing more than the tomboy they all grew up with?

They were going to have to talk about this.

And soon.

But for tonight, Anna knew it was probably for the best for them each to retreat to their own corners and be alone.

Quinn sat in the darkness. He'd been home for over an hour and didn't see any point in turning on any of the lights. Hell, it had been a while since he'd spent more than a few minutes there. Almost every night for weeks, he'd been staying at Anna's. He had loved coming home to this space—it was all his—but tonight, all he felt was loneliness.

For years, he'd been so busy just living life on his terms that he hadn't given much thought to how it would look to others. Worse, he hadn't really considered how his actions affected others.

Particularly Anna.

Well, it was becoming pretty damn clear now.

People thought he was a complete asshole.

Great.

It was one thing for his family to think it—they still had to love him—but he was slowly beginning to find out it was a more widespread opinion. He could have handled it if it just came from someone like Bobby—he'd always hated Quinn and he was Anna's brother; of course he was going to have issues. But Mark? That one stung a little. Mark liked everyone. Hell, Quinn had never even heard the guy say a bad thing about anyone.

Until tonight.

There was a reason he'd been avoiding going out on dates with Anna to any local place, but it had been based on his own insecurities and what he thought *might* happen. It was completely different when it became a reality.

He loved Anna. Loved her more than he'd thought possible. But was he being selfish? Was he banking on their years of friendship and the way she'd always felt about him to keep her in a relationship that wasn't good for her?

Not that she'd even complain—he knew that about her. She might have been pissed at him at that moment, but Quinn knew it wouldn't take much for her to get over it. Hell, he could have probably gone over to her house right then and sweet-talked her into forgiving him for acting so stupidly.

And that's when he knew he had a real problem.

There comes a time when you're forced to take a look at your life and you have to decide if you like what you see.

And Quinn didn't.

He now realized how, even though he and Anna were friends, he had manipulated her all those years. He knew exactly how to act and exactly what to say to get her to do whatever he wanted. It was usually stupid stuff, like cook for him or, back in school, do his homework for him, and it just made him feel sick inside.

Scrubbing a hand wearily over his face, an image of his mother came to mind. How many times had he sweet-talked her to try and get himself out of trouble? It had never worked, and she'd always called him out on it, but that had never stopped him from trying.

"But Aidan and Hugh are getting to stay up late! Why can't I?"

Lillian smiled down at him. "Because they're older than you and this is their reward for doing well in school today."

Eight-year-old Quinn looked up at her, and even though he was mad, he gave her his sweetest smile. "I did good in school today too! I helped Mrs. McGrath wipe down all the chalkboards, and then I got to bring the TV and VCR back to the media center all by myself."

"You did? Well, good for you, Quinn!" She ruffled his hair and then cupped his cheek. "And I am very proud of you for it."

"So I can stay up and watch movies too?"

She shook her head. "No can do, blue eyes. Not tonight."

He frowned and then inspiration hit. "If I do good in school next week, can I get a special night?"

Lillian considered it. "That depends."

"I'll do all my homework and make my bed and help with the twins and…and…I'll help Mrs. McGrath again, and then can I stay up late while Hugh and Aidan go to bed?"

Chuckling, she pulled him in close for a hug. "We'll see. Why don't you finish getting ready for bed and I'll let you have an extra fifteen minutes so you can read your new comic book. How about that?"

It wasn't a movie, but it was something. "Thanks, Mom," he said. "And when it's my special night, I'll even let you pick the movie."

"You will?" she said with exaggerated enthusiasm. "So if I want to watch…say…Mary Poppins, we can?"

Quinn wanted to make a gagging sound but decided against it. "If that's what you want, then sure." He knew he'd get her to change her mind by next week. And he could probably convince her to bake some cookies too. "You're the best and prettiest mom in the whole wide world. I love you."

Bending down, Lillian kissed the top of his head.

*"I love you too, blue eyes. Now go and see how the
Amazing Spider-Man gets out of trouble this week and
tell me all about it tomorrow, okay?"*

And he had. And she had listened.

And she had known he was trying to con her into
getting his own way.

And she had loved him anyway.

His chest felt tight, and for a minute he felt as if he
couldn't breathe. So basically he'd been manipulating
people his entire life. Great. Yeah, that felt real good. A
loud sigh escaped as he rubbed the place over his heart.
Two of the most important women in his life, and he'd
spent most of his time with them essentially conning
them into doing what he wanted.

"I'm surprised there hasn't been an angry mob after
me sooner," he muttered.

There was no way he could change the past, no matter
how much he wanted to. He could apologize to Anna
from now until the end of time. But unless he started
making some changes now and started showing her—
and everyone—how he wasn't selfish and he was a different person, all of his apologies would mean nothing.

"No pressure," he said into the darkness.

Now he just had to figure out how he was going to
accomplish it.

———

"He high-fived you?"

Anna nodded. "He high-fived me."

"Wow…just…wow."

"Yeah, that was pretty much my reaction too."

Zoe sat back in her seat and frowned. "I don't even know what to say to that. Even when Aidan was being a complete jerk when we started dating, he never would have—"

"High-fived you when you were looking to hug him?"

Raising her glass of iced tea, she saluted Anna. "I give you props for not picking up a bat and slugging him."

"It was tempting, but there were too many witnesses."

Zoe chuckled. "So…now what? What happened when you guys got home?"

"Nothing. I came back here alone, and Quinn?" She shrugged. "I have no idea where he went. Probably to the pub with everyone."

"You didn't go?"

"Between the high five and Mark's comment…I just needed to get away."

"Okay, but you've talked to Quinn since then, right? I mean, it was four days ago."

Anna shook her head. "He texted me the next day and said he needed to put in some serious time on the restoration job."

"I still can't believe he's doing it," Zoe said with disgust. "After everything Jake did—"

"I don't want to talk about it," Anna interrupted. "I told everyone I didn't mind and I don't. Sort of." She cursed. "Not really."

"Anna, come on! How can you sit here and tell me you honestly don't care? That guy is a creep! And what he tried to do to you was criminal! How can you sit here and tell me you want to encourage Quinn to do this job? There will be other restorations! Does he really want the recognition so badly he's willing to do a job that is nothing but a constant reminder of what Jake Tanner did?"

Anna hadn't really thought of it that way. With a sigh, she rested her head on the back of the sofa. "He's only doing it because I told him to. I know how important getting this restoration part of the business is to Quinn. This job was not only a big deal because of the kind of cars they are, but also because Jake had already lined up magazine interviews and deals for the big reveal. How could I take that away from him?"

"How could he not offer to?" Zoe snapped. "Honestly, out of all the Shaughnessys, Quinn really is the most clueless. And that's saying something!"

"He *did*, but I talked him out of it. So I'm partially to blame. I'll be all right," Anna said, but she didn't honestly believe it, and the look Zoe gave her said she wasn't buying it either.

"So what are you going to do?"

"I don't really know. We had a couple of weeks when we were inseparable, and that's never happened before. I know he has a lot of work that needs his attention at the new shop, and I guess when he has the time, he'll let me know."

Zoe stood, clearly agitated. "You're too good to him, too forgiving."

"What am I supposed to do?" She paused. "And besides, I told him to leave me alone."

"Oh, please. You were upset. Now, you're supposed to drive over to the shop and demand he talk to you, for starters! Then, you get in his face and tell him to man up and stop hiding when things get tough! And lastly, tell him if he ever high-fives you again instead of accepting the hug you're offering, I'll come over there and hit him over the head with one of those giant wrenches!"

Anna chuckled. "Man...does Aidan ever win an argument with you?"

A slow smile crept across her face. "Not if he knows what's good for him."

Chapter 10

BY THE TIME ZOE LEFT, ANNA FELT PRETTY RILED UP. Not that she hadn't been for several days, but there was something about a good pep talk that really seemed to help. She'd been sitting at home, wavering between self-pity and being pissed off, and at that moment, all traces of pity were gone and her anger was fresh and ready to be unleashed.

"High-five me, will you?" she muttered as she grabbed her sneakers and slipped them on. "I didn't think I was an idiot before, but if you're going to go out of your way to make me look like one now, then be ready for my wrath!" In her mind, Quinn was right there and practically quivering from her words. Anna knew the reality was going to be very different, but right then, she pretty much had a whole "I am woman, hear me roar" thing going on.

Storming across the living room, she snatched up her purse on the way to the front door. She yanked it open and froze.

Quinn.

"Hey," he said, almost sounding shy and uncertain of whether or not he was welcome there.

"Hey, yourself," she replied, and a little of the fight went out of her. He was dressed in clean clothes and he'd shaved and there wasn't a cap on his head. That told her he'd put in a bit of an effort before coming over.

"I was just coming to see you. I figured you'd still be at the shop."

"I practically slept there all weekend."

"Oh." They stood there in the doorway for several long moments until Anna finally took a step back. "So… um…do you want to come in?"

He nodded. "Thanks." As Anna shut the door, Quinn walked into the living room and sat down on the couch, waiting for her.

Honestly, Anna was a little disappointed he was so mellow. Looking at him sitting so meekly on her couch took the last of the fight out of her. With a disappointed sigh, she sat down. "How've you been?"

He shrugged. "Busy. I put an ad out for more mechanics. I can't believe how crazy things have been at the shop. It feels like everyone in town needs their cars looked at."

"That's a good thing, right?" She hated small talk. And worse, she hated forced small talk. With a steadying breath, she looked at him. "You really pissed me off Thursday night. I can't believe you freaking pushed me away when I was trying to hug you!"

She waited for his flash of temper and for him to argue with her—which he always did in an attempt to make it seem like he hadn't done anything wrong. She waited for it. She welcomed it.

But it never came.

"I know," he said quietly. "And I'm sorry."

Well, damn. Her shoulders sagged. "If you're this uncomfortable with this relationship, Quinn, then maybe we need to…"—she swallowed hard—"just let it go. I hate feeling like you're ashamed to be seen with me. I deserve better than that."

His blue eyes sparked with anger when he looked at her. "You think I'm ashamed to be seen with you? What the hell, Anna?" He stood up. "Has it ever occurred to you that maybe I'm ashamed of myself? That maybe it's less than flattering to have everyone look at me like I'm some sort of loser who isn't good enough for you?"

"That's bullshit and you know it," she snapped. "For as long as I've known you, you've never given a damn about what other people say—and you've preached it to me plenty too! And now you're going to stand here and tell me the reason you've been such a jerk is because of other people?" She snorted with disgust. "When did we start lying to each other?"

"I'm not lying!" he yelled. "Jeez, first I had your brother on my back, telling me I'm not good enough, then my whole family pretty much tells you how you can do better than me, and then at the game—"

She held up a hand to stop him. "Yeah, yeah, yeah. None of that stuff has ever bothered you before! And do you think it's easy for me? You don't think I'm afraid that when we go out people are going to look at us—and look at me!—and think 'What the hell's Quinn Shaughnessy doing with her?' I mean, look at me! I'm not your usual *Playboy* playmate wannabe like you usually date!"

"There is not a damn thing wrong with you, and I dare anyone to try and say there is!" He walked over to her and grabbed her by the shoulders and gave her a small shake. "Don't ever think that! You're ten times more beautiful than any of those women!"

Just the feel of his hands on her, the fierceness in his eyes, was enough to bring that sizzle of attraction to the surface. All she wanted to do was wrap her arms around him and jump up and wrap her legs around his waist while he kissed her.

Focus!

"Oh, please," she said with disbelief and pulled out of his grasp. "It wasn't until I was practically naked that you even noticed I was a woman! It's no different with every guy in this town. They look at me and they see Anna Hannigan, the tomboy, the chick who serves burgers and beers at the pub! That's why I had to get out of there! I'm tired of people looking at me like I don't measure up as a woman! Do you know how much it used to kill me to see you with those other girls and know that you—and everyone else—would never look at me that way?"

"Jesus, Anna…"

Tears stung her eyes and she cursed them. "I was finally starting to have a little confidence in myself and you shot it all to hell, Quinn!"

And then he pulled her into his arms and held her tight while she quietly sobbed. "I'm sorry, baby. I'm so, so sorry," he murmured as he kissed her temple and simply held her.

Anna's hands clutched the front of his shirt as she pulled herself together. When she finally lifted her head and looked at him, the look of utter devastation on his face made her knees almost buckle. With one hand, she reached up and cupped his cheek, simply needing to touch him.

"They're all right, you know," he said solemnly. "You deserve better."

She shook her head.

"It's true," he said. "We can go around in circles about this, but the bottom line is it's my fault you seem to have low self-esteem, and it's my fault you're standing here crying right now. I can't bear it, Anna. I never want to be the reason you cry."

"Walking away from me isn't the way to accomplish that," she said quietly. "That's something I couldn't bear."

He gave her a sad smile. "So what do we do? Where do we go from here?"

It may not have solved any of their problems, but Anna didn't care. She knew what she wanted—what she needed—right then. And that was Quinn.

Straightening, she looked him in the eye. "We go to my bedroom," she said, her hand caressing his face. "And you make love to me."

"Anna," he said, and it sounded like a mixture of agony and ecstasy.

"I've missed you so much, Quinn. And I need you. I really need you."

He cupped her face. "Baby, I need you too. More than you'll ever know. But...we haven't resolved anything here."

"There is no quick fix," she said. "And I don't want to fight with you. I want us to go inside and close the door and turn out the lights and just...forget about the rest of the world for a little while. Can we do that? Please?"

He looked ready to argue but didn't. Instead, he leaned forward and gently kissed her lips. "We can do whatever you want, Anna. Always."

Her heart felt ready to burst with love for him. There may have been times when she didn't like him, but in her heart, she was always going to love him.

She just wasn't sure if that proved she was weak or if it proved she was strong.

———∿∿———

If Quinn had to guess, he'd have said they were fine for a couple of weeks. They went back to their usual routine of him spending the night at Anna's almost every night, but they did start going out more.

At first, it was with people he felt a little more secure with—like Aidan and Zoe—but eventually they did go back to hanging out with their friends. And, as Quinn had figured, he took a lot of ribbing about the turn in the relationship. He had laughed along with everyone, but it was slowly eating him up inside.

It was a boring Tuesday at the shop, and he couldn't focus on anything. Deciding to just call it a day, he hopped in his truck and began to drive around aimlessly. After about an hour, he ended up at the jobsite Aidan was currently working at. He drove through the streets of the new subdivision until he spotted his brother's truck.

He parked and climbed out, and was relieved when Aidan spotted him. "Quinn! What brings you out here? Is everything okay?"

Raking a hand through his hair, Quinn looked around a bit. "Yeah...I guess. Listen, do you have time to go and get some lunch or something?"

Aidan looked at his watch and shrugged. "Sure. Just give me a minute to wrap things up. You want to ride together or meet someplace?"

"I'll wait and we can ride together." One look at Aidan and Quinn knew his brother could sense something was up. He jogged off and talked to some of his crew and then came right back over. "You don't need to rush, man. Really. If you need to talk to your guys—"

Aidan waved him off. "Everyone's good. Come on. The pub?"

"No," Quinn said a little too quickly. "Maybe someplace…" He shook his head. "Just someplace else."

Without questioning it, Aidan walked over to his truck and climbed in. Quinn joined him and they drove out of the heart of town to a small diner while doing nothing but talking about the latest sports scores and the weather.

Once they were seated inside and had placed their orders, Aidan cut to the chase. "Okay, I may be way off base here, but if I had to guess, I'd say you didn't ask me to lunch because you missed me." He shook his head. "I know that look, Quinn. I've had that look. What's going on with Anna?"

There was no point in playing dumb—this was exactly why he'd asked his brother to lunch. He sighed wearily as he played with the salt and pepper shakers on the table. "No one thinks I'm good enough for her."

Aidan sat back in his seat and studied his younger brother for a solid minute. "And what about you? Do you think you're good enough for her?"

Quinn shrugged. "I want to be."

"But?"

Pushing the shakers aside, he looked at Aidan. "You've all said it. Everyone thinks Anna should be with someone…someone better. I'm a screwup. I didn't pay attention all those years. I was a serial dater who avoided relationships like the plague. I mean, take your pick. It doesn't matter who I am now, everyone, including you, can't see beyond my past. I can't outrun my reputation."

"Okay, okay, just hang on a minute. What do you mean 'including you'? How did I get involved in this?" Aidan asked with genuine concern.

"Not just you—you, Hugh, Riley, Bobby...hell, everyone we know. You're all reminding me of the stupid things I've done and how badly I treated Anna and how she deserves better." And then, much to Quinn's annoyance, Aidan laughed. "What's so damn funny?"

"You are! Jeez, Quinn, when did you get so damn sensitive?"

"What the hell are you talking about?"

Aidan rested his arms on the table and leaned forward. "You know, out of the entire family, you have the biggest damn mouth."

"Hey—"

"Shut up," Aidan interrupted. "Every time we all get together, you're the first one to pick a fight or tease someone about something, but when we do it back, you get all bent out of shape! You've done more than your fair share of teasing me about being whipped where Zoe's concerned, and not so long ago, you told her she should leave me and marry you. Don't you think I found *that* a little insulting?"

"Dude, I was teasing!"

"Yeah, and so were we! Do you not see the irony here? It's what family does, dumbass. We tease one another. And Anna's been family practically since we all first met! Why wouldn't we all get a kick out of picking on the both of you? You need to lighten up, man."

"Yeah, well...what about everyone else?" He told Aidan about the incident at the softball game.

The waitress brought their plates out and smiled as she walked away. "Look, the fact is you do have a rather colorful past. You can't change it. And you can't expect people to simply forget it either. All you can do is your best, Quinn. You need to make people see who you are now and how much you've changed."

"What if I can't?"

"What? Change?"

He shook his head. "No. What if I can't make anyone forget or see I'm not that guy anymore?"

Aidan looked at him and gave him a sympathetic smile. "Then they're not trying hard enough to see who you really are."

"And who am I?"

"Only you can answer that."

They ate in silence for a few minutes before Quinn could speak again. "I don't want Anna feeling like she made a mistake. We've been friends for too damn long, and I don't think I'd know how to live my life without her."

Putting his burger down, Aidan's expression was serious. "What if it doesn't work out, Quinn? What if the romantic part of the relationship doesn't work? Do you really think the two of you could go back to being friends?" Before Quinn could answer, Aidan continued. "I'm not going to lie to you. I think it was a big risk to change the dynamic. The two of you were closer than any two people I know. Personally, I don't know if I could have been that brave."

"You think I'm brave?"

Aidan nodded. "You're one of the bravest people I know, Quinn. You go after what you want. You always have. I've seen you take on every kind of sport, and you were a damn legend when you were racing, and now you've got your own chain of shops. Dude, nothing scares you. But this? This thing with Anna? I can see that it does. That's not a bad thing, but you're going to have to get to a point where you're okay with it."

"You mean to tell me nothing about your relationship with Zoe scares you?"

"At one time, sure. Hell, everything about my relationship with her scared me in the beginning, and because of that, she almost moved back to Arizona. I had to come to grips with my fears and insecurities, my crazy beliefs about how life was supposed to be. And, if memory serves, you made fun of me because of them."

"Yeah, well—"

"Bottom line: Do you see yourself marrying Anna? Having kids? Settling down, buying a home, and doing the forever thing? Or do you see yourself with Anna in your life the way things were?"

"Why can't the two be combined?" Quinn asked, his throat tight.

"Because they can't," Aidan said simply. "It's always a great thing when you marry your best friend, but there needs to be more, Quinn. You can't expect Anna to be content with having you just as a sex buddy for the rest of her life. You need to figure out how you really see your future. And then you have to figure out if it only benefits you—or you *and* Anna."

Unfortunately, Quinn felt like he already knew the answer.

—⁓—

It had been a crappy day.

Anna had shown six houses to an extremely demand-ing couple, and she was mentally exhausted. There had been a problem with some of the permits for Hugh's property, and he had called her having a bit of a panic attack because he thought everything was already lined up for him to move forward with his plans. On top of that, as low man on the totem pole at the agency, it had been her turn to pick up everyone's afternoon coffee, and she had dropped the tray getting out of her car. The amount of ribbing and teasing she had gotten—on top of dealing with her coffee-drenched clothes—had been all she could stand.

The only bright spot in her day was that she and Quinn were going out to dinner that night. And not to the pub or for pizza, but he was taking her out to one of her favorite steakhouses—in town. They would have dinner and do a little dancing, and just the thought of it was enough to get her through the drive home and put the thoughts of her day behind her.

She took her time getting ready—showering and shaving and using enough scented moisturizer to make sure she was smooth and silky all over. Her hair was beginning to get on her nerves because it was longer than she'd ever worn it, and rather than being able to simply blow it dry, she had to take out her curling iron and do something with it.

"Well, this sucks," she murmured after she burned her fingers for the third time and gave serious thought to grabbing a pair of scissors and just hacking it all off.

Looking over at the clock, she knew Quinn would be home soon. They'd already talked about him coming over directly from the shop and getting ready at her place. Even though Quinn still had his place, he spent most of his time at Anna's and even had a small collection of clothes he kept there—including the suit he was going to wear tonight.

Just the sight of it hanging in her closet made Anna smile.

How many years had she dreamed of this? Of finally having Quinn love her and being in the kind of romantic relationship that made her heart skip a beat and her toes curl? They'd made the transformation from friends to lovers with such ease, she knew they were destined to be.

With her hair and makeup complete, she walked over to her closet and pulled out the dress she had purchased especially for tonight. Red silk with spaghetti straps, the bodice hugged her almost like a second skin. It hit right at her knees, and she'd found the perfect pair of matching sandals to go with it. It was so different from anything she'd ever worn, and yet when she saw it in the little dress shop she drove past every day, Anna had known she had to have it.

And she couldn't wait to see the look on Quinn's face when he saw her in it.

Her phone rang and she smiled when she saw Zoe's face on the screen. "Hey! What's up?"

"So tonight's the big date night," Zoe said giddily. "Did you get the dress?"

"I did! I still can't believe I really bought it, but once I went in and tried it on, I was sold. It's so bold and sexy and—"

"Sweetie, you should have started showcasing your curves a long time ago," Zoe interrupted. "Quinn is going to swallow his tongue when he sees you."

"That would be something," Anna said. "I think the last time I really gave him that kind of reaction was before your wedding when he saw me in the bikini."

Zoe chuckled. "That was a great day! I think it was almost cartoonish the way his eyes popped out!"

"Yeah, well…he wasn't so happy about it then. I can only hope he'll have a better response tonight."

"You and me both."

"Anything else going on?"

"Actually, yes. I just got off the phone with Aubrey, and Hugh has to be out of town for a few days. She's going to be home alone and asked if maybe you and I would come and hang out with her. My schedule's fairly flexible, but I wasn't sure about yours."

"I can definitely move things around," Anna said, going over her next set of appointments. "Is she all right? Is there a reason why she can't travel with Hugh?"

"Yeah, he's making her crazy!"

That had Anna laughing. "No!"

"Yeah, apparently she needs a little time without him hovering, and she's hoping with him away for a few days, he'll see she's not an invalid."

"I can see how his behavior could start to get annoying."

"It's sweet, don't get me wrong, but she's not allowed to just enjoy being pregnant because Hugh is so worried and cautious. She wants to prove she can still do all the things she loves to do and be pregnant at the same time."

"I'll definitely move my schedule around. When did you want to leave?"

"Hugh's leaving tomorrow—which is Wednesday—and I figured she'd want at least a day to herself to do whatever it is around the house that he won't let her do, so maybe Thursday afternoon? What do you think?"

"That should work. That will give me tomorrow to get my stuff in order. Is Aidan okay with you going?"

"Absolutely. I admit I'll miss sleeping beside him, but it's for a good cause. Besides, he's putting in a lot of extra time on this new subdivision because he wants to get a little ahead of schedule."

"How come? Everything okay?"

"We kind of started talking about going on vacation—a real one this time, when we seriously get out and leave the hotel room."

"Oh, really? Where to? Please tell me you're not going back to Mexico because that would just be sad. You blew your chance with that one. You need to move on."

"No, no, no, we're thinking either Hawaii or checking out Hugh's place in Sydney."

"Wow! Either of those would be amazing."

"I know! So if we do it, Aidan wants to make sure he's leaving at a point when things are somewhat under control. I mean, he knows anything can happen, but he's trying to get everything in order now in hopes it will stay that way."

"That's great, Zoe. I'm so happy for you guys." Anna looked over at the clock. "But I need to get moving. Quinn's going to be home soon, and I want to be dressed when he gets here."

"I'm going to want all the details on his reaction!"

"You got it! I'll see you Thursday! Your car or mine?"

"Yours," Zoe said with a chuckle. "It's new and pretty."

"Yes, it is. Okay, I'll talk to you later!" She hung up and immediately jumped up and finished getting dressed. Looking at herself from every angle in her full-length mirror, Anna was feeling pretty damn confident in herself.

She looked longingly at the jeans and sneakers in her closet. She missed them, missed being comfortable all the time. This being a girly-girl thing was exhausting—the hair, the makeup, the shoes! Why did society act as if it were all a good thing? Then she looked back at her reflection and smiled. "Oh yeah," she said. "Because I look really good!"

With nothing left to do, she went out to the kitchen and got herself something to drink and then waited.

And waited.

And waited.

She knew Quinn could easily lose track of time when he was working on a car, but she couldn't help but be annoyed that he'd do it tonight. They hadn't ever gone out on a real romantic date, and the fact that he would choose this night to be late really ticked her off.

Calling the shop, she cursed when no one answered. She got the same result when she called his cell phone.

That's when she began to worry.

Certainly he wouldn't ignore his cell phone—he kept it on him at all times. What if something had happened to him? What if he was hurt and alone in the shop? All of her anger instantly fled as she scooped up her purse and ran out the door. His shop was only a few minutes away, and she knew she could get to him quickly.

Dressed in her killer dress and heels, she pulled up in front of the garage and saw his car was still there, along with several others. Climbing from the car, she immediately walked around to the back of the property where Quinn did the restorations.

Pulling open the door, she was struck by the sound of male laughter. The loud slam of the door behind her had the space going quiet for a second. Quinn looked over at her, and she knew the instant he realized he'd screwed up. He jogged over to her.

"Shit, Anna. I'm sorry. I lost track of time and—"

"Who is he?" she asked, motioning to the man Quinn had been talking to.

"That's Ken Bishop. He's with *Classic Cars* magazine. He came to check out the cars and see what I'm working on and get some preliminary stuff out of the way for the article he's going to write. It's going to be a series, and he believes this kind of exposure will lead to me getting more clients. These two cars will—"

"Jake's cars?"

He nodded.

"You do realize we had plans tonight?" she said with a little snap to her tone.

"Yeah, yeah, I know. But he showed up here unannounced and we got to talking and the time just got away from me." He wanted to touch her, but his hands were dirty and he reconsidered. Then he finally noticed what she was wearing. "Damn, Anna. Your dress is amazing. Red looks really good on you. You look beautiful."

"You're joking, right?"

"What? I'm serious. You look amazing. I've never seen you in anything—"

"No, you haven't," she snapped. "I bought this dress

especially for tonight. I thought tonight was a big deal. Apparently I'm the only one."

"Okay, look, give me five minutes and I'll get this guy out of here and—"

"It won't matter! We've missed our reservation!"

"So we'll go someplace else. Really, just let me—"

She held up her hands and took a step back. "You know what? No. I have tried to be understanding, and I have tried to be supportive. Always. Everyone told me I was being too generous in not making a big deal out of you working on Jake Tanner's cars and I sided with you. I *defended* you. And when it came time for you to choose between those damn cars and me, you chose the cars."

"Anna, if you'd just listen—"

She shook her head. "No. I'm done listening to you. You'll always have an excuse. You'll always have a reason why you're right and I'm wrong. God, I'm such an idiot!" she cried. "I knew this about you and I still let it happen!" Her brown eyes welled with tears as she poked him in the chest. "I knew you would never put me first, and I let myself believe you would change!"

"I have changed! I made a mistake. I screwed up!"

"Yes, you did," she said sadly.

"Baby, I'm sorry. Let me get rid of Ken and we'll talk. Let me make it up to you. Let me—"

She shook her head again. "I can't. I can't do this anymore, Quinn. That's your go-to line: 'Let me.' Let me explain. Let me make it up to you. I need someone who doesn't have to keep explaining why I'm not a priority and why I'm not enough."

"But you are enough! Anna, you're everything! Please, you have to know that!"

"It's what I try to keep telling myself, but even I don't believe it anymore." Her heart ached and she knew if she didn't leave soon, she would simply crumple to the ground. "It hurt when you did things like this when we were just friends, but it's killing me now." She took a few more steps away from him. "We could have been so good together, Quinn. I gave you everything—I always have—but it's never going to be enough."

At least he was smart enough to know to stop arguing and trying to correct her.

"I don't want you to come by my house. I don't want you to call. I'll make arrangements to get your things back to you."

Quinn's expression was of pure devastation. "Don't do this," he said quietly, his voice shaking.

Anna took a steadying breath. "I have to. It's the only way I'll survive." She didn't allow herself any more time. Carefully, she turned around and walked to the door and out of the garage.

And out of Quinn's life.

———— ∿ ————

"Are you sure Aidan doesn't mind? I hate dragging him into this."

Zoe smiled sadly. "He doesn't see it like that. You're like a sister to him, and if doing this one little favor helps you, then he's happy to do it."

Anna had packed for her stay at Aubrey's and had also packed up all of Quinn's things and brought them over to Aidan and Zoe's place. "I feel like a coward."

"Don't you even think that! I think you're handling

this incredibly well. I know you're hurting, and I'm sure getting all this together wasn't easy."

"It wasn't, but it was worse having to look at it all over my house."

In truth, it wasn't that much stuff—a couple of changes of clothes, some hats, toiletries—nothing major. She just knew she didn't want it there when she came back from Aubrey's. Maybe by that time, she'd be a little more in control of her emotions, but the fewer reminders she had, the better.

The pictures that were scattered all over her house had all been taken down and packed up in a box and put away. She'd replace them all eventually, but she couldn't bear to keep looking around and seeing Quinn's face everywhere.

Zoe took the box and placed it in the house before locking up. "I texted Aidan so he knows it's here. He'll take care of it."

"Thanks." They climbed into Anna's car and she sat there silently, not starting the car, not moving.

"Anna? Sweetie? Are you okay? What's going on?"

"The car."

"What about it?"

"I can't keep it."

Zoe sighed. "Let's not think about it right now. Do you want to take my car? We can move everything into it pretty easily and then hit the road."

Shaking her head, Anna turned the key. "I'm being stupid. I don't have to have all the answers right now, right?"

"No, you don't. Just don't do anything hasty."

"I just…I need to sever all ties. I can't… I don't want…"

"I know." Reaching over, Zoe squeezed Anna's hand. "I'd say this little getaway was perfectly timed."

"You got that right."

"Come on. The sooner we get there, the sooner we can help you figure out the best plan for your future."

Right now, the only plan Anna had for her future was remembering to breathe.

"I'm not sure what we're supposed to do in this kind of situation—drink, eat, cry, throw things. Seriously, I'm clueless," Aubrey said when she and Zoe were alone for a minute. Anna had gone to the guest room to put her things away, so they were taking the time to discuss strategy.

"If it were up to me, we'd leave her here and go and beat Quinn upside the head with a heavy object," Zoe hissed, checking over her shoulder to make sure Anna hadn't come back into the room.

"I don't think it would solve any of this."

"Yeah, but I'd feel a lot better." With a sigh, Zoe sat down on the sofa. "The thing is, I'm proud of her."

"What? Why?" Aubrey looked completely confused as she sat down next to her sister-in-law.

"I've known Anna for a while now, and I've watched her fawn over Quinn for most of that time. Don't get me wrong. I love Quinn. I really do. But he is beyond clueless."

Aubrey nodded. "Aren't they all?"

"Oh, absolutely! But out of all the Shaughnessys— hell, out of all men—right now, he takes the cake."

"I thought he had potential." She looked over at Zoe with a sad smile. "I really did. The weekend they came and stayed here with us? I watched the two of them and thought, 'Okay, he's finally getting it.' Even Hugh kept commenting on how nice it was to see his brother finally get his head out of his butt."

Zoe laughed. "Yeah, Aidan thought the same thing. I'm sure most people would look at the situation and think it wasn't that big of a deal. So he forgot about dinner. It happens. Hell, there are times it still happens to both me and Aidan—you get caught up in work and next thing you know, you're late."

"I don't know. I don't think it's so much the dinner as much as what he was doing. I knew those stupid cars were going to come back and bite them eventually. He should have walked away from them right after the whole incident with Jake."

"I agree. Hell, we all think that, but Anna—being Anna—didn't want to jeopardize the chance of Quinn getting some publicity for his restoration business. Personally, I would have just told him to suck it up and find another classic car enthusiast to do business with, but that's just me." She shook her head. "Quinn's just used to doing things his own way and not really having to think about anyone else."

"We all can have that tendency, Zoe," Aubrey said. "But once you get into a relationship, you tend to make an effort to change. He's too smart not to know that by now. It's almost as if he sabotaged the relationship on purpose."

Zoe shifted in her seat and faced Aubrey, her gaze narrowing. "Go on."

A small smile crossed Aubrey's face. "Okay, Quinn's been upset about how everyone keeps bringing up his past, that he's selfish, blah, blah, blah... It bothers him."

Zoe told her about the lunch Aidan and Quinn had

had. "I know he told me in confidence, but I don't think the rules apply here. So, okay, Quinn was upset and feeling insecure. But why would he just jump ship like that? It seems cowardly."

"Or maybe he was being proactive. You know, forcing her to leave him now before things got serious."

"Please, they've been serious for a long time—long before they started dating, the two of them were serious. It was weird, and Quinn was the only one who didn't see it."

"Wow, he really is clueless," Aubrey said and sighed. "Well, then I'm stumped. I'd like to think he was being a gentleman and hurting her now rather than devastating her later."

Zoe shook her head. "Anna's been in love with him for so long, she was going to be devastated no matter what. I hate that for her."

"But you said you're proud of her. Why?"

"She always made excuses for him—or accepted the excuses he gave her. In the end, she knew she was going to be devastated and knew walking away was going to hurt. But she did it anyway. For once, she really stood up for herself and put herself first. It's not an easy thing to do."

"Tell me about it."

Zoe smiled. "Exactly! You did it with Hugh, so you know exactly how it feels. You walked away because you wanted Hugh to have the life you didn't think you could give him. It hurt and you were miserable, but at the time, you were being selfless. Our girl had to do something she'd never done before; she had to be selfish. And she's the least selfish person I've ever known. And I know it's killing her."

"So my original question stands: What do we do? Eat, drink, cry? Are we supposed to find pictures of him and throw darts at it or something?"

With a sigh of her own, Zoe rested her head on the back of the sofa. "Unfortunately, I think we're going to have our hands full with all of the above."

Aubrey stood and stretched. "I'll get started baking the brownies."

Zoe followed her into the kitchen. "What other kinds of junk food have you got?"

"Not much. Hugh's been a bit militant about what kind of things I eat and drink. He wants to make sure the baby and I are healthy."

Zoe glanced over at her. "Come on, you know you've got a secret stash hidden somewhere. And if you don't, I'm going to the store and making sure you have one after we leave."

With a laugh, Aubrey reached into one of the kitchen drawers and pulled out a pad and pen. "You have no idea what a lifesaver you are! I was planning on going to the store while he was gone, but I was enjoying the peace and quiet too much to get out yesterday." She began to quickly make a list and soon tore the paper off the pad and handed it to Zoe.

"Chips, dip, caramels, muffins, doughnuts," Zoe read off the list. Then she looked at Aubrey and smiled. "Baby steps, little mama. We can't have you gaining ten pounds while your husband's gone. He'll never let me visit you again!"

They were both laughing hysterically when Anna walked into the room and eyed them curiously. "What's so funny?"

They walked over and flanked her on both sides. "We're going food shopping," Zoe said, "to make sure Aubrey has a secret stockpile of junk food to tide her over for a while when Hugh gets back."

Anna chuckled and took the list from Zoe's hand. "You might want to add fried chicken, mashed potatoes, ice cream, peanut butter, and gummy bears."

"Um…that's kind of specific," Aubrey said. "And I don't think I'd be able to hide all those things from Hugh. And I'm not particularly fond of gummy bears."

"Oh, that wasn't for you," Anna said and walked over to grab her purse. "That's for me. And that's just to get me through lunch. We'll decide the rest while we're roaming the aisles at the grocery store."

Zoe looked over at Aubrey and shrugged. "You wanted to know how it works? We'll go in stages. Eating is obviously going to be phase one. Remind me to add tissues to the list because the crying phase will be here before you know it."

Chapter 11

FOR MORE THAN THIRTY YEARS, IAN SHAUGHNESSY had been there to pick up his kids when they fell. It almost became a full-time job after his wife died. And at that moment, he'd have given anything to have been dealing with something more straightforward, like a scraped knee or losing the big game. When he stepped into the restoration garage his heart broke.

His son—his strong and confident son—was sitting on the floor in the middle of an empty garage. He looked beyond sad—he looked broken. Ian wasn't a fool. He had found out what had happened a week ago, but he knew that his son was going to need a little time before anyone would be able to talk to him. From the looks of it, maybe he'd waited too long.

Without a word, Ian walked over and sat on the floor beside him—not an easy task for a man his age, but sometimes you had to take the pain. They sat in silence for a few minutes. Quinn didn't even blink when Ian sat down. If there was one thing Ian knew about his son, it was how stubborn he was, and he had a feeling that if he didn't say something soon, Quinn would be content to just let them stay like this.

"Business is booming up front," Ian said mildly. "There're a lot of cars lined up to be looked at. This town's needed a quality mechanic for a long time. I'm glad we have that now with you."

No response.

"You missed dinner with everyone Sunday. Owen surprised us all and showed up just as we were sitting down." He chuckled. "I haven't seen this much of that boy in I don't even know how long. It's nice that he takes the time to get away and come home more often. Of course, I wouldn't mind a phone call or two in between visits so I'd know when he's coming home."

Nothing.

It was time for a different approach. "Your mother used to call you her all-or-nothing child."

Quinn turned and silently faced him.

"Did you know that?"

Quinn shook his head.

"We used to laugh because there was never any middle ground with you—from the time you were a baby, you were the one who took things to extremes." He chuckled. "You'd spite yourself and I don't even think you were aware of it."

"What—" Quinn cleared his throat. "What do you mean?"

"Well, there was the bicycle thing. You were told you could ride it as long as you didn't race it." He looked at his son. "But you wouldn't compromise, and you raced until the bike got taken away." Ian shifted to try and get a little more comfortable. "Then there was baseball. My God, were you gifted. You were one of the best players I ever saw. But when your coaches reminded you how they had to let everyone play, you quit."

"Yeah, well…some of those guys had no right being on the field."

"Oh, I agree. But part of good sportsmanship is letting

everyone have a turn—even if it means losing the game. You can't tell me you didn't miss playing."

Quinn nodded. "What's the point in playing if you aren't allowed to win?"

Ian chuckled again. "I can see your point, but you're missing the bigger picture here. Rather than follow the rules, you chose to walk away. The team went on without you. The only one missing out was you."

"It wasn't that big of a deal."

"And what about racing?"

Quinn frowned. "What about it?"

"You walked away at the height of your career. Why?"

"My best friend got killed in a crash, Dad. It was horrible. I didn't want to put you and everyone through what his family was going through."

"How many crashes had you witnessed during your time on the circuit?"

"I don't know…dozens."

"How many deaths?"

Quinn shrugged. "A few."

"Over the course of your life—just your everyday life—have you seen people get hurt and die?" Ian asked quietly.

"Dammit, Dad!" Quinn shouted and jumped to his feet. "What the hell kind of question is that?"

Slowly, Ian stood up. "Accidents happen all the time, Quinn. Whether you're on a racetrack or running errands or standing in your own home. Your mother was a perfect example of that. Did you love racing?"

"You know I did!"

"Then why leave?"

"I just told you," he replied with an angry huff. "What's your point?"

"The point is you have a tendency to walk away when things get tough or they don't go your way."

"I didn't walk away from anything," he said with a low growl.

"And yet I'm standing here in the middle of an empty garage." Ian gestured to the open space around them.

"Yeah, well, that wasn't walking away. It was the right thing to do. I should have done it months ago. I got so caught up in something that could possibly happen two years down the road that I wasn't paying attention to what was happening right now."

"You've turned down a couple of decent restoration offers since though," Ian pointed out.

"I wasn't feeling them."

"You love cars. You've always loved cars. I think you're full of crap."

Quinn's eyes went wide. "Excuse me?"

"You heard me. I think you're full of it."

"Dad," Quinn said with a slight stammer, "what's gotten into you?"

"I think sending those cars back to Jake Tanner was the right thing to do—and so was telling that reporter the reason why."

"I didn't... I never said..."

"Yeah, well, you're not the only one who was going to be part of that interview."

Quinn rolled his eyes. "Dad, please tell me you didn't tell Ken what Jake did."

"Why not? Why shouldn't I? What that man did was criminal, Son! And all he got was a slap on the wrist and probation! He pulled the celebrity card and got to go on his merry little way! I don't think it's right, and I certainly don't think it's fair to Anna."

At the sound of her name, Quinn winced.

"Now I don't think Ken's going to write about what I told him, but I'm pretty sure his magazine won't be doing a story on Tanner either."

"I guess that's something."

"Anyway, he sent you two potential clients and you blew them off. Why?"

Quinn walked over to his tool bench and began moving things around. Ian came over and stood beside him, waiting. "I just... I can't."

"Why?"

"It's because of my selfish behavior and because of this business I was so hell-bent on having that everything went wrong. Maybe it just wasn't meant to be."

"Hmm...maybe," Ian said with a shrug. "Or maybe you're just following form and running because it didn't go your way."

Quinn threw a wrench across the garage with a feral growl before facing his father again. "You know, why is it that you're compassionate and loving when everyone else has a problem, huh? You give everyone these heartfelt pep talks to lift them up, and all you've done since you got here is kick me while I'm down!"

"It figures you'd see it that way," Ian said. "Because I see it as giving you the lift you need to get up off your ass and finish something!"

All the fight left Quinn as confusion took over.

"When Aidan came to me about his fears about Zoe, we talked. He didn't sugarcoat it and he didn't lay blame on anyone. We talked until he figured it out. Then we cried." He paused. "When Hugh came to me about Aubrey, I had to point out to him how his obsession about always wanting to be safe played a big part in why they didn't work out. But in the end, I encouraged him to take a risk. Do you think it was easy for either of them to admit they were at fault in any way? Do you think it's easy for any of us to admit to that?"

"I don't like to think about having any weaknesses," Quinn said. "I don't want anyone to see that side of me." He looked up at his father sadly. "Anyone."

"You're human, Quinn. We all have weaknesses. It doesn't make you less of a man." He looked around the garage. "You've always required a bit of a different approach. Aidan and Hugh are a little more sensitive. Don't get me wrong. They're tough and dependable men, but in their own ways, they were always ostensibly cautious."

"But you're basically telling me I am too," Quinn reminded him.

"You're cautious in a way that doesn't make you seem like you're cautious. Only someone who really looks would see it." He smiled. "I'm really looking, Son." When Quinn didn't respond, Ian continued. "I'm not going to sit here and wax poetic with you. I didn't do it with your brothers either. I can only guide you to the best of my ability. And you don't need to hug it out. You don't need to cry. But you do need a solid kick in the ass."

"Hey!"

"It's true! I want you to finish something," he shouted—and Ian never shouted. "Just once, I want you not to walk away because something got tough. Here's a bit of news for you, Son: not everyone gets their way all the time, and they don't all take their toys and go home." He huffed and raked a hand through his hair. "That's not who I raised you to be and that's not who your mom wanted you to be."

Quinn took a shaky breath. "Oh man…"

"She said you were her toughest—and she meant it in the best possible way. You do hate to show weakness and sometimes that's a good thing. Other times, well… not showing your weaknesses is what makes you weak. Make her proud, Quinn. Show her, and the whole world, how tough you are."

"What if the business fails? You know, on its own, because I'm not as good as I think I am?"

"What if it succeeds?"

Quinn frowned. "Things fail all the time, Dad. Even with all the attention in the world."

"That's true. But then you can look back and know you did everything possible and gave it your all. And when that's the case, no one can look at you like you're a failure."

They stood in companionable silence for a few minutes. Ian walked around the shop, touching tools and simply checking things out. He turned back toward Quinn. "Martha and I had dinner with the Hannigans last night." He almost smiled at how Quinn paled, although he wasn't sure if was the mention of Martha or the Hannigans that did it. "It was kind of nice. We barbecued and played cards and just visited."

A weak smile and a nod were Quinn's only response.

"By the time we got done talking about all of you kids

and how everyone is, half the night was gone. Bobby's thinking of transferring to South Carolina," Ian said with a shrug. "He says it's just time for a change."

"Good for him," Quinn mumbled.

"And we talked about Aidan and Zoe planning their Australia trip, Aubrey's pregnancy, Riley's music, Owen's promotion, Darcy's school, your shop, and... Bobby's move..." He paused and sighed. "Hard to believe there are so many of you." Once again, his son's reaction was pretty funny. "Oh, I know who I forgot."

Quinn seemed to perk up.

"Stanley."

"Excuse me? Who's Stanley?"

"He's Martha's French bulldog. He's the funniest little thing!" Ian chuckled. "Honestly, that dog has the personality of a human. I never considered myself a dog person, but he has me reconsidering. Sometimes I think he's going to just get up and talk to me!"

The poor boy looked deflated. "That's nice, Dad."

"Anyway, I guess I should be going. Martha and I are going to the movies tonight." He pulled Quinn close and hugged him. "Think about what I said."

With a nod, Quinn said, "Okay. I'll make some calls and get those cars in here."

Ian shook his head and patted his son on the arm. "You don't really think this was all about some cars, do you?"

"Hell no. But I've got to start somewhere, don't I?"

—⁓—

Life was moving on—just barely.

Hugh had finally closed on the property and Anna

had received her commission. It was really quite exciting to get that large of a check. After paying off some bills, she put another chunk into savings and then knew what she needed to do next.

Picking up the phone, she called the car dealership she knew Quinn had purchased her car from. After thirty frustrating minutes, she wasn't able to convince them to let her pay off the car. "Well, now what?" she murmured. A knock at her door had her looking up just as her brother walked in.

"Hey, squirt! What's going on?" he said with an easy smile. He kissed her on the head and noticed her frown. "Seriously, what's up?"

She explained the situation about the car. "I know I don't have to do anything, but I need to. Every time I get in the damn thing I think of Quinn." She looked up at him helplessly. "What do I do?"

Bobby quietly studied her. "This is just a suggestion, but..."

"But?"

"I'm going to be out of town for a while, so why don't you take my car?"

She looked at him oddly. "Why? Aren't you taking it with you? You're only going to South Carolina, not South America."

He chuckled. "Yeah, but...I'm sort of ready for a complete change. I already have a new car picked out, and the financing is good to go without using my car as a trade-in. So why don't you take my old car and give the Honda back to Quinn."

Unable to help herself, she lowered her gaze to her hands. "I don't think I could handle seeing him, Bobby. Not yet."

His arms came around her as he hugged her tight. "No worries there. I'll drop the car off."

Anna immediately lifted her head. "Oh…no. I don't want you to do that."

"Why not?"

"Because you'll just use it as an excuse to start a fight with Quinn."

"So? He deserves it! Dammit, Anna, I hate seeing you like this!" He looked like he was about to say more and then stopped and seemed to relax. "You know, you should come with me to South Carolina."

"Are you crazy? Why?"

"I would think it was obvious—you need a fresh start too. Look, I don't want to upset you but it needs to be said. This is a small town. You're not going to be able to avoid Quinn forever. There's gonna come a time when he moves on and, true to form, he's not going to give a damn if it hurts you."

"He wouldn't—"

"Just stop, okay? Are you prepared to run into him and one of his bimbos?"

She sighed with irritation. "Do people even use that term anymore?"

"Trust me, I'm toning my choice of words down to be nice. Think about it, Anna. If you stay here, there's always going to be that possibility. The two of you have been in each other's pockets since you were kids. He's always going to be there—or here. With this new shop he's got, it seems like he's going to be here even more than he used to be. He's not traveling as much and he's not in a rush to go anywhere. How are you going to handle it?"

"I don't know, Bobby!" she shouted. "But that doesn't mean I want you to go to the shop and pick a fight with him!"

He huffed with frustration. "Fine. I won't fight with him. I promise. I'll drop the car off, give him the keys, and leave."

"You promise? Really?"

"Unlike some people, I'm not looking to make you upset on purpose, Anna. I may be a jerk a lot of the time but not to you."

She rolled her eyes. "You did not just say that."

He chuckled. "Okay, fine. I'm a jerk to you too, but this time I promise not to be. It's part of my whole makeover." He smiled. "You inspired me."

"And why are you suddenly giving yourself a makeover?"

He shrugged. "I've been here my whole life, kiddo. It's the same thing day in, day out. I'm just ready for something new. Nothing's happening for me here. You said the same thing about yourself when you left the pub."

"How do you know something's going to happen for you in South Carolina?" she asked quietly.

"I don't. But I'm willing to give it a shot." He pulled her in and kissed her. "Come on. Give me the keys and I'll take care of this car thing right now."

"How will you get home after you leave the shop?"

"I'll give my partner a call."

"Wait...you have a partner? Since when?"

"Since about a month ago." He made a face. "There have been some changes in the precinct and I feel like I've taken about ten steps backward."

"Ah…so there's more to this makeover story than meets the eye."

"Sort of. Anyway, I'll get a ride. I don't want you to worry about it."

Slowly, Anna went and got both sets of car keys and handed them to Bobby. "I'll walk out with you and clear all my stuff out." Together they walked outside, and within five minutes, she had her few meager belongings in a pile on the grass.

"You sure about this?" Bobby asked.

"It's the last tie to him," she said and cursed the fact that she was close to tears.

Bobby pulled her in for one last hug before getting in the car and driving away.

—◆◆◆—

"What the hell do you mean?" Quinn angrily tossed a rag aside as he approached Bobby Hannigan.

"I thought I was pretty clear, dude. Anna doesn't want the car, so I'm bringing it back for her."

Everything inside of Quinn went cold.

Then he looked at Bobby's smug face and that instantly changed. "You talked her into this, didn't you?"

"Sorry to disappoint you, Shaughnessy, but it was her choice. She even tried talking to the dealership first about paying the car off, but they wouldn't let her do it." He glared at Quinn. "I'm sure you had something to do with it."

"Hell yeah I did!" Quinn snapped. "The car was a gift to make her life easier! If she knew she could just swoop in and take over the payments she would have done it sooner." He cursed. "She needs a car, Bobby.

You know it and I know it. Just…convince her to keep it. I'll transfer the payments over to her if she really feels so strongly about it."

Bobby shook his head. "She already has another car and she doesn't want any reminders of you. For once, do the right thing and just let her have her way."

Even though Quinn knew Bobby was right, it still irritated the hell out of him. "You're loving this, aren't you?" he finally asked.

Bobby laughed darkly. "Believe it or not, I'm not. You think I enjoy seeing my sister this upset? I really thought this was going to be the one time you proved me wrong." He shook his head. "I thought for her…"

Quinn looked away.

Bobby shoved him on the shoulder to get Quinn to face him. "Hey, I'm not here to gloat and it doesn't do shit for me to be proven right. I would have put up with your sorry ass forever if it made Anna happy."

"Yeah…well…now you won't have to."

"You just don't get it, do you?" Bobby said in disgust. "All these years and you haven't figured it out." When Quinn just stared at him, he continued. "Ever since she started crushing on you in the seventh grade, I've wanted to kick your ass. At first, it was just on principle. My sister liked you, and you didn't like her in return. Then the older we got, and the more she refused to move on, I started to resent you. By now I should hate you, but all I can do is pity you. You're the one who's going to miss out on an amazing life, because there's no one better than my sister."

Quinn couldn't have uttered a word even if he'd wanted to—his throat was so tight he almost couldn't breathe.

Bobby tossed the keys at him, which he readily caught.

"Most guys would kill for what you had," Bobby said, almost with a hint of sadness. "And they wouldn't have been stupid enough to let it slip away."

When Quinn was alone in the shop, he looked at the keys in his hands and closed his fist around them. He'd gotten all of his clothes back, Anna had quit the softball team, and now she'd given back the car. Short of hiding in the bushes with a pair of binoculars, he had no excuse to see her. And what was worse, no one would talk to him about her, either. It was almost as if they were all trying to make him crazy.

He'd seen Aidan and Zoe several times over the last few weeks, but no matter how many hints he'd dropped, neither of them had talked about her. Even after Bobby's little speech, Quinn was no closer to knowing how Anna really was other than her not wanting the damn car.

He'd respected her wishes and kept his distance— everyone thought he was doing it of his own free will, but he wasn't. No one could possibly understand how hard it was to stay away.

Just as no one could possibly understand how much he really did love her.

Could barely breathe without her.

Hadn't slept in weeks because of her.

Tossing the keys on his workbench, he stalked across the garage and out the door, locking up behind him. He needed to get out and clear his head. He needed to get out and find something to do that wouldn't have him thinking of Anna. Aching for Anna.

He cursed. There was no such thing and he knew it.

He could drive from one coast to the other and back

again and nothing was going to be better. Nothing was going to be right. Unfortunately, he knew he had to keep moving forward. The pain he felt was self-inflicted and he had to learn to live with it.

He drove through town in his truck. It was a quiet Tuesday afternoon. No traffic. No distractions until…

He'd have known that blond hair anywhere.

Sitting at a table of one of the café's that had outdoor seating, he saw Anna. Carefully, he pulled over and just… watched. He knew it was wrong and creepy, but it had been so long since he'd seen her that he couldn't stop himself.

She was sitting alone, talking on her phone. Even from this distance, he could see she was sad. She was laughing at something, but Quinn knew her well enough to know her heart wasn't in it. He knew her body well enough to know that her fidgeting was because she wasn't comfortable. The constant toying with her hair was because its length was annoying her. When her shoulders sagged, he wanted nothing more than to jump out of the truck and go over and hold her.

Quinn watched as she put her phone down on the table and looked around. He hoped she didn't see him. Then she stood and smiled at someone…a guy. What the hell? She was sitting there waiting for a guy? Like a date? He's sitting there like some lovesick puppy and all the while she'd been waiting for her new boyfriend?

Unable to watch anymore, Quinn pulled back onto the main road and drove away.

―∾―

"Congratulations," Anna said with a bright smile. "You've bought yourself a house!"

She had been saying that phrase a lot lately and found that it was fun to see the smiles on her clients' faces. Anna had been on a bit of a selling streak. In the last month, she'd sold four houses on top of closing on Hugh's property. She still didn't love real estate, but right now it was being very good to her. Sitting at the café table, enjoying the sunlight, she collected all the paperwork and put it in her folder.

Dan Michaels leaned back in the chair and smiled back at her. "It certainly looks that way." He paused. "I can't thank you enough, Anna. You really listened and found me my perfect house. How about we go out and celebrate?"

Celebrate? Hell, it had been weeks since Anna had wanted to celebrate anything. It was one thing to not see Quinn when he was traveling or when they were each away at college, but this? This variation they had going on, where they were deliberately not seeing each other, was slowly killing her.

Her smile fell slightly but she forced herself to keep her tone light. "I wish I could but I'm supposed to meet up with some friends after work for drinks."

"Anyone I know?"

She should have said no, but her mouth got away from her. "Aidan Shaughnessy and his wife, Zoe."

"Oh, wow. I haven't seen Aidan in years. I heard he's got a construction company now."

Anna nodded. "He's the best in the area."

"I considered calling him if I didn't find what I was looking for and seeing if he could custom build something for me. Looks like I won't have to now."

"I'm really glad you like the house, Dan. It's beautiful."

"Listen," he began as he leaned forward, "I know this

sounds forward but…would you mind if I tagged along? I really would like to see Aidan, and even though I don't need a house built, I do have some business projects in the works that might be of interest to him."

Her immediate thought was to tell him no, but how could she deny Aidan a potential opportunity for his business? So with her smile—stiff though it may be—still in place, she agreed.

"I do need to run by the office and get these processed. Why don't you follow me and we'll go from there?"

Dan readily agreed and Anna was thankful to have a few minutes to herself. Back at the office, Dan sat and made some calls while she finished with the paperwork. When she couldn't delay any longer, she went into the ladies room and freshened up and then walked out to tell him she was ready.

Twenty minutes later, they pulled into the pub's parking lot—separately—and Anna was relieved to spot Aidan's truck already there. For some reason, she was uncomfortable with the entire situation. She didn't really want to be out, and she certainly didn't want to be out with Dan, but Zoe had been after her pretty much since the breakup to leave the house and engage in life again.

So here she was. Engaging in life.

And hating it.

Dan walked over and met her as she was climbing from the car. "I don't think I've been here in years," he said with an easy grin, taking her hand to help her. "I actually came here for my twenty-first birthday and had my first official, legal drink." He chuckled. "A bunch of us came here and drank until they threw us out. It was a great little bar."

Anna chuckled. "Well, brace yourself. It hasn't changed much."

Together they walked in and she stiffened slightly when Dan's hand rested on the small of her back as they made their way through the crowd toward where Aidan and Zoe were sitting in a booth.

"Hey!" Zoe said. "Glad you made it." She looked past Anna and her eyes landed briefly on Dan before zeroing back on Anna as if to say, "WTF?"

"Oh, sorry," Anna said as she stepped away slightly from Dan. "This is Dan Michaels. We went to school together and he just signed a contract on a new house on the beach."

"Dan, how are you?" Aidan asked, standing up and shaking his hand. "You used to play ball with my younger brother, right?"

Anna could tell Aidan was deliberately trying not to say Quinn's name, and as much as she appreciated it, she just wished everyone would act normal.

Or just let her go home where she could curl up in a ball and be by herself.

"I did, way back when," Dan replied. "It's good to see you." He reached over and shook Zoe's hand, and then they all took their seats in the booth.

"So...I take it Anna sold you the house," Zoe said, grinning.

Dan nodded. "It was the very first one she showed me over a month ago. I kind of dragged my feet a bit—I had several business trips to take that sidetracked me—but luckily the house was still available when I was ready for it."

"It's a beautiful house," Anna said and then launched into all the amenities. "You would go crazy for all the finishes, Zoe. It was all done over just before the house went on the market. And the view is breathtaking."

Dan turned to her and smiled. "It certainly is."

Zoe arched a brow at Anna who, in turn, blushed. "So," she said brightly, "have you ordered yet? Are we just doing drinks? Or food? Or…"

Zoe shook her head. "We just got here about five minutes before you did, so we figured we'd wait and see what you were in the mood for."

Aidan motioned to the waitress and once they all gave their drink orders, Dan immediately began talking business with Aidan. Anna was grateful for the reprieve, but she desperately wanted to talk to Zoe—alone. Unfortunately, they were on the inside of the booth and sort of trapped in their spots. So she went for small talk—the beach, the weather, shopping.

"I was talking to Aubrey last night and she really wants to come for a couple of days and visit."

"Is Hugh going out of town again?"

Zoe nodded. "Although I kind of think Aubrey orchestrated this one."

"Uh-oh."

"Nah. It's nothing bad. She really wants to do a little shopping for the nursery and wants to get a feel for things before she and Hugh go together."

"Okay. As long as they're fine and happy and still in love."

"Almost sickeningly so," Zoe laughed.

"So when is she coming?"

"I was thinking maybe we'd hit the outlets next weekend if…" Zoe began and then her eyes drifted to the door of the pub and she stopped.

"If…what?" Anna asked and then followed Zoe's gaze.
Quinn.

It was the first time in weeks that she'd seen him, and her heart seemed to kick her in the chest right before stopping altogether.

He looked good. Really good. He must have gotten out of the shop early because he'd obviously showered and shaved, and he had on clean clothes. She watched as he shook hands and greeted a couple of people, and then she felt as if she were going to be sick.

He wasn't alone.

She didn't want to stare—she really didn't—but for some reason she couldn't seem to look away.

The girl was her every nightmare—tall, thin, big boobs. The centerfold they used to joke about. And she seemed to need to have her hands all over Quinn. And he didn't seem to mind.

"We can go someplace else," Zoe whispered as she reached across the table and squeezed Anna's hand.

But Anna shook her head. No. She was going to have to get used to this. Hadn't Bobby warned her of this exact scenario? They lived in a small town and they were bound to run into one another.

She just had hoped it wouldn't happen quite so soon and that her heart would be a little more intact to handle it.

Slowly, she leaned back in her seat and nearly jumped when Dan's arm came to rest behind her.

Worst. Night. Ever.

The waitress delivered their drinks and they toasted the sale of the house. Neither Dan nor Aidan were aware of her emotional state, and she hoped it stayed that way.

Anna couldn't help but smile—it was a great thing for Dan and it was a huge commission for her. Between this commission and the one from Hugh's property, she finally had some breathing room to get part of her life on track. The sensible part.

The emotional part was still a mess.

"Best of luck to you with the house, Dan," Aidan said.

"Hear, hear!" Zoe chimed in.

And as they all clinked glasses, it seemed as if all the noise in the room faded away. Anna took a sip of her beer, and when she looked up, her eyes met Quinn's. His gaze narrowed at her, and when he spotted Dan, his gaze turned dark and thunderous. It was all she could do to not slide under the table and hide.

"Actually, this might be of interest to you too, Zoe. Aidan says you're a decorator. I've got a building downtown that I was thinking of…" Dan was saying.

Anna knew they were all talking. All around the room, people were talking and there was music playing in the background, but all she heard was her heart pounding in her ears. The beer tasted vile in her mouth and she knew if she took another sip, she certainly would get sick.

"Excuse me," Anna interrupted, hoping she sounded normal and that no one detected the tremor in her voice. "I just need to run to the ladies' room." Zoe gave her a sympathetic smile and normally Anna would have wanted Zoe to go with her, but right then, she needed a minute to herself to calm her nerves and break away from Quinn's stare.

Anger built with every step she took. He had no right to look at her that way. This was what he wanted whether he admitted it or not. What did he expect—that she'd just sit at home and mope for the rest of her life? Well, that was kind of exactly what she wanted to do, but no one needed to know that.

Maybe Bobby had been onto something—maybe she did need a fresh start someplace else. She'd hate moving away from her parents and Zoe and all her friends, but there was no way she wanted to keep feeling like this every time she happened to cross paths with Quinn. Maybe it would get easier over time, but somehow Anna doubted it.

Her mind flashed back to a conversation she and Zoe had had way back when, while Zoe and Aidan were broken up and Zoe was all set to move back to Arizona.

"It's just too hard. I don't want to have to look over my shoulder and wonder if I'm going to run into Aidan, or any of the Shaughnessys for that matter. This is for the best," Zoe said.

"For whom?" Anna asked.

Only now did she fully understand just how much Zoe had been going through, and she knew if she went to her friend and told her how she felt, Zoe would support her. Aidan would too. Hell, half the town probably would.

And it just made her feel even more pitiful than she already did.

Inside the ladies' room, she took several deep breaths to calm herself down and then washed her hands just for the sake of having something to do. Looking up at her reflection, she wanted to cry. She didn't even look like herself—her eyes were sad; she looked pale—it was as if Quinn had taken all the life out of her.

And he was here on a date.

With a centerfold.

Bastard.

Turning off the water, she reached for a paper towel to dry her hands and forced herself to relax. She breathed through the nausea rolling through her as she kept envisioning that woman with her hands all over Quinn. "You can do this," she murmured. "It's not like you haven't seen him on a date before." All she had to do was go back out to the booth, finish her drink, and leave. No one could accuse her of hiding out or being rude. She'd come, she'd socialized, and that was that. Zoe would explain to Aidan why she was leaving so soon and she'd deal with Dan another time.

One last look at her reflection and she fussed with her hair—not that it was helping. Just another delaying tactic. Maybe she could escape out the back door and just text Zoe that she'd left. She sighed. No, that was just rude, and it wasn't who she was. Dammit. One last attempt to finger comb her hair, and then she just gave up. It was getting too long and it occurred to her she no longer liked it. She wanted her old hair back. Hell, right now, she just wanted her old life back. *One thing at a time*. "Note to self, call the salon," she muttered as she took a steadying breath and opened the door.

And immediately walked into someone. "Sorry," she mumbled and moved to walk around them. Then she noticed it wasn't another woman trying to get into the ladies' room, but Quinn.

He didn't say a word; he simply moved forward until they were both in the bathroom and he locked the door behind him. The look in his eyes was murderous.

"You can't do that," she said lamely, pointing at the door. Quinn continued to advance on her until her back hit the wall. Her brown eyes went wide looking up at him and her throat went dry. Her fingers twitched with the need to touch him, but instead she just inhaled deeply. Then cursed herself because she loved the scent of his cologne. Up close, he looked weary, tired, and she wanted to stroke his jaw, his temple, like she used to, to ease his tension away.

"I guess everyone was right," he said, an edge to his voice. "You do belong with a guy in a suit."

"What? No, I'm not… I mean, we're not…" she said weakly as she shook her head. "That's Dan Michaels, remember? We just signed the papers on the beach house. He wanted to talk to Aidan about some business and so…" She couldn't finish the thought; her heart was racing and she could feel herself trembling.

"And you couldn't just give him Aidan's number?"

She rolled her eyes. "I mentioned how I was meeting Aidan and Zoe here and Dan asked if he could join us." Then she paused. "Why the hell am I even explaining myself to you?"

He shrugged and crowded her in even more. "Habit," he said, his voice sounding gruff. "You used to tell me everything. There was a time when you didn't turn and run away when things didn't go your way."

Anna raised her hands to shove at his chest, and he grabbed her wrists to stop her. "You have a hell of a nerve."

"I never claimed otherwise," he said. "If you're not dating him, he hasn't gotten the memo yet."

"What are you talking about?"

"You looked pretty cozy in the booth."

Anna rolled her eyes. "Oh, that's rich coming from you, the man who was getting felt up at the bar. How long have you been dating Miss September out there? An hour? Twenty minutes?"

He chuckled but there was no humor. "An hour. Why? Keeping track?"

Beyond angry, Anna pulled her wrists free of his grasp. "No. It's just humorous to see how quickly you reverted to type."

His gaze hardened as he leaned in closer, until they were almost nose to nose. "If memory serves, I was more than willing to go against type and I loved it." He cursed under his breath and looked away for a minute. When he lifted his head, his expression was unusually calm. "And really, the same could be said for you. Dan's exactly the type of guy you used to always go for—the type of guy everyone thought you'd end up with. I guess they were right. So why is it all right for you to revert and not me?"

She didn't have an answer—mainly because she knew he had a point. Her mind was screaming for her to just move around him and leave—she knew Quinn wouldn't hold her there against her will—but being this close to him after so much time apart was almost a sweet form of torture.

"Quinn…" She meant to put a little force behind her words, to make it seem like she was strong, but it came out more like a breathy plea.

"Yeah…I know," he said as he lowered his head and captured her lips with his. His hands immediately cupped her face, his thumbs stroking her cheeks. Over and over his lips slanted over hers, his tongue teasing hers.

A helpless moan came out before she could stop it as her arms came up and wrapped around him. In the back of her mind, she knew this was wrong, this wasn't going to make walking away again any easier, but right now she wanted him, needed him. Her hands came around and rested on his chest and just as they were about to curl into his shirt, he pulled away.

His breathing was just as ragged as hers, and she knew immediately that he was frustrated and angry but didn't understand why. Instead of speaking, Quinn turned and punched the wall. The sound echoed in the small confines of the room, causing her to jump. He reached for the door and looked at her over his shoulder.

Tears almost blinded her as she looked at him.

"Good-bye, Anna," he said, his voice low, broken.

Once the door closed behind him, Anna sank to the floor and cried.

Chapter 12

TWO WEEKS LATER, ANNA WAS BACK AT THE PUB.

The only reason she was able to convince herself to do it was because it was a private party. Her brother was leaving, moving, and they were having his going away party. Steve, the owner of the pub, was standing with his arm around Anna as they watched everyone mingling.

Steve was a sixty-five-year-old Navy vet, and this place had been in his family since forever. He'd always treated Anna like the daughter he never had. Steve had no kids, no family left, and it always made Anna feel good to help him out and take care of him.

"You know, this place hasn't been the same since you quit," he said. She'd had more than her fair share of guilt since leaving, but Steve had understood her reasoning.

"You seem to be doing okay," she said, smiling up at him.

He shrugged. "I'm getting too old for this. I'm thinking of moving someplace tropical."

"And then what would you do?"

"Open a bar," Steve said with a big grin.

Anna elbowed him in the ribs. "Then why move? You already have a bar!"

"Anna, I'm getting old. Other than my time in the navy, I've lived here my whole life. I think I'd enjoy someplace tropical. Plus, a couple of buddies of mine are thinking of going in on it with me."

"Not you too! What is it with everyone suddenly needing to move away from here? This is a great place to live!"

He nodded. "No one's saying it isn't, but I'm ready for a change."

She sighed. "What about the pub?"

"Well, I heard there was this sassy new Realtor on the block who seems to be responsible for selling half the houses around here." He looked at her with pride. "You did good, kid. I know it's not your dream job, but as usual, you totally rocked it."

Tears welled in her eyes. "Yeah, well...sink or swim, you know?" She shrugged. "I chose to swim."

"You always do." Steve looked around the room and took a step away from Anna. "I need to go and check on the food and make sure Johnny's okay in the kitchen. I hate leaving that kid alone back there."

"He's not so bad, Steve."

"Yeah, but he ain't you, Anna," he said with a wink. "Do me a favor? Hang around after the party. I really want to talk to you."

"You got it." Watching Steve get swallowed up by the crowd, Anna couldn't believe just how many people were there. Besides her own family, Ian and Martha were there along with Aidan and Zoe and Hugh and Aubrey. Hugh and Aubrey had surprised her, but it seemed Hugh was finally starting to relax with his wife and come to grips with the fact that she was more than capable of leaving the house without being encased in bubble wrap.

It was incredibly sweet.

There was a large percentage of the local police force in the room, and while Anna knew most of them, there were a few unfamiliar faces. Zoe stepped up beside her. "How's it going?"

"Good," Anna said. "I still can't believe he's leaving. I thought he was just going to go for a week and check it out and decide it wasn't all he thought it would be. I never thought he'd really move."

Aidan walked over and kissed Anna on the cheek before putting his arm around his wife. "What are we talking about?"

"I was just saying I can't believe Bobby's really moving," Anna said with a bit of a pout.

"He's not going to be that far away. It's going to be good for him and he seems happy about it," Aidan said.

"I suppose." Anna looked around the room and spotted a woman she had never seen before. "I wonder who she is?"

"She's Bobby's partner. On the police force," Aidan said as if it were obvious.

"Wait…*what?* But she's a…a… She's, um…"

"A she?" Zoe said.

"Exactly!" Anna cried. "No wonder he was freaking out."

Aidan looked around uncomfortably. "Anyone need their drinks refreshed?"

"What?" Zoe asked. "What do you know?"

"Nothing. It's…it's nothing."

"Uh, yeah. Okay," Anna said with a chuckle. "You know something, so spill it."

"You mean you know something and you didn't share it with me?" Zoe asked with mock offense. "I thought we told each other everything!"

"Okay, fine." Aidan sighed dramatically. "Bobby

was a little put out that they paired him up with a woman and at the same time they almost demoted him while they restructured the department."

"That's just crazy. I can't believe my brother is so sexist."

"It's not that," Aidan said and began to look around for an escape.

"Then what is it?" Anna asked impatiently.

"He kind of... He's... Well..."

"Oh, just spit it out, Aidan!" Zoe demanded.

"He's kind of really attracted to her!" he hissed.

"*No!*" Anna and Zoe said in unison.

Aidan nodded. "But you did *not* hear it from me," he warned them both and then rolled his eyes. "Honestly, when did I become the town gossip?" he mumbled as he walked away.

"That was fun," Zoe said as she watched her husband's retreating back. "So you really had no idea about this female partner thing?"

Anna shook her head. "Not a clue. Bobby hasn't said a word. At least not to me." She sighed. "I guess I've been so busy having my own pity party he didn't think he could talk to me. I hate that. I'll have to make sure we get some time to hang out, just the two of us, before he leaves."

Zoe nodded and took a sip of her beer. "I saw you talking to Steve earlier. Was he begging you to go and help out in the kitchen?"

"No." Anna chuckled. "But he did mention wanting to move to someplace tropical and open up a bar with his navy buddies."

"But what about the pub?"

Anna shrugged. "I think he's going to sell it. He

asked me to stick around after the party to talk to him about it and he was praising my real estate skills, so I'm guessing that's what he wants."

"Wow…just…wow. Too many damn changes lately."

"You got that right." And as true as it was, Anna knew not all of them were bad. She was surrounded by so many amazing people, and even though she contemplated jumping on the moving truck with Bobby, she knew she would miss all of this far too much if she did. The people. The places.

Quinn.

Dammit. She had sworn to herself she wouldn't think about him tonight. That lasted all of thirty minutes. Good grief, when was that going to end? If she was going to stay in town—and she was—she was going to have to learn to coexist with Quinn. They'd known each other too long and knew too many of the same people to avoid each other forever.

"So what about you, my friend? What's next for you?" Zoe asked as she maneuvered the two of them to a quieter corner.

"I'm not really sure. Things are finally going well with real estate. It's not my dream job, you know, but I'm finally out from under the mountain of debt I had."

"I know that's got to feel good." Zoe smiled.

"It does. But other than that, I don't have any plans. Work, work, and more work. I think I may want to do some renovations and updates on the house."

"Why don't you sell it? You can afford something a little bit newer and bigger now."

"What do I need a bigger house for? It's just me," Anna said sadly. "Maybe I'll get a cat. Or two."

"Oh no you don't. You're not going to become that person. I won't allow it. There's no need to do anything drastic!"

"For crying out loud, Zoe," Anna laughed, "it's just a cat!"

"That's how it starts! Then it's two cats, then four, and the next thing you know, you're sleeping on the couch because the cats have taken over your bed!" She grabbed Anna by the shoulders and shook her. "Don't do it!" They broke out in fits of laughter and Zoe pulled her in for a hug. "It's gonna get better, sweetie. I promise."

———

It was two in the morning and Anna was exhausted. She was helping Steve clean up—all of the guests were gone and only a couple of pub employees were still there. She yawned widely and Steve chuckled. "Subtle, Anna. Come on, come sit down and talk with me."

She followed him over to a booth and sat. "So I'm guessing you want me to get the ball in motion for you to put the place on the market."

He shook his head. "No. I've been thinking about this for a while, and this place has been in my family since I was a kid. My grandparents started it—hell, my grandfather built it. It's not a great place, but it's been good to me and my family." He shrugged. "I worked hard to keep up with everything and I'm proud of all I accomplished."

Anna reached over and squeezed his hand. "And you should be! This place is a local legend. An institution! Everyone who grew up here has a memory of coming to the pub. You and your family created something great, Steve."

"That's why I can't sell it, Anna," he said, smiling sadly at her. "I'd rather see it close down than have strangers in here changing everything. Or worse yet, having some big corporation buy it and turn it into one of those chain restaurants or something."

She didn't think he had to worry about that but decided to keep it to herself. "I hate the thought of this place closing, but I understand."

Again he shook his head. "But I'm not going to close it. I'm going to give it to a family member."

She looked at him oddly. "But you don't have any family left. You've always said that." Then she gasped. "Did you find some long-lost cousins or a secret child you didn't know you had?"

The bark of laughter nearly shook the walls. "Oh, Anna! You have quite the imagination!"

"I don't think it's so out of the realm of possibility," she said primly. "You hear about things like that happening all the time. You watch daytime TV. You know I'm right."

"Sweetheart, believe me, there are no Steve Jr.'s running around in this world. I can guarantee it."

"And the long-lost cousin?" she prompted.

"Afraid not."

Anna leaned back against her seat. "Well, then I'm stumped."

Steve seemed to blush a little as he fidgeted in his seat. "Anna," he began, "I took a risk hiring you when you were fresh out of college. But you were a fast learner and you always knew how to make everyone around you smile. Hell, I was a grumpy old man even back then, and you came in here like a breath of fresh air and a ray of sunshine rolled into one."

"Steve," she said with a soft sigh.

He reached out and took one of her hands in his. "I watched you grow up here. You came here at a time when I was ready to call it quits. I was tired and unmotivated and pretty much resented everything and everybody."

"You weren't so bad."

He tugged on her hand and laughed. "You don't need to sugarcoat it. I was a pain in the ass, and you used to call me on it daily." He paused. "You turned this place around and breathed new life into it. Now, I know you've been working in real estate for a while, and I know why you went into it, and if you're happy, then we'll just forget we ever had this conversation. But if you...you know...if you want to take on something else, something of your own, I want to sign the business over to you."

"What?" she gasped.

He nodded. "You're the only family I have, Anna. You are like the daughter I never had, and I would be honored if you'd let me do this for you."

"But...but...Steve, I don't have the kind of money it would take to buy this place! I couldn't possibly—"

"You're not listening to me, Anna. I'm not asking you to buy me out. I want to sign it all over to you. We can just put your name on the corporation and all the accounts, and it would be a done deal. I'm debt free," he went on. "The business has been doing really well, and I have an account set up for business expenses that would be yours. There's enough to cover all the monthly stuff for at least a year, plus money to do any improvements you'd like."

She stared at him wide-eyed, certain she must be

dreaming. "I…I don't know. I mean, it's not a big secret that I'm not in love with selling houses, but…wow. This is huge, Steve. This is really, really huge."

"I know," he said solemnly. "And I don't want you to answer me right now. I want you to take some time to think about it. I'm not in a rush, and we can take our time transitioning, and then when you're ready, you can throw me out."

"I would never do that," she said, unable to help the smile on her face. "I don't even know what to say."

He squeezed her hand one more time. "Promise me you'll think about it."

As if she'd be able to think about anything else.

***

For three in the morning, Anna was pretty wide-awake. She'd left the pub after hugging Steve until her arms went numb and then sat in her car for several minutes still trying to wrap her brain around what had just happened. At one time, she had considered the possibility of buying the pub from Steve, but she knew, financially, she couldn't do it.

I want to sign it all over to you.

Right then, she really wished someone would pinch her so she'd know she hadn't had too much to drink and was only dreaming. "I need to get home," she murmured, starting the car. Sitting still, Anna let the car warm up a bit. She was grateful to her brother, but this car wasn't in as great condition as Anna would have hoped. There was a bit of a chill in the air, and it took a few minutes for the heat to kick in.

Dammit, she missed her Honda.

And not her old Honda, but the new, shiny one she had stupidly given back to Quinn. "Should have kept it," she said in disgust. "I'd be on my way by now, and warm."

Pulling out of the parking lot, Anna drove the deserted streets with a smile. This was her town. Her home. What Steve was offering her was an amazing opportunity and, if she was honest, a dream come true. She wasn't happy selling houses, but it had helped her achieve financial stability. Anna knew if she did take over the pub, she'd not only have the financial backing from Steve and his business accounts, but she'd also have breathing room because of her own smart decisions from her commissions.

Maybe she'd hold on to her real estate license and do it as an on-the-side thing if need be but put her primary focus on the pub. "Okay, pros and cons," she said out loud. "Pros, no more dresses and high heels. Cons, go back to everyone looking at me as Anna the tomboy."

Hmm…not off to a solid start.

Racking her brain, she tried to think of more pros. "I can cook as much as I like—pro! I'll never have to be the low man on the totem pole—pro!" She giggled, feeling a little bit giddy. "I'll be spending every day surrounded by friends! Pro!" She laughed again. "This is kind of fun! I could redecorate a little bit with Zoe's help and then—"

POP!

Anna let out a small scream as the car immediately began to swerve. She tried to regain control but wasn't sure what exactly had happened. She hit the brakes and carefully pulled over to the side of the road. Cursing under her breath, she shut off the car and took a few seconds to let her heart rate slow back down.

"Holy crap." Climbing from the car, she walked around it and found she had blown a tire. "Well, this just sucks." Stamping her foot, she popped open the trunk and was grateful she had taken the course that taught her how to change a tire.

The only problem? It was pitch-black outside and she was on a side road with nothing around, and she was majorly freaked out. Jumping back into the car, she slammed the door, locked it, reached for her cell phone, and immediately called Bobby. She hated to do it at such a late hour, but it was an emergency.

"Hey, you've reached Bobby. I can't take your call right now—"

"Dammit!" she yelled and disconnected the call. She thought about calling her dad, but she knew he'd never even hear the phone at this hour. With no other choice, she dialed Zoe's number and prayed their friendship could withstand a middle-of-the-night tire change.

"H'lo."

"Hey, Zoe, it's me," Anna said softly.

"Anna? You okay?"

"Yeah…kind of. I blew a tire and I'm over on Elm and it's pitch-black, and I was wondering if you could send Aidan to help me."

No response.

"Zoe? Zoe, you there?" she asked a little louder.

"What? Oh, shoot… Sorry, Anna. I sort of dozed for a minute."

"Crap, I'm sorry. I know it's late but I don't know what else to do. I think I can change the tire myself, but it's so dark out and it's freaking me out."

"Okay, okay…o…kay…"

Anna heard a very distinct snore and then the connection was lost. "Well...shit!" Unwilling to give up just yet, she tried her parents and got no answer and even went so far as to call the pub, but Steve was already gone and she knew he'd had enough to drink that she wouldn't feel good about having him driving around any more than he had to tonight.

She wanted to cry. How was it possible that she knew so many people and there wasn't anyone to help her? The clock on her phone now read three forty-five and all she wanted was to be home in bed.

Her last resort was to call AAA. She waited through all the recorded messages, and when she finally got a live person on the line, she told them her issue, her location, and her member ID number and was finally feeling optimistic.

"We'll have a tow truck to you in three hours," the operator said.

"What! How is that even possible?"

"There was a multicar accident on Route 74 and all the local trucks responded to it. There's a chance one can get to you sooner, but I can't guarantee it."

Anna groaned. Her first thought was how she hoped no one was injured. And while she desperately needed help right now, her only problem was a flat tire. A multicar accident usually meant much more extensive damage. There was no way she could begrudge them for getting the help they needed. The reality was that she could change the tire. She just didn't want to.

"Ma'am? Are you still there?"

"I am."

"Someone will call you when they are thirty minutes out. Will that be all right?"

"You know what? It's okay, just cancel the request."

"Ma'am, are you sure?"

"Yeah. I'm sure. I'll...I'll just find another option. But thank you."

"Okay. Have a good night!"

Anna wanted to reach through the phone and slap the operator upside the head. "Have a good night"? For real? This was a nightmare and she had clearly exhausted all of her options.

With a huff, she climbed from the car again with her phone in her hand for light and began to search in the trunk for everything she'd need to change the tire. On a good day—as in full daylight—it took her almost thirty minutes to change a tire. There wasn't a doubt in her mind she was going to double that.

Ninety minutes later, she was done.

She was exhausted, sweaty, and filthy, and was practically seeing double from lack of sleep. Slamming the trunk closed, Anna stumbled to the driver's side door and pulled—and almost fell back on her ass. On her second attempt, she managed to get it open and then just stood there as if trying to remember what she was doing.

Off in the distance, the sun wasn't even close to being up but she did see a light. "This is it," she sighed wearily. "This is how it ends. I'm seeing the light. Changing a tire killed me." She yawned and rested her head on the roof of the car. "I hope they don't put that on my headstone."

Somewhere nearby, she heard a car door slam and her head shot up as she looked around. Was she in the car? Did she close the door?

"Anna? What the…?"

Quinn? Now she knew she was dreaming.

Or dead.

Quinn didn't talk to her anymore and that was just fine with her. She looked over her shoulder and saw him sprinting toward her just as her knees gave out and everything went black.

———~~~———

Quinn drove with one eye on the road, the other on Anna. She had taken twenty years off his life when he watched her eyes roll back in her head and she started to fall to the ground. All night, he had cursed how he couldn't sleep but now he was thankful for it. It was why he was driving around at this hour—he was going to the shop because he couldn't stay in bed staring at the ceiling any longer.

He wished he knew what had happened to her but she was out cold. Pulling up in his driveway—his house was closer than hers—he quickly jumped out and ran around to the passenger side and picked her up. Once he had her inside, he strode through to his bedroom and placed her down on the bed.

"Anna? Anna, baby? Come on, wake up for me, sweetheart." He stroked her cheek and looked for any signs of injury. Other than being dirty—like she'd been working on a car—she appeared unhurt.

Running from the room, Quinn went to the kitchen and poured her some water and then was immediately back at her side. "Anna, please, honey. Open those eyes. Let me see those beautiful brown eyes. Please."

She didn't stir. Not sure of what else to do, he was

about to call 9-1-1 when she moved. He whispered her name and watched as she tried to open her eyes and focus on him. He said her name again.

"Dream Quinn…you need to stop talking," she mumbled and rolled over.

Dream Quinn? "Wait…Anna…what happened? Why were you on the side of the road?"

She sighed loudly and rolled over. "Jeez, even in my dreams you can't just be quiet and let me have my way, can you?"

She was so adorable and obviously not really awake and yet Quinn couldn't stop looking at her, talking to her in hopes of figuring out what had happened. "Baby, I need to make sure you're all right. Are you hurt?"

A loud yawn was her only response.

Quinn repeated the question.

"Just my heart," she said as her eyes started to close. "You broke my heart."

"I know," he said quietly, and leaned in and placed a kiss on her temple and then watched in mild amusement as she kicked her shoes off. She was dressed in a pair of jeans and a plain blue T-shirt and looked every inch the girl he'd always known.

"Sleep," she slurred. "Flat tire. Too hard to change… even with the classes, but I did it." Another yawn. "I don't need you anymore, dream Quinn."

And with that one statement, he felt his own heart break again. Unable to help himself, he ran his fingers through her hair and caressed her cheek. She hummed for a minute—just like she always had in her sleep when he'd touched her. With a sigh, he rested his forehead against hers and whispered her name.

"But I miss you," she whispered and then her head lolled to the side and she let out a soft snore.

It wasn't much.

Hell, it was barely audible.

But those few words gave Quinn more hope than he'd had in a very long time. Standing up, he covered her with a blanket, turned out the light, and left the room so she could sleep. Out in the living room, he got things in motion to get her car towed to the shop and to have all the tires checked.

Once that was done, he made a few other calls—and woke a bunch of people up—to let them know he wasn't coming in to the shop today, he'd be in touch, and he wasn't to be disturbed unless it was an absolute emergency.

He put the phone down and looked toward his bedroom door. Anna was here and he wasn't going to let her leave until they finally talked things out. He'd given her the space she asked for, and ever since that kiss two weeks ago, he'd barely been able to think straight.

He loved her.

That wasn't going away, and it wasn't going to change.

And after hearing her small admission that she missed him, Quinn was hopeful that maybe Anna still loved him too. Somehow, they had to make things work out. Yeah, he had a little explaining to do—like why he'd been out on a date—but she'd been out on one too! After seeing her at the café with that guy—who he now knew was Dan Michaels—Quinn had gone a little crazy.

The date had been a mistake. He'd known it as soon as he'd agreed to it. Sandy was someone he'd gone out with a time or two a long time ago, and when he'd run into her that same afternoon and she'd invited him to go for drinks, he'd said yes mainly out of desperation. It had killed him to think of Anna with someone else, but he knew if she was moving on, he had no choice but to move on as well.

But after he had kissed Anna in the ladies' room, Quinn knew he couldn't do it. He'd gone back out to the bar and faked an emergency at the shop and left. Sandy hadn't seemed overly upset and he hadn't heard from her since.

It wasn't until a week later that Aidan fessed up and told him how Anna really wasn't dating Dan and it had been a business meeting. Quinn wanted to kick himself. She had essentially told him the same thing in the bathroom, but he'd been too riled up to listen. Seeing Dan with his arm around her and sitting so close to her in the pub had pretty much pushed every one of his buttons.

And now look where he was.

A quivering mass who was afraid to go into his own bedroom. Anna had obviously had a rough night, and the last thing he wanted to do was upset her even more.

Unfortunately, for the first time in months, he genuinely felt ready to go to sleep. He looked over at his couch and grimaced. It was too small and it wasn't comfortable. He kicked off his shoes and poured himself a glass of juice. He finished it in two great big gulps and then looked toward the bedroom again. He wanted to sleep, and he wanted to hold Anna while he did it.

"Of course you do, you selfish bastard," he cursed himself. "Glad to see you're only thinking of yourself, as usual."

Yeah, he pretty much despised himself right now.

Walking around the house, he locked up and turned off the few lights he'd turned on. It was a little after six in the morning, and he had a feeling Anna was going to sleep until at least noon. He had a second bedroom and Quinn had resigned himself to sleeping in there when he heard Anna call his name. It was soft at first, then a little louder.

Cautiously, he opened the bedroom door and stepped inside. "You okay?" he whispered.

"What…? How did I get here?"

Quinn sat down on the edge of the bed, not trusting himself to get too close to her. "I just happened to be heading in to the shop early and I found you parked on the side of the road. What happened?"

Slowly, Anna sat up and ran a hand through her hair and Quinn could tell she was still disoriented. "What time is it?"

"It's a little after six."

"We had Bobby's going away party at the pub last night. I stayed afterward, to talk with Steve." She yawned. "I didn't leave until after three. I blew a tire. I tried calling everyone and no one answered."

"Why didn't you call me?" he asked softly.

She gave him a wry look. "I know how to change a tire. It was just a little more…challenging when it was pitch-black out."

"So you changed the tire?"

She nodded and yawned. "It took me over an hour. By the time I was done, I was near delirious. I guess that's when you found me."

"I'm glad I did." He was almost shaking with the thought of what would have happened if he hadn't come along at that point. "I'm glad you didn't try to drive home."

"Speaking of…I really do need to get home. I'm exhausted and…and…and I shouldn't be here."

"Anna, it's really early and you're exhausted, and to be honest, so am I. I was just going to the guest room to grab a couple hours of sleep."

"But you just said you had been heading to the shop," she reminded him.

He nodded. "I was, but you scared the hell out of me and I haven't been sleeping well, and suddenly I feel like I might actually be able to sleep."

"Oh."

He looked at her, studying her face in the dimly lit room. She was so beautiful. How had he looked at her face for so many years and not realized that?

Anna made no attempt to lie back down.

Quinn made no attempt to get up and leave the room.

He saw her swallow hard and then lick her lips. He wanted to do that for her—lick her lips and then every inch of her. But it was too soon to hope he'd ever be allowed to do that again. He willed her to say something, anything—preferably to ask him to stay—but she just continued to watch him warily.

Resigned, he stood. "Get some sleep. I'll take you to get your car later. Don't be mad but I had it towed to the shop. You know, just so it wouldn't be sitting there on the road. You need to be safe."

Silently, she nodded.

So did he. "Okay then." Quinn turned to leave the room when Anna whispered his name. He stopped and looked over at her. "Are you okay? Do you need something? I put a glass of water on the nightstand for you."

"Don't go."

If he hadn't been watching her, he wouldn't have been sure she had indeed spoken the words. He sighed her name.

"Please."

And then he was lost to anything and everything but Anna. He pulled his shirt over his head and watched as she slowly stood and peeled her jeans off. He followed her lead, and in seconds, he was down to nothing but his boxer briefs. Anna did that funky little trick where she took her bra off without taking her shirt off. He loved that trick but would have loved seeing her without a shirt too.

Crawling back into the bed, Anna lay back and waited for him. Unsure of how he was going to survive being this close to her and just sleeping, he said a silent prayer and then climbed in beside her.

Without asking, she curled up beside him—her head on his shoulder, her hand over his heart. Which was just as well, because it belonged to her.

~~~

The next time Anna opened her eyes, she really believed she was still dreaming. She was in Quinn's bed, in his arms, and everything seemed just right. Sighing happily, she snuggled closer. She loved these dreams. In them, they were always still together and he loved her and had begged her to take him back—after she'd made him grovel for a little while.

Yeah, she loved these dreams.

His arm tightened around her, and if it was possible, that one simple act made her feel a myriad of emotions—safe, protected, cherished. Another sigh.

Her thigh was wrapped around his. In her dreams, they were both always naked—mainly because of the hot and steamy sex they always had. But when she shifted her leg, she could feel his boxer briefs. Then she moved again and realized she had on a T-shirt.

Oh crap... Everything came crashing back to her. The party. The tire. Quinn. Her mind began to scramble for a way out—a way to excuse her practically begging him to sleep with her without making her look pathetic. Plus, she really wanted to leave just in case one of his new girlfriends decided to drop by. Ugh...that would just about kill her.

"I never thought someone's brain could be so loud, Anna, but yours could compete with a freight train," Quinn murmured right before placing a kiss on the top of her head.

She squirmed against him, but Quinn held her firm. "I need to get up."

"No."

She struggled a little harder and cursed a blue streak when he wrapped his other arm around her. "Dammit, Quinn...let me up!"

"I don't think so," he said mildly.

With a loud sigh, she ceased moving. "Fine. Happy now?"

"Did you sleep okay?"

Anna wanted to punch him. Like seriously inflict major pain on him. "I guess."

"Mmm...good," he said.

They lay there like that until Anna was certain she'd go mad. "You can't keep me here forever, you know. Eventually you'll have to move."

"I'm not so sure. I'm pretty content just like this. I don't have any place to go and no one's gonna call, so... really, I'm good."

Yeah, she was gonna punch him hard. "Dammit, Quinn, come on. Maybe you don't have anything to do today, but I do." His grasp instantly loosened, and she took full advantage to put some distance between them and sit up. Frantically, she looked around the room and spotted her jeans and bra, and was about to swing her legs out of the bed when Quinn reached out and put a hand on her arm.

"Don't," he said softly. "Not yet."

Anna looked over at the clock—it was almost one in the afternoon—and groaned. "It's late. I need to get my car." When she met his gaze, she saw the defeated look on his face—it was something she'd never seen before. And suddenly, she didn't feel so good about herself or about how she was just thinking about him. She started to say his name, but he was rolling out of the bed and pulling his jeans on.

"Just give me five minutes and we'll go," he said as he walked out of the room.

That was it? He wasn't going to argue with her or force her to listen to him? She looked around in confusion—as if she were in the middle of a *Twilight Zone* episode. Jumping up from the bed, she stepped over her pile of clothes and walked out of the room after him.

Why she couldn't just be thankful he was being agreeable she couldn't say. But for some reason, his quiet acceptance was more irritating, more insulting than his arguments ever were.

"So that's it?" she called after him. He was standing

in the middle of his living room and he turned and looked at her in confusion. "You hold me in a death grip, telling me I can't leave, and then just—"

"Agree and let you leave?" he finished for her, but there was very little emotion in his voice.

"Well…yeah." She studied him. He'd lost weight, he needed a haircut, and…he bore little resemblance to the man she'd always known.

He shrugged. "What is it you want from me, Anna?" he asked sadly. "When I argue with you, you're pissed. When I playfully disagree with you, you're pissed. And when I give you exactly what you ask for, you're pissed. Baby, I can't seem to win. So if you'll just tell me exactly what it is you want, I'll do it. I'd do anything for you, Anna."

Slowly, she advanced on him, her eyes never leaving his. When she was only inches away, she stopped.

For a minute, Quinn looked hopeful—like he took it as a good sign she wasn't fighting with him and maybe, just maybe she was coming to him to hold him, hug him, forgive him.

He was wrong.

With everything she had, Anna reared back and punched him in the stomach. His loud *oomph* filled the room as he staggered backward. "What do I want from you?" she cried. "I want to know why it is you can go from being this amazing man one minute to a colossal jackass the next!"

"What? When…?"

"Every day, all the time," she responded sarcastically. "Do you have any idea how many changes I put myself through to be the perfect woman for you, you big jerk?"

"I never asked you to!" he said defensively. "There wasn't anything wrong with you!"

She punched him again—this time in the arm.

Hard enough that her knuckles stung.

"I changed the way I dressed! The way I did my hair! My job! Hell, I even took some stupid classes on automotive repair so we'd have that in common! And you know what? I hated it! All that engine grease and dirt—it was disgusting!"

"You said you enjoyed learning about all that stuff!" he argued.

"Yeah, well…" She huffed. "Okay, it was interesting. But I don't want to make a career out of it. And that's not the point! I did so much and made myself crazy to get your attention! But did you even notice? No!"

Quinn quickly stepped back and moved behind one of the living room chairs to put some distance between them. "I didn't know! I never wanted you to change, Anna! You were perfect the way you were!"

"Clearly I wasn't!" she argued and began to walk toward him. She chuckled when he looked around for an escape route. "For years I did everything I could to make you see me—really see me—but you didn't. And then finally—finally!—you did, and I still wasn't enough for you!"

He held up a hand to stop her advance. "That's not true. Anna, I swear. It's not true."

Something in his tone made her stop. She waited for him to continue.

"You know me better than anyone, Anna. You know me better than my own family—you always have. I may come off as being confident and self-centered, but I'm really not. I'm afraid to fail. I've always been afraid to fail. And if I ever think there's a chance of that happening, I bail." He shared with her the conversation he'd had with his father. "And then there was you."

She looked at him quizzically. "Why would we fail?"

He stepped out from behind the chair with a bit of fire in his eyes as he turned the tables and began to advance on her. "Why would we fail? You mean other than the fact that every single person we know pointed out how I didn't deserve you? Like I wasn't good enough to even touch you? Or maybe because no matter what I tried, I was never going to be as considerate and thoughtful toward you as you are to me? And believe me, people had a field day reminding me of that one!"

"Why didn't you tell me? You know, you and I used to tell each other everything. Some would say we shared too much! But as soon as we went from being friends to lovers, you stopped talking to me!"

"I did not!" he denied fiercely. "We talked every day, all damn day!"

"No, we talked about safe stuff—work, what we wanted to eat, or what movie we wanted to watch, the basics—but you never shared with me how much everyone was freaking you out. Not until I pushed. And I never had to do that before."

His shoulders sagged. "When have you ever known me to admit a weakness?" He waited a moment and before she could answer, he added, "But I never had to with you—because you always knew. You knew and you helped me. Only now…now you weren't looking, and I felt like you were judging me for them."

"Me?"

He nodded. "For as long as we've known each other, we talked about everything, and you stopped talking just as much as I did. And when everyone was making those comments about me not being good enough for you, you didn't exactly correct them."

"What was I supposed to say?"

"Oh, I don't know, how about that I *was* good enough? Or maybe that you loved me for who I am and not some stupid image everyone had built up for you?"

He had a point there. She hadn't said a whole lot to defend him. Wait…he almost had her again! "So because I wasn't playing cheerleader for you, I deserved to be taken for granted?"

"I'm not perfect, Anna!" he shouted and raked a hand through his hair. He began to pace and let out a growl of frustration. "I'm never going to be perfect! And you know what? I didn't think I would have to be with you! Everywhere we ever went when we were just friends, no one questioned us being together. But suddenly I've got my arm around you or look at you differently, and all of a sudden people are looking at me like I've committed some federal offense by touching you! Do you know how it made me feel?"

Anna opened her mouth to speak, but he stopped her.

"But now? Being without you all this time? I'd gladly take the comments, the looks, the sneers…all of it. I'll take it, and hell, I even agree with them. I don't deserve you. I never deserved you. But I need you." His voice cracked. "I love you, Anna. I know I screwed up and I hurt you, but if you could find it in your heart to give me another chance, I promise to spend the rest of my life making it up to you."

"Quinn," she sighed.

"I sent Jake's cars back," he said quickly. "I never should have agreed to work on them. Even though you said it was okay, I should have known you were being selfless—for me. I was so busy paying attention to what I wanted for the business that I let you down. I don't need that kind of fame and attention. Not if I have you."

"Quinn," she said a little more firmly, a smile beginning to form.

"I know I'm begging... Hell, I'm groveling. I'm not good at it, and you're probably wishing you could just leave—my truck keys are on the counter. You can take them and go. I won't stop you." He shook his head. "I should have just taken you home earlier. I took away your choices—again. Shit. See? I'm standing here talking about trying not to screw up and I'm even screwing that up!" He closed his eyes and turned away from her. "Really...just take the keys and—"

Anna's lips claiming his stopped his words. She had to work a little harder to get him to give in, but once he did, he simply consumed her. Quinn's arms instantly banded around her, pulling her close, and he kissed her until they were both falling to their knees, gasping for air.

"I love you, Anna Hannigan," he said, raining kisses all over her face, her throat. His hands reached down to the hem of her T-shirt and began to wander upward, taking the garment with him. "I love you so damn much."

"I love you too," she sighed, relishing the feel of those work-roughened hands on her skin. She never thought she'd feel them again except in her dreams. "I missed you."

"I missed you too, baby." He sighed and then groaned when his hands cupped her breasts. "This may not be the right time, but it kind of feels like it is, and I need you, Anna. It's been so long. Please, baby."

Leaning back, Anna pulled her T-shirt over her head and pressed against him. Quinn's chest was still bare and the skin-on-skin contact was glorious. "Yes," she sighed, anxious to feel the rest of him.

She gasped with surprise when he scooped her up in his arms and walked across the room. She was perfectly content right there in the middle of the living room, but the thought of Quinn and a soft mattress was far more exciting.

When he had her sprawled across the bed, he simply stood back and looked at her—like a hungry man eyeing a feast. "You're mine, Anna," he said, his voice a low growl. "You've always been mine, and from this point forward, everyone's going to know it."

No words had ever sounded sweeter.

"Of course, they're not going to know it today because I plan on keeping you right here with me for the rest of the day, all of the night, and probably well into tomorrow." Shucking his jeans and briefs, he joined her on the bed and then froze. "Oh shit…wait. You said you had someplace to be." He started to jump up. "Okay… okay. I can wait. We can go and do whatever it is you need to do and come back here later."

The poor man was sweating and trembling, and Anna started to laugh.

"What? What's so funny?"

She rolled her eyes. "I don't have anything to do. Well, I do need to make some calls, but other than that, I'm completely free."

"But you said—"

"Yeah, yeah, yeah…I was being a brat and making you suffer a little bit. I was embarrassed about my behavior earlier, how I practically begged you to sleep with me."

"Believe me, you didn't need to beg." And then he crawled back onto the bed and covered her body with his. "So we're good here? No one needs to leave?"

Anna shook her head. "Not for a very long time."

A slow, sexy grin crossed his face. "That's good because the things I have planned are going to take a very long time."

"Quinn?"

"Hmm?"

"Stop talking. You know how I love a man of action," she said with a sexy grin of her own.

And then he spent the rest of the day being exactly the man she wanted.

Chapter 13

"I SAW YOUR PICTURE IN THE PAPER LAST WEEK," Anna said. It was two in the morning, and they were in bed after just finishing a late-night dinner of leftover Chinese food.

Quinn groaned. "I didn't mind the article, but the picture was corny."

She chuckled. "It certainly wasn't your best photo."

He pulled her in close and kissed her. "That's because you weren't there with me."

"So tell me about these cars."

He sighed and shifted to get comfortable, hating to bring up a sore subject. "Remember the reporter who was in my shop that day?"

Anna nodded.

"Well, when I sent the cars back to Jake, he reached out to me and said he knew a couple of collectors who were looking for a restoration guy like me."

"Quinn, that's great!" She turned her head to look at him.

He shrugged. "There's more. Basically, the magazine likes to have several restorers they keep on staff, so to speak, and are able to follow their jobs from start to finish. They offered me a position."

"Oh my gosh! That's even better!" She leaned forward and kissed him and then pulled back. "Wait...why aren't you more excited about this?"

"Well…I don't get to pick the cars. So I could get some really cool cars, and I could get some not-so-cool ones."

Beside him, she groaned. "Dude, all cars can be cool. You need to change your attitude a bit. I mean, you probably won't get to work on any Australian muscle cars—they are considered some of the best in the world—but…"

And then he laughed and rolled her beneath him. "God, I love you," he said and then kissed her thoroughly. "You're perfect for me, Anna."

"Yeah, well…sometimes you just need a swift kick in the ass."

He chuckled. "I've heard that before—recently, as a matter of fact."

"Whoever said it was extremely wise."

She had no idea how accurate she was. "You're right. I need to have a better attitude. I haven't given them my answer yet, so—"

"Why not?"

Quinn rested his forehead against hers. "Because I would need to make this shop my home base, and all this time we were apart, I was going crazy. It was hell for me to live this close to you and not see you. So I was thinking of going back on the road and doing that whole lifestyle again."

Anna cradled his cheek in her hand. "It was pretty hellish for me too, you know."

Rolling off her, he got comfortable. "Okay, so here's the thing—if I do this, then I'm pretty much staying here. This is where I'm going to be. I never thought I'd stay this long back in the place I grew up, but there it is." He paused. "I don't want us living in two separate houses." He turned his head to look at her. "I want to be where you are, but I want it to be a place that's ours—not your house I move into or my house you move into. Do you think with all your real estate savvy you could find us a place?"

They were words she never thought she'd hear from him.

"I know we never talked about it before," he went on, "but it's something I've been thinking about. Honestly, I thought about it a lot before. I probably should have said something sooner. I used to hate coming home to get a change of clothes or to sleep alone." He stroked her cheek. "I want to be where you are. Always."

"Oh, Quinn," she sighed. "I want that too."

"I want us to find something we can grow into… someplace big. With a huge master bedroom, so we can have a king-size bed and one of those big bathtubs, because the thought of being in one of those with you has kind of been a fantasy of mine."

She elbowed him. "Stop. It has not."

He nodded. "Has too. And we'll need a room big enough for a game room—you know, pool table, dartboard, maybe a foosball table or one of those air hockey ones."

"You've really put some thought into this," she said with a laugh.

"Definitely. And we'll need an outdoor kitchen with one of those huge grills because you know how much I love it when you make things on the grill."

She nodded. "Anything else? An indoor basketball court? Olympic-size swimming pool?"

"Nah, I think I hit all the important stuff. And word around town is you are the queen of finding the perfect house for interested buyers. So what do you say? Know of any houses that fit my description, Miss Realtor of the Month? Who am I kidding? You'll end up being Realtor of the Year in no time."

"Um, funny you should mention it because…I think I'm giving up that particular career."

He let out a very loud sigh of relief. "Thank God."

Raising her head, she looked at him questioningly. "What? Why do you say that?"

"Baby, I knew it wasn't the right career for you, but I wanted to support you. I knew pretty much from the beginning you weren't happy, and I hated it for you, but after a while, you were making it work, so I kept my mouth shut. Whatever it is you want to do, I'm here for you. I'm sure Steve would give you your old job back, and if it's not enough for you, I'm sure one of my brothers would love to have you working for them. I mean, Aidan's company is growing and he could use someone like you in the office, and with Hugh's resort getting ready to start going up, you know he'd need the help. And—"

"Slow down, slow down," she chuckled. "I don't need your brothers to help me out. I actually got a pretty sweet offer last night." Then she laughed even harder when she felt him stiffen beside her. Playfully, she smacked at his chest. "Oh, don't go getting all freaked out. Steve offered the pub to me."

"Seriously? Anna, that's freaking fabulous! And I think it's the perfect job for you because you love that place!" And then he kissed her again and relaxed beside her.

She told him of Steve's plans and how she felt a little

guilty for even considering his offer. "He deserves to make some money off the sale of the business, Quinn. It just feels wrong to let him sign it over to me like that."

"Steve doesn't strike me as the kind of guy who would make an offer like that if he wasn't financially able to do it. He's been single his whole life, with no one to take care of but himself, and the pub has been a very lucrative business. If he's able to offer it to you on those terms and go into business with his buddies someplace tropical, then he must be doing all right."

"I guess," she sighed. "But I still feel weird about it. I just don't know how to counter his offer."

"How soon do you need to give him an answer?"

"He's not in a rush, but still, I feel like I should have something in mind."

"Well, to be fair, you only found out last night and you've had an eventful twenty-four hours since."

"Eventful, huh?"

"Mmm-hmm," he hummed as his lips began to kiss a trail across her shoulder. "Some might even say adventurous."

She purred when he reached the sweet spot between her neck and shoulder. "Adventurous? Hmm…I'm not sure if that really describes this. I mean, we haven't left the bed other than to eat cereal and cold Chinese food."

"Yeah, I probably should buy some food," he murmured and then went back to gently biting her earlobe. "Later though."

"Yes. Much, much later."

—∿∿—

"I am so, so sorry."

"I know."

"No, I'm serious. I can't even believe I did it. I'm, like, the worst."

"It's really not a big deal. I think things worked out for the best."

Zoe slouched down in her seat, arms crossed, and pouted. "Dammit, Anna! Would you just yell at me or something? I can't believe I fell asleep on you when you were stranded on the side of the road! I'm a horrible friend!"

Anna shrugged. "I'm not gonna lie to you. I pretty much wished hateful things on you right after it happened, but, like I said, I think things worked out for the best." Both women turned and looked at the brothers who were standing by the grill in Aidan's backyard, talking.

Once Anna and Quinn had resurfaced from their twenty-four hours in bed, Anna had found that Zoe had left multiple voice mail messages for her, each one desperately begging for forgiveness. Apparently, she had thought Anna was purposely ignoring her calls. It wasn't until Anna finally called her friend back that Zoe had realized Anna had had a good reason for ignoring everyone's calls.

As much as Anna was enjoying reuniting with Quinn and all the ways they had been rediscovering one another, when Zoe extended the invitation to dinner a few days later, Anna had accepted. Luckily, Quinn had readily agreed.

"You must have a guardian angel watching over you, my friend, because it was dangerous for you to be out there by yourself."

"What was I supposed to do? No one would answer their phones, and those who did fell back to sleep," she said with an evil grin.

"Thank you! That's what I needed!" Zoe cried. "Be sure to throw it back at me a few more times. I mean it."

"Oh, stop. I'm fine, the car's fine…"

Zoe leveled her with a glare. "By fine I hope you mean Quinn put it out of its misery and got rid of it."

Anna nodded with a big smile. "I have my Honda back and all is right with the world."

"Thank God. Not that I'm saying Bobby did anything wrong, but clearly the dealership must have refused that thing as a trade-in."

"Yeah, I haven't gone there with him yet, but at some point I will."

"Have you talked to him at all? Is he settling in?"

"It's really only been a few days. I talked to him briefly yesterday, but he was dealing with the cable guy and getting all his games and gadgets hooked up, so he was a little distracted."

"Did you tell him about you and Quinn?"

"I did," she said with a nod. "And believe it or not, he was happy. Genuinely happy. He even invited us to come down and spend a weekend with him." She chuckled. "I never thought I'd live to see the day when my brother would be willing—and happy—to spend time with Quinn."

"How does Quinn feel about it? Do you think they finally had it out with one another?"

"Neither of them mentioned anything. I just think Bobby knows I'm happy and he's happy for me. I think his issue with Quinn had a lot to do with the way he didn't return my feelings for all those years."

"Well, duh. We all knew that. You're the only one who seemed to not get the memo."

"Yeah, well, sometimes ignorance is bliss."

"So what's next for you guys? I heard about the restoration gig Quinn got offered. Is he going to take it?"

Anna shared with Zoe all their plans—the restoration work, the pub, and the house.

"That's awesome!" she squealed and then leaned in close. "But don't tell Aidan about it. If he hears about the game room idea, he'll want one too and I just cannot handle the thought of it."

"Oh, come on. It could be fun. You could convert the room over the garage!"

Zoe shook her head. "No way. No one is changing that space. It's the first place Aidan and I..." She stopped and cleared her throat. "Never mind. Let's just say that space is not an option."

"Ugh, too much information."

Zoe merely grinned.

Aidan and Quinn walked over. "The steaks are almost ready," Aidan said, kissing Zoe on the top of her head. "What else do we need to do?"

Zoe stood and kissed him back. "I've got everything else ready in the kitchen. All you need to do is bring the steaks in. Anna made potato salad, and I've got a big tossed salad ready and waiting." She walked away and Anna followed. Together, they put everything on the dining room table and soon the four of them were sitting down to eat.

"I talked to Riley yesterday," Aidan said to no one in particular.

"Oh yeah? How is he?" Quinn asked.

"Weird." He took another bite of his steak. "He's moved on from that annoying state of paranoia he's been in and onto some sort of needy, clingy…I don't know. All he kept talking about was the importance of family and how great it is how we're all so close. He mentioned us all going away together on vacation—something about how our wedding was so magical because we were all together under one roof."

"Yikes," Quinn said and took a sip of his drink. "That's not weird. That's scary weird."

"Oh, stop," Anna said. "Has it occurred to either of you that maybe he's just lonely? Maybe being surrounded by a bunch of kiss-asses isn't all it's cracked up to be?"

"Hell no," the brothers said at the same time and then laughed.

"I don't think it's a bad idea," Zoe said. "Maybe we should give it some thought. Instead of going to Australia, we could—"

Aidan immediately cut her off. "Don't even think about it! We have been planning this and planning this and planning this," he repeated for emphasis. "I am not giving that up for anyone—not even my brother!"

"Sheesh, relax," Zoe grumbled. "It was just a suggestion."

"Well, don't go suggesting it to anyone else," Aidan said. "If Riley's got a need for some family time, he's going to have to come to each of us individually. We all have lives and we can't just drop everything to accommodate him."

"I agree," Quinn added. "This is essentially where he'd get to see almost everyone, but with me getting the restoration business off the ground and Anna taking over the pub—"

"Hugh building the resort and Aubrey's advancing pregnancy," Zoe added.

"I've got two subdivisions going up and Zoe's business with Martha is expanding," Aidan said.

"Okay, so we've pretty much established how we all lead very busy lives," Anna finally said. "But it doesn't answer the question of why Riley's looking for some family time."

"He mentioned he's having some issues finishing the new CD," Aidan said after a minute. "And he knows he needs to do something about it and needs to start getting some publicity for it."

"He better not think we're going to jump on the PR bandwagon," Quinn said with a laugh. "Can you imagine? Like a Shaughnessy reality series or something?" Then he laughed even harder.

"Oh, good grief," Aidan said in disgust. "No one needs to see that."

"Exactly. Maybe I should give him a call tomorrow and feel him out a bit," Quinn said. "What do you think?"

"I don't know. Maybe."

"Maybe one of you should talk to Owen first," Anna suggested. "You know they're the closest out of all of you. Maybe he'll have a little insight into what's going on with Riley."

Aidan and Quinn looked at one another. "You may be onto something there," Quinn said, winking at her. "I'll do that."

Anna smiled at him.

"So, Australia…" Quinn said—officially changing the subject.

Later that night, Anna was curled up against Quinn's side, this time in her bed. "I hate to say it, but I like your bed better. It's much bigger."

"Yeah, but there's something to be said about a smaller bed—you're forced to stay close to me. Where you belong."

She couldn't help but sigh when he said things like that. Knowing him for as long as she had, Anna knew he didn't normally talk so sweet, so mushy, to anyone.

Only her.

That put a smile on her face.

When she remained silent, Quinn said, "I want you to know I'm going to try very hard to be a better man, Anna, someone who's worthy of you."

Raising her head from his shoulder, she looked at him. "Let me tell you something, Quinn Shaughnessy—you're a good man. One of the best men I've ever known. Remember how you once told me I didn't have to change—how I was fine the way I was? Well, I feel the same way about you. There's nothing wrong with either of us. We need to remember that even though our relationship has changed a bit, we're still the same people. We need to talk to each other when something is bothering us."

Quinn chuckled.

"What? What's so funny?"

"The last time I tried telling you something was bothering me, you kind of beat me up."

That had her laughing too. "And how many times in our lives have I done that to you?"

Quinn thought about it for a minute. "A lot."

"Okay, so why would that change? I've always been

prone to doing that when you're being a jerk."

"And yet I don't retaliate."

"Maybe not with your hands, but certainly with your attitude," she replied.

"Attitude? Me? I don't know what you're talking about."

That had her laughing even harder. "Quinn, you are the king of attitude."

"But you love me anyway, right?"

Slowly, Anna crawled on top of him until she was straddling him. "Yes."

"Say it," he whispered. "I need to hear you say it."

Reaching out, she skimmed her fingers across his cheek. "I love you, Quinn Shaughnessy. From the very first day when we snuck into my house and stole those chocolate chip cookies and then hid behind the jungle gym, I was hooked."

"You may not believe it, but that day I got hooked on you too. It just took a little longer for me to realize it."

"Twenty-four years, but who's counting," she teased.

One of Quinn's hands came up and curved around her nape. "I'm a slow learner."

"It's okay. You were worth the wait."

"You're not going to have to wait anymore."

She looked at him oddly.

Carefully, he sat up, keeping his hands on Anna's hips to keep her in place. "I had lunch with Aidan a couple of weeks ago, and he asked me where I saw our relationship going. At the time, I was feeling scared and insecure, but it got me thinking. All these years that I was—as everyone has reminded me—serial dating, it was because I couldn't see myself with any of them."

"Quinn—"

"No, no...hear me out. Please." He paused. "I couldn't see myself with any woman, and yet whenever I thought about my future, you were there. Always." His hands left her hips and traveled up until he was cupping her face. "You're my past, my present, and my future. You're my life, Anna. I love you."

She sighed and leaned down to kiss him. "I love you too."

"I know I just said I was a slow learner, but it's one of the things I'm working hard to change. Anna Hannigan, will you marry me? Be my best friend, my partner, my wife? Will you stay by my side and kick my ass when I need it, and love me and bake me cookies in the middle of the night?"

She smiled. "That's a pretty specific list you got there."

"Well, the cookie part is negotiable, but not the rest. What do you say, Anna? Will you marry me?"

Tears filled her eyes and emotion clogged her throat. All she could do was nod as her hands went over her heart.

Quinn's thumbs instantly went to work wiping away her tears. "I told you I never wanted to be the reason you cried."

"These are good tears," she finally said. "Really good tears."

He visibly relaxed and let one thumb glide across her bottom lip. "Good or bad, I hate to see you cry, baby."

"I'm afraid you're stuck with this," she said. "If we get married, you're going to have to deal with the fact that I will cry from time to time."

"*If?* If we get married?" he croaked.

She chuckled and leaned her forehead against his. "I meant when. I'm marrying you, Quinn. You're not getting out of it."

"I don't want to get out of it. You're it for me." His arms banded around her as he twisted until she was sprawled out beneath him. "Forever, Anna."

Yeah…she really liked the sound of that.

Epilogue

Six months later…

"THIS IS HOW LIFE WAS MEANT TO BE LIVED."

"You got that right."

"Why don't we live this way?"

"Because we're poor and have to work."

"Oh yeah. I temporarily forgot about that. Thanks for the reality check." Anna stretched out on the chaise lounge by the pool on her belly and simply sighed with happiness.

"It's what I do," Zoe said from her chaise beside her.

Aubrey hummed her approval, rubbing her hand over her very swollen belly. "Although I have a feeling we're going to get caught."

The three women were out in Quinn and Anna's new backyard, sitting around the pool in new lounge chairs. The sun was shining, there was a beautiful breeze, and right then, it was downright heavenly.

"I have to agree with Aubrey," Zoe said.

Anna lifted her head and looked at her. "What makes you think that?"

"We've been out here for almost thirty minutes and we were supposed to be making lunch. It's only a matter of time before one of the guys comes looking for us — and food," Aubrey said. "And to be honest, I am kind of hungry."

"You're always hungry," Zoe reminded her.

"I do feel a little bit guilty about it," Anna said. "Not that you're always hungry, but how I don't have a whole lot here for you to nosh on."

"So maybe we should go and fess up and ask the guys to take a break. We can go into town and grab something to eat," Aubrey suggested.

"Nah. There is so much stuff still on the moving truck. There's no way they're going to even notice we're not around or that lunch isn't ready yet."

The sound of a male clearing his voice had them looking up.

"Uh-oh," Zoe murmured.

It wasn't one Shaughnessy male; it was all of them. Plus one Hannigan.

Anna jumped up from her chaise and stood, almost falling over. "Oh, hey, guys! How's it going?"

"We're all busting our asses getting the truck unloaded and you're out here sunning yourself?" Bobby snapped. "How the hell is that fair?"

"Okay…I know it looks bad, or like we're just slacking off, but—"

"It looks that way because it is that way." Aidan chuckled. He looked at his wife and shook his head. "I'm ashamed of all of you."

"Um, Aubrey," Hugh said, "I don't think it's a good idea for you to be out here in this heat. You should be inside where the air-conditioning is running."

She waved him off. "I'm fine. It was just so relaxing out here, *was* being the operative word."

Quinn stepped forward menacingly, but there was a glint of humor in his eyes as he made his way toward

Anna. "We just spent the better part of an hour getting our bedroom set up because you specifically mentioned it was the most important room, and instead of making lunch, you're out here sunning yourself. Do I have that right?"

She took a step backward and knew she was in trouble. "Okay, I'll admit it was a little wrong of me to take an extended break while you're all working so hard. But...but..."

"An extended break?" Quinn repeated with a grin. "Is that what we're calling it? When did you even have time to unpack your bathing suit?"

Okay, that one will take a little explaining, she thought. "I...um...I wore it under my clothes so I could cool off if I needed to."

"We'd all like to cool off, but you said we needed to get the truck unloaded first."

"All right, I'm sorry!" she said, a nervous laugh escaping as she noticed she was getting dangerously close to the edge of the pool.

"No, no," he pressed, "you said you needed to cool off..."

"Quinn...don't you dare," she said, holding her hands out to stop him. "I swear I'll go inside right now and make lunch."

He shook his head. "Not good enough."

Anna shrieked when he lunged at her.

"Wait a minute, wait a minute, wait a minute!" Zoe yelled, coming to her feet. "It's not her fault."

Quinn paused and turned to look at his sister-in-law. "I'm sure you're just trying to buy her some time, but go ahead and humor us. How is this *not* Anna's fault?"

"Zoe," Aidan began a bit hesitantly.

"No, no, no…it's okay. First, I ordered pizza for everyone for lunch, and it should be here soon."

"You did?" Anna asked. "Why didn't you tell me?"

Zoe shrugged. "I got sidetracked."

"Ooo…so there's food on the way?" Aubrey asked, slowly coming to her feet with her husband's assistance. "Please tell me one of those pizzas has bacon on it!"

Zoe grimaced. "I cannot wait for you to have that baby because your food cravings are making me queasy!"

Quinn looked between the two women quizzically. "Okay, so you ordered lunch. That still doesn't excuse Anna's hanging out here relaxing—in her bikini, no less—while I'm sweating my ass off!" He tried to sound angry, but he didn't quite pull it off.

"I asked Anna and Aubrey to come out here and sit with me because I needed to talk to them. But then we got all comfortable and talking about the house and I never got to tell them what I needed to."

Anna stepped forward. "Are you all right? Is everything okay?"

Aidan came to stand beside his wife and wrapped his arm around her waist. Zoe looked at him and smiled. "We're having a baby!"

In the blink of an eye, everyone was around them, offering congratulations and hugs and well wishes.

"When did you find out?" Anna asked, squeezing Zoe's hand.

"I went to my doctor yesterday to confirm. Looks like we conceived him or her while we were on vacation in Sydney!" Zoe looked over at Hugh. "Your resort there was especially romantic and will always hold a special place in our hearts."

Hugh grinned. "That's great! But I hope you won't mind if I don't use that blurb in a travel brochure or anything."

"Shut up," Aidan said, but he was smiling from ear to ear. He looked at everyone. "I told Zoe I didn't want her lifting anything heavy today so that's why she lured the girls out here."

"Not that I could do anything either," Aubrey added and then looked back toward the house. "So...do we know exactly when the pizza is going to get here?"

"Oh, for the love of it," Anna said. "Go inside. There's some fruit and crackers in the kitchen." She looked at Hugh. "Go and make sure your wife doesn't pass out from starvation," she teased.

Everyone was talking at once, and a few minutes later, the sound of a car horn beeping quieted them. "I bet that's lunch," Zoe said and led the group out of the yard and into the house. Everyone followed except Anna and Quinn.

She looked at him shyly. "Are you really mad?"

He grabbed one of her hands and pulled her in close before kissing her soundly. "Mad?" He shook his head. "Not really. Although I hate how you're parading around here in this bikini while everyone's here."

She rolled her eyes. "We have been over this before— multiple times! It's not a big deal!"

He shrugged. "To me it is."

Wrapping her arms around him, she pressed up against him. "I'll tell you what, when everyone's gone, I'll parade around all you want, just for you."

A grin slowly crossed his face. "Oh yeah?"

She nodded. "Yeah." Looking over her shoulder to make sure no one was within earshot, she added, "I'll even parade around back here in nothing at all and we can go skinny-dipping."

He groaned. "I'm going to hold you to that," he said and kissed her again.

"Now come on, or all the pizza will be gone." She turned to walk away, but Quinn grabbed her hand.

"Not so fast."

"What? What's the matter?"

Without a word of warning, he tugged her in close, and before she knew it, Quinn had swung her up in his arms and was moving close to the side of the pool.

"Quinn! No! Don't! I said I was sorry!" Then she was flailing in midair before splashing into the icy-cold water. She went under and quickly came up sputtering. Swimming to the side of the pool, she shook her hair out and away from her face. "You are going to pay for that!"

"You'll have to catch me first," he teased, but made no attempt to move.

"I didn't say you'd have to pay right now," she said calmly, climbing from the pool. When she was standing right in front of him, dripping wet, she looked up and smiled.

Quinn's eyes were locked on her glistening body, and he swallowed hard. "We…um…we should get inside," he said, his voice low and gravelly.

"Mmm…we should," she said quietly, closing the distance between them. Her arms went around his shoulders as she plastered her wet body against his. She was just about to kiss him—distract him, actually—before dragging him back into the pool with her, when Bobby shouted from the door.

"We've got an emergency in here!" he yelled.

Anna and Quinn instantly broke apart and dashed for

the house. "What is it?" Quinn asked as they stepped inside. "What's going on?"

"Aubrey's water broke!" Zoe said with a huge grin.

Hugh was running from room to room, collecting their things, while Aubrey looked at everyone and smiled. "Sorry to cost you a mover," she said and then winced with pain. "But we really need to be going."

Riley looked over at Bobby. "Come on, Mr. Policeman. We're going to need a designated driver who can get us to the hospital and knows the fastest way to get there."

"Yes, please," Aubrey said with a tight smile. "I don't think Hugh can drive right now. Or at least he shouldn't."

Bobby looked over at Quinn and Anna and smiled apologetically. "Sorry, but duty calls."

"Don't worry about it," Anna said. "Just go. We'll be there as soon as we can!"

Five minutes later, Hugh, Aubrey, Riley, and Bobby were gone. Anna looked around and quickly did the math—Quinn, Aidan, Ian, Owen, and her dad, plus herself and Zoe were all that were left. Everyone was eating pizza and talking excitedly about how there was soon going to be a new family member joining them.

Anna felt slightly overwhelmed—not about the move, but about life. So much was happening, changing. Quinn looked over, caught her expression, and instantly walked over and wrapped her in his arms.

"You okay?" he whispered.

"For so long, it seemed like nothing ever happened around here. Everything was always the same and I used to almost resent it. And now, in just a short amount of time, everything's changed."

He tucked a finger under her chin and forced her to look at him. "But they're all good changes," he said.

She nodded. "I know. But we have so much going on, and yet I look at Hugh and Aubrey and now Aidan and Zoe and…I'm envious."

His eyes went a little wide. "Yeah?"

She nodded. "Yeah." Then she shrugged. "I know we haven't talked a lot about it and we're so busy and we're planning a wedding, but…I wouldn't mind doing something small like Aidan and Zoe did and…and starting our own family."

Quinn looked around the room and frowned. "I kind of wish we weren't talking about this with our families here."

"Why?"

"Because if we were alone, I'd strip that tiny bikini off you right now and start working on that family," he growled against her ear. "Then I'd book us on the next flight to Vegas and marry you tonight."

She almost swooned at his words. "And I would love every second of it."

"How about we—"

"Okay," Ian called out. "Break time's over. We have a lot to do and I know I'm not the only one who is anxious to get to the hospital and wait for the baby to be born."

"How much is left on the truck?" Anna asked.

"If you hadn't been sunbathing, you'd know that," Quinn teased, and she elbowed him in the ribs. "Ow!"

"We have two rooms of furniture left and about two dozen boxes," Ian said. "Now I don't mean to be rude, but I think we should just get the boxes in their proper rooms and get the furniture unloaded, and we can come back tomorrow and help you get it all in place, if that's all right. I'd really like to run home and shower before going to the hospital. It's not every day a man gets to meet his first grandchild for the first time."

Tears were back in Anna's eyes and Quinn pulled her close before addressing everyone. "Okay, I agree with Dad. If everyone can give us an hour, I think we can empty the truck. If anyone wants to shower here, you're more than welcome to, but I can't guarantee I know where the towels and soap are just yet."

Rather than answer, everyone sprang into action. Anna pulled on her shorts and T-shirt over her bathing suit and joined in. She assigned Zoe to unpacking the master bathroom box just in case anyone took Quinn up on his offer to shower.

In an hour, they were done and people were all filing out the door with the promise to meet up at the hospital. When the last car pulled out of the driveway, Quinn turned to Anna and swung her up into his arms.

"Quinn? What in the world?"

"This is our first home and I am carrying you over the threshold."

"That's what you do when you get married," she said with a laugh.

He shook his head. "Well, I'm changing things up and doing it now." He walked them into the house and kicked the door closed behind him. Carefully he locked the door and continued to carry her up the stairs of their new two-story home and into their bedroom. The room was a mess—the furniture was all in its place but there were no blankets or sheets on the bed and no curtains on the windows.

When he placed her down on the bed and smiled,

Anna smiled back. "Wow! That was kind of fun. We may need to make that a thing."

"Don't get used to it. That was a lot of stairs."

"Hey!"

He chuckled. "Just kidding." And then he stretched out beside her. "Welcome home, Anna."

"Welcome home, Quinn," she replied. They lay there in companionable silence for several minutes before Zoe said, "I think we need to get showered and changed and head to the hospital. I know first babies normally take a while, but nothing about Aubrey's pregnancy has been typical. I wouldn't be surprised if everything went really fast."

Rather than moving and getting up, Quinn began to kiss her shoulder, then her neck and her cheek.

"Um…this isn't helping us get ready," Anna purred.

"I disagree." His hand trailed up her thigh to the button on her shorts and quickly popped it open.

"Quinn…we need… We have to—"

His lips claimed hers, effectively cutting off anything she was about to say. When he finally lifted his head, he gazed into her big brown eyes. "I was thinking about what we talked about earlier. I'm not saying we have to run off to Vegas tonight—or at all—but I certainly wouldn't mind getting in a little practice on making a baby before we head to the hospital."

Anna smiled up at him and continued to smile as he stripped off her shorts, shirt, and bikini. His hand rested on her flat belly, and he smiled as she sighed his name.

"This would be a big change," he said softly.

"Quite possibly the biggest one yet."

"Are you sure about this?"

As much as she wanted to accuse him of being a chicken, she suddenly was one too. "Maybe we can talk about it a little bit more after we come back from the hospital. Or after we babysit a couple of times."

Quinn stripped his shirt off and grinned. "I think that sounds perfect." He stood and kicked off his jeans, sneakers, socks, and briefs before joining her back on the bed. "We should probably let Aidan and Zoe have the spotlight for a little bit longer too."

She nodded. "And when it's our turn, we'll know it is the perfect time."

"You know it."

Even though they knew there was someplace they needed to be, Quinn made love to her slowly, sweetly, perfectly.

And later, as they stood side by side smiling into the nursery to meet their new nephew, Quinn squeezed her hand. "Yeah, I definitely want one of those with you."

"Just one?"

He shook his head. "Hell no. We're going to need our own little league team!"

She rolled her eyes.

"Just think, we can have our own team and challenge all the other teams in the community, and I can train them at home. The yard is big enough for a T-ball stand. How early is too early to start kids on learning how to hit a ball?"

Anna could only chuckle. There was one thing she was certain of—her life with her best friend, the man she loved, was never going to be boring.

And she wouldn't have it any other way.

Can't get enough of the Shaughnessys?
Look for:

This Is Our Song

The Shaughnessy Brothers, Book 4
Coming soon from Sourcebooks Casablanca

As soon as Riley got a glimpse of his manager, he knew something was up. It was written all over the man's face. "Okay," Riley began as soon as they sat down. "Out with it."

Luckily, Mick wasn't the type to play dumb. "I spoke to Rich Baskin earlier—that's who called when I was here."

Rich was the head of Riley's record label. It was all Riley could do just to nod.

"I told him you really weren't on board with using outside writers to finish the album."

"And what did he say?"

"What do you think he said? He's pissed."

"Great."

"However," Mick went on, "he is willing to give a little."

Riley's head shot up, and for the first time in what seemed like forever, he felt hopeful. "Okay. How?"

"Do you know Tommy Vaughn?"

Riley's eyes went wide. "Of course I do! Who doesn't? The man is right up there with Jagger, Mercury,

Lennon, Bowie... I mean, the guy is a rock god. Why? Is...is he one of the song writers? Does he want back in on the music side rather than writing about it?"

"Okay, so you're aware of his magazine."

Reaching over the side of his sofa, Riley pulled a copy of *Rock the World* magazine. "Aware of it? I subscribe to it!"

"That's good," Mick said. "Because you're going to be in it."

Riley pulled back and frowned. "What do you mean?"

"Look, I don't play dumb with you, don't do it to me." Mick paused. "Tommy wants to do a big piece on you—possibly multi-issue, something he doesn't do very often. He's got someone lined up to work with you. Rich wants this. So if you're hoping to get back in anyone's favor, you're going to do this."

"Mick, you know how I feel about interviews. Especially right now!"

"Then you're going to have to get over it. Fast. Because if this deal doesn't happen, they'll pull the plug on the album—and think of the lousy publicity *that* is going to cause. 'Riley Shaughnessy cut loose because he didn't want to do publicity and couldn't write any songs.'"

"That's pretty low," Riley growled. "Even for you."

"I'm not here to candy coat it for you. I've been doing that for too long, and now look where we are." Mick shifted in his seat. "You never asked for much and you were never complicated to work with—you were certainly never a diva—so when you started to struggle, I let it slide. Well, I'm done with that now. It's time for some tough love. You need to stop with the pity party and get your ass back in the game." His phone beeped and Mick looked at it and stood. "I've got another appointment to get to. You're gonna get a call from the magazine. Take it and be thankful."

"Mick—"

"I'm not kidding, Riley," Mick interrupted. "Everyone's done playing around. We want an album from you—we wanted it six months ago. Don't turn into a diva on me now. Do the interview. Hell, who knows, maybe talking to someone—even a magazine reporter—can be... what's the word? Cathartic. Maybe you'll finally get out of your head and get the music down like you need to." With a pat on Riley's back, Mick walked to the door. "I'll talk to you in a couple of days. Think about it. I don't want you to screw this up."

Riley stood and stared at the closed door for a solid minute before he could force himself to move. When he did, it was to go back to the couch and collapse.

He'd sworn he wouldn't do any interviews until the album was done and he knew it was perfect. Now what was he supposed to talk about? How he couldn't write? Couldn't play? Couldn't sing?

Yeah, the fans would love that.

Unfortunately, he knew there was no way out. So he'd give the interview...a superficial one. No one said it had to be deep and meaningful. Nowhere was it written that he had to be sincere or enjoy it. The label wanted this? Fine. He'd do it. But he'd do it on his own terms. He'd say all the right things and smile at all the right times. They could take their pictures and think they were getting a glimpse into the real life of Riley Shaughnessy.

But they wouldn't.

They never would.

There was a time when Riley had loved the interviews, the press tours—when they were fun. Now they felt like a chore—one more thing to make him resentful toward the talent that had deserted him.

Jumping to his feet, Riley walked to the window and looked down at the city. Somewhere out there was some reporter thinking he'd struck gold by getting the chance to sit down with him. Riley had a reputation for being a great subject. Well, news flash, that guy was gone and no one had seen him in about a year.

God, he sounded morbid.

He honestly felt sorry for whoever Tommy Vaughn gave this interview.

—⁓—

"I can't believe you're doing this to me," Savannah Daly grumbled at her boss.

Tommy studied her thoughtfully. "Hey, it's not like I'm sending you on tour with a boy band or something."

Just the thought of that made her stomach clench. She'd been there, done that, and had the heartache to prove it. Not that she'd ever share that bit of information with Tommy Vaughn.

Or anyone.

"You might as well be." She sighed and sat down in the closest chair. She took a minute to get her thoughts together. "Okay, say I decide to take this on…"

Tommy's bark of laughter shook the walls of his office. "Seriously? Did you just make it sound like there's a possibility you won't?"

Savannah shrugged. "Maybe I miss cutting hair."

"Yeah, okay. And I miss eating ramen noodles ten

times a week. Cut the crap, Savannah. You and I both know you're going to do it."

She acted as if he hadn't spoken. "If I agree to this piece, how do you propose I get Riley to agree to an interview? He's been turning down people left and right for a year. I heard he turned down Ellen! And you really think I'm going to be the one to convince him to sit down for a conversation? You're crazy!"

Tommy smirked as he slowly sat down behind his desk. He took his time getting comfortable and folded his hands in front of him. "Sometimes it amazes me how little you think of me."

She rolled her eyes.

He held up a hand dramatically. "No…no. It's all right. Let me enlighten you on how I make things happen. For starters, I know *everyone* in this business. Everyone. Secondly, Riley's people are just as anxious to get him back out in the spotlight as his fans are. So much so they're guaranteeing that he'll agree to this interview."

"You mean…"

Tommy grinned. "They're probably breaking the news to him as we speak."

"He'll never agree to this," Savannah said hopefully.

Tommy shook his head. "We nailed the exclusive. You've got an all-access, monthlong pass to work with Riley Shaughnessy."

"*A month?* Tommy, I'm writing a piece for the magazine, not his autobiography."

"Yeah, well…from the way I understood it, Riley may be a little gun-shy, so this isn't something you're going to accomplish in a couple of sit-downs. Hell, for all I know, you may get enough information to make it a multi-edition story, and I'm okay with it. But we've got a basic timeline. All you have to do is reach out to him." He handed her Riley's number.

Stuffing the paper in her pocket as she stood, she glared down at him. "You know, you can be a real jack-ass sometimes, Tommy."

He stood and chuckled. "Only sometimes? I'll take that as a compliment."

———

Back at her desk, Savannah sank down in her chair and sighed. In the past year, she'd done more than her share of second-tier interviews. It was supposed to build character, Tommy had told her. Only she had hoped that by now she'd built enough character and she'd start getting the assignments she really wanted. She had set her sights on Coldplay.

No such luck.

Tapping her keyboard, she watched her computer come back to life and immediately began a Google search on Riley. Instantly there were dozens, if not hundreds, of pictures, links, and blurbs about him. Her first hit went to Wikipedia.

Riley Shaughnessy is an American singer-song-writer, record producer, philanthropist, and actor, best known as the founder and front man of the rock band Shaughnessy. During his career, he released four studio albums with his band, which to date have sold over fifty million albums worldwide, making them one of the world's bestselling music artists. Currently Riley is embarking on a solo career.

"Bor-ing." Savannah sighed and then clicked through photos of Riley throughout his career. Tall, lanky, dark hair...all things she normally found very yummy in a man. He had the look—the sexy grin, the earring, and probably had a tattoo by now. She snorted. "Typical rock star."

She skimmed the rest—four brothers, one sister. Mother dead, father alive. Grew up in North Carolina. No marriages. Just the basics.

With Riley doing his solo thing, Savannah did a quick search to see what the rest of the boys in the band were doing with their time. "Hmmm," she began, unconsciously reading out loud, "Matt 'Matty' Reed is writing the music for a Broadway musical and starring in it. Not bad."

Scrolling down a bit, she continued. "Dylan Anders, the partier of the group, has been popping up onstage with various other artists...drunk. Lovely." *Scroll, scroll, scroll.* "And last but not least...Julian Grayson." She sat back and almost smiled. "Just got married and has a baby on the way. He's taken up photography in his downtime and has no musical plans at the present." She nodded with approval. "Good for him."

Okay, maybe this assignment wouldn't be the worst thing...

"Hey, Van," Blake Jordan said as he sauntered by her desk, using the nickname he knew she hated. "Tough break about the Coldplay story. I promise I'll give Chris and the boys your regards."

Once he was out of sight, she flipped him the bird. "Bite me."

Now she was even more ticked off. Knowing she wasn't going to accomplish anything here, she packed

up her laptop and made her way out to the parking lot.
The sun was shining as she fished around in her oversized purse for her sunglasses. Sliding them on, she
hastily combed her long black hair out of the way and
trudged to her car, cursing Tommy, Blake, and Riley
Shaughnessy the entire time.

———~~~———

Savannah kicked off her shoes and headed to the beach,
lugging her giant purse and laptop. To sit and watch the
sun set over the Pacific Ocean seemed like a great way
to end the day.

Midway to the water's edge, she pulled a sweatshirt
out of her bag and spread it on the sand. Once she got
comfortable, she pulled out her laptop and then inhaled
deeply, taking in the amazing scent of the ocean, and
exhaled slowly.

It took all of thirty seconds for her to realize that
wind, sand, and her laptop did not make a good combination. With a sigh, she stuffed the computer back in the
bag and decided to just relax.

"Yeah," she purred. The beach was her happy place.
Someday she'd have a place of her own where she could
have a view of the ocean whenever she wanted it. For
a while, Savannah was content to sit and listen to the
waves crashing.

One minute everything was peaceful, the next all hell
had broken loose. A rumble of thunder and a flash of
lightning had Savannah springing into action. She pulled
her sweatshirt on, raised the hood up, and began to jog
back to her Jeep. With any luck, she could get there
before the rain came down too hard.

Unfortunately, she wasn't the only one going in the direction of the parking lot, and there was a brief moment of panic when she almost got caught up in the mob and knocked off her feet. Dodging quickly, she picked up her pace and made it to her Jeep just as the sky opened up.

"Thank God for small favors," she said with relief as she climbed in. She was slightly sweaty and out of breath, but she was glad to have cover now that the rain was really coming down. It didn't make any sense to try and pull out of the parking lot just yet—it seemed like dozens of people were doing the same thing—so she waited.

The windshield wipers were swishing back and forth and Savannah sat back and people watched for a few minutes. And then she found herself focusing on one person.

Riley Shaughnessy.

He was standing at the front of her Jeep looking a little lost. For a minute, she just watched him curiously. Why wasn't he going to his car? Was he looking for someone? His driver? And then, as if it was happening in slow motion, she saw the crowd gather around him. Girls were screaming his name and in the quick glimpse she got before he was surrounded, she saw a look of pure panic on his face.

She should have pulled away sooner.

She should have taken her chances with the traffic jam.

The crowd seemed to be a little overzealous and Savannah felt an uncharacteristic and overwhelming need to help him. The Jeep was running, most of the cars that had surrounded her a few minutes ago were gone. She opened her door and stood on the side step and called his name.

"Riley!" Unable to believe he'd heard her over the crowd, she was surprised when he looked up and caught her eye. "Get in!" she cried and watched as he broke through the crowd, grabbed the passenger side door like a lifeline, and swung inside.

About the Author

New York Times and *USA Today* bestselling author Samantha Chase released her debut novel, *Jordan's Return*, in November 2011. Although she waited until she was in her forties to publish for the first time, writing has been a lifelong passion. Her motivation was her students: teaching creative writing to elementary-age students all the way up through high school and encouraging those students to follow their writing dreams gave Samantha the confidence to take that step as well.

When she's not working on a new story, Samantha spends her time reading contemporary romances, blogging, playing way too many games of Scrabble or solitaire on Facebook, and spending time with her husband of twenty-five years and their two sons in North Carolina.

I'll Be There

The Montgomery Brothers

by Samantha Chase

New York Times and *USA Today* Bestseller

—⁓—

This Montgomery has a head for business

Working for Zach Montgomery is challenging on many levels—coming from a wealthy and powerful family, he lives by his own rules and doesn't answer to anyone.

And a heart for adventure

Zach's perfect world is turned upside down when a climbing accident leaves him broken, angry, and maddeningly dependent. In his slow quest for recovery, Gabriella Martine is always there to help...but as Zach comes to see his assistant in a new light, he is forced to reevaluate what it really means to be a man worthy of her love.

—⁓—

Praise for Samantha Chase:

"A perfect happily ever after." —Carly Phillips, *New York Times* bestselling author

"Samantha Chase makes your heart skip a beat and leaves you smiling." —Tome Tender

For more Samantha Chase, visit:

www.sourcebooks.com